SECOND SIGHT

SECOND SIGHT

A NOVEL

RICKEY

GARD

DIAMOND

Cliff Street Books
An Imprint of HarperCollinsPublishers

This book was originally published in a slightly different form by Calyx Books in 1997.

HarperCollins books may be purchased for educational, business, or sales promotional use. For information please write: Special Markets Department, Harper-Collins Publishers, Inc., 10 East 53rd Street, New York, NY 10022.

FIRST EDITION

Designed by Nancy Singer Olaguera

Library of Congress Cataloging-in-Publication Data
Diamond, Rickey Gard
  Second Sight : a novel / Rickey Gard Diamond.
    p. cm.
  ISBN 0-06-019203-8
    1. Female friendship—Michigan—Upper Peninsula—Fiction.
  2. Women—Michigan—Upper Peninsula—Fiction. 3. Upper Peninsula
  (Mich.)—Fiction. 4. Family violence—Fiction. 5. Psychic ability—Fiction.
  I. Title.
  [PS3554.I2447S43 1998]
  813'.54—dc21   98-42115

99 00 01 02 03 ❖/RRD 10 9 8 7 6 5 4 3 2 1

For Ray and Elinor

Earth cure me. Earth receive my woe. Rock strengthen me. Rock receive my weakness. Rain wash my sadness away. Rain receive my doubt. Sun make sweet my song. Sun receive the anger from my heart.

Nancy Wood
from *Hollering Sun*, 1972

CONTENTS

I

THE HUNT

Gabrielle has seen deer sign, fresh tracks along a trail at the bottom of the draw behind the cabin. Beyond the run, a gradual elevation rises to meet a high cedar brake that stretches for several miles, all the way to M67, the route back to Clearwater. More than once that summer, when she'd climbed high enough on the ridge trail and the wind was blowing in her face, carrying away her scent, she'd jumped a doe, sending it up over the top. Wherever there are does there are bucks.

Gabrielle had been living away from home a good ten years. Long enough to be nearing thirty now, long enough to have been married and two months divorced, but all of that unimportant in the moments she thinks of the hunt. It gives her some relief from the silent stare of self-reproach, from unspoken recriminations she's been defending against in her night dreams a long time—all unimportant because the bucks still move down at dusk to feed in the speckled alder near the lake at the farthest end of the cabin's peninsula.

A shrubby swamp shelters willow and red-osier dogwood in the wettest spots, and young birch and aspen still grow along the edges. Pa used to take her there to wait for the half-light of dusk and watch the bucks' silhouettes, bowing and dipping above the browse. When they paused to watch for danger, stretching their necks, lifting their racks up high as talismans, her father, whose Catholicism had lapsed just this side of her baptism, used to whisper they were like priests raising the host.

He will miss the hunt this year, sick at Pinewood—maybe too sick ever to come home again, but she doesn't put words to this last, only sends the thought packing, bad luck to acknowledge it. He has left behind two shotguns, a 12- and a 16-gauge, a new sporterized Mauser with a scope, and a flintlock he'd built for himself several winters before. The gun case still holds the .30–30 he'd taught her to shoot. She's bought cartridges for this one out of tradition, wanting to stay connected to him somehow. Or not to *him* exactly, but connected.

The rifle is customized with a cheek piece to bring it flush to her face, and after all these years it still sets right—not comfortable, just safer and under control. She has practiced her shooting all summer, since she first settled in. She still feels wary every time she fires the rifle, plagued by unease whenever she lifts its weight and gazes down the barrel. Some people say they feel power when they hold a gun. Gabrielle feels danger and the certainty of sorrow.

Tomorrow will be Thanksgiving, and the clouds have yet to give up their snow. Hunters coming into Shub's store at Five Corners up the road complain they might as well be walking through cornflakes, trying to stalk a deer through all these dry leaves. The deer are spooked, the kill is down. But Gabrielle knows a hollow sycamore that stands near the deer run at the bottom of the ridge. She's seen scat there, as fresh and dark and glossy as clumps of coffee beans.

Getting ready by lamplight, she eats her breakfast in silence, thinking of her father and the first time he took her out with a gun. She'd been tense, careful, twice as attentive as Robert had ever been— her brother, Robert, who had stayed in bed again that morning to rankle the old man. Her excitement, barely contained, had to be borne in quiet. She was only eleven, but she knew she had to prove herself.

People had thought it odd, Henry Bissonette's taking a daughter out on the hunt, giving his son such freedom. The hunt was all-important to the old man, but Robert, always a hellion, had gotten downright wild once he started driving, and never went out with his father anymore. It was hard to figure why Henry put up with it, but folks chose to admire his lack of complaint, saying, "Goes to show you what kind of a man that Henry Bissonette is."

That only made it harder for Gabe. She was glad for a chance not to let him down and terrified that she might. He'd spent years teaching Robert to track, all for nothing. By the time he resorted to Gabe, he must have run out of patience, or maybe he never had any real faith a girl could learn to track. Instead he set her up on stand and drove the deer to her, teaching her the easier way: to stay perfectly still, to look carefully and constantly, not for a deer but for a piece of a deer—an ear, a haunch, a foreleg—there! Behind that stand of trees, that outcropping of rocks.

Gabrielle laces up her boots, stuffs her down jacket into a backpack to put on once she's on stand, and heads out, flashlight in hand.

She walks quickly to make the hollowed-out tree well before daylight, choosing a trail that cuts through a grove of ancient white pine. It's the long way around, but the thick pad of needles batten her steps and she moves almost as silently as she would have through snow.

By the time she reaches the stand, she is panting frigid air into the deepest parts of her lungs, each breath like a dive slicing icy water, each breath shocking her more awake. She is so alert she imagines herself one of those watchers of the woods who stare out of the dark with green heat showing in their eyes, a luminous heat close to freezing.

She puts on her jacket, squeezes into the rounded curve of the hollow tree, facing out toward the deer run, picks up her gun, and loads it. Gradually, her eyes adjust and find what little light there is. At first she sees only the rounded outlines of small hemlocks and aspen, but then she can make them out branch by branch, needle by needle. The sky to her right begins to lighten, a brighter, more metallic gray above a break in the overcast.

Daybreak comes slowly, no sudden line crossed to mark it, but eventually the ability to see and, here and there, a pale hint of color warming the grays. Higher up the ridge a raven calls. A sound like a cabinet door opening accompanies the wind, the creak of trees swaying and rubbing against each other. She hears chickadees sound an alarm and gets ready, hoping it forewarns something is coming. She waits and there is nothing. She waits some more.

She expects the deer to come from the right, headed back to bed higher up, but, unsure of herself, she also watches the ridge trail, keeping an eye out for either possibility, up or down. Her old man would have known which way they'd be heading.

Warm weather this year has delayed the rut, though by now it's surely safe to count on the deers' preoccupation. The first cold snap always makes their blood run hot, the bucks' necks swelling up to show their readiness to mate. They make scrapes and mark them with urine, follow the does with their noses low to the ground, groaning, intent on one thing.

It always seemed unfair to hunt them when they were so taken up with sex, but Gabe has learned to accept this. Her second season out, when she was twelve, she shot her first buck, a little spikehorn too intent on the smell of rut. Her heart pounded when she sighted him moving quickly along the run. She followed him with the barrel, half expecting him to bound away before she could squeeze the shot off, half hoping he would. Double-mindedness spoiled it: She had a perfectly good shot at him and missed an easy kill, wounding him instead.

He reared away while the roar of her gun wavered in the air. He was trailing blood. She ran from her stand, following the deer run, to find him lying in a hollow on the bank just off the path. By this time she was crying, and his looking at her didn't help—ohgod, ohgod, why did I do it, why would *anybody* do this, no time for that now, look down the barrel, get it right this time, you screw-up, mygod, ohgod— and she did it right. She did it right that time.

When Henry found her, she was sitting in the snow next to the dead buck, the cold soaking her wool pants. Knees drawn up, head buried in her arms, she choked down what felt like stones, trying not to cry. He didn't ask what had happened. He'd followed the trail. He could see what a mess she'd made.

It was one of the few times she remembered his ever touching her. He sat down next to her, placing his arm on her shoulder briefly. Then he got out his pipe, lit it, and sat there smoking next to her, the scent killing any chance he might have had for more tracking. She sat hiccoughing and staring straight ahead, her eyes burning, barely able to breathe except through her mouth. The longer they sat in silence, the sillier she felt. The wind began to pick up, ruffling the fur on the flank of the deer, a lovely gray down next to immaculate skin, and she had to fight hard to swallow down another binge of sobs.

Pa said, "It's not so big. We'll drag it out and wait to dress it at home. We're not that far." She knew this was for her sake, putting off the gutting. He started to get up then. After a pause he said, "From now on, you won't be soft about it. You'll do him honor, clean and quick."

He never told her, the way he never told her anything of deepest importance to him, but she knew this was one time he didn't mind her wanting to cry. It was too much to imagine he might have felt the same thing himself once, though maybe his first time he had. Whatever the reason, he seemed to respect her grief.

They didn't speak of this, and certainly not to Robert, who came bursting out of the cabin and hung over the porch railing as they unloaded the buck.

"Who got it? You, Pa?"

"Gabrielle. This is Gabe's buck."

"No kidding. Well, what's the matter with *you* then?" he demanded of Gabrielle, who was still glum and standing aside, slump-shouldered. "You mad 'cause it's just a little spikehorn? I never thought you'd get *anything*."

"Well, that's what *you* know," she said fiercely, at once discovering it felt good, this shoving away softness. "Who's mad anyway?" she dared him, and hoped the bravado in her voice would disguise her stuffed-up nose. "I'm not mad. You're probably the one who's mad, sleeping in like that."

Robert glanced toward the old man to make sure he was still turned away, then mouthed the words silently, so only Gabrielle could see how he'd make her pay for this later: *Fuck face!*

By now he had spotted the second wound, and he said, "What was she trying to do, Pa, make Swiss cheese?" This was aimed at the old man's back, a jibe at her, and at the old man for hunting with a girl, but Henry ignored him, and Robert went back inside.

This had only fueled her determination to finish well. She helped her father gut the deer, not just watching this time, but placing the warm kidneys and liver in a plastic bag as he handed them to her, thinking, never, *never* again would she eat these. Huffing and puffing, she had borne the weight of her deer, helping Pa to hoist it over her head and hang it. Then he'd had her sponge the ribs inside with salt water until the cavity was free of blood, the peritoneum clean and pearly.

Except for giving her instructions, Henry Bissonette was silent. His tone, when he did talk, was aimed at the buck, not at her—the attentiveness, the tenderness, different from the heavy sound of duty she usually heard in his voice or in his quiet. "Not a white spot on it," he said, holding the heart in his hand, talking to it. "A good life, plenty to eat."

Years before he had rigged up an elaborate cooler on the open side of the basement, under the porch. The room had a big table and an ancient band saw from Shub's store that Pa used for cutting and wrapping game. The buck would be bled out by tomorrow afternoon, dripping onto the dirt floor. In the cooler the meat would keep for a month, would be better for the aging. In the old days, if the temperature outside went up over forty degrees, they'd have had to butcher in twenty-four hours. All of this he explained to her, and had explained before.

She was alone with the feelings she had. Talking about these, making sense out of these, wasn't done in her family. What was, simply was. Feelings were something like demon possession, sometimes descending on you from someplace else and occasionally overtaking, but always best resisted and cast out finally.

Gabrielle dozes off, remembering. She awakens with a start, amazed to have fallen asleep, cold as she is, while leaning against the inside of the sycamore. But standing stock-still is tiring, and so is watching constantly. After a while, delirium sets in. Pa always told her not to worry about that, to use it. There's a place you get to when you concentrate on what's coming and you picture it over and over in your mind, seeing the deer coming, getting ready. As if you had second sight, everything changes and comes alive in the moment something moves—like you *make* it happen, he told her, like you have prophesied he will come.

Gabrielle's brain cells are sparking in astonishing directions, not the sort of trance Pa had talked about, not like being anchored, more like being swept over rapids by a strong current, a surge over one rock, then the next, and the next. The current sucks her into a stuporous sleep for several moments again before she awakens to find her face dropped forward in the folds of her scarf, moist breath warming her cheeks.

What summons her is an insistent whisper of small noises, orderly noises that signal something is walking toward her. She holds her breath, raising her rifle up with infinite slowness to sight it on the deer run, waiting for a buck to walk into view. A haunch flies by and is gone, headed up the ridge on the high trail—a button buck, young enough that he hops a little. In three bounds, he is at the foot of the ridge trail, crouching to a stop. He whirls completely around once, rearing up. Then as suddenly as he came, he's gone, the flashing white of his tail melting, vanishing, the way she's seen so often.

Once before she's watched young deer play like he did, but in a group. Pa had told her of times he'd seen deer eat fermented apples and get tipsy. Maybe that's what had happened to this one, maybe he'd been over on the old farm road.

She waits to see if a female follows, another possible explanation for his showing off. But no—she waits. The deer is alone. A button buck is all she's going to see.

Another raven calls. Thoroughly awake again, Gabe realizes how cold she is. By now it must be close to ten o'clock. The deer would be finished feeding, bedded down in the draws at the top where they command the winds and their scents. She could track them to the cedar yard on top, the way her father used to sometimes, but that would mean crossing the footbridge, up higher, across the deep ravine. Just the thought of this deepens her chill until she shivers.

Bad as she needs the meat to make it through the winter, she has studying to do—writing her thesis the other reason she's up here, alone. Plenty of time to read and reflect about great literature. That was the plan at least, she thinks with a grimace, emptying her rifle. Her faculty adviser keeps saying that Ernest Hemingway should be at the top of any American literature reading list. Yet she can't get into him and is worried she's incapable of understanding what great literature really is. She wants to give Shub a hand at the store, he's so busy this time of year, and maybe she can read while she's doing that. And maybe she should go visit Pa.

She will try her stand again before dusk, when the deer head back down to the shrubby swamp browse. It will have to be reward enough for now just to unwedge herself from the sycamore, to move about freely again.

Hitting her stride on the trail back, Gabe thinks again of the buck's dance and can't keep from smiling—his crouch, the little whirl, his oblivion. A pulse of fear washes over her, but she refuses to indulge it. Misplaced, any wanting to *save* the buck.

There's her connection to Hemingway right there, she glimpses, but the thought bounds away. She is scared about her lack of nerve, eaten alive with it really, like that self-loathing hunter of his in "The Snows of Kilimanjaro." She'd read the hunter's dying words again last night and had wondered if they were the writer's own, "Now he would never write the things that he had saved to write until he knew enough to write them well. Well, he would not have to fail at trying to write them either. Maybe you could never write them, and that was why you put them off and delayed the starting."

A Hemingway story made death seem preferable to making a fool of yourself. Not like real life, she decides, thinking again of the silly buck, only wanting him to live, wanting to finish her degree however she can. She has a proposal due in two weeks and, rolling the gun back farther on her shoulder, quickens her pace. Survival will depend on the buck's being smart enough and lucky enough. Nothing she can do about that.

November 1, 1983
Five Corners, Michigan

It's snowing outside my window already. I should have covered up the woodpile, but I've been busy poking around upstairs, sorting things out. I've been thinking maybe I do stay to myself too much, like Shub says. Only living alone I never have to explain myself. Today Kate surprised me with a letter—round handwriting, address full of palm trees. She asks so many questions. So point-blank. I had to laugh because people have wanted to grill me like that for years—I still catch people looking out of the corners of their eyes at me, trying to judge if what they've heard can possibly be true.

At the conference, Kate never let on she knew a thing about my story, but if I know Anita, she must. Anita and all her social-scientist friends love to talk these kinds of things to death—yada-yada, the personal is political—my own fault for going to a women's conference in the first place. I only went because Anita was presenting on Hemingway, my subject, and I felt I owed her for putting her butt on the line, hiring me. By rights, she shouldn't have. I can't even say now how I got up the nerve to apply after so long. It was that professor, on vacation at the lake, who said she remembered me from years ago, admiring my presentation. Orbach had retired, she told me, and her friend Anita had taken over and would like my work. But as I told Kate at dinner, I only just started this teaching business. And not because I wanted to change the world.

I remember her smiling when I said that, watching me. Kate's the same age as Anita but acts older, sturdier, more down to earth. Wears her hair short like mine and stands very straight, clasping her hands in front of her, the way a mother waits for the school bus—watching, watching for her children. That's the impression she gives. I mean she actually muses. Always half smiling. It's irritating and at the same time fascinating—what did she see when she studied me, trying to draw me out?

"Anita tells me you're something of a legend on campus—what's behind that?" she asked, tipping her head closer.

"I suppose she means the way I stick up for Hemingway," I blurted, sounding defensive even to me. "I'm a hunter myself." The others at the table looked uncomfortable. I think I wanted to punish the whole bunch, shaken by their speeches on domestic violence, all the new research. They knew too much about me already. "I'm not one to go baring my soul in public," I said, deciding to tone it down, aware of Kate's calm gaze.

"Silence is often a sensible strategy," she answered. I felt relieved, until she added it was common enough among the women she'd been interviewing. Putting me in that company. Now I have to read her book.

NOVEMBER, 1973

"You wanna know why it hasn't snowed? The trouble is," Shub is saying as Gabrielle comes out of the meat cooler, carrying a tray of chops, "see, the whole planet is shiftin' on its axis—whatsa matter? You don't believe me?"

His chin is challenging a man dressed in a one-piece Day-Glo jumpsuit, who looks surprised to find himself in the middle of an argument he hadn't known existed.

He hesitates, and Shub jumps in to continue the debate, on his own. "I read this in *Reader's Digest*. Just the tiniest shift, and everything—the weather? the tides?—they get all mixed up. And that's just what I'm talkin' about, only people don't pay it any attention. What do you suppose happened to the dinosaurs? You ever think about that? I suppose you never thought about that, now did you?"

"Well, *acourse* I—" the man's expression is blank, except for embarrassment at being blank.

Shub looks around, wanting to make sure that Gabe and anyone else in range is listening. "Well," he explains, "the Earth started shiftin' on its axis is what they say, and then when these magnetic fields or something got all caught crosswise, why then, damned if the Earth didn't flip right over. Zoop! Like that." Shub illustrates the flip with his hands, upending the planet's poles with such zest it is dizzying.

The Day-Glo man turns his head to look at Shub sideways. "Get out," he says, disbelieving.

Shub's chin sticks out, more emphatic. "Yes*sir*, the god's truth. Happens every few million years or so. How else you think they'd find fossils of ferns and stuff down under the ice at Antarctica? And the mammoths? Froze so quick they still got buttercups in their bellies—I *read* this, it's science! Zoop, and that's it, folks. Bye-bye and you are freeze-dried."

Shub glances Gabe's way again, nodding his head once, and she leans both elbows on the counter, giving him the signal of her attention that he wants.

The man takes a moment, first blowing a scoffing breath through his nose, then saying: "Well, doesn't make much *difference*, does it? What are *we* gonna do about it? I don't see where worryin' about the weather is going to *help* us any."

"Besides, Shub," Gabe calls out, "the radio says snow. Things will be normal soon enough, and you'll be wishing they weren't."

Shub makes a face and waves this detail away. He's not about to let Day-Glo off so easily. "You mark my word. That Christmas last year? When everything was so warm? That frost they had in Florida, in June or something? Somethin's going mighty screwy. But you go on. Pay no attention." He waves his arms in Day-Glo's face. "You got nothing to worry about."

The man looks to Gabe for a rescue. Forgiving her dark hair's wool-capped utility, he eyes her big-boned frame, which enables her to look at him eye-level, squarish chin leading. He grins to win her over. "Snow's on the way, is it?" he says. "Just my luck. I could have waited and done some tracking. Guess I done all right though." He motions out the window where his car is parked, a buck roped to the trunk.

"No prizewinner," Shub comments, and gestures toward the bulletin board where Day-Glo's photo is the last in a small lineup of snapshots.

Gabe goes to take a look. Four points, 112 pounds. Nobody is getting much this year.

"To tell the truth," Day-Glo is saying, "I gotta admit it was dumb luck. I must of sat for a good four hours this morning, and I give up. Started making all kinds of noise, blew my nose, you know, lit up a cigarette, coughed like hell. And then here he comes. Out in plain sight. I think maybe he was *deaf* or something!"

Shub scowls at the man, but Gabe has to laugh. Because it's true. Luck does play a big part in hunting, especially the sort that downstate once-a-year hunters do, crashing around through the woods.

This guy's a troll, Gabe decides. She and Shub are yoopers from the upper peninsula, or U.P., as people put it. They call downstaters trolls because they live under the Mackinaw Bridge on the map, and because they're too stupid to know they'd have better luck downstate using a shotgun, with their cornfields and shrubby half-grown pastures perfect forage for the whitetail. Gabe used to see plenty of deer sign when she lived in Benton County, but her husband-at-the-time wouldn't have owned a gun, so she kept her interest in hunting a secret, just as she keeps quiet now. Not so much out of shame as a sense of efficiency. People like to hold certain things sacred—why waste her breath? With high-powered rifles allowed up past Muskegon, the north woods is a troll's idea of where a hunt ought to happen.

By early November, Clearwater's stores are jam-packed with Hunter's Specials: Buffalo plaid jackets on sale this week only, thermal underwear, two-for-one, buy now, save! Windbreakers, ammo vests, camouflage hats, electric socks, plastic hot seats, and every kind of knife there is—bowie knives, jackknives, Swiss army knives, skinning knives. Wool gloves, wool underwear, wool socks, wool shirts, red plaid, blue plaid, green and black plaid, Day-Glo. All of it going for top dollar—yeah, some special sale. All of it sold out before season's end. Sid Nichol's Friendly Tavern cranks out its world-famous french fries and stocks up on beefsteak and hamburg. No Friday night All-You-Can-Eat Fish Fry during deer season. Men who have been outdoors crave red meat, not fish, and they pay for it, every ounce premium price.

Sid makes a fortune in beer alone each year, and it rips him he can't get a license to sell it except on tap. Abe Foreur has the case lots all sewn up at the Red Owl. And he sells them too, every last one. Shub likewise stocks up on beer, but he keeps this in moderation, enough for when trolls come in at night and need to relax, not so much they get tanked up with a snoot full. For that, he prefers they go into town. In fact, about the only thing a hunter can't get in Clearwater during deer season is the deer itself—but for most who come up, that's minor.

"And, man," Day-Glo is saying, "*now* what I gotta do with him? Not gonna have to *eat* that whole damn deer, am I?" His shoulders hunch up and down as he laughs.

Shub pulls himself straight and walks behind the counter next to Gabe. "Well, don't you go and waste it," he says, rummaging under the counter, searching for his Alka-Seltzer bottle. "You throw it out, and we'll have dogs runnin' wild, maybe wolverines. Besides, there's folks around here who could use the meat."

Shub is a butcher. For friends in this situation, he might offer to make some of his legendary venison sausage. For a good business prospect, he might cut a fifty–fifty deal. This guy gets a lecture.

Day-Glo is embarrassed again and, loathe to show it, reaches for a couple of cans of corned beef hash, saying of course he is taking the meat home. His buddies will be coming in soon from the field. They are dying for venison, just dying. He's shooting his mouth off, is all, happy to have a trophy to mount. His voice trails off as he goes up the aisle, putting creamed corn and Spam and a box of lime Jell-O in his basket.

Shub's store is set up in an old house. Two oak pillars separate the front room with its bay window and its shelves from the room where Gabe sits at the counter. Behind her is the curtained doorway to a tiny kitchen and living space. The ceiling has been lowered with fluorescent light panels in the years Gabe's been away, and she can't shake the sense that everything seems small and out of proportion. The hardwood floor is some comfort. It still dips alarmingly toward the front as if something important had collapsed, although nothing has—it's always been that way.

Gabe sighs so Shub will notice her. She's worked through lunch, but it's quieted down. "Put me down for these," she says, and Shub gets out a small tablet, shuffles through a half-dozen slips, and pencils her charge for a quart of milk, another box of shells. "Unless you need me, thought I'd head over to Pinewood and visit my pa a little."

Shub looks up, stares a moment, then says, "That's right. Thanksgiving's Thursday, ain't it? I better get the turkey thawing." He slams down the pad on the counter, hard. "That's a hell of a note, being in a place like that on Thanksgiving. I didn't think of it that way till now. Here, you take him this," and he goes over to a display where knickknacks in cellophane packages hang from hooks. He picks up a folded ornament, a paper turkey whose tail will open up into an orange tissue fan. "Take two," he says. "One for dinner at your house. No, go on, take 'em. Be ready for me for dinner about four?"

"So early? What about the store?"

"Oh, hell. I haven't had a decent Thanksgiving dinner since we opened this place. Used to make Elsie mad as a hornet, you know that. A damn shame the way she had to live."

"Well, it's not gonna be fancy," Gabe warns him.

"Don't you worry about that. I'll bring the bird, all cooked and stuffed. I'll do it back there, nothing to it." He motions toward the curtained doorway behind him, where the television is droning away, unseen. "You make potatoes and we're set. If we're sittin' on chairs, that'll be something. All the gol-darned meals I eat on my feet!"

He walks with her to the door, saying, "Ain't gonna be any hardship on me, sitting down to a warm meal for once, and takin' time to get away from the likes of"—he makes a face and jabs his finger in the direction of Day-Glo, who has turned away—"the likes of this place!"

The bell overhead jangles as Gabe opens the door to a rush of chill air. She walks behind Day-Glo's Buick to get a look at his deer. Its forelegs stick out, suspended in air, the head flopped forward on one shoulder, half resting on the back window. Against the glass, the deer seems in flight—but as if his long stretch of a leap had gotten hung up here, head down on his shoulder, ashamed at his shortfall and where he has landed.

November 10, 1983
Five Corners, Michigan

Just finished Kate's book. Anita was thrilled to lend it, of course, raving about its revelations on patriarchy and women's oppression. She's so annoying. There isn't anything of that in Kate's book—not the blaming—she just describes what is under our noses. Things I knew, but hadn't thought about or connected.

Now she's asking for my help. She told us at dinner after the conference about her newest research project, something for a book she's calling *The Secret History of Home.* "You could be my narrative consultant," she says in her last letter, wanting a peer who can talk about the experience of being interviewed in rhetorical terms afterward. Anita told her I'm good at helping comp students write what they mean. Really I think she wants me to be her guinea pig.

She says she doesn't care whether I show her my answers to sample questions—just my reactions to the process and suggestions for structuring interviews. But what self-respecting sociologist could pass up learning more about my family's history? It's weird how this reminds me of Valley. She could wrap me around her little finger too. Even weirder—I wish Valley were here to help me decide. And when did she ever have answers? If she had them, she'd tilt her head and disguise them as questions—wasn't this what I really felt, what I really thought? Putting words in my mouth. She used to shrug out of habit, pretending not to care what I answered or even whether I answered—when I know she did.

I always thought I had to forget about her if I wanted to get over what happened. Now it seems obvious. I never stopped thinking about her, not for a moment.

NOVEMBER, 1973

"Pa?" Gabrielle leans forward in her chair, across from Henry Bissonette. They sit in a corner of the lounge where a nurse has walked him to an orange vinyl chair with chrome tubing side arms. Her father is dressed in pajamas and a pale blue cotton wrapper. Behind him, a stand of pines is framed in a picture window, its heavy draperies billowing from the sill heater's warm air. He has already sat for several minutes, not seeing her. He doesn't respond to her voice.

Gabrielle walks to the window and turns the dial of the blower for something to do, then sits back down. "It's awfully warm in here," she says. Then louder, "I turned down the heater."

Henry sits and stares. He is thinner than last time, she thinks, and far paler than she remembers ever seeing him. He is like some other species of her father, an overbred version without the coppery color of outdoor skin, dressed in clothing he would never have worn at home. At home, he had slept in his long underwear and, getting up in the morning, had merely slipped on his overalls and added a flannel shirt, maybe a ratty sweater. Her real pa would think this outfit sissy.

He is only sixty-eight, and his heart, they say, is the heart of a racehorse. She can picture it pumping blood through glass-smooth veins, keeping his body nourished out of habit in the absence of his mind, trusting him to come back. Some crucial underpinning has been sliced through by this last stroke, leaving the right side of his face adroop, his right arm and leg immobilized, severing his already slender will to communicate.

Other than that, and a slightly pickled liver, his body is as good as any man twenty years younger. As if this were cause for celebration, the doctors say that he is likely to live a good long while yet. He sits slumped over a little, leaning to the right. His hands are bent up at the wrists, gone off in strange directions, and his eyes stare away from her. His face is frozen in an off-kilter moan, like a theater mask.

He looks appalled. After so many visits, she doesn't think it's about his being here, alone in this place—he doesn't seem to know about that. Maybe he's fixed on some memory. He could do that sometimes. His eyes seem a paler blue under fluorescents. Still they pierce, a look enhanced by the taut skin of his face, pulled thin over a bony edge of nose. A hawk's face, she thinks, with his hair like a falconer's hood, still as dark as a young man's, and longer than he wore it. The nurse has combed it back in wet strips.

Gabrielle opens the paper turkey and spreads out its rounded tail so that it can sit upright on the table between them. Her arranging is elaborate; she turns it by nudges, left and right. "Shub says to tell you he'll be coming to visit you, once everything quiets down. It's season, Pa. Did you know that?"

He still looks appalled.

"It's Thanksgiving tomorrow."

A gust of wind hits the window and rattles it. Gabe looks up to see a fine, swirling snow, what all the hunters have been praying for. It hisses against the glass.

She doesn't know why she should be here to celebrate Thanksgiving. They had never had a turkey dinner at home until she'd learned how to cook one. And then when she had, more often than not Pa left early to go hunt, and Robert too, unless he was going out somewhere else.

It's just that you're supposed to think of family at a time like this. Shub and Elsie tried to. She and her ex, Dennis, and his family, *they* always had a big to-do. Marrying him, she learned what she'd missed, silver candlesticks and cornucopia. Sugary yams and cranberry sauce. Murmured grace with heads bowed over lace and linen.

"I keep forgetting to tell Robert," she blurts out. "I keep putting it off, really. Marquette's not that far away. Really, he should know."

After Pa's first stroke, when everything still seemed all right, she had gone to tell Robert what had happened. It was the last time she'd been to the penitentiary. The news had panicked Robert, and she was in bad enough shape herself. She didn't tell him she'd just filed for divorce, though he'd have loved to hear that. She didn't feel like putting up with his sarcasm, didn't want him to have anything on her.

The first time Robert had met Dennis, she was living with him in Lansing, her first year away from home. That was 1968. She and Den were both going to Michigan State. Robert, newly discharged from the Army, had dropped in on them on his way back to the U.P. Two years later, Robert would land himself in jail. There had already been warnings in his letters, bragging about fights in the bars of Da Nang, a talent which his superiors were too stupid to use when the Tet offensive started; they had thrown him in the can instead. In those days, the bravado had seemed something he'd outgrow, something he could give up once he was home again.

So Robert had surprised her, flying into Lansing from California, fresh off the boat, still wearing his uniform. He and Dennis had a thing between them from the start, Robert seeing in the college student every peacenik he'd ever heard of and every excuse for America's pussyfooting around—when what we should have been doing was winning the war. Meanwhile Dennis projected onto Robert the imperialism of "Amerika," a veritable picture of it, the way he strutted around in uniform.

Dennis had been planning on graduate school at the time—a ruse to avoid the draft, Robert said privately to her. She'd defended Dennis fiercely. When he got his 4-F with one deaf ear a month later, he promptly dropped school to go into business full-time with his father, who owned two drugstores. Robert was right; Dennis never did go to another anti-war demonstration and became impatient with her involvement in it.

Dennis went on to keep his father's books, join the Rotary, take up golf, and insist that she cook his mother's seven-layer dinner topped with a can of tomato soup every Wednesday. She sees now that the thing between Dennis and Robert hadn't been entirely Robert's fault. Maybe the Dennis she'd married had been made up in her head.

"Got any big *scars* you want to show us?" Dennis had grinned at Robert that first night and then ducked down, still smiling into his drink, just kidding. Later, he would tease her own aspirations of graduate school with the same smirk, "Read any great *lit-cher-cher* lately?"

When Pa had his second stroke, Gabe never got around to telling Robert about it. She hadn't seen the point of watching Robert turn it into his crisis somehow. Soon she would, though. She promises herself she'll tell him face to face about how Pa had to be at Pinewood, and how she was back up at the cabin again, living nearby. She *would*. At the very least, she'd write.

And she'd tell him Shub had been the one who'd insisted they put everything in Gabe's name after the first stroke, just in case her pa ever had more trouble. It could happen, Shub warned them, still mindful of disaster so soon after Elsie's death. "That way, if Henry ever needs nursing care—god forbid, knock on wood," he said, "at least the whole thing will be paid for. Otherwise, there'll be nothing left for nobody."

Her father, never one to take charge of such matters, and suddenly scared enough to be cowed into action, had gone along with Shub's suggestion. And so had she, Gabe suddenly wants to tell Robert. To make sure Pa would be cared for, that's all, the only reason. Only later, only after she'd gotten the divorce and decided to go back to school—that's when she began to think about living at the empty cabin. She knows the cabin is Robert's too. She would tell him. The papers were just a legality.

She's ashamed for staying away from Robert for so long. She had something of an excuse when she lived downstate with Dennis. It doesn't hold up now. She keeps putting off seeing him or writing him, and it doesn't seem right, not with the holidays coming.

Though that's a crock. When had they ever been close? They'd never been close. When she and Robert were really young maybe, the two of them, trying to hold it all together when they moved up north. The two of them had been it, after their mother took off.

Gabe looks at her father across the table, thinking he should have been the one to hold the family together, but he never had. Right away she reproaches herself. That's too much like *Pa*, blaming, the way he always had their mother. In his mind, their mother was the one supposed to hold it together, and *she* never had. At least he'd stayed around, Gabe had to give him that much.

Pa and Gabrielle had gone together to see Robert at Marquette only once. It was close to a year after he'd been incarcerated for voluntary manslaughter, nearly six years ago now. She'd come up to see Pa without Dennis that time, and in fact, from then on, always came alone. Dennis had had his fill of her family by the time Robert's trial was over, the year they were married.

She forces herself to smile at her father now and turns the paper turkey toward him, making it walk a little. He doesn't notice, doesn't mind at all that she's been absent herself, deep in thought.

That visit was three years after Robert came back from Nam. Pa had been adamant about going to see Robert. He got these fixations sometimes. It was hard to know if he'd made up some kind of rule he had to obey, or if he really wanted to do a thing. They had gone, bearing the sight of windowless halls together, and the hollow sound of metal gates, clanging deep inside the belly.

She remembers sitting at a visitors' table like this one, with her hands in her lap, waiting for Robert, ashamed of his being in a place like that, ashamed of being there herself. Robert had been cool at first, saying, "Wellwellwell," standing in the doorway and looking at them for so long the guard finally gave him a nudge forward. He sauntered to the table and flopped into his chair indifferently. After sitting sullen, half-listening to their small talk flounder, he finally answered their many questions with "How do you *think* I am?"

Along the same long table, divided down the middle by a wire net, sat a row of men dressed in denim shirts with bold numbers stenciled on the pockets. On the family side, people in their best clothes leaned forward, whispering, talking, laughing softly—crying, some of them, and all straining for privacy where none was possible. At the narrow end of the room, high windows reinforced with wire let in a light that was harsh, without any softness of green or dappled shadows. Before she sat down, Gabe had spotted the gun-metal color of Lake Superior meeting the horizon, Lake Superior with its reputation for being so deep it won't wash up its dead the way most lakes do.

Exasperated by Robert, Gabe had finally jumped in to excuse herself. "It's not like this is easy for any of us, Robert. And it's not like I can come up and drop in every week. I drove six hundred miles to see you, didn't I? And this is how you act?"

"So the mail doesn't deliver all that distance, is that it? I'm not counting those sappy little cards you send. I haven't heard word one from you."

"Or me from you! Maybe I don't know what to say."

"Maybe you don't, is right."

They were silent, Robert looking down at his hands on the table between them. After a moment, he said, "I'm all right, I'm okay. Christ, I'm behaving myself, I guess." He looked up, smiling. "Doing carpentry! Can you beat that? Poundin' goddamn nails like my ole man."

Pa pulled back in his seat. "You could do worse," he said. "It's honorable work, using your hands."

"Yeah. I been doing the honorable thing. Just like Nam, the honorable thing." He looked down and stared again, then up at Gabe as he said: "And how about you? You livin' honorable, sis? Say, how is ole Dennis? Now *there* is an honorable man. Still sellin' Ace bandages and liniment? Still taking money off his poor, rich daddy?"

"Shut up, Robert! Why are you doing this?"

"But at least you're still married, baby sister. When I heard he'd turned 4-F, why, I figured he wouldn't be needing you anymore. Do you know, used to be I could get a mama-san to do for me what you're doing for ole Dennis—cleanin' his house, fixin' his dinners, sleepin' in his bed—for about, say, a buck-fifty a week."

Gabe's mouth had dropped open, as if she'd taken a punch in the stomach. She looked for some clue as to why he had said this to her, but Robert's expression was pointedly friendly and open, head tipped to one side.

She said, "I don't have to take—"

Pa, half-rising out of his chair, interrupted with his own response, "That's *enough!*"

Robert leaned back, satisfied at what he'd accomplished so easily, even the old man's silence overcome. "I just had to get a few things off my chest, that's all. Don't blow a gasket, old man."

"We're pretty sick of you and your gettin' things off your chest," Pa said. "We are up to here with your gettin' things off your chest. Like killing Fatty Wilson, gettin' things off your chest, pick a shovel up and whack him in the head, gettin' things off your chest."

As Pa's voice rose, the room grew quieter. People nearby glanced at him, hurrying to finish mumbled confidences. The guard, unsure, took a step in their direction, ready for the worst. Pa throttled his anger with a whisper, but its hissing carried farther than a normal tone would have. "You better *face* a few things!" he said.

People always said Robert should be an actor, he was so good looking. Blue eyes, blond curly hair, a face that Raphael might have wanted to paint on one of his angels. He sat with a smile on his lips, until the murmurs around them started up again, signaling they were safe. Watching him wait for the room to go back to normal, Gabe thought the trouble was people didn't know how accomplished an actor Robert already was.

When he finally leaned forward, he bit off his words and smiled. No one would guess there was anything wrong. "Okay, old man, I'll face a few things. Like how this family can't stand the sight of one another. I'll face how you drank yourself into a stupor every night you couldn't find some reason not to be home with your snotty-nosed kids. Is it okay if I face that? Or why our mother walked out, you want to *know* why? If she wanted any love she sure wasn't going to get it from you, was she? Nobody would. You just face a few things, old man. God *damn*. *You* better face a few things."

Gabe watched the color rise up her father's neck, spread to his face. Mean as the two had gotten, she had never before heard Robert challenge Pa's version of their mother. She felt Pa struggling with his breath, racing around inside himself to answer this. Finally, he countered, "You were a trial sent to punish us both. And I'll *tell* you about your mother. She came close to a nervous breakdown after you, and the two of you, together—you think it's easy? Trying to make ends meet like we did all the time? You don't need to look any further than yourself to find the reason your mother run off. She shoulda *beat* you more, but she didn't have the *spine* for it. I shoulda beat you more myself."

While Pa talked, Robert had straightened in his seat, keeping his face calm, glancing off to the side, crossing his legs. When he was finished, Robert sat there and stared, not saying anything, just pinching the bridge of his nose with his left hand, closing his eyes as if they hurt. He shook his head from side to side, slowly, back and forth, before opening his eyes. "Sssh-iit. You just don't get it, do you, old man?" he'd said.

Now she and Pa sit at a different table. Heat fills Pinewood's curtains as if they were sails. "I can't stay long," Gabrielle says after several minutes of watching them, listening to the blower in the sill. She can see the snow dashing itself against the glass, melting and running in tiny rivers. She speaks to the father who does not hear and is careful to explain herself, tone apologetic. "I should give Shub a hand. If there's snow, there'll be more deer checked in. It's been lousy tracking. I saw a little buck myself this morning. At the bottom of the ridge trail, remember? Below the ravine?"

Henry Bissonette takes a deep breath and then sighs, moving his left hand, the first detectable movement he's made. He must remember, she thinks. He wants to be out tracking. She asks, "What, Pa?" leaning forward, looking for some flicker in his eye to mark the passing of a thought, a recollection. But he's silent.

"Pa, you've got to try and talk. You can't get better unless you try. I hate to see you like this. People still tell stories. They talk about you and your tracking."

She hopes the mention of tracking will trigger another reaction, but after several more moments, decides it was coincidence, that's all, his earlier move unconnected to anything she's said. That feels familiar enough. At Marquette that day, listening to Pa's long speech at Robert, seeing the bitterness between father and son and feeling how palpable their anger, she had felt an odd loneliness, a dreadful envy.

She is tired of trying to get her father to see her, of not mattering, of feeling outside and removed from whatever is most important, whatever is *male*, she thinks, and at the center of things, and god, she is sick of it.

She shifts in her chair and looks down at her hands, because as soon as she thinks this, she wants to take it back, wants to tone it down. The male part, especially. It's not like she's some women's libber.

She's tired. From getting up before dawn. From working at Shub's. Besides, if she could say what she was thinking, and if her father could hear her, he'd only be annoyed and deny there was anything to it. He'd dismiss her, say she was crazy, maybe chuckle if he were in a good mood, but he would never fight with her.

He stares out past her, his expression unchanged. His eyes are empty of her.

November 18, 1983
Five Corners, Michigan

November makes you feel reckless—perfect for remembering the year I came back here. Outside, the clouds have been hanging low for a week, pressing down like some fur-covered belly. You start wishing the snow would just go ahead and let loose, even if it is that grainy, pebbly stuff that bites when it blows. Already it's pelting the ground with what looks like cornmeal, freezing mud solid. Walking out to the woodpile tonight will be pure misery, like a stroll on an iron washboard with iron boots on.

Kate's first questions about "home" as a place seem a pretty wise strategy for getting the weight of the story rolling behind anyone—even me. But as she says, nothing can make this easy. Everybody up here asks themselves similar questions, about this time of year. Why do I stay? Here, of all places? The one bright spot is deer season. More important than Thanksgiving in Copper County. More festive than

Christmas. Deer season, everybody at Five Corners wears hunter's red plaid or Day-Glo vests twenty-four hours a day. We stand ready to duck on our way out to the mailbox or just dumping the garbage. Downstaters with factory-fresh guns flock up here, camping in motels along M67, some of them sleeping at the lakefront cabins across from Shub's store.

My pa used to work at driving the deer for them whenever he was hard-pressed for money—most of the time, that was. It went against his grain, but there were always hunters at Sid's Friendly, and if Sid prevailed and got enough money for his best guide, he'd escort them out to Lake Nekoagon and Pa would drive them out some logging road in his pickup. You'd see them squeezed in shoulder to shoulder, their legs hanging down along the tailgate, arms cradling rifles like long-stemmed bouquets, looking bashful as suitors.

If he could've, Pa would have ignored buck fever, the place gone crazy with wanna-bes showing off. He hunted alone usually, out before dawn and again at dusk. I follow his example yet, sticking close to home, and though I don't study the bucks for size the way he did, most years I still tag my allotted deer. Like the news stories all said, I handle a gun well enough. You don't live up here and not.

Pa never let on he cared a thing about the hero worship waiting for him back at Shub's weigh-in station. More often than not, he brought in Five Corner's heaviest buck, and sometimes a trophy rack that'd bring the Boone and Crockett Society running. Wasn't any secret to it, he said. He'd single a buck out and track him all year—till he knew him like a brother was how he put it. The way he said this, you knew that was only the whole point of it. Although it's odd, thinking about this now—I mean if you knew him, because really he didn't know anybody like that, like a brother, nobody but the deer, and he shot them.

Nobody knew him either. When he brought a buck in, they'd all act like it, maybe, but that was about as close as anybody ever came. Shub's Economy Mart is where you can go for a little friendly "knowing" if you happen to need it, but relax, it's not going to go too far. Folks go to Shub's to hear themselves talk.

I know I felt safe there—the only place I did for quite a while. Does that make it home? After what happened, I kept on working there, getting by hunting, forgetting about old ambitions. For years, Shub tried to connect me with any likely suspect that came through the store—a guy from Al-Anon, some therapist from Escanaba, finally the professor who said there were part-time jobs opening up at Fond du Lac. People told me about books, some of which helped. But what helped me most was that Shub grieved what I grieved.

He's as old as the mountains now, older than my father was when he died. Just this morning I saw a downstater posing on his porch, a deer hanging from the scale's hook. You have to cringe at the way these guys will beam at Shub and his camera no matter what—eighty-nine pounds and a spike-horn?—they beam, proud of themselves.

Hunting's not about trophies. But what is it exactly—and why should it matter to me so much? How is it part of what I think of as "home"?

Maybe if Pa'd had the words for saying what he loved, our family could have been different. But that's too simple. He had more power in his silence than I've got blathering away here for pages. Probably I'm just messing myself up with this nonsense—off on the wrong track or something. I want to talk to Kate about this—but how?

NOVEMBER, 1973

Gabrielle takes the long way home from visiting her pa, stopping in Clearwater to buy some cognac, special for Shub. This will please him like nothing else, prompting his stories of WWII. His marching through France, seeing Patton—the bastard—and drinking his first toast with a mademoiselle whom he later found out was a madame with a kid. Not that he blamed the poor woman for it, she and the kid were both hungry, and he'd given them all the chocolate he could. But of course, if he'd known Elsie then . . .

Yes, the cognac would do it.

Bottle on the seat next to her, on M67 again, she drives past Sid's Friendly Tavern and sees the parking lot is jammed already with hunters quitting early in honor of the holiday. Sid has a portable sign out front, flashing lights atop a message that reads: BETTER THAN HOME! GOBBLE-GOBBLE ALL YOU CAN EAT! TURKEY AND THE FIXINS, $5.95 THROUGH THURSDAY!

The turnoff that leads to Five Corners changes to dirt, the trees close in overhead. To the side of the road, bare huge beeches and maples stand far apart, stripped of leaves. Light that had been shut out during summer now fills the open spaces with an incandescence, the feel of an empty cathedral. On impulse, Gabe turns off on a logging road she'd forgotten about, one that ends with a trail to the top of the cedar ridge above the cabin. This late in the day, she might catch something heading back down to feed. The snow might help.

She puts on her down vest and a second pair of wool socks she keeps in the glove compartment, tying on a bright red tunic for other hunters. Deer see only in shades of gray. What they pick up on is the slightest movement and human scent. Gabrielle tears a small branch off a pine tree at the edge of the road and, crushing the needles, rubs their spice on her clothes.

The trail she remembers cuts south, crossing the logging road about where an outcropping of rock forces it to curve. A spring-fed trickle of water winds its way around the base of the rock and following it is a deer run. She squats near the rock at a spot where icy pellets look kicked up. Carefully, she picks wet leaves away to look more closely. An imprint in the soil just fits the vee of her two fingers—deer sign, and fresh.

She follows the trend of the land downward. Where the trees are not so lofty, an understory of aspen shivers, whispering with coppery leaves intact. Here and there a hemlock grows, its green surprising. The wind is quieter, blowing into Gabe's face from the northwest. Luck is with her.

Every so often, the sound of rifle fire comes quavering through the air, a far-off report that echoes in waves in the ear, sometimes repeated: four, five, six in a row. Most of the fire seems to be coming from miles behind her, over nearer to Dumpling Hill beyond Five Corners.

She looks more closely at the trail, aware suddenly that it is much more obvious than it should be. Someone has been here earlier in the day. No deer would have kicked up the trail this badly, no herd of deer. She stoops to look and thinks she sees something new. What is that? A smear of blood. A sticky wad of fur. Leaves sprawl, upended from some great lunge. And there are the deep, slashing tracks of an animal on the run.

Someone has wounded a deer and not brought him down. The longer she follows the trail, the surer she is. And the hunter has given up. There, in that mound of snow, Gabe sees part of a boot print headed back. As she studies it, the heel fills in with granular snow, pelting down harder.

She is hooked now. She follows the trickle of water to where it widens enough to be called a creek. Eventually it will seep down the hill and empty into the swampy outlet down the shore from the cabin. This area is on Bissonette land; somewhere back there she has crossed the line that marked it. She is closer to where Pa's footbridge crosses the deep ravine. On a rock, she spots another splash of near-fresh blood.

It is possible to climb down the rock side of the ravine and back up the other to continue along the deer run. She has seen deer do this, bounding without effort, straight down, straight up again, thirty feet on each side. Her guess is that this is what the deer she is tracking has done, though more slowly, headed for the safety of the cedar. It might have found cover at the bottom of the ravine, but from here it looks too bare, too narrow, and wet. If she had time, she'd take the climb on foot and scare it up if need be, but the day is growing dimmer. She decides to use the footbridge and gamble on the deeryard, knowing that habit is a driving force too, for anything wounded.

She begins looking for the bridge, at the same time checking to see whether she's remembered the small flashlight she usually hangs around her neck. It is still there on a thong and working. She judges it close to three o'clock. There should be a pulley that she can use to bring the deer back over, but she'd almost prefer to drag the buck down the hill to the cabin, the shortest way. Her breath comes faster.

Near the edge of the ravine, the gorse thickens. She makes out a rub where a buck has exercised his neck, polishing the bark of some young saplings with his antlers to mark his territory. She hears the trickle she's been following drop into the ravine to join Brushy Creek at the bottom. About a mile to the east is the stand of spotted alder where Pa had taken her as a girl to watch the bucks feed.

In the spring, Brushy Creek is noisy, rushing with melt-off, in a hurry to sweeten the lake. But now the brook is close to silent, soaking under snow that is mounding on rocks and icy banks. The ravine's crags aren't the usual Copper County ore, but something softer, a tan sandstone that has yielded to the water and been cut deep and narrow, left with pits and cavities where small hemlocks and spruce have taken a foothold. Here and there, one has lost its grip, falling forward, upended, turned brown and brittle from the air striking its roots.

The bridge, slung over wide-open space, unfurls in front of Gabrielle like a hammock. Her pa had cinched two heavy pieces of cable at the base of sturdy white pines on opposite sides of the ravine. Like two parallel sides of a ladder, the cable is connected by wooden rungs that are flat slats to walk on. The sides of this ladder move and reflect back the crosser's weight, bobbing and swaying.

On the left side of the cable, Henry Bissonette had bolted a rickety wood railing to guide one hand. In the middle of the span, though, he had run out of wood. Both enterprising and lazy, he'd continued on with a piece of plastic-covered clothesline and had never gotten around to finishing the thing off properly.

This transition where it dips lowest is always the worst moment on the bridge. Gabe remembers how the sturdy feeling of wood gives way to slender rope and jars the body, disrupting the rhythm of walking. The trick is to ignore the jounce and keep on going. She fears getting stuck on that bridge and being unable to deny the sickening loss under her hand, unable to push past the point where her heart jumps up and flies away.

Her pa, mindful that he couldn't keep hunters off his land or off his bridge either, has posted a sign in case one of them decided to sue him. Nailed to the white pine, a board with red, drippy letters spells out his warning: USE AT YOUR OWN RISK. The paint looks relatively fresh, so Gabe guesses he'd continued to check on the bridge until this past year. She tells herself there is little that can go wrong anyway.

Gabe makes certain her rifle is empty and slung firmly back on her shoulder. She rolls both shoulder blades around to get comfortable, kicks her boots against the pine to make sure any ice is knocked off. Two deep breaths and she reaches out to touch the rail and puts her foot on the first slat.

At the beginning, close to the ravine's edge, the cable is taut. She feels a gentle swing back to the pressure of each step, a swing that grows a little deeper the closer to the middle she gets. Rhythm is everything. She begins pacing herself to step regularly, inhaling evenly. The rhythm is the thing, like dancing.

The railing ends and the rope begins, the swaying deeper-seated here. She has to lean out a bit, depending on the rope to tighten. It does finally, but her foot slips on a hint of ice. Her straightened arm pushes harder on the rope, its movement out, farther out—taking her breath away. The treble of water far below becomes loud music.

Gabe holds her breath in close to her spine. She straightens. She keeps on going. The cable grows taut again. Step-two-three, *there*-two-three, *there*-there-there, *across*—she hops onto solid ground, bends over and, bracing her hands against her knees, takes several deep breaths and blows them out forcefully to calm the drubbing against her chest wall.

The bridge sways from her last step. She can't help smiling at it, riding her breathing, reining it in. She can feel every muscle, shot through with adrenaline. Maybe this is the real reason Pa built the bridge. No deer could outrun her now. She pulls her breaths deeper until they satisfy. Then she shrugs off the rifle to load two cartridges.

It is another ten minutes to the knob that marks the beginning of the white cedar, a winter deeryard. She had expected to follow the buck farther in, but he is there, just on the edge of a small meadow, facing upwind of her, so that she gets closer than she might have otherwise.

He struggles to get up as soon as he spots her movement. Bleeding at the chest, forward of the right shoulder, he stumbles as he gathers himself to leap away, his mouth open a little, panting.

He never completes his vault. Later Gabrielle will not remember raising her rifle or aiming. She only hears the blast of her gun and watches the untying of bones. The buck collapses.

She comes at him from the saddle to make sure he is dead and, seeing his size, wants to leap and whoop with elation, except that at the same time, she is wrestling with a numinous dread that radiates out from her belly. One of the buck's slender legs is drenched in half-dried blood, the hair matted with it, and his muzzle too, from trying to lick the wound.

She squats next to him to feel the wiry coat and make this real. He is healthy, his hooves dark and polished as hardwood, his flanks well muscled and warm. Six points, a good 140 pounds. Shub will appreciate this one.

The snow is beginning to blow in heavy waves, turning to big flakes stacking in mounds on the ground and along tree branches. The gray of the sky has deepened ominously. She has already decided to take the shorter route downhill to the cabin on foot. She can pick her truck up tomorrow when Shub comes. Dressing the buck out here in the field will make dragging him easier.

Moving quickly, she pulls the buck over next to a rotted log, propping it on its back, hooking its forelegs under the antlers to keep them out of the way. She draws out her knife, aware suddenly that Dennis and his family, seated at Thanksgiving linen, are watching, aghast. She waits for her hand to take the chill from the metal handle.

Every time it comes to this, there is a moment longer than a moment ought to be, when she is certain she will not be able to finish. She keeps seeing the buck, gathering himself to leap—at odds with the buck on the ground, whose eyes are as bright as they had been in life, whose nose remains wet, a succulent black.

She opens him then, releasing his warmth to the cold in a cloud of raw-smelling steam.

November 21, 1983
Five Corners, Michigan

Barraged by memories and feelings. Not sleeping. There's this one time especially I have to write down—the year I moved back here. I'd bagged a deer late in the afternoon and decided to drag him back down the ridge trail—steeper than it looks, coming down. I was only worried about running out of light until what was forecast as flurries turned into a regular snowstorm. You'd think someone who'd grown up here would have had more sense. But I was feeling as though I could do anything. You feel that way sometimes after a hunt. It was the first time I'd ever tracked a deer, not waiting on stand the way I usually did. I felt full of myself. Unbeatable.

It got dark sooner than later, and I wasn't as strong as I thought. I'd made a sled for the buck with a pine bough and some rope, but steering it was tough and wherever it was steep I had to turn around and brake the thing to keep from getting run over by my own contraption. I reloaded it so the antlers wouldn't do me in because turning the whole sled around was impossible on the narrow path headed down. But flopping the carcass over was as bad—gripping the slope with my toes through my boots, one leg up to brace the sled, my arms the only leverage.

I kept falling, stumbling. The next steep place I decided to slide down on the seat of my britches so the buck's gravity sat against my shoulders. I scootched forward, braking with my legs. But this tore up my pants and soaked my fanny so that after a while I lost feeling in my butt. I mean, it was funny, but at the same time I knew it was dangerous to do nothing but laugh.

I stopped and stood up a lot, rubbing myself hard, shaking my legs and squatting to keep the circulation going. And I started remembering hunting stories. The time Sid Nichols sat down too hard on a rock and broke this little whiskey bottle in his hip pocket. Sliced a vein in his leg, soaked his whole pantleg with blood—he might not have made it out alive if Pa hadn't known about pressure bandages. Another time Shub fell off a ledge and knocked himself out so he couldn't feel one leg had broken through the ice and was soaking in the river. Thought he might lose some toes that time. Another guy, Whitey Turner, shot himself accidentally and did lose some toes, and lived to thank god that was all he lost. Now you talk about being lost, like I was, and that's another whole subject in itself.

The thing about being outdoors is the way it pushes out whatever doesn't count right now this minute. Every bit of you has to find the right footing to keep your balance and watch for weather and tracks and direction and do what has to be done and done now, done right. Living at the cabin is something like that for me—just staying warm or planning well enough ahead so that I'm not going to starve to death if I get snowed in. Keeping to essentials suits me. I mean, it was clear enough that night. What matters is staying alive.

Except for the strangest part—with me half frozen, half dead, and worn out. The part I want to get to for Kate. I mean how beautiful it was. I couldn't help seeing this even in the shape I was in. Or maybe the shape I was in made seeing it possible. The clouds stayed thick, but the north wind had picked up—part of my misery. It was breaking up the cloud cover and every so often, this full moon would come sliding out. Whenever it did, the snow sparked and flashed. Even when clouds muffled the light, a spooky radiance backlit woolen sky and shone on the ground, until the moon seemed to be coming out of things, the snow glowing from the inside and everything blanketed, white, still.

I knew I'd be all right once I got to the edge of the ridge. I could see Five Corners down below. Shub's Economy Mart across the road from the cabins and Mrs. Snow's place—she was still alive back then—and the ranger Natty Raison's house. The hunters in Shub's cabins had already put out their lights. Or at least I imagined them there, already tucked into their beds, the air moist and warm, silent except for when their space heaters kicked in maybe, or when somebody let out a moan from a dream.

While I watched, Lake Nekoagon bulged toward their doors thick as syrup, chunking up with slush. Standing there, I felt like I could see and understand everything in the world. All these slivers of ice connecting and joining until everything would be tempered white, every liquid solid as stone. No compromise. Everywhere there was water, everything that was alive would be growing the same icy razors. Alone on a hill with your feet growing numb, watching the world freeze, you remember: It gets cold enough and the sap in the trees will crack timber wide open with a sound like gunfire.

By then, the buck and I were coated with snow. Inside, where just that morning blood had rushed to keep him warm, his hollowed-out center was crusted with ice needles. They were stitching his eyelashes, binding his liquid eye. Now there was only the press of the cold, the weight of his carcass, the coming stone of the lake. Whenever the moon eased out from behind a cloud, its face was the picture of grief.

The snow kept on sparkling, and right after that my life came undone. Though in another way, it came together. I've never thought of the deer story quite that way before—not as gateway or boon until just now when I wrote it, imagining Kate unblinking as the full-eyed moon. Maybe it's time, maybe I can tell this.

II

AND THESE
THY GIFTS

Moonlight paints a trapezoid of pallid light on Gabrielle's quilt. She believes those stories about people going mad from lying in the moonlight just enough that she remembers them, lowering herself down into the stuff. Somehow the cool, sad glow from the moon's face seems companionable.

She pulls the quilt up over her nose and through her window watches clouds breaking up from the wind. As if blown by the same gusts, her own aches are opening, stretching out in every muscle and joint of her body. The bedding is chill against her skin, but her cheeks burn and so do her right arm and thigh, rubbed raw by her sliding, made rawer still by soaping them in the shower. She smells good, at least, no longer damp and sour. After a moment, she begins to warm the space. Her muscles unclench, elongate.

Without trying, she begins to float, the cleft between her legs the only place heavy on her, weighing her down. She is swollen, and a vague pleasant pulse wambles down her thighs. If she weren't so exhausted, she'd be horny. She always gets this fluid-laden ache with her period. She was surprised, undressing for her shower, to find the stain in her panties. She never pays her rhythms any attention, so the sight of blood there, an echo and so close, had unsettled her.

Down in the cooler beneath the cabin, the buck hangs where she's hoisted him with a pulley, his hocks punctured by her knife to take the rope. He's suffered a beating, just as she has, coming down the hill. But there'll be plenty of meat for the freezer. She'll eat well this winter. She turns on her stomach, feeling satisfied, cupping her pussy with one hand to connect with that other side of bleeding.

Growing warmer, sleepier, her deep breathing overtakes other rhythms. If she could observe herself, she'd see her eyelids beginning to flicker, eyeballs sliding underneath, turning from side to side, trying to look everywhere at once. Inside, she is much younger, in a dress of purple seersucker, a dress she remembers loving, and on a journey, meeting magic at every turn. There are convoluted pivots and inter-twinings, and then, at another turn, some menace she runs from.

Her hair streams out, in danger of being caught by the thing behind her, but she can't run fast enough. Her legs are so heavy she can barely lift them. Behind her comes a pounding, like feet on a wooden floor, like hands at the hold, demanding to get in. She wants to see who is there, wants to do the right thing, open it. But that would let the water in, and then she might die—yet the voices cry, the hammering persists.

Gabrielle sits up, startled at being awakened when she hadn't even known she'd been asleep. A chill line of sweat edges her upper lip. She can hear a pounding at the door.

"Aaah, that's hot," the girl says.

"No, it's not. Your feet just think it is. Here. Tell me if it gets to be too much."

Gabrielle tinkers with the faucets on the tub, adding tepid water little by little over several minutes, warming it very gradually. "How's that?" she asks at intervals. "Still hot? Better?"

Eventually the water feels baby-warm to the touch. The young woman has been silent, unmoving, but now she begins swishing a foot around. "Still moves," she says, then tries the other foot, then both of them together, like two fish swimming, and adds, "They're not aching like they're going to fall off anymore. They still burn though."

The girl lifts one foot onto her opposite thigh, trying to look at her toes more closely in the light of the kerosene lamp while she balances on the edge of the tub. "Hey," she says, "aren't you going to turn the light on? I want to count and see if they're all still here."

"There isn't one. Just in the kitchen and at the back door and downstairs where I've got some power tools. Come out here and we'll have a closer look." Gabrielle hands her a towel and the girl pads out behind her. They study her feet under the kitchen light, her toes and the edges of her feet still bright red. "There's no white," Gabe pronounces, and bending to pinch the girl's big toe, she asks, "Feel that?"

"Yes!" the young woman says, looking annoyed and surprised. She flops down in a chair, sighing, obviously worn out and able to feel it now. Her long blond hair falls forward around her face.

"Put these wool socks back on. Go on. Get close to the stove."

Gabe goes to the back door and looks out at the driveway, where an orange rusted Volkswagen Beetle is parked. She wonders how the girl made it so far. And dressed in that absurd wine-colored cape—no mittens, no boots. She's a tiny thing, no higher than Gabe's shoulder, and fine-boned, hatless, too vain to cover her hair.

The girl had rolled her eyes with relief when Gabe opened the door, but she couldn't speak, her chin was chattering so violently. Her whole body was shaking. It had taken several seconds for Gabrielle to take in the strange vision. The girl's ankles were bare, she had on a pair of strapped Mary Janes without so much as a pair of nylons, and she was in trouble.

It was this last realization that broke through Gabe's fog of sleep, and without speaking, she'd led the girl to the cookstove. "Get those shoes off," were her first words, and after the girl had obeyed, Gabe watched her gasp at the alarming red of her toes and the bottoms of her feet, heard her say, "Oh I *am* stupid, aren't I?"

Gabrielle had thrown another log in and, leaving the oven door open for extra warmth, went to the bedroom to get warm clothes: wool socks, a wool shirt, some sweatpants.

"Here, put these on," she had said, helping her slip out of a longish dress, which was wet around the hem. The girl was maybe twenty, more likely younger. She had the sort of body Gabrielle had wished for when she was that age: petite, small-breasted, slight, her long fingers ending with polished oval nails. A kind of doll, Gabe thought, though more wholesome than a Barbie—a Debby or a Heidi, maybe.

As her feet came back to life, the girl had started moaning a little. "Ohh! God, *ohh!* They're killing me, god, what did I go and do? Are they frostbitten? My toes are gonna fall off, aren't they, right here on the floor. Ohhhh. I never knew you could ache like this. Ohgod."

"Come on," Gabe had said, fearing the worst, and walked her to the bathtub, filling it with cool water the girl had felt as hot.

Back at the stove, the girl says, "Guess I'd better introduce myself." She takes Gabe in with a gaze that assesses, appearing to find her hostess in need of a makeover. Then she straightens her face, polite in view of her situation, and motions her awareness that Gabe has on pajamas, apologizing with a limp gesture. "I was so scared," the girl says. "I was ready to break a window or something just to get in here. My name is Valley." She puts out her hand and pumps Gabe's, adding in a burst, "I guess I got lost in all this snow. I've been driving for hours, I should have started out earlier, you know, but that's always been my problem—sleeping in. Like I'm on some different biological wavelength or something. Biorhythms, that's what they call it. I can't get up in the mornings. Like right now? Tired as I am, I'm wide awake." She shrugs helplessly, letting go of Gabe's hand. "Listen, can you get me a hanger for my cape? It's gonna be ruined if I don't hang it up."

Gabe, surprised by this outpouring, gestures to some pegs on the far kitchen wall, near the back hall. She watches the girl busy herself straightening the folds of the cape, fussing with it, smoothing it. Every so often Valley purses her lips and bends her toes upward, checking to see if they move all right, but she never stops talking. "Oh, brother. It's really soaking wet. I don't know how long it's gonna take, drying. Maybe a long time." She looks at Gabrielle then, who takes a few moments to understand her real point.

"You'll have to stay here while it dries," Gabe finally answers. "I've got plenty of room, it's no trouble. Anyway, with this snow, you're only going to get hung up on the road. I can't believe you made it this far."

"Neither can I! I must have gotten stuck about fourteen times! I never felt so desperate. Or so stupid. Can you believe I didn't wear boots! I mean, I have some somewhere, but they're not very warm anyway, and I thought I'd be fine, sitting in the car. It wasn't snowing when I left Marquette. Like I never thought about having to get out of the car fourteen times! I was ready to sleep in the thing, but then I worried that maybe I'd freeze? And that was when I saw the top of your house here and I thought, hallelujah! Civilization!" She smiles and lifts her hands, wriggling her fingers like a holy roller, tipping her head, side to side.

"I mean, I really appreciate your taking me in. I promise I won't be any trouble at all. As soon as the snow stops, I'll be on my way again." She says this last part with intense, unwavering eye contact so sincere that Gabe finds herself doubting it. Then Valley suddenly flops forward and begins rubbing her ankles, her hair hiding her face.

"Where is it you're going anyway? Maybe I can help you with directions."

"Oh, I'm looking for this *old* geezer. He lives alone in a cabin somewhere around here. For all I know, he may be dead by this time, you probably don't even—well, maybe you do know him. Henry Bissonette?"

The girl is still bent over, her body perfectly relaxed. It can't be a joke.

"Why do you want to see *him?*" asks Gabe.

"Why? You know him? What is he, an ogre?"

"I'm just surprised *you* would know him, that's all."

"Oh, I don't. I never met the guy."

Exasperated, Gabrielle comes closer, wanting to see the girl's face. "Then why are you looking for him at two o'clock in the morning?" she demands.

"Hey, what's with you?" Valley answers, looking up, her tone just as annoyed. "You know this guy? Is he something to you? Look, I'm supposed to go to my boyfriend's house and his father, Henry Bissonette, is going to put me up for a while, see? I'm meeting my *boyfriend*, Robert Bissonette, not the old geezer. Does that explain it? Jeez."

"Robert? What do you mean you're meeting Robert?" Gabrielle feels balanced on a wire, swaying alarmingly. Who is this girl?

"God, you act like you're gonna have a litter of kittens or something. What's so awful about me meeting Robert Bissonette?" She pauses and purses her lips. "Oh, I get it. You know about his being a con, is that it? Well, look, don't worry, I'll be out of here and you'll never know the difference. You can cross the street if you see the two of us in town, okay?" Valley goes back to rubbing her ankles, furiously now, and Gabe hears an exasperated, half-whispered "God!"

"Well," Gabe matches her tone, "why don't I just introduce *myself*. How would that be?"

"Yeah, that'd be good. What *is* your name?"

"Gabrielle Bissonette."

Valley sits up straight. "You're kidding."

Her mouth drops open and Gabe sees that she understands Gabe isn't kidding, not at all. She watches a horrific possibility cross the girl's face. This frump in plaid, who never plucks her eyebrows? "You're his *wife*," Valley says. "I shoulda known he'd have a wife! Oh, he is such a smooth talker, and *no* respect, bringing me all the way out here—*telling* me all that stuff—Jesus *Christ*—"

"No, you've got it wrong. Look, I'm his sister. This is the Bissonette cabin you were looking for, you've *found* the place he told you about."

"You're kidding. This is it? You mean I did it? I wasn't lost?" She is elated, beaming at the discovery of her good sense. "I found this place all on my own? And I thought I was *stupid* for getting myself lost. This is it? Whatta you know? This is *it*!"

She is grinning widely and then suddenly covers her mouth and ducks her head, looking around the room, sheepish. She whispers, "So where *is* Henry? I don't even know if he's old, really. I didn't mean to call your *father* an old geezer. Sorry." She shakes her head. She goes back to her rubbing, but keeps glancing about the room, ducking, waiting for him to pop out.

"He's not here. He had a stroke. Didn't Robert tell you he'd had a stroke?"

"Well, yeah, but he said he was better. So is he really sick? Is he in the hospital or something?"

"No, he's out now. He's at a nursing home."

"Oh. So that's why *you're* here?"

"Sort of."

Gabe picks up the poker and thrusts it into the firebox, making room for another log. She slams the stove door shut harder than she needs to. "I'm not even going to ask how my *brother*, who must be a good fifteen years older than you, managed to have a relationship with some girl while he was in *jail*. I mean, how old *are* you?"

"Older than I look. Twenty-four."

"Right."

"I am!"

"And he's coming *here*, you say?"

"Yes. In a couple of months."

"A couple of months. As in sixty days?"

"More or less. He gets out in"—she shrugs—"February. Near the end of February, I guess."

"That's more like three months. You planned to stay here with my father for three months?"

"Robert said he'd be happy to have me."

Gabe thinks, Right, that sounds like Pa. Picture him with a tea towel draped over one arm.

Valley adds, "Look, I didn't *know* he was sick. Robert didn't tell me he was sick. He said you told him he was all right after the stroke. He said he had a sister lived downstate. He called you Gabe, that's why I didn't recognize your name."

Gabe has been sitting, twirling the poker in her hands. Now she stands to set it upright in the nearest corner. "Yes, Pa was all right after the first stroke. And Robert didn't know he'd had another. I kept putting off telling him. I—" She heaves a loud, exasperated sigh, shaking her head. "I kept putting it off." She shakes her head harder. "This is great, just *great*. What a royal, stupendous mess."

"What's a mess? *I'm* a mess?"

"No, this. *This* is a mess. Me here, the old man sick. You, Robert. All of it, a mess."

The lights overhead go out suddenly, and the room is pitch-black. Valley's voice trembles, politely alarmed, asking, "What happened?"

"It's the snow. You'd better get used to it." Oh, she'll fit right in, Gabe thinks. The girl would probably start in crying next. Probably steal Gabe blind if she's anything like most of Robert's girlfriends. Christ! The girl can't stay *here*.

Gabe waits for her eyes to readjust, then opens a cupboard and brings down another kerosene lamp. She lights it and, reaching to turn off the switch for the kitchen, walks in the dark to the back door to flip the switch there.

The clouds are blocking much of the moonlight, but she can still make out the Volkswagen, which by this time is piled even higher with snow. Gabe's eyes ache and she's getting cold again. She shivers, thinking of her warm bed, chilly again by now. Damn, *damn*, she has to figure this out, but she has to get herself some *sleep* first.

"I'll set you up on the day bed," she calls, opening the hall cupboard and pulling out some extra blankets. "You'll be comfortable enough for tonight anyway. We'll worry about the rest of it tomorrow."

Valley's voice, calling from the dark, is a compliant little girl's. "Okay."

Gabe sets the kerosene lamp on a table in the far corner of the front room and Valley helps her make up the bed in dim light.

Through the porch windows facing the daybed, the moon's struggle with cloud cover is casting a shadow that moves like water, darkness writhing with the lamplight's reflection. "I can close the curtains if the moonlight bothers you. Might be warmer."

Valley nods she'd prefer that.

"You climb in and I'll turn the lantern off."

"Do you have to?"

"What do you mean?"

"Can you please leave it on, just real low? It's safe with the glass over it, isn't it?"

"It won't smell very good."

"Please? I'm kinda shook up."

Gabe shrugs and adjusts the knob to a low flame. When she turns around, Valley is curled up under the covers. "I'm exhausted," the girl says. "My biorhythm's just pooped out on me I guess."

"I guess. Well, good night now."

"Good night. Sleep *tight*," the girl chirps.

Pausing at her bedroom door, just off the kitchen, Gabe looks back at the lantern's flicker, the shadows on the draperies. She hears the rustle of bedsheets, the girl making her nest.

Exhausted is what she is herself, Gabe thinks, climbing into bed, feeling the ice of the sheets again—damn, *damn* it all, and she'd had it so warm. She pulls her knees up to her chest, hugging herself, trying not to give in to the shiver that is gathering in her belly.

Her eyes beg for closing, she is tired, so tired, but closing them only makes clearer what a tangle this is, nothing to distract her but the spinning sensation behind her eyelids, bright bits of color floating in the black. She opens her eyes, turns over, and her quilt wraps and snarls itself around her legs. She kicks herself free, wanting the air on her feet. She wants to be able to hit the floor, running. Damn, she thinks. A girl who's afraid of the dark. Plumping up her pillow, she drops her head down hard, plumps it again when that's not comfortable.

Outside her window, the moon has traveled across the sky, lower now and nearly out of sight behind the ridge. The back-lit clouds are changing their shapes like ghosts, moving, never still. Gabe folds the lumpy pillow in half and gives it a sock, feeling her fist sink into softness next to her face, socks it again, again.

THANKSGIVING DAY, 1973

The snow on the sill is a good two feet deep and, although the stuff is still falling, it falls with less vehemence, the sky over the lake clearing, looking colder. Gabe stares at the view several moments, until she is sure it is staying in one place. She feels strangely unsteady. Maybe she has fluid in her ears from having gotten so frozen on the hunt. Maybe she's awakened in the middle of tossing and turning.

She gets up to restoke the cookstove fire and makes coffee as quietly as she can. When she hears the squeak of springs coming from the front room, she feels a sinking sensation, but puts on a face that gives nothing away, not friendly, not unfriendly.

Valley comes tiptoeing into the kitchen, her face puffy from sleep, hair pulled back in a knot. She's draped a brown wool blanket over her shoulders. "You have guns," the girl says, and her tone makes Gabe look up. She might have said, "You have boils."

Gabe crosses her arms and answers, "Most people do around here. You ready for breakfast?"

The girl eats so much Gabe wonders when the last time was. She is glad she bought fresh fruit when she was in Clearwater. She sets this out in the cornucopia for a second course, explaining she'd intended it for the Thanksgiving table but probably there will be no turkey today. Shub, the turkey-bearer, will never be able to get through all the snow. They'll likely be stuck here for a while.

"Well, at least we're warm, you know?" Valley hoists the blanket up higher around her neck. "Anyway, I hate that whole turkey scene, poor naked thing. I don't eat turkey, not even if it *is* Thanksgiving—I don't eat meat ever. People look at you weird, you know, like you're un-American or something. But I don't care. I'm not any carnivore."

"You've never eaten meat?"

"Oh sure. My mom made me eat it when I was a kid. But I never did like it."

"Does Robert know this?" Gabe asks, coffee cup up to her lips, arms held tense in a casual pose. "Last I knew, he loved a good steak."

Valley shrugs nonchalantly and chases a last spoonful of oatmeal in her bowl.

Gabrielle is tempted to ask her how she had met her brother. What did they plan once he got out? He has always talked about going away, to California, which he'd seen when he got back from Vietnam, or out to Nebraska where the family of an Army friend lived. Another part of Gabe wants to remain separate—not to know any of this has been a blessed state.

"I might as well tell you. We got married at Marquette," Valley confides suddenly. "Did you know you could do that? There were thirty or so of us getting married all at once. Like the Moonies or something. I never knew a guy in jail could get married, but they say they do it all the time." The girl smiles, hugging her knees. "I can't get used to it. I still call Robert my boyfriend."

Gabrielle stares at the girl's flawless skin. Wherever light finds downy hair—on her cheeks, above her full mouth, her forearms—she is golden. There's a tiny cleft in her chin, an angularity to her face that hints at strength and will.

Gabe says, "I can't believe you. Why would a girl like you—no, why would *any* girl—tie herself down like that? With somebody you can't even know, except that he's trouble, that's all you know about Robert."

Valley looks at Gabe as if she has just said something in Greek, and mouths her answer carefully: "If you love someone, you're *already* tied down. No ceremony does that, it's just something . . . you know . . . that you *want*." She shrugs, signaling an end to the matter.

"I see." What Gabe sees is the futility of engaging. She gets up to concentrate on stacking the dishes, deciding to dismiss the girl. What is the point of talking to someone who thinks like this, in homilies?

"You're married, aren't you?" Valley calls to her back. "Robert said you were."

"Divorced. This summer."

"Oh."

Valley seems to be waiting for Gabe to tell her about it, but Gabe only runs water in the dishpan, splashing soap bubbles with her hand. Outside everything is stacked with snow, branches of young pines and underbrush bowed over with the weight of it, a million white arches.

"When I wake up some more, I'm gonna go out to the car," Valley says. "My clothes are all out there. I wanna give you back your things." She holds out both her legs, her feet in Gabe's woolen socks.

Later, they both get dressed and venture outside, Valley in Gabe's wool jacket and some extra boots. The temperature is colder and the snow crunches under their feet. Snow is still falling, but it's finer, brighter in the sun.

"I always hate being the one to spoil how perfect it looks, don't you?" says Valley, looking back on her trail. "We should make angels." At that, she flops backward, laughing breathlessly, sweeping her arms and legs in the snow.

Gabe watches her, unamused, then begins stacking firewood on the back porch. Valley doesn't seem to mind her glum stares. Still smiling, half-playing, the girl brushes the snow off her car with a broom. The door on the driver's side is ornately wired shut, slightly off kilter. Valley crawls in from the passenger side and struggles with pulling things out over the gear shift. Her winnings are two brown garbage bags that apparently hold her belongings. Gabe watches while she lugs them to the cabin.

"Don't tell me you don't have a car!" Valley calls back over her shoulder. "What do you do? Snowshoe? Dogsled?"

"Oh, I have a truck. It's just not here. I left it up at—" She remembers Valley's tone about the guns. "It's a long story. I have to get it later."

"Well, you can use my car if you ever need to," Valley calls, her inflection screaming she is anxious to be of service, dying to be of help. While Gabe pretends to be too busy stacking wood to notice, she watches the girl's belongings pile up by the back door.

Back inside, Valley begins pulling out dozens of small brown bottles filled with aspirin-like pills, rubbery yellow and brown oil capsules, and one horse pill that is filled with tinier yellow and green pellets. *Timed C*, the label says. A miracle, Valley calls it, sniffing loudly and rubbing her nose with the back of her hand, explaining that she hasn't had a cold since she discovered it. She swallows a handful.

Next she reaches into another bag and pulls out a long flowered skirt, holding it up to herself. The kitchen looks ransacked. This is the third outfit Valley has pulled out and discarded, flinging all of them over the backs of chairs.

"Wait," Gabe says. "Before you drag everything out here, underfoot, why don't I show you the room upstairs. If we leave the hatch open, it'll get warm up there. I used to sleep there myself when I was a kid."

She knows getting Valley out will be harder now, but at least the girl will be out of sight and the space down here will be hers again. Gabe gathers the clothes, folds them, places them in the garbage bags, and drags both bags to the top of the stairs. Pushing the hatch open, she feels a rush of cold air against her face. Her old dresser with the carved handles still stands in the corner. At the foot of the bed is her cedar chest. The blue ticking mattress looks bare, but there are still ruffled curtains at the windows, pale yellow against dark logs.

Coming after her, obviously pleased, Valley cries out: "It's a garret! Perfect for the starving artist!" She smiles, opening several drawers, running a hand along the bureau. "This is wonderful. What's in there?" She points to the door at the far end.

"Robert's old room."

Valley opens it and peers in. Another cold blast of air rushes in. "Brrr," she says. "Pretty bare."

"It's bigger, but this is nicer. You have to leave the trapdoor open though, or you'll freeze. Listen, there should be linens in here." Gabe opens the chest and pulls out some worn sheets, a blanket made of scratchy wool and her quilt, her favorite old quilt. Everything smells of cedar and mothballs.

"Make yourself comfortable," Gabe says as a leave-taking, straightening up to put her two fists at her waist. But realizing as she says it that this sounds too open-ended, she adds, "It'll do for a while anyway."

"This is really nice of you. I know I'm—well, I'm horning in on you, that's the truth, and it's a lot to ask, but it's not like I can go anywhere else, not with this snow," she adds, smiling a little. "And if I stay up here, out of your way, I promise you won't even know I'm around. Honest. It's what Robert said, I mean, he thought it would be Henry who'd put me up, but up *here*, he said, out of the way, there's really plenty of room. It won't be such a long time, Robert'll be here in no time, really."

Gabe opens her mouth, trying to put her thoughts together solid enough to lob back Valley's words. She wants to say something sensible that makes irrefutable this is only until the roads are clear, only until then. She doesn't know Valley from Adam—and what kind of a name is *Valley*, anyway? But the words and her feelings get all tangled up and something strange comes out, an echo of sorts, sputtered awkwardly. "But I wouldn't necessarily—I don't think you should—"

Valley must see on her face what is coming. She is faster on her feet than Gabe. "Look, I have some books out in the car. I think I'll go get them too, while I'm at it," and she bolts back down the stairs.

Come back, Gabe thinks, reaching out a hand after her. But this is inside-out, what she really means is *No, go away!*

The gable window rattles and she sees the wind is picking up again, blowing the snow in deep drifts. Probably Valley is practiced at this sort of thing, she thinks, studying the round, full, garbage bags. The girl is clearly a drifter. When Gabe finally manages to lumber back downstairs, her arms feel strangely heavy.

Valley continues to haul things in. The kitchen counter is lined with little plastic bags and jars of raw nuts and brown rice, kasha and sesame, dried fruit, molasses and tamari. Gabe can't imagine what it all means, even though Valley explains it with passionate detail, unasked—now holding a bottle close to her nose, now lowering a paper bag, demanding Gabe peer in. Half-listening, Gabe stares at the stuff, wondering vaguely what the yellowish powder is, not asking, not caring.

Valley talks to her about the labels, the contents, talking, talking. Her books, a whole pile of them, extoll the excellence of her nutritional path, the spirituality of it even. Illness is largely a matter of ignorance, she says, of having failed to eat the right things or enough of them, or in some cases, in the right combinations or with the right mental attitudes. Valley hates to poke her nose in where it's not invited, honestly, she does. But she thinks there is help in here for Henry, and she turns to a chapter on strokes and how to prevent them.

"Animal fat? Very bad." She points out the passage to Gabe. "And vitamin E is crucial. See? At least four hundred units, mixed tocopherals, not just alphas."

Gabe stares into the brown bottle Valley holds out, filled with tiny oil-filled eggs, all rubbery. Good for the heart, for virility, the girl adds. Taking one of what she holds out, Gabe thinks it couldn't hurt anything but half-wonders if it might, feeling reckless as she swallows. Maybe the girl will be quiet after this.

Close to dusk they hear the whine of a snowmobile and, hopeful, Gabe goes to the back door, looking up the drive.

"Maybe we'll have Thanksgiving after all," she says to Valley, who is craning her neck behind her to see. "Here comes company."

Shub stomps in, blustering, "What the hell! So here you are!" He is holding a box out in front of him. Natty Raison with the State Park Service stands behind him. "The ranger's been worried since he found your truck up on the knob, isn't that right, Natty? You have engine trouble, Gabe? You gave us a scare."

The whole time he is talking, Shub is sizing Valley up, not taking his eyes from her. "Say," he says to the girl now, "you the one driving that bucket of bolts outside?"

"Be nice, Shub. You're never going to believe who she is. Robert's wife, Shub, come to wait for him. He's getting out soon. Come on in, Natty, shut the door. Robert's *wife*, I said."

"I ain't deaf."

Valley, looking embarrassed, holds out her hand in greeting.

Shub sets the box with the turkey roaster on the counter and takes off his gloves. "Shub Walters, glad to meet you, ah—"

"Valley," she says, shaking his hand.

"Vall-ee—" he nods.

Talking above their handshake, Gabe explains her car situation to Natty. "I started tracking and got carried away. Ended up dragging a buck all the way down Brushy Creek side, definitely the hard way."

Natty pays scant attention, following Shub's example. "Glad to meet you, Valley," Natty repeats, and shakes her hand. He is dark and muscular, jaunty-looking in his plush knife-edged hat. Gabe sees the recognition of this in Valley's sudden shyness, a coy downswept glance, a quick smile.

"Well, this is a surprise, all right," Shub says. "And here for Thanksgiving too, when I wasn't even sure I'd find *this* one alive. Say, you haven't even got the table cleared yet. What is all this mess? What'd you think, Gabe, I'd let a little snowstorm stop me? They got the main road cleared past the store. Probably have your road done before I'm ready to go home. Where's the cranberry sauce?"

Natty pinches the knife-edge of his hat, inclining his head. He needs to check on the houses up the road from Shub. Summer homes, most of them, but he'll feel better just checking on them. And then, his family is waiting dinner for him.

"Yeah, and besides, first ride of the season on *that* thing, ain't it?" Shub laughs at Natty's love for his snowmobile.

"You call me after dinner," the ranger says, reaching for the door. "I'll come and take Shub home and take you to your truck."

"No phone," says Gabe.

"Not *yet*? What have I told you about that? You gotta get a ham radio then. It's not good to be out here alone and no way to get word out. What if you broke a leg?"

Gabe shrugs. She's thought about this, but hates worse to break tradition. Once she got a radio, she might be tempted to get a telephone and then a TV. But she says, "You're right, Natty. I'll think about it. And if the road's not clear tonight, Shub can sleep here. Yes, you can! They'll have it clear by morning for sure. We'll dig Valley out and she can help me get my truck and then *we'll* take Shub home. You enjoy your Thanksgiving, Natty."

Natty claps Shub on the shoulder, waves good-bye to the women who are within hand-shaking distance, and heads out.

"Those things make a hell of a noise, godawful!" says Shub, listening to him take off. He puts his hands over his ears, muttering, "Like mosquitoes before we got DDT. I suppose you like all those fast new gadgets." He stares at Valley a moment. Squinting, he asks, "How old are you?"

"Let's get started with the rest of this," interrupts Gabe. "I have to put potatoes on, and squash. I'd given up on you! Valley here doesn't like turkey but we'll make the best of it. Where's that crazy decoration you gave me? I had it. See, I do have the cornucopia out. Except we ate half the fruit."

"Doesn't like turkey!" Shub says, but he doesn't get an immediate explanation because of Gabe's commotion. She is clearing a space on the table, unwrapping the newspapers he has put around the turkey roaster. She wants to put it in the oven to keep the bird warm. "Careful, careful," Shub says, giving her a guiding hand. "She's really juicy."

By the time they have potatoes peeled and squash cooking, ready to sit and take a break for coffee, they notice Valley has disappeared. "Where's the little thing gone to?" Shub asks, and Gabe conjectures she's escaped upstairs, to the space they'd fixed for her temporarily. Maybe this business of turkey dinner was a shock to her system.

"She's something of a hippy-dippy. Can't you tell by the way she looks? Doesn't eat any meat. Look at this." Gabrielle opens the kitchen cupboard where she's stuffed Valley's vitamins and lecithin and brewer's yeast. "She prefers this stuff. The miracle of Timed C. Fatty acids."

"No meat?" Shub looks astonished. "Up here?" he asks, meaning he has heard of such things in California maybe.

"I dunno, Shub, that's what she says. Guess she wouldn't think much of my six-point buck. That's right, you heard me, he's under the porch, down in the cooler. Somebody'd wounded him, but I tracked him, Shub, from up top the knob all the way over to the footbridge. By the time I brought him down, I decided it was as close to home dragging him down the hill as bringing him back over the bridge. But I'll tell you, I didn't know the half of it. Almost *froze* to death."

"D'you bring in your tag?"

"I've got it downstairs, you can check him out after dinner." She hasn't exactly forgotten this legality, but she thought she might be allowed to skip it this one time, given the circumstances. Pa or Robert or some others would have bent the rules a little, and she looks at him to convey this.

Shub lets it pass, but she knows he means for her to go by the rules. She will have to keep to her limit. He opens another cupboard, looking for plates to set the table. "Pretty funny, isn't it."

"What is?"

"Robert showin' up for Thanksgiving dinner, that's what it's like. You know, I am *glad* to be thinkin' of him after all this time, he's been gone too long. I'm gonna set the table for three, anyhow. Maybe she'll come down."

Gabe stares out past him. Six points, she'd been in the middle of saying again, but Robert's intrusion, just like Valley, so easy, takes the steam out of what she was about to say: I *tracked* him, Shub, and you know how that bridge always scared me.

Instead, she lets herself be distracted by the stains on the Melmac plates, which she's irked to see—never mind the white tablecloth she's laid out, trying to make things nice. Something else pops into her brain then and this she does manage to say out loud, though her voice blazes, all sharp-edged, and she isn't sure why. "Oh, *damn!*" she says, throwing a potholder. "I forgot this beautiful bottle of cognac in the truck! And I could have had Natty get it for us!"

Valley does surprise them with a late appearance. While Gabrielle and Shub watch from the table, she comes down the stairs in a mid-calf-length blue velvet sheath, an old one from the thirties, with folds draping from one shoulder. She's done her hair up in a twist and wears a blue feather cloche that hugs one ear and then veers off in a surprising flourish: one thin feather, an aristocratic signature. Though she is shoeless, her toenails are painted bright red and she wears a silver ankle bracelet.

Her posture plays the part, hands carried in front of her, elegant and perfectly at ease with asymmetry—her feather, her drapery, her chin upturned but off center. She must be pleased at so stark a contrast with crockery bowls and plaid flannel shirts. Or so Gabe thinks until the girl seats herself. On the breast of the sheath, which gapes out a bit from her bony chest, is a rhinestone cowboy throwing a silver lasso, secondhand kitsch from some flea market.

Valley smiles shyly and excuses her tardiness, promising to clean up afterward to make up for it, telling them both what a lovely table this is, not so much as taking one squeamish look at the meat platter. She picks up the tissue-paper turkey with the tips of two fingers and studies it, smiling at it as she sets it back down.

"Robert told me I'd have to be sure and buy all my groceries from Shub Walters." She bows her head toward Shub in a courtly gesture, saying for emphasis, "The very honorable same. Robert says anyone Shub doesn't like, Five Corners doesn't like. Simple as that."

"That's because I'm about all that's left at Five Corners."

"He still runs the place. You want your mail, see Shub. You need mosquito repellent, Shub's the one. Bait? He's got it. What else would you need up here?"

"Ah, it's not like when Elsie and I first moved here. Back then, they was widening the lake road, and somebody from Mackinaw City was buying up the lumber across the lake. Remember that, Gabe? There was talk about an airport in Clearwater in those days—I don't know what happened to all that talk. We just keep goin' backwards."

"That's why I like it," says Gabe.

"I woulda thought I'd be in Florida by now, retired."

"You'd be bored. No snowmobilers to hitch with down there."

"No, but they got these flying swamp boats. I saw 'em once on Disney."

Valley has been savoring mashed potatoes and squash, eating sensual spoonfuls like ice cream while she listens. Now she says, "I went to Disneyland once. In California. Now they've got that new one in Orlando. Wouldn't it be great to have something like that up here?"

Shub thinks about this. "Couldn't be open but half the year. People would never come this far."

"That's what they said about Florida—they never settled it really until the railroads got built." Valley gestures with a wave of her spoon, elbow up on the table. "Nowadays distance is nothing to people. You've got the new Mackinaw Bridge at the straits and I-75—"

"That's *all* we need," Gabe says. "It's bad enough we have to put up with trolls for hunting season. Imagine the same kind of thing in the summer, Shub."

"I make a lot a money during deer season. Leastwise, most of the money I *do* make."

Valley smiles with a certain languor, a Cheshire cat smile. "That stuff does make the world go around, doesn't it?" she sympathizes with him, shrugging. "I hear the man with money around here is Sid Nichols."

"Outside the bank, you mean. I suppose. It's hard to say. Tight as he is, he must have money. But you'd never know it to look at him."

"Robert says he's the one I should talk to. He said you'd introduce me, Shub. Will you?"

"Sure. I suppose so. Trouble is getting us together when we're both businessmen. He works nights at the tavern and I work days. The Lions Club is about the only time I see him. Ain't no girls allowed at Lions."

"You gonna work at the Friendly?" Gabe asks, surprised.

"*No!* Well. I've done worse, I guess. But no, the tavern's not what I'm thinking about."

This whole business begins to annoy Gabrielle. She reaches with a knife to saw away at the remaining drumstick, twisting the thing to disconnect it, making it crack. "You're certainly being mysterious," she says.

"I don't mean to be. I just don't think I should talk about some things, I mean Robert's been talking to Sid about some plans they've got going and I'm not sure just how much I—"

"Sid and *Robert?*"

Valley nods, the feather on her hat chopping the air. She reaches for the dish of squash again.

They're silent for a while and then, outside, Gabe hears the rumble of the snowplow, the clink of the chains on its tires sounding oddly cheerful.

"There she comes," says Shub, hearing it too. "Now we'll be out of here. Poor bastards, out on a holiday."

Gabe tries again. "So what about Sid and Robert? What are they up to?"

Valley shrugs. "Going into a business, something like that. But really, I'm not sure what's actually going to happen. Maybe nothing."

"Going into business! You've got to be kidding. Robert? With what? His good name? Listen, Sid doesn't take partners, he doesn't need them, isn't that right, Shub? He's just cooking up some scheme, he'll take anybody's shirt who gets close enough."

"Gabe! Hear the girl out now. Keep it civil. Sid's all right." This from Shub, who loves a good argument.

But Gabe is not about to let it go. It's crazy, this idea. "What kind of business are you talking about? Come on, *what* exactly?"

Valley's mouth has dropped open and she closes it now, moistening her lips. "A tourist place. Something the tourists will like—maybe a museum. You know, nature scenes and stuff to buy. To remember the place. Copper County is really pretty, you know. Lots more people come through these parts now—with their campers? You might as well make some money off them, that's what Robert says."

"Oh great, that sounds great. And Sid's gonna put up the money for this?"

Shub is watching them both, cleaning the bones on his plate, pulling the gristle with his teeth. He is hungry for news, this is valuable news.

Valley shrugs. "I told you, I don't really know that much about it. I haven't talked to Robert since he talked to Sid last. I hope it happens. But don't say anything about it to anyone, will you?"

They go on eating for several minutes, then Shub, tossing a bone back on his plate, jumps in and restarts the conversation, his voice unnaturally cheerful. "So, young lady! I don't suppose you met Robert in *jail*, did you? Or *did* you?"

"You mean, was I serving time?" she asks. Valley leans forward, eyebrows arched, and asks his question for him. "Am I a *con*?"

Shub sits back and purses his lips, unsure of himself, sorting out how to phrase this exactly.

The girl laughs a little. "Have you checked lately to see if you still have your wallet?" And when he feels for his back pocket, she laughs louder. "Don't worry," she giggles, tone patronizing. "I just started writing Robert, that's how I got to know him."

She takes a bite of squash, then reaches to put an olive on the end of her index finger, bouncing it at them while she keeps on talking between mouthfuls. "He had a letter in the newspaper, asking people to write him and, I dunno, he sounded lonely. And I was too, you know, I mean I *had* a boyfriend but *he* was—oh, never mind." She waves her hand at Shub, then brings it back to bite the olive off her finger. "That's too much to even get started on. So when Robert started in writing—I mean, have you ever had a pen pal?"

Shub has a look on his face like a student reaching for an algebra equation, one for whom the last two or three problems were already too much.

Valley laughs again. "No, I guess not, but—well, I dunno how to explain it. I found him to be so—oh, you know, really smart—and romantic and—"

This time the laugh shivers and she smiles and shrugs from the pleasure of it, the sound making Gabe think of the snowplow's clinking chains, and underneath, the heavy rumbling that shakes the ground. "I can't explain it," Valley says, blushing.

Gabe keeps her voice deliberately bland. "Robert always did have that effect on girls." She has always disliked Robert's girlfriends, although, she tells herself now, it is only because he always chooses such inappropriate ones. Gabe was only eight or nine when Robert first crossed the mysterious boundary called sex. She hadn't known it was sex at the time; she only knew she wasn't allowed to tag along anymore and felt abandoned. Sex had always been easy for Robert. Valley might as well know it.

Valley says, "Oh, I wasn't the *only* girl he was seeing, I know that. Some women just come to the jail to visit—they don't even know the men to start with. Isn't that weird? Well, really, it's not so weird. I figured it out. I mean, I asked them about it."

"Wait. You mean they come to the jail to meet men? Like a singles bar or something?" Gabe asks.

"Yes, like that, sort of. I thought it was strange at first too. But usually they get to know the place through a friend who's got a man in jail, and so they come along . . . out of sympathy, just to be nice. And they meet men. There's plenty of men in there. They're *all* men, really, and it's kind of flattering, they're so hungry for attention, they hang on every word you say. So it kinda makes sense, you know? Like this one woman told me about her boyfriend, at least she always knew where he *was*."

"That's a hell of a note! Preying on a man who's locked up and can't even get away!" Shub says.

"They're not *preying*—"

"I didn't mean you, missy. I know you were writing to Robert, answering his letters—"

"Not the others either. They're all nice women. A lot of them had these bad relationships before and it's like these guys are safer for them. They're the only ones the women can trust a little. This one woman got to be kind of a friend and she told me, a guy in jail has to be a gentleman and behave himself. I think it's kind of sad, really. They're not *preying*."

At this, Shub looks genuinely ashamed of himself. "I didn't mean to—that was kinda—*say*! You listen to me. You just ignore an old man and him shootin' his mouth off. I can be full of it, isn't that right, Gabe?"

"Yes, but I don't think I ever heard you admit it before."

Shub looks askance at her, annoyed. He can't even take a little joke. She can't believe he's trying to make a good impression.

"Well, I for one am glad to have some word about how Robert is," Shub is going on, "and that he's got some plans for hisself, and for this one here too," he gestures. "Valley, it's good to know he hasn't disappeared off the edge of the earth, be good to see him again."

A pause. He is looking at Gabe expectantly. "Isn't that right, Gabe?" he asks, and then she understands.

Her cue. She nods and says, "Yes, of course."

With Shub satisfied, the conversation goes on, flowing around the small bump of Gabe's silence. And in a way she supposes she is glad. To know that Robert's life has gone on, that he'd reached out to people, that someone had reached back. For all she knows, maybe the girl does love him. Maybe he loves her. Stranger things have happened. The main thing is, Robert has gone on living, gone on learning probably, same as she had. He might have changed a lot, grown up some. A person could hardly get away from that after thirty-four years.

There's a lull in the conversation. Gabrielle takes note that it's growing dark outside, and she's been silent for quite a while. Valley is smiling, chin propped in her hand, elbow on the table, watching Shub finish the last of the potatoes. He blinks and looks at Gabe, then swallows and asks, "When is it you go back to school?"

"Every four to six months," Gabe explains, putting up her fingers to count. "October," she marks her first time at Fond du Lac, lowering one, two, three fingers, whispering the months. "April, next time." Turning to Valley she says, "Graduate school. A low-residency program—over at Fond du Lac College. You ever hear of it?" Valley shakes her head and Gabrielle shrugs. "I'm studying literature. Listen, when you're done," she says, "I think I'm going to go dig out that little Beetle of yours so you can take me to my truck up top. I'm feeling antsy being here without it. Makes me stir-crazy."

"Don't give me that!" says Shub. "You're after that fancy bottle of cognac. Best antifreeze there is. I could use a drink myself. Might be worth giving you a hand."

"Cognac?" asks Valley, completely lost.

"In my truck. I bought it for tonight's dinner and left it there when I tracked the . . . never mind, it's a long story."

"Well, I can change my clothes and help too. Could I borrow something warm? You mind?" Valley tilts her head and smiles.

The plow has left a small mountain of snow at the mouth of the drive. They start shoveling there and work back to the Volkswagen. The sky is completely clear and the moon, though beginning to melt on one edge, shines bright as daylight. It sparks countless ice hexagons lying crisscrossed and thatched, so that the world seems buried in glitter.

Shub shovels the stuff in sturdy rhythmic bites, solid, as if he were built of bricks. He begins singing, puffing a little breathlessly, "Dinah, won't you blow, Dinah, won't you blow, Dinah, won't you blow your ho-ho-*horn?*"

Valley, dressed in wool jacket and pants too big for her, still wears her ridiculous hat, placing it atop a wool kerchief tied under her chin. The feather bounces with her movement as she tries to match Shub's speed, sending tiny shovelfuls flinging back over her shoulder. Puffing a little, Valley joins in, "There's someone in the kitchen with Dinah, someone in the kitchen, I *know*-ho-ho-ho!"

Their playfulness irritates Gabe, who has never felt comfortable singing or letting herself be silly. Years ago, she used to listen to Elsie and Shub sing a whole repertoire of old tunes. It always made her feel shy, no matter how much she loved it, or how kind they were. Their easy, wholehearted harmony was something she couldn't feel part of.

Obviously Shub is taken in by a pretty face, she is thinking, just as Valley lets loose another peal of tinkling laughter. His being so gullible surprises Gabe, but no more than the way that this hurts her. She puts her head down and shovels more earnestly, ignoring the grand finale and the laughter afterward.

"Someone in the kitchen with Diii-*naaah!* Strummin' on the ole banjo!"

Even when she feels a pelt of snow on her backside, and hears another melodic line of laughter, she refuses to look up. Really, the girl is nothing more than a kid.

The bell jingles overhead as Shub unlocks and swings open his door. Shub insisted they take him home to have their cognac at the store. They can bring him leftover turkey tomorrow.

He has to look deep inside the cupboard out back, but finally he finds the small jelly glasses that will do as snifters. He sets them on the oak counter and Gabrielle pours three glasses a third full, swirling them slightly as she passes them out.

Shub takes a deep breath, then lifts his glass high, signaling an event. He stares off to the corner, blinking and deep in thought. Finally he says, "I want to drink to all those who can't be with us. To my Elsie first of all. And to Henry. And to Robert! And here's to the girl Robert married. And the girl who's his sister." He lifts his glass to each one in turn, saluting them. "Did I leave anyone out?"

Gabe, wanting to make up for her lack of cheer earlier, lifts her glass, closes her eyes, bows in return. She *wants* to be happy, she decides. It's a possibility—quite possibly a probability—that she is wrong about a lot of things she's been feeling. She had been put in a bad mood, having things forced upon her, whereas, if she had a choice—well, she has a choice, she still does.

She straightens and adds to the toast: "And to Shub Walters and his store, where all roads lead in Copper County."

Arm extended, Valley clears her throat a little, signaling her wish to contribute. She smiles at Shub and then says, "And to sisters and wives and all women who are also persons in their own right, not merely sisters and wives of persons. Hear, hear," she bows, and clinks her glass to their two.

She looks closely at Gabrielle, who, surprised, returns her cryptic smile.

Meanwhile, Shub has thrown back his head to down the cognac, oblivious.

Gabe and Valley drink theirs still standing near the door in their boots, making appreciative noises for the warmth they feel in their breastbones. Valley pats hers and coughs a little, clearing her throat again.

"Another?" offers Gabe, extending the bottle.

Shub holds out his glass and then Valley, stiff-armed, full of bravado, follows suit.

"This one is for the coming year, and all that we are thankful for," says Gabe, feeling warm and generous, full of the power of ritual and alcohol. "Here's to new beginnings, for all here concerned."

Valley smiles widely at this, her lips parting to show teeth that are even as pearls. Her tongue is soft looking, pale pink, a gift of clemency against that too bright edge of white. "Hear, hear!" she says.

Gabe begins to like the girl a little, despite feelings of envy for the directness of that smile, those shy, laughing eyes, the way she looks pretty even in such a ridiculous getup. There is something pleasing and vulnerable about the way she hunches her shoulders when she laughs, the way she can't look at you for long. And what about that secret toast she gave?

Robert has picked a smart one at least, even if she is a little ditsy. Gabe pours them another drink.

The last time Gabe had sat at table with Robert was the same time he'd come to visit, just back from Nam. Dennis had insisted Robert go to dinner with them at his folks' house. "Wear your uniform," Dennis suggested, and something in his tone had made it a dare. "My old man will love it."

Later, when Dennis had left to run some errands, Robert told her he was leaving early.

"Why? What about the dinner?"

"I just don't—you know—I—*you* go on without me. I can tell. His family is—I wouldn't want to embarrass you and use the wrong fork or drink out of the finger bowl or something." He kept shrugging, looking everywhere, at his hands, over her shoulder, everywhere but at her face.

"What *finger* bowl? You're crazy! Al and Ruth have a little money, but they're sweet. Ruth'll give you a big hug, probably."

"Scare me *off*, why don't you." Robert rolled his eyes, blew his breath out through his smile, finally looking at her. "I don't want to. I just—I gotta go."

"Robert, you have to go with me!"

She wonders why she had insisted. To hide behind him, she decides. Maybe to win over Dennis's father. That had certainly worked. Robert and Al had hit it off, talking about draft dodgers. They drank too many rum Cokes, got louder and louder while Dennis, also drinking steadily, grew quieter.

That was when Robert, taking off his uniform jacket, challenged all the male guests to a barefoot race down the street of their new and exclusive ranch-house subdivision, in full whooping view from every picture window in the neighborhood. The street made a clean, black circle through spans of close-clipped green, past new red hydrants and raw-looking wooden markers with orange ties flapping in the wind.

The men slapped each other on the back, shouting every comment at the top of their lungs, outdoing each other: "God*damn!* Where the fuck did all these little fucking *stones* come from! Oh, man, you asshole. Take those shoes off. Here's where we find out what you're made of—you some fucking *girl?* Oh no! your socks *too,* asshole, come on, man. I'll outrun you—ma-aan . . . get outta here!" Robert and Al hammed it up, lifted their feet high, hobbled like cripples on the fine white stones that edged the blacktop.

Poor Dennis got bullied into performing by his father. "Come on! You gonna let an old man defend the family honor by his*self,* boy? Get your socks off! You heard what the man said. Line up!"

After several false starts, they were off, running with mincing steps, yelling from pain when somebody stepped on a stone. Robert was an easy first, Dennis brought up the rear, with all of them stumbling, pushing and shoving, their laughs more like shouts, getting funnier and funnier and angrier and angrier.

From the redwood deck, Gabe could see Robert and Dennis standing closer, beginning to jostle each other. Robert put his face in Dennis's, saying something funny-mean. Al squeezed in between the two. Meanwhile, Ruth, her future mother-in-law, busied herself emptying ashtrays. "He can be such a *fool,*" Ruth commented, meaning Al, whose face looked red and sweaty even from this distance. Yet something in her tone included the rest of the male gender. Gabe and the other women had all understood this.

Shub is telling Valley about the first taste he'd ever had of cognac, back in France, during WWII. "Acourse once I knew they was hungry, why, I tried to get 'em all the chocolate I could. You shoulda seen them gobble it. I had a deal going with this Jewish guy in Supply. I give him all the cheap French wine I could abscond with, for all the chocolate he could get for me, and that worked fine, worked fine for her and the boy, worked fine for ole Hymie."

Gabe smiles a boozy smile, leaning back against the counter, knowing what comes next. The predictability of everything around her is a comfort. Though there is something else, she thinks—something glancing, frightening. She rearranges herself, avoiding the feeling, but comes close enough to remember yesterday on the trail. Tracking her buck, she had heard the snapping of brush behind her and imagined suddenly that she was the hunted, the prey. Maybe she will never be able to outrun who she is, who she has always been in this place. It's a cliché she doesn't put into words, only sensing the feeling and dismissing it, embarrassed.

Shub is talking about the time he toasted Patton, and Valley is unbuttoning her coat, stopping to smile when he swings his arm up high in defiance. "The bastard!" Same as always.

Leaning on her elbow, propped on the counter, Gabe tilts her head a little to see out the window. A nature museum—up here, where they already have the real thing. Just the kind of get-rich-quick stuff she'd expect from Robert and his friends. Always out to make a killing.

Irritation pushes fear down deep enough she can't feel it anymore. She puts her hand up to support her cheek, leaning farther, deciding to concentrate on the cognac's glow. Outside, she can see the moon, mid-sky over the lake, filling the world with cold. Only the water remains, dark, stubborn, denying its thickening. She watches it swallow the light, imagines it bent on giving nothing back, nothing in the time it has left.

November 30, 1983
Five Corners, Michigan

Kate finally wrote today. I'd been worrying that I should have kept my story out of my letters after all. But she wrote back and said I made her think. And not like some scientist pinning a bug either, the way I worried she might. I believe she really does want my ideas. She's sending me some books about women's hunting legends of all things, reminding me about Diana, goddess of the forest and a hunter, whom I must have learned about in school. Or maybe I didn't. After that story about the three goddesses who let some mortal judge their beauty, I decided mythology was silly. But secretly—knowing this wasn't what I was supposed to think.

I've always felt like an intruder outdoors. Or more like an impostor. In lots of places. Scared of being found out.

Completely different from most of my female students these days, who already are cocksure that Hemingway is full of it. This bothers me. It took me until the end of graduate school to question his version of "realism," and even then I was cautious. I rather liked his not writing about feelings—or what he called "talking a lot of rot." This was practically my family motto and he knew the family prayer too: "Hail Nada, Full of Nada, Nada is with Thee."

Last spring I had a girl in class who was quieter than the rest. She asked if "A Clean, Well-Lighted Place" wasn't being disrespectful of the Virgin Mary—and I cut her off, deciding it was a silly objection, when I might have praised such a close reading. Hail Mary, Full of Grace—I'd never stopped to notice whose prayer he mocked out of all those he could have. The girl was only following my advice never to disrespect too easily—I'd meant Hemingway, but she was more open-minded. Which is why I worry when some of my students seem afraid of me. It's because I demand their best, Anita says. But what if I'm not able to receive it?

I feel like a stone dropped into a pond. These kids don't know the details of my story either—but I'll bet I send out eddies in every direction. They must feel these—I feel them myself, writing and thinking with Kate about what happened—I thicken, grow denser just remembering.

Do your own thinking. That's what I say to my students. No wonder they're afraid of it. Before I ever heard from Kate, before she ever said a word, I was certain she would answer, "No, no, Gabe, you have it all wrong!" I can admit that now, because Kate valued what I wrote, but I was already braced, getting ready not to care what she thought. I knew how to keep my own counsel. Like that Catholic student. I taught her what I learned. I recognized her eyes, round and alert after I dismissed her, the way the set of her mouth would swallow nothing.

Kate's questions this time—about cause and effect—have me thinking about how hard it is to be authentic. What other decisions could I have made early on? I used to think it was simple. I should have nipped things in the bud when Valley first showed up at my door unannounced. But whenever I've pictured myself sending her packing with a message to Robert—or better yet, giving Robert the message myself—it hasn't felt possible. That's not who I was then. I'd already put off talking to him for months.

Lack of money backs people into all sorts of corners. Valley and I felt helpless, but we were pretty damned resourceful. Why should I fault myself for trying to help her? My family job was to keep things pleasant and smoothed over. How could I give up this imagined control over Robert until I stopped believing in it? I didn't even control myself. I should have left Five Corners, but I couldn't.

I kept what I felt hidden. Dennis used to complain that my face scowls whenever I'm relaxed. I've always had to work at pushing my lips up into a more socially acceptable smile. When I was a girl Shub showed me myself on a totem on a postcard once—third figure up, a frowning bear or a frog. I was quiet and dark and Shub, always wanting to make things more interesting than they are, told people I had psychic powers. I piped up information no one thought a little girl could know about. That wasn't magic. I eavesdropped.

You can't live your whole life by listening in on it. I had my opinions—I just kept them to myself and hoped the people in charge were as smart as they thought they were. And maybe felt secret satisfaction when they never were. God— little frog, little pond. There's my face in the dark of my window—that ugly down-turned mouth.

I read once if you put a frog in a kettle of water on the stove and light a fire underneath, it won't jump out. It won't even notice its own blood heating up.

I'd like to get my hands on the guy who thought up that experiment and then wrote about it afterward in that unfeeling tone. He should have eaten the frog at least and shed a few tears—for it—for himself.

LATE NOVEMBER, 1973

Already Gabe knows the girl's habits. She is thinking another few minutes and Valley'll be coming back down the stairs to get a drink of water, when her footfalls thud their descent to the bathroom.

Gabe has given her the chance to bring it up, but the girl still has said nothing about leaving. Gabe listens to the toilet paper being unrolled, a lot of toilet paper, then the flushing water. Then more water splashing into the sink, and she hears Valley filling her glass. The girl calls out, "Gaaabe?," and comes to stand in the doorway, another part of the routine. "Gabe, do owls fly south for the winter or do they stay here?"

"They stay here."

"Oh. Good. 'Cause I keep hearing something upstairs, something scary."

"Probably an owl in that the big white pine outside your window. I think there's a nest."

"Oh. 'Cause I heard this sound, and I wasn't sure what it was. A weird kind of sound, spooky—is that what it is?" She hesitates. "Listen, can I get you anything while I'm up?"

"Uhh . . . listen, Valley," Gabe starts to say, pulling the covers up a little as she sits up in bed, preparing herself to break the bad news. This isn't going to *work.*

But Valley sees it coming, stands closer, beating her to a speech, as if she's been dying to say something, as if this were really hard for her. "Do you think we oughta talk, Gabe? We probably gotta talk about this. I mean, you've been real nice, I don't know how to thank you, but I know I must be wearing out my welcome, and listen, I've been racking my brain, I don't know what else to do, I don't *know* what else—"

The girl turns and takes two paces, then turns again to face her, crouching down. "Listen, if you let me stay here—just the next two months? I promise I won't be any trouble to you. That's all, just until Robert gets back, just until then. I won't get in your way, I'll help out, I'll do everything—"

"I thought you said the end of February before. That's three months, Valley."

"Well, early March, something like that."

"Now it's early March! Valley, that's just the kind of thing that worries me, I don't even *know* how long it's gonna be. Every time you talk about it, it's different."

"Early March. That's when it is. You can ask Robert. No, I swear it. Three months, that's all. I just didn't want it to sound so long, okay? Listen, I don't like being any trouble to you. I don't like any of this, but please, Gabe, you've gotta help me."

"Look, *I* can't afford to feed you!"

"You don't have to—no, listen—I can live on brown rice, honest, I've done it before and I've got plenty. I can take care of myself, that's not what I'm asking—"

"And what about money, what are you gonna do for money?"

"Listen, it's not gonna cost you one red cent, no, I'll *pay* for my share, I'll get some kind of job. I'll work for Sid, anything—I'm just asking for a place to stay, just a roof over my head, that's all. I just can't stay by my*self*, I know that's crazy but—you won't even know I'm here—look, never mind me, do this for Robert's sake, will you? Otherwise, I don't know what's gonna *happen* to him. Doesn't he deserve to have something waiting for him when he gets out? Doesn't he?"

Gabe shakes the top blanket, making it flap, and she pulls it closer to her. This isn't the talk she wanted to have, not at all, not at all. She'd have been better off to just keep quiet, she had better talk to Robert and get this straight.

"I don't know," she says. "I don't *know*, I mean, we'd have to have some ground rules. We'd have to be perfectly clear about everything because it can't go on like it has—"

"Oh, absolutely. We want everything perfectly clear. I know that's the way *I* want it."

"We do our own shopping, our own cooking, our own washing up."

"I don't mind cooking, I'll do *all* the dishes!"

"*No*, we each do our own, and in the afternoons, I have to have peace and quiet, and you have to leave me alone, totally alone so I can study."

"Absolutely. You won't even know I'm around. I know how important that is to you and really, I *admire* what you're doing, you've gotta know that. In fact, the firewood and the stove? Don't you even worry, I'll take care of all that, you don't even have to—"

"No! The fire is mine. You don't touch the fire, you understand? You don't have to do anything for me. You'd better *not* do anything for me, and I don't want any of your lectures about what I should eat either."

The girl puts her hands up, in total surrender. "Okay, okay. I just wanted to help, that's all."

"I don't need your help. That's just it, I don't want you twisting things around backward—I don't need *your* help. And you're only going to get mine until the first of March when Robert gets out. Is that clear?"

"Well, Robert says it might take us a couple of weeks to find our own place—we can't just—"

"Just until then. You're gonna have to talk to him."

Valley clasps her hands together. "Yes. Just until we're on our feet, until then. And meanwhile, you won't even know I'm around. I promise." She pauses, letting her hands drop in front of her. "You won't be sorry, Gabe," she says with eyes wide and unblinking. "I swear it. I swear you won't be sorry."

The girl starts to back away into the kitchen, keeping her eyes on Gabe. She is out of sight for several moments and then she reappears in the doorway, her face leaning in. She attempts a smile. "Listen," she says, shrugging, "you mind if I borrow some tampons? I wouldn't ask, but I just started, unexpectedly. I can improvise with some toilet paper, but I'd—"

She judges Gabe's facial expression, drops the smile and straightens up, gathering her dignity. She decides to use her instructive voice. "Women who live together always do this, you know. Have their periods together. It's pheronomes or something," she says.

"Pheromones," Gabe corrects her.

Their stares lock together and the silence says all that is angry between them, all that is unfair and unplanned and unwanted, but finally Valley blurts out, "Look, do you think I'd *ask* you, if I wasn't desperate?"

After that, as they go through the bathroom cupboards, moving boxes out of the way, making soft, scuffing noises as they search for the tampons, the silence they keep is a resting place, an unwritten accord, a kind of mercy for them both.

III

LEGENDS

It's been cold and snowy enough to make Shub give up his theory of the world flipping over on its axis. Things are too goldarned *normal*, that's just the problem these days, is his new explanation. Nobody wants a little excitement anymore. They go off to Florida, to their little trailer parks, everybody just playing it safe.

"Now you take yourself, for instance," he is saying to Valley, who is wearing her wine-colored cape. Underneath she has on an orange leotard and a long Indian-print skirt, wrapped and tied at the waist. "Now I know you like to think you're not so ordinary. The way you dress and things, the stuff you eat. But I am willin' to bet that somewhere you learned that was normal, being *different* was normal. You learned that was how a theatrical girl—or whatever it is you think you are—should dress, and so now you won't put on some sensible snow pants for a change, and maybe some boots instead of them ridiculous things you got on."

He is pointing at Valley's Mary Janes, overstuffed with rag wool socks.

Valley goes on looking through the rack of cellophane-covered cards, unconcerned. She picks up one that is mint green with a smiling puppy and the words "Hello There!" printed in canary yellow.

"I am perfectly warm," she says without raising her eyes. "You can just stop picking on me and find yourself something else to do."

Most of Shub's summer rental customers are scared to death of him and never grasp this is simply the way he likes to talk, the way he makes himself comfortable. Valley saw through him from the start.

Shub turns to Gabe then. "I don't suppose you'd do me the favor of drinking some of that coffee out back? Got some gettin' thick as crankcase oil and too expensive to throw out."

Gabe allows as how she would, matching his tone like Valley, making it clear it is not as if she were *enjoying* this. She pulls a stool up to the thick oak counter, while he goes through the curtained doorway to his living space. A laugh track from a sitcom titters in the background.

Gabe knows all the details of the three tiny rooms behind her, unchanged from when Elsie was alive, filled with overlarge furniture upholstered in a rose-colored loopy fabric, walls faced with knick-knack shelves. The windows are covered with venetian blinds. Shub liked his privacy and Elsie preferred no curtains at all. They had adjusted and readjusted the light in an ongoing battle. Now the rooms are in constant twilight.

On the counter beside Gabe is a roll of pale green paper and a cone of string, mounted on a wrought-iron stand. The wood is satin where she runs her hand over it, remembering how many times she's seen a customer order, say, a pound of hamburg. Shub, standing behind the meat case, would take the metal paddle, scoop the meat into a red basket-print paper boat, lift it on to the scale, and then, adding or taking away until it was just the right weight, pat it neatly with a piece of tissue and hand-deliver it to Elsie.

More than likely she would be perched on a stool, doing her crocheting. But she'd stand up at once, tear off a piece of the pale green paper, twirl the package and tie the string in a single, practiced motion, writing with a grease pencil the amount Shub told her. "Now what else can we get you?" she'd ask then, with Shub standing ready, wiping his hands on his white cloth apron next to her.

The two had been bookends, like-minded and matched in size as well: stocky and solid, both with square-tipped fingers and well-muscled legs and straightforward, straight-nosed faces. Their hair was thin and brown back then—Shub's a slightly paler version with wisps straying in wild directions, made worse by his habit of running his fingers back through it.

He does this now, after setting Gabe's coffee in front of her. Long silvery strands stand nearly upright in places.

Gabrielle reaches out to smooth his balding head. He grimaces but endures it. "Busy day?" she asks, knowing that it couldn't have been.

He nods toward the cabins across the road. "Ah! Been waitin' for Fred Quigley to show up. Gotta get that sink replaced in Number Three, or I'll never have the chance. You two staying for supper?"

This gets Valley's attention. Supper for Shub is a baloney sandwich, followed by a chaser of Alka-Seltzer and several world-class belches—all of this while he's standing behind the counter. Valley looks at Gabe and Gabe speaks for both of them, shaking her head.

"I'll be in tomorrow all day when deliveries are due. We're just in to pick up a few things." She doesn't get up though; they're in no rush. "Valley wanted to send some cards."

"Say, that reminds me. Sid was askin' about Robert at the Lions Club. Had some nice things to say about meetin' with you too, Valley. That business deal going all right?"

Valley smiles, nodding.

"It's all right," he says, putting a finger to his lips. "We know how to keep it all on the q.t. Gotta get past the permit stage. Sid's a good one to handle that." He chuckles then, shaking his head, turning to look at Gabe. "Which reminds me, Sid got to tellin' that story about the time your old man nearly caught Robert jackin' deer? Damnedest thing—here your old man didn't have but one or two rules in the world, and that Robert had to go and make sure he broke 'em."

It was too late to stop Shub, even though Gabe had heard this one too many times before: how Robert drove up, pale as a ghost that night, the old man right on his tail. Only Henry didn't know it was Robert he was chasing, and Robert didn't want him to find out either.

"Oh, he was scared—clammy—shaking like a little kid. And Sid said he'd take the meat off his hands, had a restaurant would take it, out of season. Belle, she could use the cape and mount it. But if he wanted Sid to take care of the thing that quick, why he'd better just hand it over, and not expect to make a dime off it this time."

Shub laughs a little at Robert's predicament, the way Sid must have, telling the story at the Lions afterward. "Stuff'll bring twenty bucks a pound downstate," he says aside to Valley, and then goes on. "Well, Robert didn't like the deal much, but the old man came in just as they got the thing packed into the cooler at the Friendly. Robert and his crony with the truck hid behind the beer crates, while Sid calmed your old man down, out by the bar. Henry was wild-eyed, like he might take the place apart, and it scared everybody, you know, because he was usually so quiet—they saw as how he might let loose and just everything come pouring out."

Gabe says nothing, just puts her elbow up on the counter, clamping her jaw shut with her chin in her palm. Valley has picked out a card and is walking closer, listening.

"And so, Sid's calming Henry down, and about then he hears Robert laugh once behind him." Shub's eyes open wide to show Sid's surprise, then, with elbows out, he twists on one foot, to look behind him. "And he turns and sees Robert cuttin' up, jabbing the other kid"—Shub shoves with his elbow—"like all of a sudden, he's tryin' his damnedest to get himself noticed. They start in shoving each other, like this, you know, and pretty soon, Robert falls out into the aisle, falls right out onto the floor!"

"Now your old man happens to be looking the other way just then, trying to find a deer jacker's face in among all Sid's customers. And Sid hurries up and picks the boy up, shoves him back behind the bar. So Henry never does find out Robert's the one who did it. But not because Robert didn't go and try his damnedest to get caught. Can you figure that?"

Shub chuckles without making a sound, a little out of breath from the energy of his presentation. He rests his elbows on the counter, shaking his head as if to say: Who can figure that Robert? Now isn't he just the damnedest?

Gabrielle has been twisting a little on her stool, pretending to watch for customers out the front window, looking at the canned goods and mentally making a list. Shub doesn't notice she isn't listening, because Valley is.

This is all news to her. She gobbles up any history or lore about Robert.

Now that Shub is finished, Gabe gets up, a little tight-lipped smile and a nod her only acknowledgment.

"You gotta go?" Shub asks.

"We better get some milk. And eggs, Valley. What are we down to?" Valley has explained to Gabe that she is a lacto-ovo vegetarian, not as strict as she wants to be; when Robert comes they'll do macrobiotics. For now, every other night it's omelets.

Gabe doesn't blame Shub for telling his stories. She is used to hearing these tales about Robert and the old man. She has told a few of them herself, believed a few from time to time. Something about the two invites these larger-than-life renditions, and the stories never wear out because they never quite give up their tension, never get resolved. It isn't anybody's fault exactly.

"I don't understand," says Valley. "What *is* this deer jacking? What's so—?"

"Hunting from a car, usually out of season. Doing it with a spot-light. Makes the deer freeze, stock-still, hypnotized almost. They're like sitting ducks."

"What? Well, I don't *blame* your father for being angry, that's a terrible—but I can't believe Robert would—"

Gabe says, "Believe it."

"But he must have had some—it just doesn't sound like—I mean, probably this sounds naive, but Robert has always been so—"

"There's not a lot of work up here, missy," Shub puts in. She looks blank, so he explains, "He needed the money."

"Oh. Yes. The money, he must have *needed* it, he must have been—well, he must have just had a *terrible*—" Valley looks around, trying to see what had been so terrible, knowing it must have been something, something.

"But you see, it wouldn't matter. 'Cause Henry would have had no part of it anyway. See, he was different in that way, different from most everybody. Chose one whitetail every year and he'd trail that buck for months until he knew it backwards and forwards. And even if he had another shot at some other deer, he wouldn't take it. It was like religion. Made it a pact between them, isn't that right, Gabe?"

Shub doesn't need her answer, but he is being courteous, including her, since this is her father, after all. He leans forward against the old iron cash register, both hands on the curved front, his tale-telling posture.

"Henry used to stop in for a smoke at the end of the day and he'd say, 'I saw Brother down in the spotted alder.' Henry's a tall man, never spoke much, but he'd talk to us about the deer, callin' them by name. 'Brother's got a scrape down there, looking for does,' he'd say. And sure enough, Brother would be introduced to all of us, by and by, same day he met his Maker, same as Rusty had been met and Whiskers the year before that. Named every one, and all of them trophy bucks. Nobody could match that Henry Bissonette when it came to tracking."

"He *named* them?" Valley asks, but it is more incredulity than a real question.

Gabe knows what is coming before Shub opens his mouth. The Blue—that comes next. The big, blue-gray buck Henry'd seen once and lost and talked about ever since, the one buck he couldn't find again.

Now every time the buck got mentioned, people told his colors a little brighter and more fantastic. And every now and then, somebody will come even yet into Shub's store and claim to have seen Bissonette's blue buck. Big as Babe the Blue Ox, he got to be, and by and by, a shade just as storied as July sky and just as loved.

Everywhere there are hunters, there are always tales of blue bucks. The details might vary from place to place, as legends do, but people seem to need them. Gabe's theory is that folks talk up the Blue the way they talk up Robert's being in Vietnam, and maybe for the same reason. Robert and the old man, both bigger than good and bad, and forgiven for trespasses explained away as something other than trespasses. Bad is just another way of looking at their virtues.

Gabe doesn't know she is thinking this except by the way her body tenses. She braces her hands. She hears Shub say, "You think *that's* something, did Gabe here ever tell you about the story her old man came home with one night? Back in fifty-six I think it was."

And she waits for what she already knows is coming.

December 12, 1983
Five Corners, Michigan

I see myself everywhere in the article Kate sent on domestic violence research, especially in what women say. I guess I'm not the only one to have taken so long to talk about things. Reading this, I heard myself making excuses like they did— for Robert, who didn't fly off the handle all that often. I see now it was enough for him to slam things around and throw things—just the threat of violence keeping Valley and me in line. Maybe this habit is why I feel compelled to explain more about him and our family history to Kate. I don't want to shortchange him. Maybe I'm afraid of shortchanging him— but I don't think it's only this. He can't hurt me now. Really, he never wanted to hurt me—I know that's crazy, but he kind of took care of me, growing up.

I was only about five when we moved up here to Copper County. Robert was five years older so he remembered more. He used to talk about another downstate place we called home, a second-story apartment. I looked for it years later when I was living in Benton County with Dennis, but I never did find it. Robert made the place live in my mind, though. There was a stairway on the outside of the house and I was afraid of it, Robert said. He used to ask me if I didn't remember—and after a while, it seemed as if I might.

He told me I fell down on a nail that went into my palm. In those days we still went to catechism. When I ran, scared, up the stairs, one drop of blood fell on every step—a drop on every step. I used to look at these every time I went up or down after that, Robert said. Nobody could hurry me—it used to drive Pa nuts. Robert showed me how I'd bend over and really stare at the spots every time—and he was doing what he always did when he told stories. Moving around, changing expression, playing out every word like an actor on stage, but playing all the parts. Each time he came to that place in that particular story, he'd bend over from the waist and peer in front of him, sober-faced as any four-year-old, elbows back, fingers spread wide—a perfect impersonation.

He knew our mother a little. There had been a child after me who had died—Robert, then me, then quickly after me, a stillborn son. Robert believed our mother had been happier before that or at least he used to tell me stories of happier times—with a mother who was different from the one I remember. To me, she always seemed stiff and far away, even when she dressed me or combed my hair. "All these rats," she'd say, yanking at the comb, wrenching my head back.

Most of what I know about our family comes from Robert, from earlier times. Robert told me this: When I was two, she had a birthday party for me. She hung crepe paper strips and rubbed balloons on her hair to make them stick on the wall. I sat in my high chair with my cake, and she laughed when I put all ten fingers in the frosting, my mouth a perfect "O" from the soft, surprising feel of it. "Oh!" she said back to me. "Oh, oh, oh!" He used to show me the photo.

I had to get it out and look at it again, to make sure I remembered it right. There I am with my mother, our two faces close together, both our mouths in tight, happy circles, both of us with curly, dark hair. And now I see it: a blousy tunic hides her belly, the child who died.

She could have been a movie star, Robert always said. And it was true that our mother looked a little like Loretta Young. Soon after we moved up to the cabin, she cut a picture of Dr. Schweitzer out of *Life* magazine and put it up on the wall in the kitchen. She used to do that: There was one of a smiling sled dog, a Persian cat. But after she left, it was the picture of Dr. Schweitzer I kept.

I used to imagine her in the jungle with the good doctor playing his piano up on a rough plank stage. My mother stood nearby in a white-sequined gown, her arms full of roses. That last image definitely came from Loretta Young. Every week Robert and I watched her whirl in the front door on Shub and Elsie's TV.

My favorite photos were the black-and-white ones, the edges crinkly-cut. Robert was a beautiful child, with dark lips, round wide eyes. Most of the pictures are of him. By the time I arrived, we had color film and the light had gone out of our mother's eyes. The photos began to drop off, taken only at events like birthdays or Christmas. I can see this in the album Valley put together for us, all the old photos in order. It changes them, seeing them all together.

My mother isn't looking at the camera or at anyone else in any of the photos that follow me through toddlerhood, except for the birthday "O" picture. And one other, taken just after we'd moved to Five Corners. In that one, she seems surprised, coming in—or going out?—with her coat and hat on, pupils red. All the people in the color flash photos have red pupils, but on our mother's deadpan expression, they look almost natural.

Pa must have taken this picture. Although after our mother left, he never took any more. Robert said he always got mean when we didn't squeeze in tight enough or pay attention to the direction of the sun, so we ought to be just as glad. Back then, the old man wore a dark green work uniform and carried a lunch bucket and shined up his shoes. Mother wore perfume and toeless high heels with straps, even to go out shopping. These are memories that are one step removed from me, Robert having pointed them out in photos to prove them. He told me the story of our daily routine so often, I began to claim it, began to believe that I did remember.

We had a ritual. "And then what happened?" I used to ask him, sitting cross-legged on the chenille bedspread up in my room, envelopes of photos between us. "When did we move up here, to the cabin?" I'd say, knowing the answer, savoring its danger. On cue, he would tell me the story. She had a boyfriend. He would come to the house when the old man went to work and hang his jacket on the kitchen chair. It smelled good, like aftershave, Robert told me. But his words were at odds with his expression, his face teaching me to sniff out treachery.

How could my mother have thought we wouldn't know? Robert said I used to stand up inside the man's jacket, hiding while he took off his necktie. "I can seeeee yooo," Robert used to imitate the way the man would tease me. But I wouldn't come out. I didn't like him, Robert said. Even though he was very nice to us and Ma told us to be nice to him back. The bastard, Robert always said.

They made Robert take me outside to play, and one day Pa came home early. Whenever he came to this part of the story, Robert's eyes would narrow as he stared past me. He told me how Pa threw the guy out and almost killed him. Threw his fancy clothes after him. I must have heard this story a hundred times before I ever had an inkling of what it was our father might have found that changed our lives so drastically. But before I had an inkling, I had a dread in my stomach. It was bad, it was very bad. I could look at my mother's photographs and tell that.

Although, that's when I started to get mixed up. The bad photos were before that too, our mother's melancholy stare already set. I thought I could remember a square-roomed house with dark woodwork and inside it the sound of her crying. I'm sure that's not from Robert. I could hear her crying down at the end of the hall sometimes at night. I wanted to get out of my bed to go to her but I was afraid. Whenever I tried to tell Robert about this, he'd get mad. "Ain't it the awfulest thing," he'd scorn me for feeling sorry for her. He said she always cried when she'd been drinking.

His anger never lasted though. Most of the stories about our mother were Robert's happiest ones. Sometimes he made them up so recklessly, I knew they were made up and still I hung on every word—we both did.

I miss his telling stories. I don't know what to think now, looking at these pictures. I believe I do remember the inside of that downstate apartment, but any insights I gain about our mother at this point seem cold comfort. Robert's impersonations were warm, living, breathing. Blood relations—that's what he made us, that's what I want to tell Kate.

JANUARY, 1974

"That old car is so cold," Valley says, setting her sisal bag down near the door. She isn't frozen this time. She has learned to sandwich herself in layers of clothing and has borrowed Gabe's dress boots for the occasion. She writes long letters to Robert and has promised that once a month she will make the trip back to Marquette.

Gabe grants Valley the small amenities that are coming to her after being gone a few days' time, but she gives her no more, steering away from anything personal, saying, "You'd better have the oil changed in that bug of yours. How many miles do you have on that thing now?"

"Ninety-three thousand. Runs like a top though. Motor's still great—it's the body that's going."

"True for all of us."

Obligingly, they both smile, watching each other like wrestlers coming out of their corners. Valley peels off a wool shirt, a T-shirt, a cotton broadcloth men's shirt. Down to her long-sleeved thermals, she finally says, "They have a lot more snow in Marquette."

"They always do. The snowbelt goes right through Marquette and on up to Keewenaw."

"I thought about finding a place and just staying up there. You know? Forget about coming back here. No, I did, I hate it—being in your way."

Gabe looks up at the ceiling, bites her lip briefly. "So why didn't you?" she asks, bringing her gaze back to Valley's face.

The girl shrugs. "Robert's set on it. He wants me to keep on working on Sid. Things are coming along. Sid wants to call the place 'Wild Kingdom,' thinks it'll be the best thing ever happened here. He came up and talked to Robert about it again, I guess. Robert says once he starts working, we'll be able to get our own place."

Gabe nods, watching Valley pull off her long johns in front of the stove. She goes back to the essay she is reading, something about Hemingway's friendship with Ezra Pound in Paris and the "American-ness" of their characters. Both were active, energetic, and "violently American." The "tough guy" that made Hemingway internationally famous, the "strenuousness of him of the Big Stick" are modes of the American ethos. But she keeps missing the meaning of these words, and goes back to the beginning, over and over.

"You could at least ask."

"Ask what?"

Valley glances toward the corner of the room, then back at Gabe. "You know what. About Robert."

"What about Robert?"

"What do you mean, what about him? About how he is. About . . . about how he is."

"All right. How is he?"

Valley stares and Gabe stares back, upping the ante, determined to outbluff her. She thinks the girl looks tired. She wouldn't be surprised if she slept in her car to save money on these trips. It's possible.

Valley throws down her first layer of socks in an overhanded swat. "You don't even care," she says. "He could rot up there for all you know, all these years, and you don't even care what happens to him. You don't know what an awful place that is."

"What do you know about it? What do you know about any-thing? I've been going to write him, it's just hard, thinking of some-thing to say, he's got such an attitude. What does he talk about when you go up there? He puts the whole thing on us, doesn't he? Feels sorry for himself, blames his childhood, blames society, blames the war. That's all I ever heard him say. Why should I want to know how he is? When has he ever cared about anybody but himself? Let me ask you something, did Robert want to know about *me?*"

"Yes!" Valley's chin juts out, dares her.

Gabe looks down, searching for her paragraph with a grim determination. The girl's lying. At the very least, she is improvising. If he did want to know anything about her, it was probably whether she was moving out anytime soon. The page of her book is an impenetrable gray blur. She looks up again. "What did he ask?" she challenges.

"What you look like. He said you used to be chubby. Whether you've changed. I told him you read books a lot. He says that's no different. I told him you go outdoors a lot. He says you both always went outdoors. He wanted to know about your dad. I told him I didn't really know much. I know you go and see him sometimes, but you never really talk about him."

Gabe feels as if some crucial piece of underclothing has just come undone. Valley isn't lying. Robert really has asked about her. If Gabe's honest, she knows Robert has cared about her, about other people, even the old man in his way. But especially her. She should have gone to see him when Pa went to Pinewood. She could, at the very least, write him a letter. She's afraid of what he might say—why the hell didn't you tell me about the old man? What the hell do you mean, going to a lawyer? But she will write him, she will. Maybe she'll go to Shub's and call him, soon—tomorrow, maybe.

"You can tell him for me the old man's okay," Gabe says, trying not to look chastised. She shrugs. "And you can come with me next time, if you want to. Pa doesn't recognize anybody, but he's all right. They say he could come out of it, but probably he won't."

Valley opens the belly of the stove, bends over and stares into the fire as if judging the need for another log. Gabe waits for her to cross the line she's drawn. The fire is Gabe's job. Actually she is aching for Valley to cross it, but the girl only stands and studies it.

Finally Gabe says, "Look, I told you I wasn't going with you to make small talk with Robert. I don't especially want to hear it secondhand either. There's a lot between the two of us you don't even know about. A lot I haven't even *thought* about in years. We are not the Beaver Cleaver family here. We never were. There's bad stuff. I'm afraid of getting sucked into that again. I want it to be different and I don't know that it can be, I really don't know. What is it he wants me to know? Just tell me. I'm going to talk to him. I *will*."

Valley straightens up. She is stripped to her bra and panties, toasting herself. She turns her back to the stove. "Robert says you used to be really close."

"Maybe when I was eight," Gabe says after making a scoffing sound. She draws in her chin. "And being close to Robert . . . that's kind of a mixed bag. You already know *that*, don't you?" She sees that Valley doesn't. She goes back to her book and reads with determination:

After the initial meeting, Hemingway visited Pound at his apartment, but came away irritated by his egocentricity. Shortly afterward, he vented his anger in an obscene lampoon of the poet, which he showed to the French writer Lewis Galantière, whom he met through Sherwood Anderson. A few weeks later, however, Hemingway brought Pound the manuscript of one of his short stories—probably "Up in Michigan"—and the poet praised it warmly. Hemingway then informed Galantière that they "were now getting along fine. I'm teaching Pound how to box. . . ."

Valley interrupted her again. "I think he's changed a lot, Gabe. He says he has."

Gabe shrugs.

"You know, it's not like I came from the Cleaver family either."

Gabe laughs a little, surprised at this new direction. "No," she says. "I never thought so."

"No, I mean, I know what you're saying. A mixed bag. That's a good way of putting it. All mixed up. I only had a mother, and I know she really loved me, but sometimes—maybe most of the time now that I think about it—she hated me a little. She was sick, you know. Do you know what it's like, never having enough money?"

Gabe has been sitting with arms crossed over her chest, knees crossed, not meeting Valley's eyes. She's said nothing to encourage this outpouring. She gets up to put a log in the stove, ignoring the obvious question and making the girl move over so she can open the door. She jams the log in, then pokes at the coals underneath it. Why does she need any of this? Why doesn't the girl just shut up?

Valley squirms. "I wonder if he realized what it would mean—his committing suicide," she says.

"Who? What are you talking about?"

"My father. I told you about him. We were in New York. He was on his way to being famous—no, I mean it. I have his book—my mother kept it for me. Do you want me to show it to you?"

Gabe feels a little seasick from following Valley from one non sequitur to the next, but the girl always talks this way, with zigs and zags.

"We traveled all over, from one dinky college to the next, taking whatever low-life job my mother could get. She was a good writer too. But after my father, she couldn't get full-time teaching. Do you know they blackballed her? Everybody blamed her for what happened."

"So where *is* she?" Gabe asks, feeling a pinpoint of hope, hearing about this other possibility, a mother, Valley and Robert going somewhere else perhaps.

This possibility is dashed by Valley's answer. "She died. After I ran away. She had this horrible family. German? Midwestern? They wanted to take me in. They hated me, but they thought they could fix me—you know? It was funny, all of them, men and women, they wore these knit pant suits, green ones mostly, like—"

Valley stares off in the distance a moment and wrinkles her nose. "Like big, lumpy dumplings, spinach ones. Do you think they were part of some weird kind of cult?" She smiles a little from the satisfaction of this revenge on their memory. "I've been all over the place since then—mostly with men. Don't tell Robert, but I went to Iraq once, honest. I had a *really* crazy boyfriend there. He didn't want to ever let me out of the house." Valley tips her head to one side, then asks, "You a dyke?"

Taken by surprise again, Gabe laughs a bit defensively and, catching herself, stops. "No!" she answers too strenuously, then trying to sound more thoughtful, adds, "I mean, I don't *think* so. We're all homosexual, part of us, probably, given the right circumstances. But ask anybody, I'm pretty conventional. Why do you *ask* that?" Gabe demands. She looks down at her hands, aware that she has been watching Valley as she talks, Valley who is half dressed and slim and pink and somewhat wondrous.

"Robert was speculating," Valley answers. "He says you've got a certain—I dunno, a certain—*air* about you."

"Oh, an air. Now what is that supposed to mean?"

Valley doesn't seem to think it necessary to answer. She takes six long leaps to the front room to fetch her quilt, wrapping it around her as she walks back, saying, "You know the reason I ended up with Jack? *He* was the guy I was with in Menominee when I first started in writing Robert—because of my friend Sundew. She was a dyke. I worked with her in Petoskey at the health-food store there, and she had a friend who had a women's bookstore and, I don't know, there was this whole group of us used to go to music festivals. That's when I took my name. Did you know Valley's not my given name?"

No kidding, Gabe stops herself from scoffing. She wants to hear this story.

"We had this Corn Mother ceremony. The Navajos have this Blue Corn Woman, see, who's associated with femaleness, and also the White Corn Maiden, who symbolizes maleness—don't ask me why when they're both women. But see, whenever a baby is born, they have two naming mothers take the baby outside at dawn with these two perfect ears of corn, one blue and one white—to perform this ceremony. Like it's kind of bisexual, or something? It's funny, but in folklore whatever's female is usually something dark. Or hidden or on the inside and secret? Maybe because of our wombs or something. That's what Sundew used to say. So anyway. She and this other woman were my two naming mothers."

She was quiet a moment, studying Gabe before she spoke again. "I mean, I didn't know they were lesbians or anything—I knew they were *something*—but then Sundew started in on the men I took up with—she hated all of them, and she said I must be looking for my father or something—god, I hate that, when somebody starts in analyzing you? I told her, *you're* not my shrink. But then, you know, it started in being more than that. She listened to me, and that was great, but then she started in pushing me too—telling me what to think, like a man? It was weird. She kissed me once—"

Valley pauses. She has her legs crossed at the knees, and she extends the free one toward the stove and rubs her exposed arm with the other hand. "Her mouth felt . . . *small*, like flower petals." She sits up then, wrapping the quilt tighter. "And then I ran off with Jack Lundeen. I never would have taken up with him if it wasn't for Sundew. I mean, he was *worse* than usual."

"So that's when you connected with Robert."

"Uh-huh. Like I told you. He wrote this letter to the editor. And there was something about the way he put things—I dunno, I wrote him and we hit it off. And then he started in begging me to come and see him, and at first I was dead set against it. I mean, why should I want to go and ruin a perfectly good thing? Who needs sex and all that other stuff messing it up? I had just about had it with men by that time, thanks to Jack, and I was thinking, maybe Sundew was right about me, maybe I oughta be a dyke? But then I went, and—you know, the first time I laid *eyes* on him—"

She smiles a deliberately dippy smile, eyelids half lowered and fluttering. She shrugs. "So you think I'm just crazy?"

"Like I said, a lot of girls have felt that way about him." Gabe bends over to pick up one of Valley's socks and fold it.

"You can be so *mean*!"

"Well, Robert's the bad boy, like Marlon Brando in that motorcycle movie. And you're the only one who'll ever be able to tame him—that's how *that* story goes."

Valley tries to look haughty. "Maybe. Robert does listen to me." She goes over to the refrigerator and gets out a beer, twisting off the cap before she raises it in a salute. "So why don't you come loose, Gabrielle. If Robert doesn't know your story, why don't you tell me? What about you?"

Gabe reaches out for the offered bottle. "There's nothing much to tell. Married a guy in college. Not good looking particularly, but steady, dependable. Everything a girl would want after living with the Bissonette men. Except he bored me to death. I tried to be Mrs. Drugstore Owner. He'd walked into this really nice setup from his father. Plenty of money, enough to send me back to school. I had an affair. Couldn't make things fit anymore. Then when the old man got sick and suddenly the cabin was empty—*voilà!* The divorce settlement made a case for finishing up my graduate work while I figure out the meaning of life. And here I am. You know all the rest."

Valley studies Gabe a moment as she reaches in for a beer of her own, clearly disappointed that this truly does seem to be the sum total. She takes a swig, throwing her head back to gulp from the bottle. "The thing is," she says, plopping down into her chair again, "the thing I don't understand is, why there's such bad blood between you two. Why are you so mad at Robert? Because you wanna know the truth? I think he's scared of you."

"You're joking. If anyone's entitled to be afraid, it's me. You know that's just *it*, that twisting things around, that's just exactly what I'm mad about. Somehow it always ends up being me, all twisted around," she snaps, thrumming on her chest with an index finger, "It's me, me, always *me* gotta do something." She stops, then dares to say it. "It's not like *I* ever killed anybody."

Valley looks as if Gabe's broken some rule. Not fair, this hitting below the belt. "Look, you know he didn't *mean* to do that. No, I know that's what you'd expect me to say. But I believe it, I do. And he *is* afraid of you. He is. I don't know how else to explain it exactly. He's intimidated, 'cause maybe you know him too well and you're smart. You really *are*, Gabe."

Fat lot of good it's done her. Worn out, Gabe rests her chin on her hand. With no supper, she can already feel the beer loosening the hinges of her jaw and she wiggles it a little. "Maybe he's afraid of being outnumbered for once," she says, a bit weakly.

Valley raises her beer to that. Glad to have a laugh as exit, she's a little too loud, too giddy. "That must be *it*!" she crows. "Conspirators, that's us. Hey, you know what Sundew used to say? Long live the bitches! *Off* with their balls!"

Valley laughs, taking another sip, but by the time she sets her beer down, she is serious again. "I mean, I never thought it was that funny," she says. "In a way, I mean, women must be sort of scary to men—their starting off being their mothers and everything. It's not all *that* big a joke, do you think?"

Gabe is tipsy and glad of it. She answers, "We all have mothers, Valley. *And* fathers."

January 4, 1984
Five Corners, Michigan

Between the lines Kate is asking how my family created a feeling of safety, of happiness, who did what. I suppose she's trying to discover if people's families fall out in the expected ways—mother wiping kids' noses, dad bringing home the bacon. Or maybe to uncover how often they don't match ideals. I remember Shub and Elsie never divided their roles the way they were supposed to—unless you count Elsie's wearing a dress when she pumped gas, or Shub's frowning whenever he was kind. In my family I keep coming back to Robert for both functions—mother and father.

Our mother wasn't physically there, and Pa most often was absent even when he was around. So Robert and I filled in for each other or we didn't. I think we'd learned to want more of a mother because our disappointment at her abandoning us was a daily, abiding one. Our father, we never held culpable.

I was more eager to excuse Pa than my brother was, smart enough to recognize early on my low place on the totem pole. For Robert it was different. Firstborn and a son, he could afford to be angry, was probably even cultivated for this, if Kate's book is right. My place was to define his privilege. If I slammed a door, it was back talk. If I were smart in school, I overreached myself. But people stood back and made room for Robert's banging and crashing, sassing his way to self-reliance.

I suppose that's why his anger or his intelligence or his anything became more important to me than whatever I was or wanted to be. Robert was changeable as the weather that blows up on Lake Nekoagon, and I became his little weather station, taking in data. He'd cloud over, seethe with waves—and then the next moment, all was calm and he'd be playing the role of wise teacher, savior, friend. He liked these nicer roles the best, but he needed me for confirmation. I was the one who laughed when he was silly or who felt bad when he skinned a knee. I was the one who could keep the secret of our mother, the one he could show his feelings to. Since these tended to be wild and wide-ranging, I was also his target.

I think self-reliance isn't all it's cracked up to be. Being a pinnacle of certainty in one realm only guarantees a handicap in others. And it never develops on its own. It sits on the heads of those who uphold you. My hidden support was probably more important to Robert than either of us knew. I remember we never troubled Pa with our childhood dramas.

He seemed lost without a partner to buttress his feelings—more a child himself. Robert would deny this, though Pa said it himself once at Marquette. He didn't much like being a father. There wasn't anything personal in this. It was just that what we wanted—for him to be more motherly—he would have considered a character flaw.

A child can't understand these kinds of things. It can end up feeling personal. When Robert couldn't get Pa's love, he settled for hate and at least that way sometimes got Pa's attention. I had the relative freedom of being small game. We could all understand his indifference to me.

That's the value of family roles I suppose—they bring some security you can agree on, whatever misery they separately contain. But feelings have a way of busting out and surprising you, revealing what you really think. Robert had that trouble all his life. I had my hard feelings too.

If I'm honest, just now what sat me down to write was the shock of rivalry I felt—jealousy—seeing Kate with her family in the Christmas picture she sent. I wasn't thinking of her as someone else's mother. As an ideal—yes—she was everything my mother wasn't. She could meet every need. But now here she is—with grown children, an ex-husband, a grandchild even, and complicated stories to go with them. What do I do with this new image? I'd been loving the idea of her sitting up nights in her office, poring over books, so brainy she needn't bother with the body and its needs. An old dream, this—one that would require a wife. I'm as bad as Kate's own children, who joke about her book writing as an elaborate ruse to get out of housekeeping. I just have a different ideal for her.

I don't know why I hold on to these notions of male and female anyway. Maybe I'm more like Hemingway than I know. I'll have to tell Kate about the biography I'm reading about the women in Hemingway's life. I've always hated how his female characters seem cut out of cardboard. But there they are—the real women in his life. His mother earned her own money teaching music—rather radical in those days. She used the cash to build herself a cabin getaway. They say the whole family knew she wasn't to be bothered when she stayed there. She fought to win women the vote, began painting. More than once Hemingway told interviewers that his mother was a domineering shrew, an all-American bitch. He even blamed her for his father's suicide, but I'd respect her better, even as shrew, than any of the women he imagined.

Robert and I learned to hide from our real mother too. She always rippled the surface like something lost or submerged—weighed down by ideals maybe—the same that sank me. From the moment Robert reentered the picture, we both remembered who had taught him he had power, that he could be the one to make somebody else feel pain and fear. He'd found some relief, terrorizing me with regularity. When I failed to expect and tolerate torture, I was cast as uncaring. Unfeminine. I could pretend this didn't hurt, with Valley there to play my role and prop him up.

FEBRUARY, 1974

On one thing at least, Valley and Gabe agree. Neither of them is a slave to fashion.

"I got these at the Salvation Army," Valley says, lifting both feet off the floor and holding her legs out straight in front of her to show off her black Mary Janes. "They're perfectly good. I hope they never wear out." Gabe never sees her wear any other shoes, though often Valley goes barefoot or wears slippers or borrows Gabe's dress boots.

The way their freedom from fashion plays out is entirely different though, Gabe dressing simply, for comfort and convenience, Valley not so much dressing as costuming. She has a collection of dramatic scarves and costume jewelry, vintage dresses and Eastern saris, but sometimes she puts on an old cotton housedress and still manages to look stylish.

Her secret, Gabe decides, is her willingness to exaggerate. If she wears a housedress, then she braids her hair and pins it in a peasant crown or adds a cotton babushka. Her look for after-bath is overdone frumpy. Until she dries and powders her feet, she keeps them wrapped in hideous multicolored crocheted booties she got at a church bazaar. She wears a flowered cotton wrapper with hot pink rhinestone-centered plastic buttons, and pads around the kitchen, fixing herself tea, arranging crackers in a circle on a saucer.

She bathes frequently and likes to read in the tub by candlelight before she comes out to finish reading a chapter with Gabe at the kitchen table. Often she will read aloud some particularly important passage from one of her self-help books, as she does this afternoon. Already it's nearly dusk. She'd been complaining of feeling low. The days are so short, the nighttime so lonely, and now she has the antidote.

"You must envision your success now, just as you have always envisioned your doom in the past. Let go of those images that portray you as defeated, unsuccessful, disheartened. Paint yourself powerful now, see yourself move with complete confidence, addressing friends in wisdom and with assurance. Breathe deeply as you create this inner vision now."

Valley shuts her eyes then, taking a deep breath. The steam rises up out of the teapot's spout like a genie. She is no longer a girl in an old lady's cotton wrapper and slipper socks. She is a seer, a woman of mystical powers.

When she opens her eyes, she looks annoyed to find Gabe studying her, as if it were unthinkable that Gabe hasn't also shut her eyes, and has missed this moment. She breaks a single cracker in half. "You are so resistant to new ideas, Gabe. I worry about you."

She gets up, still nibbling and clearly irritated, though Gabe also sees embarrassment. Frowning, Valley undoes her hair and goes to fetch her comb. She sits down again, smoothing every tangle until her mane lies flat as a wide, shiny ribbon down her back.

She says, "You look like a lumberjack sitting there, do you know that?"

She is trying to hurt Gabe's feelings. The girl gets up and walks past the kitchen window next to the door. Just outside is where Valley has been routinely dumping the parings and vegetable scraps from their meals. Gabe believes this a poor practice, but the first time Valley set out carrot peelings, something in the way she moved as she opened the door overtook Gabe—a memory of her mother doing this very thing, her one winter here. Her mother with the full mouth, the tense laugh, fighting with Pa about this one thing, frightening them all because she was usually not so fierce.

So Gabe had let Valley go ahead with her ill-placed charity, because other memories, or the possibility of them, still shimmer occasionally in some gesture Valley makes. Especially when she is quiet, Gabe thinks, wanting to soothe the girl, not particularly taking in the connection she's made.

There's a lot of activity out by the parings, and Gabe motions to Valley to come nearer the window. Their red squirrel, its tail flicking with a life of its own, is sitting upright on a branch of the maple tree, above the pile of scraps. A crow, wings spread wide, bumps down with a caw, makes a sharp jab with its beak, and, grabbing up a carrot end, flies off. But it's a field mouse Gabe wanted Valley to see.

It has come skittering across the clearing on important mouse business to find a hole under some tree roots where it disappeared. Through all of this, the squirrel keeps lookout on its haunches, holding food in its tiny, handlike paws, nibbling at a furious pace. Suddenly it drops down on all fours, tail jerking up in alarm. Gabe looks down, close to the glass, trying to see what's up, and sees a slim outline, a weasel, by the corner post of the porch. The thing must be starving because usually they hunt by night.

The weasel pauses a moment, then bounds across to the tree root, arching and extending, like a high-speed inchworm. It slips down the mouse hole and then, very quickly, reappears with the mouse entrepreneur in its jaws.

Valley makes a small sound of discomfort as the weasel sits up with the mouse dangling from its mouth, then, with prize still held high, disappears with the same undulating hop. Valley looks stricken. "Poor mouse," is all she manages, her voice higher than usual. Her expression says she has witnessed the death of a mouse martyr. "Why did I have to see that?" she asks plaintively. "Was that why you called me over to the window? To see *that?*"

"No. I didn't know that would happen. How could I? Honestly, though, it's bound to happen. If you put food out and attract animals, why then naturally you attract their predators too, Valley. That weasel would have to be stupid not to take advantage of a setup like that. I tried to tell you it might not be a good idea to put out the garbage. You don't know what you might get. It could be wolverine next time."

Valley only continues to look as if she's been dealt a blow.

"Look, don't feel bad. There must be a million mice out there. If it weren't for weasels, we'd be overrun with mice. As it is, I have to trap them in here by the dozens."

"Oh, you *trap* them? Don't you ever let me see that! I mean it, I couldn't stand it, I couldn't *stand* it—oh, just the thought!" She puts her hand over her mouth, looking sick.

"Valley. You can't spare every mouse in this world. I mean, we are talking about a little mouse here."

"Shut up. That doesn't help. That doesn't help. I am sick of your always telling me stuff like that."

Gabe puts her hands up in surrender. "Okay, okay."

"I don't care what you say, I don't ever want to see that again. The next time that weasel comes around, I am going to smash him flat with the shovel, I am just going to smash him so he never does that again!" Valley says this with such venom Gabe has to look closer at the girl's face. The mystical woman of spiritual power has her jaw set, her teeth on edge, and the look in her eye might cloud the heavens, striking infidels dead with a thunderbolt.

MARCH, 1974

Winter's worst behind them, the snow is melting, turning into crusty lace. The sunlight stays for respectable visits in the afternoons and makes their days more bearable. Valley has rescued the old worn box in the corner of Robert's room, the one filled with the black pulpy paper of their photo album, the pages come undone. Underneath the book are more wads of unsorted photos. She's bought a new album, one with a red padded vinyl cover, and has been reconstructing the old one, aiming for its completion by the time Robert arrives.

He was the firstborn and the photos get scarcer after Gabrielle arrives on the scene, but even these are of Robert—Robert looking into the buggy where presumably Gabe slept, Robert standing with their mother in front of the buggy, the birthday-O picture with Robert in the background sticking a balloon up on the wall, his long curly hair sticking up from static. Finally, Valley finds a photo of Gabe and two friends, sitting on the front steps of an apartment with three tiny kittens on their laps. In the background Gabe can see the staircase where she fell on a nail and bled on each of the steps.

Valley uses a special fountain pen with white ink she's bought for this project, writing on the black paper to caption each photo after she's attached it with black corner mounts. "Robert welcomes the new arrival—Gabrielle," "Robert and his mom," "Three tiny kittens, three musketeers." When she isn't sure how to label something, Valley asks Gabe about it. And Gabe does feel some pleasure, looking back at an orderly past, seeing things in starker outline, clearer for the distance and the way the camera's eye will leave things out.

There must be a million families who have mothers who drink or are unfaithful. But their husbands don't turn mean and silent, and their sons don't grow up wild and go to jail. It can't all have hinged on her mother, the way they made it seem. In fact, for the first time it's clear to Gabe, as she looks at the photos, that Margaret, her mother, had next to no influence. If her father said, move, she moved. If her father quit his job, then she had to make do.

Margaret's actions and motives seem chopped into small pieces, captured in something thick and gelatinous. She was a drunk, an adulterous slut, but on the other hand, a social climber, spoiled by her big ideas, who wanted things nice. Perhaps her mother didn't leave, not really, but had only faded slowly, slowly away. Then maybe days or weeks after she'd completely vanished, someone noticed. So that it seemed sudden—her leaving—as if she'd walked out the door— when really she'd been disappearing by little bits for a long, long time.

The last photo of their mother was taken when Gabrielle was five and a half and Robert just eleven. They are all three dressed up in their best, standing near the Christmas tree set up in the front room of the cabin. Lengths of plastic, ugly and gaping, wet with condensation, are stapled to the row of windows behind them. Their mother has her coat on, though neither Robert nor Gabe do, and this seems odd to Gabe—as if their mother knew she was already headed out the door and wanted them to have some clue.

Gabe is the deadpan one in that picture. Maybe I noticed, she thinks. But more likely it is resignation, her typical resolution not to extend herself too much and risk getting into trouble. Robert is squirming and shrugging his shoulders so that his face is a little blurred, and their mother is looking askance at him, as if contemplating reaching out a hand to calm him, though Gabe is sure that she didn't.

Probably the old man was shouting at him. Probably Robert straightened up for a moment and, beside himself, slugged her a couple of quick jabs in the back. Gabe would have kept her face calm, just wanting to get through it, because if she reacted or moved her face, she'd ruin the picture and get into trouble, even if Robert were the one full of piss and vinegar.

Just as if their mother were unhappy and unfaithful because of the way their father treated her, she would be the one to get into trouble, not the old man. Because he had a photo to take, a family to support, a reputation to keep. Her mother had a duty. That's all. One word. One two-ton word.

Gabe wonders, Did her mother have a hard time making the decision to leave without them? She looks at those pictures and Robert is gangly by then but still handsome; Gabrielle is the prettiest she will ever be. There are dimples on the tops of her babyish hands and nothing in her eyes accuses anyone.

Pa never tolerated questions about where their mother might have gone. One night not long after she'd left, Robert had asked some question about her. Their father's tone had leapt up in such heat, it surprised them both.

Gabrielle was already in bed, but Robert had been resisting, as usual, standing in the doorway between their two rooms. He'd been whining, needling the old man with all kinds of unanswerable questions: Why can't we stay up later? Why does it get dark so quick? She can't remember now what question of Robert's had prompted her father's outburst. Was it: Why can't our mother come tuck us in?

Whatever it was, she remembers Pa's answer. "Shut up," he'd said. "Just shut *up* about it. Don't you talk about her, do you hear me?" he'd said and put his hands up over both his ears. This had struck her, even then, as a childish gesture. Pa had stomped downstairs after that, forgetting to say good night to her—to her, the child who had been so good and quiet and had not asked any questions.

Robert didn't speak to her either. He put his arm up on the doorjamb and placed his face in the crook of his elbow for the longest time, swinging a little from side to side. She watched him until the light faded to a deep purplish slate, until she could barely make him out, a darker blue against the black logs.

"Robert?" she whispered once, but when he didn't answer, she held her breath, barely stirring, afraid to say anything or move, not even when she heard a shuffling noise and guessed that she must be alone again.

Valley has mounted the last Christmas picture. "This is the most recent I can find of your mother. You don't have any more somewhere, do you?"

Gabe shakes her head no. "They all peter off after that one."

Valley is trying hard to look nonchalant before she comments, "Robert told me that your mother left. I guess he doesn't know where she is."

Gabe nods that she doesn't know either.

"It makes you wonder, doesn't it?"

"About what?"

Valley is smoothing the page in her lap, sifting through the box of pictures, studying a few. Behind her, the window glowers with dim light. Damp hangs in drifts above the warming ground, which is grimy and wet and laden with smells, as ripe as a logger's wool cap at the end of the season. Patches of dirt-pocked snow are growing smaller by the day, melting away at their icy edges, though probably it will snow again.

"How she could do it? I never had any kids, but I don't think I could do it. Look at you, you're so cute in this picture. It goes against nature, don't you think?"

It isn't until she hears herself talking that Gabe understands what she does think about her mother, that she has on some deep level forgiven her without knowing it. "Women get blamed for things," she says. "Especially in families. We put them in the center and if they screw up, everything is *their* fault, the whole center falls out. And if they do what they're supposed to, then they're nothing but some fixture."

Valley looks stymied. "A fixture? You mean, like a bathtub or something?"

"Yeah, like a bathtub. No, like an institution, an edifice! Or *wait*, maybe you're right. A bathtub's more daily, isn't it? Turn a few knobs—*voilà*! A nice, hot soak, just what you needed. A good woman is like that—everyday magic."

Valley thinks about this a moment, shuffling through the piles of photos. Then she says, "When we went to Iowa, after my mom was sick? I finally met my great-grandma, this saint I'd been hearing about for years, everybody always called her a saint—and the whole family went to her house for every holiday? She never said a mean word about anybody, *ever*, and god, everybody just loved her to death. And there she was, this sweet, sweet person, hugging everybody, loving everybody.

"And you know what I thought? I thought, Man, her love is worth about nothing. I mean, what does it mean if she loves you the same as she loves everybody? A saint *has* to love everybody. I mean, if she'd bite somebody's head off every once in a while, then maybe you could believe that she loved you. It might mean something then."

Valley has been intent on the photos as she blurted this confidence out, the way she always did, carelessly. Gabe is surprised that she's been heard so well, and despite Valley's casual demeanor, she risks answering her more fully, "There's more to my mother too, but I don't know what. You have to figure they *must* have been more complicated somehow, these mothers. But you know, the story goes, you're either a saint or you're a bitch. What I want to know is, who put women in charge of family anyway? Or in charge of sainthood, for that matter? Who *asked* for it?"

Valley licks the corner mounts, then presses a photo down. "Personally," she says, "I think my great-grandma was pissed off that my mom and I just dropped in on her, and then the whole bunch came over and tromped all over the house. They had her cooking enough for an army and I think she'd been watching 'Jeopardy' or something. I kind of felt sorry for her. But I dunno. I still think it's kind of unnatural. Your mother just taking off like that. Here," she says next, changing the subject with another photo held out. "Who's this guy with Elsie and Shub?"

"My ex. We came up here for a visit after the wedding."

"No kidding? That's him? Well, what's the matter with Robert then? He's not all *that* bad."

January 14, 1984
Five Corners, Michigan

It begins to come easier. I'm less self-conscious and some of the memories—not the ones Kate wants necessarily but the ones released like worms from all this spading—won't let me alone until I write them down. I'm learning not to fight them.

This one time when I was about ten years old, Robert had holed himself up in his room, threatening to quit school. We both had a long bus ride into Clearwater every day, but that year he had started high school and went to a different building farther out. He didn't like it and quit going. He said the kids were all snobs.

He wouldn't come out of his room even for dinner, just snuck out once in a while to raid the kitchen. He told me through the door that he peed in a can and not to worry about it. The old man got sore. He didn't need some truant officer coming by asking him for excuses that, by god, he was not about to give. Robert managed to barricade the door and even after dark fell and Pa had worked himself into a fury, he couldn't get Robert out. The next night Pa drank a lot before he climbed up to my room and bashed the door to Robert's room with a steel beaver trap he swung on its chain.

Robert stayed put. Pa threatened to get his gun out and blast the door open, but I hung on to him and begged him to come sit down on my bed for just a minute, and once he did, he passed out. I fell asleep at his feet, wrapped up in my robe, too afraid to sleep downstairs. The next morning, Pa got up without saying a word to me and all day he pretended he had no son.

Neither of us spoke about Robert. And then about night-fall, when Pa had gone into town to the Friendly to meet with Sid Nichols about something, Robert appeared at the table. He wanted me to come and look. I followed him upstairs through my room and he opened the door to his. It was pitch black in there. He'd put blankets up over the windows. He told me it was all right but I remember I was scared. He had to shove me inside.

He shut the door behind us and lit the lantern on his bureau and then he clicked another switch. What I saw made me gasp.

He had plastered the walls, the ceiling, the floor, everything on one end of his room with aluminum foil. And inside this silver cubicle he had built a huge mobile of the solar system with glistening chrome wire and glass tubing to mark the orbits and clay models of the planets, painted and shellacked and glowing with color.

The sun at the middle was huge, a ball of crumpled cellophane. A yellow light lit all the intersecting planes from inside the ball, setting it aflame as it slowly twirled and reflected on the foil all around us, traveling out and out and out.

However he did it, I thought it the most gorgeous thing I'd ever seen. Robert had this look of satisfaction on his face like he'd gotten even with somebody who had it coming. He told me it was better than any shit they'd ever see at the Science Fair.

I saw it instantly. Yes, he had to enter this in the Science Fair. He'd win hands down. I'd help him. My mind was racing with the status this would bring. My brother, the genius, the one with such creativity and, yes, he was rather good looking, wasn't he? This kind of achievement would mark him as college material, would capture the likes of Linda Carpenter and Debby Finster, girls to whose parties I had never been invited.

Robert told me not to be a jerk. Did I think they were going to give first prize to somebody who'd been skipping school and was probably on probation right now? And where did I think he'd gotten all this shit? They were probably looking right now for the guy who'd cleaned home ec out of its tin foil. Hell, he'd gotten all the wire and tubing right out of the science lab.

I remember him holding up a handful of glass, with the light from the mobile shining on his face. He wore a braggart's smile, his eyes laughing at the joke of an orderly cosmos built out of stolen parts. "I got a bunch more of this stuff," he said, motioning toward a pile in his closet. "Enough for the whole fucking Milky Way."

If I'd told on him, Pa would have washed out his mouth. But at least Robert went to school after that. Pa blustered to Shub how it was about time the boy shaped up and if something like it happened again there'd be hell to pay. All of it a sham. At home Pa avoided Robert more than he used to and drank more too, and Robert stayed gone most of the time or locked inside his room.

When things quieted down that time, Pa's bluetick hound disappeared—Boomer, the old man called him. A few days after Robert showed me his model, I was walking along the trail next to the lake and I found Boomer at the water's edge. He had a piece of glass tubing broken off in his rectum and there was blood on the ground next to his tail.

I never told Pa. But I felt guilty for the way my silence made me part of what happened. Smoothing things over—important for keeping tensions intact until they build up to a blowout. Another fight, something with scuffles and fists, did come after that, though I don't remember the reasons exactly—I only know it did and that saying something about Boomer might only have set off the explosion sooner. Maybe I couldn't have made any difference. At the time, I thought what happened to Boomer said something dangerous about Robert, too dreadful to expect Pa to deal with. Now I see Boomer also says something about me.

Shub used to say that Pa and Robert couldn't mix, like oil and water. That wasn't it exactly though, because in this case the oil needed the water, was practically dying of thirst. So I guess none of us were surprised when Robert shook things up, first with the old man, finally with Fatty Wilson and the Big Man—the law. We expected it. Maybe we halfway approved.

I think we wanted to make it up to Robert somehow. Shub and Elsie always tried to believe the best despite what they saw when Robert got back from Nam. Sid had nothing but hope and praise even after he'd been put in jail. The warmest, the funniest stories will always be about Robert. He had something hard to describe that some people have and can't get rid of, even if they try, and I think Robert did try.

The thing's drawn from the gut, passes clean by reason, out-runs caution, flies straight in the face of experience—I mean, people loved him.

APRIL, 1974

The bell over the door rings, and everything about the man who opens it says, This here's not just anybody coming in through the front door. This here's Big Frog, owns his own little pond. He says, "Well now. Lookit here, Belle. I guess I know a little gal who's been beside herself, getting ready for *this* day." Broad shoulders, booming voice, cowboy boots, and oversized silver buckle holding up his jeans, Sid Nichols is standing with the door open at Shub's Economy Mart. He looks around as if he is pricing everything, about to reach for his wallet. And next to him, here she comes, queen of all the lily pads hereabouts.

"Don't stand there lettin' all outdoors in. I ain't doin' so well I can afford to bring spring to the whole upper peninsula," Shub calls from behind the meat case. He is busy slicing a ham loaf on the cutting block, for a tray beside him decorated with plastic parsley.

At this reprimand, Belle, who is short as her husband is tall, tucks her flat bottom in and minces away from the door, purse held up high in front of her. She has on tall heels to match her bag and a two-piece knit dress, light mint green with a touch of angora. Underneath that, some undergarment with intense powers of elastic separates breasts from midriff and tummy, all of which bulge fulsome and unnaturally stable, pent up with a visible tension. The door slams behind her, bell tinkling overhead, and she says, "Well now, isn't that *pretty*."

Both are looking at Valley's banner. Cut out of an old sheet and unfurled between the pillars that mark the store's front room, each letter is a different bright color, festooned with climbing vines and flowers, and butterflies flitting from word to word: WELCOME HOME, ROBERT! NEW BEGINNINGS.

Sid's boots resound on the wood floor as he strides to the counter and slings a six-pack and a large bag of pretzels there. "So where's the party boy?" he brays. Belle, holding up her purse with both hands, smiles like a girl apprentice at a magic show, watching him pull out a beer bottle and—*voilà!*—knock the cap off against the oak counter.

Gabe had heard them from the kitchen where she was opening a pack of gold-printed congratulations napkins. She comes out from behind the curtained doorway in time to see the beer cap flying.

"Hello, Sid. Belle. Glad you could make it."

"Well, look here now. If it's not a family reunion. Gabrielle. You're looking the same as always. Up here to stay awhile too, I hear. That's good, that's real good. A sign of the times, when bright, educated people like yourself come up here to stay. Things are turning around for Copper County, you wait and see. It's not just the end of the line anymore."

Gabe had been ready to make some excuse about why she hasn't yet stopped in at the Friendly to see them. But they're as relieved as she is that she hasn't stopped by. No excuses necessary. She says, "Belle? You wanna put your things back here?"

Belle has opened her purse and set down a tiny wrapped package on the counter.

"Sure, go on Belle. Powder your nose. I know you want to look your best. I tell you, she is rarin' to see him. Go *on*—I know all about that, you dirty old girl." With that, Sid gives Belle an elbow in her considerable port side and she flops a hand at him in fake protest, giggling and following Gabrielle.

"Oh," she says, at the sight of the snowy picture on Shub's round-eyed TV. "Isn't that 'General Hospital'?" She puts her purse and the present on the nearest chair, then bends to peer closely at the television. Mounds of tweedy, monographic snow are shifting and moving, accompanying voices laden with emotion. After a few minutes, half to herself, Belle comments, "She's just a tramp. I can't believe he hasn't woke up to her."

Gabe is busying herself at the sink and pauses.

"Terry," Belle explains then, straightening up and pointing to the screen for Gabe. "The doctor's wife. She started having affairs the minute they were married. Say, can I help you with that?"

"I'm just pouring the punch into this pitcher. You could slice some orange for it, if you want."

"Oh, isn't *that* pretty."

Valley has broken all her nutritional rules and ordered a sugary white cake with blue roses. It sits on foil-covered cardboard on the table. Belle studies it a moment after paying this compliment, but there isn't much else to say about it, so she goes back to watching the tweedy mounds.

After a while, Gabe ventures back out to the store area and half-listens to Shub and Sid. They are talking about the new highway going in at Galesburg and how that is going to open up the whole plateau from Dumpling Hill on over, and maybe bring in more business to the state park up the road, and to Shub's store.

Gabe hears Valley's VW before she can see it. As she watches out the window, the orange Beetle pulls into the parking lot. Valley is behind the wheel—Gabe knows this from the way the car's nose plunges to a halt. The door on the passenger's side swings open first.

Sid has come over to stand next to Gabe and is commenting, "I don't know how anybody living can stand to sit in them cars for long."

From behind Sid, Shub says, "Lookit that, he looks *good*."

Robert, the one they're all watching, stands up next to the car, one hand on his neck as he rolls his head around, loosening his muscles. Next he stretches both arms up over his head and puts one foot out, shaking it slightly.

He is dressed in a knit shirt, no jacket, and brand-new jeans that are smooth and stiff as poster board colored an unbending blue. He looks uncomfortable. He is thinner than Gabe remembers, but broad-shouldered, as if he's been doing work, and outside, because he is tanner than when she saw him last. Valley has told her about the carpenter crew he works on, and how he's been lifting weights. His curly hair, cropped short, is thinning in back, the blond mixed with a little silver.

He cups his hands to his face to light up a cigarette while Valley, still inside the bug, struggles with unwiring her car door. Straightening, Robert takes a deep drag, glancing at Valley, whose longish skirt has gotten tangled on the gearshift somehow.

Sid and Shub walk out on the porch, loudly welcoming the two of them. Robert walks over to the steps, smiling with the cigarette still in his mouth, eyes scrunched up from the smoke rising in front of his eyes. He pumps their arms in a noisy handshake, clapping them on the side of the shoulder each time. "Shit," he says, over and over. "If you two aren't a sight for sore eyes."

Belle has heard the arrival and comes rushing out the door past
Gabe, squealing a little, and Robert says, "What is this place, the
fountain of youth? Look at you, Belle—you haven't changed a bit.
Come-*eeere*," he growls, and Belle rushes down the stairs to give him a
squeeze.

While they are busy, Gabe slips out past the doorjamb, holding
the screen door open, half shielding herself with it. Valley finally
extricates herself from the car and comes up to stand next to Robert,
holding his arm, while Belle continues patting him, one arm around
him. "Come on inside now," she says, nudging him forward. "You
should see what Valley has gone and done for you."

The whole group comes up the stairs toward her, and Gabe feels
the breeze pick up, the air and its smells rushing against her face. She
stands tense, listening for something to alarm her. She thinks she sees
a light go out in Robert's face when he sees her, though this is so fleeting, the next moment she isn't sure.

He comes to stand in front of her. She stares, still waiting. The
skin around his eyes crinkles as he smiles. His cheeks, pulled up into
little humps of pleasure, flush pink. He makes no move toward her,
and they don't touch. "Little sister," he says.

"Hello, Robert."

He flips his cigarette down to the ground then, stepping on it
with a graceful twist of his foot as he looks back over his shoulder at
everyone, and they, who have been quiet in this moment, begin talking again all at once, pushing him along inside. Gabe opens the screen
door wide as he walks by, sucking in her breath as she feels the heat
from his body, senses the weight of the warm, moist space surrounding him. She remembers it now, the way he takes up room and fills it
solid.

Indoors, there is awkward, loud conversation to avoid any lulls,
more talk about things they've already hashed over: the highway
going in at Galesburg, the sign that Valley has made, the unthinkable
possibility of sitting in a Volkswagen for any length of time. And as
they talk, warming up to the occasion, the whole of Five Corners
begins trailing in, and some from far away as Clearwater and
Galesburg.

Valley looks as if she is at her first prom, the way she hangs,
beaming, on Robert's arm. He is in his glory, beginning to spin off

stories to beat the band, oiled with the beer he has told everybody his parole officer had better not find out about. "Say, you think this Black Label is bad, we had winos up at Marquette so desperate for anything, they'd cook up a can a Sterno, drain off the oily stuff, and drink that. Called it Pink Lady Sque-*eeeze*," he said, drawing the name out through smiling, clenched teeth, face squinched up. "Make you blind, that stuff!" he half shouts, showing the effect with a cross-eyed stagger, everyone laughing.

Natty Raison is there in his ranger uniform, and Barney Guilmette, president of the Lions Club. And so is Mrs. Snow, newly arrived from Florida with a paid companion, a redheaded woman whom Robert eyeballs whenever she's not looking. He has this in common with a couple of surveyors who have come down the Galesburg Road and dropped in at Shub's Economy Mart to buy some packaged pies and milk for their lunch. They get handshakes all around and welcome-home cake instead.

Gabe can see they don't know what to make of it, especially when Sid and Shub fall on them with questions about what they are surveying, and just when the new highway will be done. But they don't look a party horse in the mouth; they swallow down cake between questions and soon are joining in the wise cracking as if they were old friends.

For his gift to Robert, Shub has cleaned up his best cabin, Number Three, for the honeymoon and stocked it with ham and eggs and sliced bread. He tells how he's stacked dry wood up on the porch, at his age, though it's damn hard to come by this time of year, and everyone jokes they'll be plenty warm enough without it.

Mrs. Snow has made up little bags of rice to throw, anxious to publicize that the happy couple is, in fact, married. She holds the brown paper bundles up, but hardly anyone notices.

Robert is holding center stage, spinning stories and opinions. He has had much time to reflect on current events and has strong feelings— about Nixon "and his kike friend, that Kissinger"; about the Paris peace talks, "That's a crock. What the hell were we doing over there, huh? Tell it to the guys in body bags. We shoulda bombed the shit out of 'em when we had the chance, and finished it a long time ago."

It's the tension or the excitement or maybe just everyone getting well primed. More than an hour goes by and Gabe can hardly hear herself think, the talk is getting so loud, the outbursts of laughter so regular they are almost constant. And then Sid wants to give a speech. He raps a pencil on the neck of his beer bottle to start with, and when that doesn't work, yells, "Shut *up!*"

Everybody gets quiet.

"Now Belle and me got a little something for the honoree of this here party. No, no. Ain't no gettin' *out* of it. Come over here, boy. We wanna give you this."

Everybody cheers and crowds around, anxious to see what is in such a little present, and from Sid, who they know just doesn't go around giving stuff away, never. Gabe can see Robert doesn't quite know what to make of what he's found inside. He holds up a set of big plastic keys on a round hoop, the kind you give babies to teethe on. On the ring Belle has attached a big label that says, "Jailhouse," only that is crossed out with a big crimson "X." And under that she has written the word in the same red, "Opportunity."

Then Sid gives a speech with his legs spread like a gladiator, looking into Robert's face, his hands on both of Robert's shoulders, saying how nothing should stand in Robert's way now, because after he's done with his honeymoon, Sid is puttin' him in charge of Wild Kingdom and the two of them are practically partners—they might as well just come out and say so. This is seeing as how the whole thing really wouldn't have come about at all, unless Robert had first come up with the idea. And Robert's own little wife helping Sid get the thing all planned and started. And now there's no telling what the future might hold for them, the way Copper County is opening up, they might all be richer than Croesus before long.

At this, everybody cheers again and whistles and claps. And Robert, maybe half out of embarrassment, maybe just drunk, grabs Valley and mashes his mouth against hers, tongue kissing the likes of which Five Corners doesn't usually see in public.

"You better go on your honeymoon now, you horny ole bastard," Sid Nichols half-shouts and shoves Robert a little, slapping his shoulder. Sid grabs Belle and tries to give her a kiss, but Belle smiles tightly and turns in a practiced motion, deflecting it onto her cheek.

Gabe watches Robert move and speak, with everyone surrounding him like planets around the sun, and she knows somehow in that one hour, everything has turned. It is nothing he does or says, exactly, nothing he accomplishes by himself. It's the way everyone gives him importance without his even asking, how they listen and receive what he says with regard. A vague gnawing in her stomach tells her she is thinking this, but she accepts the order of things and on a level she doesn't question, knows it is she who is living in *his* house now.

Later on Robert comes to stand near her while she busies herself with keeping napkins on the table and the punch bowl filled. He eats a piece of cake as he talks to her, pausing to watch the crowd, listening. Gabe tries to be nonchalant.

"Valley took me by the place before we came over," he says finally. "Looks real nice, Bean-o."

She had forgotten all about this nickname for her. And looking at him then, his adult face blurs into memories she has of him—the brother protecting her, explaining the way of the world to a little girl. It's why she's gone along, unprotesting, with all of them on this party. But she doesn't for a moment believe what Valley's told her, that in just a month or two they'll have their own place.

"Who'd a thought you'd come back to Five Corners, huh? Same for me, you know, same for me," he is saying.

He turns his fork over and looks at a blob of frosting before putting it in his mouth. "So what happened to old Dennis boy? I thought you had it *made* with him, the happy housefrau with money to burn, an' all that."

"I was never cut out for it. You know that."

"True enough, I guess. And no *big* loss, if you ask me."

Gabrielle looks away, forcing a smile. "That's what you always used to say. It'd been nice if you hadn't said it in front of Dennis, that's all."

Robert shrugs. "He had no sense of humor, that was his whole problem. No backbone either, unless you want to count that pipe up his ass."

"That's enough, Robert, I mean it." She is aware of how ineffectual this sounds, but she does mean it. This is her marriage they are talking about, her life. He can just back off.

To her surprise, he does. He changes the subject. "I guess you took over the old man's room, huh? Got lacy curtains on the windows. Looks real purty."

Gabe's stomach jumps over an incoming wave. She hadn't thought about the possibility Robert and Valley might do that, tour the cabin on their way back to Five Corners, walk around her room, sit on her bed, open the drawers to her dresser. She feels out of breath. She's forgotten to exhale. She does this now and forces herself to look into his face.

"I didn't want to heat the upstairs. I thought it'd be simpler to just live on the first floor."

Robert pulls his lips up in an exaggerated smile. "Yeah," he says. "That woulda been simpler. Way it is now is *real* complicated, isn't it? Guess you forgot about *me*." His eyebrows arched high to pose a question it's obvious he's already answered for himself.

"No. I didn't forget exactly. It's like you said, it was more I didn't think you'd be interested in coming back. The old man said you never wrote."

"The old man, yeah." Robert heaves a sigh and turns to stare straight ahead a moment. Then he turns back to Gabe, full face. "You know, I wanna see him right away. I wanna know how bad he is. Doesn't seem right, his living in a *home*. You shoulda talked to me about that. He oughta be with the rest of us, in his own place, especially now that we're both back here. It's his place, after all."

"We can't do that. He's not himself, Robert."

"How *could* he be? Locked up in a nursing home, in some goddamn institution—him of all people. He could never stand the smell of hospitals, couldn't even stand being indoors. He oughta be home where he belongs, with the rest of us."

"Robert, I put him there because not just anybody can take care of him."

"Well, now there's more of us, isn't there? We can probably manage. It isn't right having him there, Gabe. You know that as well as I do." He looks away again, watching the others to see if his voice had given him away, and when he looks back his anger has gone underground. He changes the subject again. He says, "Valley says you're going to school again. You're gonna be gone for a couple of weeks?"

Gabrielle looks down and nods.

"Well, Number Three is nice enough meanwhile. We'll wait until you go before we move ourselves in. Give us all more adjustment time, this way. We'll park ourselves up in my old room. That way you can have your old room back if you want it."

Gabe looks up, alarmed. "No. I want my privacy, Robert. I'll stay downstairs where I am."

"Okay. I was just thinking of the old man."

"Look, don't you do anything until I get back. You can't just bring him back without talking to me about it. I'm his guardian, Robert."

Robert's eyebrows fly up again in an exaggerated arch. "Oh, his guardian! His *guardian!*" He puts his fist up to his lips, curling his forefinger up, tapping his upper lip. He says, "Well, it so happens I am his *son*. I think they will listen to his son, don't you? I think his son oughta have some say in it. Besides, little sister, aren't we talking now?"

Then as suddenly as his tone had changed, he sighs and it changes again, the rest of his words covered in velvet. "I wanna give you credit, Gabe. You did a nice thing, nice thing, taking care of Valley. You didn't have to do that. Some people might not have taken to her—god knows, she doesn't take to most people."

He puts his head back to gulp a swig of beer, then stands, holding his lighted cigarette in one hand against the neck of the bottle. "She told me you two fed the little bunnies and the deer all winter. That'd go a long way with her." He chuckles a little at this. "She'll cry if the littlest beetle gets squashed. I guess you figured out she's a little on the flaky side."

The lighted end of his cigarette glows bright as he inhales again, smiling, and he bumps into Gabrielle's shoulder as he exhales, waiting for her to join in on the joke. "Oughta fit right in with the rest of us crazies."

"What are you saying? You talking about *me?*" Valley comes up and puts both hands around his upper arm.

"Just about what a sweet little dingbat you are, honey-melon."

"I am *not!*"

"You are *not!*" He mimics her and laughs good-naturedly, tossing his cigarette butt to the floor and putting it out with his foot. "I think maybe we oughta head over to Shub's super deluxe honeymoon cabin. What do you think, sweet thing?" He pulls Valley, and when she giggles, he buries his face in her neck, brushing his hand against her breast in plain sight of Gabrielle, who, flustered, puts her back against the wall and looks straight ahead.

"Can't get so carried away like that, kumquat," Robert says to Valley, straightening up and catching Gabe's eye. "Let's go, dingding. I am serious." The two of them head for the door, making hurried good-byes to all who reach out for them. They walk faster than Mrs. Snow and Belle can grab for their little bags of rice, waving to the people behind them, joining in the laughter.

"Hold on there, you can't go without a picture," Shub calls, waving his Polaroid at them. They stop in the road long enough for Shub to take one from the porch.

"Thank you, thank you, everybody," Valley calls to those who are standing there, heaving ceremonial rice at them. Barely a grain reaches the couple. They turn to walk hurriedly away.

When Shub peels off the backing, the crowd takes turns watching the photo darken, darken, until Valley and Robert are standing there, smiling. The rice whitens the wet mud in front of them and lines the hollows of their footprints leading up to where they stand facing the crowd. Gabe tells herself to stop being so traditional, wanting to cry at a wedding. She looks at the picture and thinks of the waste in such a stupid custom, all that lovely white rice gone to waste, thinking only of that.

There's a thick-feeling thump in her side, Shub jostling her. "Come look at this, Gabe, you'll want to see this one," he says, and she follows him, past loud voices and pats on the back, to the kitchen. He has remembered another photo, one he had wanted to give to Valley for the photo album she's put together and has out on the table with the guest book. "Lookit here," he says, and reaches for a glass dish where he collects paper clips, rubber bands, and odd coins. He hands her a photo with curled edges.

Two women dressed in pith helmets and hiking boots are standing close together. Gabe peers closer at the faces, shadowy from the hats. That's Elsie with binoculars around her neck, and next to her, with Elsie's arm around her shoulder, is Loretta Young—or *wait*, her mother! Her mother, Margaret, dressed in khaki with her long hair up off her neck, and she's smiling.

Gabe asks, "What are they doing? I didn't even know they knew each other that well." She finds herself smiling back at Elsie and her mother, just for this sight of them, together.

"Oh, they hit it off pretty well. Took a bird-watcher's course together or some such silly thing. They had a good enough time though, hiking around, just the two of them."

"I always thought she hated it up here, the woods, I mean, being so far away from everything."

"She might have, I heard that. All I know is Elsie was sure sad when she left. You know, sad for you kids, acourse, but sad for Margaret too, and sad for herself, I think. After that, she was the only woman around the place, except Mrs. Snow in the summer and she always complained too much, even before she got old."

They both look at the photo again.

"It's only the second picture I've seen where my mother looks happy," Gabe says after a moment.

"Well, she was up against it. God knows I love your old man—but then I never had to *live* with him." He claps her on the shoulder, gives it a shake, then nods once before starting back to the front room. The party is getting louder, someone's asking, "Hey, remember that time—"and Shub doesn't want to miss anything.

"Do you *know*," he adds, turning to look back at her, "your mother, Margaret Bissonette, could add a whole row of double-digit numbers right in her head. Helped us put up stock sometimes, and damnedest thing I ever saw, how fast she could do it."

He opens his hands then and shrugs as if to say, Who could figure a thing like that? It will stay just between the two of them, this story that is so unlike all the others. But just the same, who could figure?

IV

EDUCATION OF A GIRL

The Faculty Chair for Independent Graduate Studies is pinching back the leaf tips of a wiry ivy plant on his desk, looking at it, not at Gabrielle, as he smiles with lips together. He has reddish whiskers with streaks of silver and well-scrubbed cheeks that reflect light almost as well as the wire-rimmed glasses he wears low on his nose.

"You have a good enough mind. Trust it," he says and lifts his nose to see her better through his glasses. She can see the wall behind her mirrored in them, its large four-paned window covered with a trumpet vine. "The best learning comes when you question long-held assumptions at a very personal level," he goes on, reciting Fond du Lac philosophy. "My advice is to pay attention to what your gut tells you."

She offers, "Like my hating Hemingway, for instance."

Professor Orbach throws his head back and laughs so abruptly that Gabrielle feels jarred. She can see his teeth when he smiles at her and it's not an altogether pleasant thing.

"No," he says, "no, it's *good* you've spouted off about him, but you need to work on understanding better *why* you hate him so much. You have to analyze your reasons, convince a reader. Visceral *thinking* is what we're after, Gabe, not just *viscera*."

"But what if I . . . I mean, *how* do I—?"

"Look, the reasons you feel as you do are there. You're not crazy and you're not bad. And he's not a god the way you may have thought. Neither are the critics who lionize him. That's what I'm talking about. Assume you are entitled to be in the critics' company," he says, pinching another leaf. "Change a few minds, if need be." He pinches twice more for emphasis. "And remember to be open. If he's not god, he can't be the devil either. Don't lose sight of the fact that he *is* a great writer."

She can't tell him this is the part she has trouble with. She doesn't *know* how far to go; she isn't sure what crazy is. Last night she'd written pages about Hemingway's pathetic sense of superiority. She'd discovered *Torrents of Spring*, written early in his career, a book so funny she thought she'd found something new to admire in the writer—until she learned it wasn't the good-natured invitation to laughter she'd imagined. He'd written it with deadly precision and the steady hand of a rifleman. The laughter was only a decoy.

She'd learned the publishing world had been shocked by *Torrents of Spring*, recognizing a slap in Sherwood Anderson's face. A calculated parody of the older writer's style was fair enough in itself, but it was well known that Anderson had been the first to stick his neck out and give Hemingway a helping hand by putting in a word with his publisher, who then became Hemingway's own. It was almost as if Hemingway wanted to destroy any claim Anderson might have made on him. She had seen this dynamic close at hand too often not to recognize it.

Hemingway thrived on one-upmanship. He used the language of combat to describe the literary, once bragging of knocking Turgenev out of the ring. Miserable whenever F. Scott Fitzgerald was praised, he preferred to think of himself as Scott's mentor and helper, referring to "Poor Scotty" this, or "Poor Scotty" that. Everything Gabe read showed her a man she already knew, a man frightened of losing an inflated sense of himself. He repeated his treatment of Anderson with others who had helped him, such as Gertrude Stein, who had considered only one other American writer in her Paris salon, Gabe noted, to be on a level with Hemingway—Sherwood Anderson.

But Gabe says nothing about any of this. She is worried she's so warped that all her ideas are ill-gotten, her thinking process itself all skewed. Who did she think she *was*, anyway?

Orbach is making little marks on a form, one of Fond du Lac's endless assessments and evaluations, far more intimidating than grades. "And what about resources, Gabrielle? Are you having any problems there?"

"No, the library here is very good, and you were right, I can get books through the interlibrary loan in Clearwater. That's not far, I go into town all the time."

"Excellent." Orbach nods, tight-lipped again.

"There is one thing," Gabrielle says, jumping in. "Financial aid. When I started, you see, I thought my housing was all taken care of, but now I'm thinking about some other arrangement, maybe moving back to Benton County where I lived before, I mean, most recently. Or maybe something nearer by." She shrugged. "I'm not sure what I'll do, frankly."

"But I thought your moving back to your family home was an important part of doing this here. Too much solitude for you? Clearwater is pretty deep in."

"It's even farther than Clearwater, but no, I *love* that part. It's money, and it's—" She chuffs a little sigh. "It's a long story basically. So what else might be possible, do you think? Are there loans? Special grants? Maybe work study?"

"Oh, you'll have to speak to the financial aid office. I don't know a thing about the details, although, at this stage of the game, I'd be surprised if you could get anything for this semester. Work study? Not for nonresidents, I think. But check with Paul. He'll help if he can. Dear, dear, and didn't you say your *father* was ill? Is that part of it, Gabrielle?"

"Well, yes, in a way, but not really. Well, it *is*, but— Look, I better not take up more of your time. I'm sure your students are always in one fix or another. I'll work something out." Gabe stands up and holds out her hand.

Orbach matches her handshake, firm and hearty in his grip. His face, the picture of reason, looks full of faith that all will go well for such a capable student.

Her chest constricts even while she beams back at him—she wonders how such things as she fears can *live* in the same world as his. She promises to keep him posted, shaking his hand vigorously. But all the while she is imagining Robert walking into the room, bumping into Professor Orbach with a shoulder, demanding, Who the hell did he think *he* was?

February 3, 1984
Five Corners, Michigan

Kate says she went to a women's conference at Fond du Lac around the time I was a student there. She was impressed by the college's progressiveness and I guess this matches with what we locals saw of it. My father thought the place was nothing so much as an excuse for artsy-fartsy types to waste their time, making clay pots for god's sake, painting pictures that some chimpanzee could do. Robert said rich kids went there to goof off and smoke dope and get out of the draft. People always wondered what kind of an education you could get where there wasn't a set curriculum, no courses everybody had to take, and this strange fact—no grades. I used to kid Valley about how she'd fit right in. I think I was covering up my embarrassment at going there, but somewhere along the line this stopped being funny.

I wish she could have gone—she loved novels and books. She thought it a splendid ambition, wanting to teach literature. Valley was smarter than I ever thought of being. And if Robert hadn't had his manly reputation to keep up, he'd have done twice as well as I ever did in school. Valley, too. I get so mad at myself, thinking I was such great stuff going to graduate school when I should have been finished with my education by that time. It was something to do after my divorce. I harassed myself about finishing my thesis precisely because I was so unsure I could even find a thesis topic—much less one I believed in.

I can almost hear Valley laughing. "Oh, lighten up— pleeease!" she used to say. I was always trying to frighten her with my evil imagination when I was working on Hemingway, but she saw through me. I worried I wasn't going far enough and then I worried I might be going too far—how would I ever know for sure? How do you know when you know something?

I think I knew for a while in the tension between Valley and me. "What do you want to say?" she asked me one time, out of patience. "That there aren't any such women? That they're a lie?"

"Of course not." I explained in my most erudite voice how that would be far too simple. Hemingway may have been rather selective about the women he portrayed, but it was likely they were the only sort he had known in his circle. These were higher-class women. She blew through her lips and covered her mouth with a finger, looking down as I spoke, playing with a piece of celery on her plate. "What?" I demanded.

"Oh, just that his women—they never had any friends, did they? Can you name me a woman who hasn't ever had a girlfriend? Wouldn't you go crazy if you didn't?"

I guess I did go crazy a little. I don't think I even knew that until the night I went out with Kate and Anita and their friends—the excitement I felt even when I didn't dare speak. Measuring my ideas against theirs, listening to them talking and thinking out loud together.

But what would they think of me if I told them the truth? I withdrew and avoided problems with Robert, I indulged in do-gooder fantasies with Valley and obsessed over school— pretending to be doing something too important to look up and notice what would only scare me. They'd be ashamed, embarrassed for me. Although Valley would say I'm being too hard on myself. Kate would tell me I was being sensible.

They'd both say these things don't make me responsible for what happened. But what's the alternative? Believing I was helpless? Here's something I do know—it would be sin to gloss over my faults and paint Robert and Valley in paler colors than they lived.

APRIL, 1974

The last night of her second residency, Gabrielle sits in the garden outside Nicolet Hall. The garden is hedged with privet and headed by one moldering wall where a gargoyle is poised to spit water into a shell-shaped basin. The water line, like most everything else on campus, is out of repair, the shell crumbly-dry and silent, though Gabe waits patiently, staring at it, almost convinced it will start to trickle. The night air, surprisingly balmy and warm and moist, seems to be drenching the quiet.

Gabe takes another sip of the Rusty Nail she has brought with her from inside the dorm, where the end-of-semester farewell blowout is still going on. Behind her comes the murmur of voices in civilized argument and even farther back, from nearer the center of the party, comes the pounding beat of Stevie Wonder. A student from Illinois, taller than she, rangy and big-boned, had been eyeing her inside. She toys with the idea of taking him to bed, though he looks too young and earnest.

An ancient black locust holds court over the garden, its high-reaching branches looking as if they were making supplication on behalf of the primroses and bleeding heart, the campanula at its feet. "What is it you're asking for?" she says to it out loud, forgetting herself, half aware that the question is really for her. Clapping her hand over her mouth, she looks around to see if anyone has heard.

She wants to think for herself the way Orbach is demanding, but she cringes at what she finds in her head when she tries—a little girl begging not to be left alone, a scared little whine: I'm not sure, I'm not sure, I don't *know*.

For two weeks, in between seminars and presentations, she's tried to fix the problem of going home. She's learned there are no grants, that she could do work study if she moved to Fond du Lac and took out a student loan. Meanwhile, she'd have rent to pay. She's also considered the idea of going back to Benton County where she could get a better-paying job and avoid more debt, pay for her rent, but she'd be leaving the old man to the wolves, and she wouldn't be any better off.

She could try to outlast them. Valley'd said they were going to move anyway. Robert and Valley surely would want their own place if she stayed underfoot, there in the cabin.

The only sure thing in her life at the moment is the next year or so in school. That's what she has to concentrate on. She has to go through with that no matter what. Her studies are her own, free from courses and teachers and books chosen for her, because Fond du Lac has given her an outlandish freedom—heady and terrifying all at once, like the rest of her life. So every few months, she'll come to residencies with preliminary work. At the end, finished with her master's thesis, she'll take her turn formally presenting her findings to the faculty and the rest of the students.

At least she isn't a kid anymore, when she didn't even know that she had any options. Now she has *options*, only none of them is good.

In a moment she will go inside and have a drink with the long-limbed fellow. She's heard him give a presentation, something about a leap of existentialist faith. She didn't quite follow it all, so she'll ask him about it, certain he will want to tell her. He will talk and talk and never think to ask her a question about her studies. For a moment she fantasizes telling him about Hemingway's recurring plots and heroes, always singular in their masculinity, testing themselves against great risk as they face those questions her tall existentialist seems fond of—how to live and how to die. Wouldn't he be surprised at all she knows?

She stares at the gargoyle's profile, the lips pursed to spit out something that will not form. Probably it has been here for years, helpless in its ambition and stuck here, she thinks, watching as she takes another sip, concentrating on the way her drink numbs her.

"Mind some company?" comes a deep voice behind her, and she knows who it is before she turns to see him. She will not bring up the subject of Hemingway or anything she knows that will put her in the limelight. She takes another sip of her Rusty Nail.

A subterranean discourse has been going on all night. Gabe feels worn out by it, though shaking her head, she knows she's slept the sleep of the dead. The earnest young philosopher next to her snores on, giving off a slight reek of alcohol and sweat. He looks older in the daylight, with crow's-feet next to his eyes, a few singular gray hairs.

She'd awakened still dreaming of J. Gordon, the deer Valley has named—J. Gordon, who is tamer than all the rest, bolder and greedier. In midwinter, a good two months before Robert had come home, Gabe and Valley had located the deeryard up from Brushy Creek. It lay in a depression on a high plateau, where northern white cedar crowded together, cutting down on snowfall and wind. Here the deer had tamped the snow flat. They could walk without too much effort or the danger of falling through an icy crust. Even so, the deer moved about as little as possible. Survival in winter was a two-pronged strategy—eating, but also conserving hard-to-come-by calories.

Gabrielle and Valley heard dogs baying one night. Gabe had suspected it meant they'd found the deeryard. If they chased the deer beyond the cedar into deep drifts, many would never make it back. Half starved, the exertion would be too much for them, even if the dogs didn't catch up.

At first light, the two of them made their way to the cedar, the sky overhead a dim, backlit gray. They found a young doe's carcass in a deep drift on the way, the snow around her torn up and bloodied. Valley had made a groaning sound as she sat down on the drift, mittens up to her mouth. "Hoodlums," Gabe said, "doing this for fun, not food." She picked up one of the doe's hindquarters. "If it's any comfort, looks like this one might not have made it anyway." She showed the severed bone to Valley, whose eyes widened above her mittens.

Inside, the bone's center was blood red, not the thick pink marrow it should have been. "Whitetail can lose a lot of their body weight each winter and still make it okay. But when this happens," Gabe explained, "when they start burning the fat in their marrow, you know they're pretty well done for anyway."

Gabe had brought a hatchet with her and, with Valley's help, following orders to pull down certain branches, she hacked off some of the cedar above the browse line, higher than the deer could reach. They left the branches on the ground at the edge of the yard. "Maybe we can save a few of them anyway," she said, and for the next few weeks, until there was a thaw, they routinely trimmed trees and left the branches on the packed snow.

But Valley went further. On one of her trips in to see Sid, she picked up two large bags of cracked corn. Gabe had no idea how she paid for it. She mixed this with raw oatmeal and began bringing a bucketful with her to the clearing outside the deeryard, trampling the area wider with her boots. Gabe didn't think this a good idea. Even trimming branches was a step her father wouldn't have taken. From the beginning the deer always cleaned the grain up thoroughly. Valley was thrilled whenever Gabe showed her the tracks and described who had come there.

After the grain became a twice-a-day habit, Gabe and Valley occasionally jumped a deer as they neared the clearing. Eventually a few of the creatures were only a few steps removed from tame. Instead of bounding off when the women approached, they went off a short distance, watching Gabe and Valley put out food.

J. Gordon, named—incorrectly—by Valley for Watergate's Liddy, was always the first to walk up to the food left behind. Gabe predicted that, like his namesake, he was sure to pay for his crimes, though she feared for the deer in a way she didn't for the guy in Washington. J. Gordon had a tolerance for human movements and this put him at an advantage for the time being. Eventually the buck found his way to the cabin, following the path they'd made from all their treks, to find Valley's vegetable parings just outside their door. This was such unusual behavior, it made Gabe uneasy.

It wasn't good for a deer to be complacent about humans and their scents. Come fall, he had better spook at the first whiff, because anybody he saw would be carrying rifles, not corn mash. It was hard for Gabe to argue for the natural scheme of things, the inevitable leveling of the deer herd, when the extra food made such a difference. J. Gordon had been gaunt, his coat scruffy and unkempt looking. Now he was growing sleek, his eyes bright and alert. J. Gordon was an individual they were getting to know, the way her father had always known one buck each year. That too had made her uneasy.

All this is enfolded in her memory of the dream that awakened her. She sits up in bed, next to the sleeping philosopher, trying to make the images coalesce. She dreamed that Valley and she were girls together, Valley feeding J. Gordon out of her hand, Gabe, nervous about it.

"Come on, Gabe," Valley said, making her hold out her hand and filling it with a small mound of cracked corn. Gabe felt the muzzle of the deer in her palm, the wet, whiskery tickle, the crunching noise of his chewing.

"Hold your hand flat," Valley instructed. "He might bite you otherwise. He wouldn't mean to, but he might."

And just then, up in the tree outside the kitchen window, Gabe could see the squirrel who regarded their yard as his personal property. He was scolding them. But there was something different about him too, something human, she thought, and she was trying to analyze this—what was it, *what* exactly?—when he dropped down on all fours in alarm, knocking a branch loose from the tree.

Startled, J. Gordon lifted his head up with a jerk, and one of his antlers fell loose to the ground as he leapt away.

"Look what you've done!" Valley cried out, and in that moment Gabe looked down to see four little fingers nipped off neatly and lying in the palm of her hand. Yet this wasn't what Valley meant. She was holding up the antler, all smooth except for the main beam, which was ridged like bark, streaked with brown. At its end was a whitish, rounded piece, the part that connected to the buck's skull, dotted with tiny specks of blood and giving off a heavy musk scent. Valley's mouth fell open, the way it did whenever she was shocked.

"You act like *I* did it," Gabe had said, sounding defensive. "They always come off. They grow new ones every year, didn't you know that?"

But Valley wouldn't be comforted. Not even when Gabe, who in the dream was more certain than ever that Valley was just a child, only a child, and possibly growing smaller as she spoke, opened her fist to show Valley the fingers, each one with bloody dots on the end like the antler. This image stays with her, though Gabe is quiet—so as not to wake her lover as she dresses and leaves for her own room, as she loads her suitcase into her truck. At breakfast, she finds herself glancing at her hand, held open and secret on her lap where the others can't see.

Nancy Jo and Elaine are exasperated with her because they want to know all the details of last night.

"There's not much to tell," is all Gabe says, shrugging. They believe she is tantalizing them, Gabe thinks, withholding lusty details because they are both married and have children. But it's the truth and it doesn't matter. They'll supply their own details, better than the reality.

Gabrielle says her good-byes as if nothing heavy were weighing on her. Bye-bye, she says, smiling and waving, then gets into her truck, puts her key in the ignition, all the while thinking, Where to? This is not so much a thought as it is a muddied pool of emotion, and she is up to her neck in indecision. She seems doomed to go back to Five Corners for want of a solid alternative with a name and a plan.

Finally, to avoid what feels like capitulation, she simply turns in the opposite direction, toward Chicago. Not intending Chicago precisely, just telling herself that she needs the time.

With wheels rolling beneath her, she remembers suddenly that there isn't any rule that says she has to decide by today, or tomorrow, or by the next day for that matter. She can take her time until she feels sure of what she wants. She can make up her mind as she goes along, and then she can change it again, if need be.

Besides, she thinks best on the move, with her vehicle sucking the highway's middle line up underneath her flying weight. Something in the rhythm of the cars humming by, of the poles rushing past at a slant, will put it all together for her, like a dream she is having while awake, like a dream that will do her thinking for her.

February 21, 1984
Five Corners, Michigan

Kate says it's survivor's guilt. Maybe so. But I'm the one who has lived this story. I'm the one who has to be the expert here. She's the one who told me that. Only now she says I'm worrying too much about being fair to Robert and Valley. That I need to put myself and my own experience at center stage. But I meant what I said about its seeming important not to put myself as central. I was part of this story. If I tell it the way Kate wants me to, I'll see what happened all cockeyed. I want to feel and remember what was true for me. And I've never liked being at the center.

After what happened, it seems more important than ever not to see anyone alone and central—the way we saw Robert—the way he saw himself. Kate can read the damned police report if she wants facts strung out in a line and dead certain. They have them all typed out in their boxes on their triplicate forms. But she'll hardly find me in there—or any of us really. She wants this story firsthand—and all I have to give her is this trembling doubt.

When I falter and shake, I imagine I've caught something alive in this spider's silk of questions. But I suppose I could be the victim, stuck here and wriggling. Kate's probably right about my disparaging myself. But why be so quick to count this against me? This is how I have seen the world, and myself related to all the other pieces, and none special, all special. She'll want me to have a thrusting point to it all, like my thesis. I meandered too much with that too, looking for what was revealed to me, not created by me. But that's my point—that meandering connections are the point, the creation. You can't ever be that sure of yourself. Maybe you shouldn't be.

I think Hemingway knew this—I should send Kate something I found in my old school papers. An interviewer was asking the great artist about his art—why he chose to represent a fact, rather than giving us the fact itself. And he answered rather grandly, "You make something from things that have happened and from things that exist and from all things that you know and all those you cannot know, and you make something through your invention that is truer than anything true and alive, and if you make it well enough, you give it immortality." Then he said, "But what about all the reasons that no one knows?"

I love that he finally answers with a question, when for just a moment he stops pretending to sound so profound or to know all the reasons why people have always made up things they hoped would outlive them. He didn't know why he told stories—he just loved that he did. And I think he was right, not choosing between facts or their representation— because really what else is possible?

I understand artifice. This has always been the way things get explained at Five Corners. Facts I know less well. I want to ask Kate, What are facts anyway? Things you can hold in your hand? You take a fact's blood sample, you staple a fact's ear with a numbered metal tag. So how do I report the facts of what happens between people who love each other and hurt each other?

APRIL, 1974

She keeps on driving downstate, through Wisconsin. Though Lake Michigan stretches to the east of her for the length of her journey, she never sees it, however much she cranes her neck to look. The day is the color of dishwater, mist hanging in the air so thick she wants to squeeze it out like a sponge.

Seeing the cities of Green Bay and Milwaukee settles her mind on one thing at least. Not here. Famous places these may be, but famous football and famous beer look tedious and dreary up close. They will not do.

On and on she drives, past places clustered with people—how could there be so many houses and towns, with people in every one of them, their lives all a snare, like hers? Or at least she wants to believe this, doesn't want to believe that other people live their lives more effectively than she does, though maybe they do. A good distance from the city, identical subdivisions of identical houses begin, miles of them, crisscrossed nets of them, thrown over the sprawling slopes, row upon row. She imagines hordes of people heading out every day with their lunch buckets, heading home every night after work, day in, day out, down the streets, through the maze, like drone bees to their hives, mile after mile after honeycomb mile. And she strains to see what her naked eye can't, because there has to be something, something she doesn't understand.

She thinks about a phrase she's just read, Robert Penn Warren's description of Hemingway's code. "The discipline of the soldier, the form of the athlete, the gameness of the sportsman, the technique of an artist can give some sense of the human order, and can achieve a moral significance." But she wonders. Was it this same moral order that created the heroine of *The Sun Also Rises?* She gives up the man she loves, certain she will ruin him—saying at the moment of her sacrifice, "You know it makes one feel rather good deciding not to be a bitch." Gabe thinks of Orbach then and the way his glasses won't let her see into his eyes, and the closer she gets to Chicago, the more she suspects that maybe people do know something secret that they haven't let her in on.

The traffic thickens. By now it is past noon. The mist that had followed her all the way south jells and curdles here, weighed down by chemical smells. Everything on the highway that outskirts the city is bigger than Gabe and faster and more certain and reckless. Trucks swoop in front of her, squeezing ahead into just enough space. Their brakes make schussing noises that mimic Gabe's relief each time they make the squeeze and remain intact.

She has to pull off the highway for a fill-up, and the exit takes her to a one-way street so that she can't retrace her route. Making a new way back is complicated by street repairs and a detour, but finally she finds what looks to be the direction out.

She is sitting at the intersection at a red light, beginning to catch her breath, when someone behind her lays on his horn. Looking back to see what the honking is about, she sees a long line of cars behind her, all of the drivers angry looking in a personal sort of way. The man who has honked his horn leans out of his car window and yells, "Don't you know how to *drive*, lady?"

She's forgotten that she can turn right on a red light here and lurches forward to make up for her stupid mistake. She's also indignant at the angry faces, the only personal side she has seen of the city—except for that pimply boy at the gas station who for some reason had been loath to give her the key to his filthy rest room. He had taken her money without so much as looking at her, careful not to touch the flesh of her hand.

Back on the highway again, she determines to get out of the city as quickly as possible and to skip lunch, despite a growling stomach. Afraid of somehow taking the wrong turn again, of being in the wrong lane and rushing along at seventy miles per hour past her turnoff, she grips the steering wheel hard. Driving slower is impossible; a dozen trucks would barrel right on over her.

Her improvised plan is to take route 294, which goes round the city from a distance, and then hook up again with I–94, heading up through Gary and on to Michigan and home turf. But she's unsure if she's on the right highway. She's definitely headed down some main artery, sucked along faster by traffic thickening on both sides of her. The haze on the horizon is beginning to break up, and she makes out what looks like a crest of skyscrapers—god, no—the Loop—the opposite of what she wanted. Like a log churning downriver, she's washed along the highway, down under bridges of other expressways crossing overhead from a dizzying array of directions, and passed by cars—other logs, mindless, heedless of the rapids ahead. She squeezes the steering wheel harder and sits up straight.

The lanes grow narrower, the cement banks on either side, higher. Cars swooping in from either side of her speed up to make their turnoffs. Unsure, Gabe maintains a middle ground, afraid of being forced to exit where she doesn't want to go, yet her timing is off, distracted by cars too close to her. By the time she notices an exit she might want, the sign is already slipping by, missed.

She shuts out the fear of crunching metal and trains her eye to look for the signs far ahead. But she's already deep in the city, too far gone. She feels close to crying, but glancing at the driver next to her, a beefy bald man with mirrored sunglasses who doesn't take his eyes off the road, she sits up straighter, clamps her jaw, and leans forward.

She drives fast enough to keep up with the bald man, pretending to know what she is doing, and then sees an exit name she recognizes, Michigan Avenue, and turns off. She follows close on the tail of a bus she theorizes must know its way, but the bus goes into an underground garage and she's on her own again. She goes around some alarming curves, an exit that spits her out finally onto what is street, not highway, the traffic thick but not so hair-raisingly fast.

A canyon of brick and metal and glass, some of it gleaming copper and aquamarine or spiked with tall shafts of crystal, surrounds her. Gabe has to scrunch down to look up through the steering wheel at the buildings that seem to lean together overhead, reaching for some single precise point—so high they shut out the light, so tall she can't see the tops.

There are small locust trees just beginning to leaf out in a yellowish shade of green along one section of street. Something about this makes her feel more at home. In fact, she thinks she is driving some part of the route she and Dennis took to see the Cubs at Wrigley Field. The possibility makes her heart jump, glad at the notion of feeling something familiar, though she isn't certain yet—the green of the trees might have tricked her.

If she's made it this far into the city, then maybe she can make it out again. Dennis had left Chicago on Lakeshore Drive that day. From there it was a straight shot up to Benton County. Not bothering now with the signs that mumble all around her, she begins to function on gut instinct and memory. Timid at first, she reclaims a shred of confidence, defending herself against the bullying shoves of traffic. As things look more familiar, she begins to feel a bit of sympathy for honking horns, shaking fists, insults flung from rolled-down windows. Human beings like herself, being asked for more than is humane.

Then she sees it.

Lake Michigan, straight ahead, stretching as far as the eye can make out in either direction. Not beautiful. Fearsome. Enormous and gray. It is shrouded in the same dirty mist that has plagued her trip since the morning. The lake's surface is as drab but more solid, drawing the haze down and distilling it into something close to peace. Drop the whole city in and it would swallow all the noise and frenzy and filth.

Gabe can hear the lake's swelling roll when she cranks her window down, and its cold, watery breath rushes in to dampen her cheek. Everything that touches the lake, the fog, the noise, the confusion, resurfaces in rhythm, answering Gabe's breathing as she turns onto Lakeshore Drive. Heading north, she can hear it. She can hear it calling her back to what is green and alive and home and herself.

March 30, 1984
Five Corners, Michigan

I can't believe how light I feel. I didn't know I'd been braced for Kate's cutting me off. She confesses to doubts of her own as if we really were collaborators. She says she's really not after "an answer"—like me, she believes that thinking about things that way is all wrong. Or not wrong exactly—it's not right or wrong. But see how automatically I divide things, opposition embedded in my brain. I'm not sure how this perspective can live side by side with my need to see things fitting together. Yet both are in my head.

Kate's given me some silly exercises that remind me of Valley—"Breathe deeply. Imagine this, imagine that." I won't be able to. But at least we agree that I should go on giving myself words, however it's easiest. I've been thinking about storytelling, the way people count on it to make sense of things. Hemingway's last novel, *The Old Man and the Sea*, was about this tired old guy all alone out in his boat, but somehow people of his generation felt as if his story were their own. Sometimes people think you're saying more than you're saying, and they're right. An old man out at sea. What a metaphor after the logic of Hiroshima.

We always used stories at Five Corners to discover who we were. I heard Kate's friends telling stories at dinner, Anita and the others using erudite phrases like code words for some club they belonged to, and I wanted to be part of it. But wanting this can make you vulnerable too. Can make you afraid to step out of line. Kate says the pain becomes unbearable when differences between people's versions of things stretch too far. You can change your story here and there, and it won't matter so much, if you happen to love the other person. But if your senses report something far different from what's being told around you—then the truth only deepens your loneliness. I think you fear this most when truisms you'd relied on are threatening to break apart.

One time I took Valley out to find some wood frogs, the kind my pa always called "bandits" for the dark patches around their eyes. There was still snow on the ground but I finally found one, frozen solid, hidden under a pile of leaves that hadn't gotten sun. The frog wasn't breathing and its eyes were clouded over. Naturally she got all broken up about it, as I knew she would. But I said she should just sit quietly awhile before we buried it, knowing what would happen. Meditate, I told her, putting it in the sunlight at the edge of the water where the ice was breaking up. And while we sat there, the frog thawed out—its sides moving in and out, throat bulging.

She didn't realize this happened every spring, and was wide-eyed to see the thing bounce away into some leaf litter to hide, as good as new. It never crossed her mind that I'd been playing a mean trick on her. She told everybody the story afterward, saying our quiet was the moment she knew I was finally her friend—not just a relative. Anything was possible after that resurrection, she always said.

I think at some point I started to lie to myself. Sometimes I'd want to accept the bogus version of what was happening at Five Corners just so as not to be alone. I stopped thinking about what my own brain reported I had seen and smelled and felt. I'm not sure I can follow Kate's advice, not even now. "Stay in touch with your body," she says. "That's all this has to be about." Not so easy when you've been numb.

APRIL, 1974

Gabe has stopped for a fast-food dinner at a Benton County spot, unsettlingly close to her mother's family farm. Or what had once been a farm. But her mind is on another piece of property. She takes her tray to a booth with hard plastic seats and looks out past hanging plants to the Dumpster. She could go back and show Robert the will Pa had signed, announce that it's her land, announce that since he has a job, he can move somewhere else, but she's not sure this would hold up in court. The property wouldn't be hers until their father died, and he might hang on a long time. Then hating herself for even thinking this, she replaces it quickly with another legal thought.

Possession is nine-tenths of the law. She had possession before Robert did. Now she sees she shouldn't have gone to her residency at Fond du Lac and left Robert in charge of the cabin. But she had to. She couldn't let him take school away from her too.

She has been going in circles for so long with this, she can put it on automatic pilot for a moment. She stops a girl in an orange and brown uniform who is mopping the floors near her. "What are they doing with that house?" she gestures. "Do you know?"

The girl is what Shub would have called heavyset, a plain Jane. She looks up and her eyes, small in a round moon of a face, register surprise at being seen. "*That* house?" she asks, glancing out the window and up the slope. "I hear they're moving it. Yeah, it's awful big to move, isn't it? But that's what I heard."

"Where to? Move it for what?"

"I don't know. See, it's apartments now, but I hear they are going to make it into an inn or something. I hope they put it some place nice. I always thought it was kind of a shame, it being here."

Gabe nods, looking at her grandma's house again. Finished with her burger, she throws her trash into the bin and goes outdoors. She walks across the parking lot and steps up onto the lawn, which has been sheared off, leaving bare sand edging the asphalt. The place seems smaller than she remembers, less imposing, and this fits with her changed perceptions. Not even a year ago, she had set off from Benton County by herself to start her new life, full of big plans that now seem puny.

Then, looking off in the direction where the vineyard used to be, she remembers something so vivid it doesn't seem possible she could have forgotten it for a moment. At the end of the summer when she'd stayed here at the farm, alone with her grandmother, she'd discovered green frog eggs in the pond and had put some in a big quart jar. She wanted to impress her new second-grade teacher, Mrs. Bucking-ham—young Mrs. Buckingham, with the smooth auburn pageboy and the suede open-toed platform heels like her mother had worn.

All the long bus ride home to the cabin, she'd been certain of glory, hiding her secret jar with a jacket draped over her lap. It wasn't until she held the greenish murk of pond water up to the light of the cabin's porch windows for Robert to see, that she considered the possibility of disgrace. The jar had been closed up, had gotten warm in the sun and smelled bad. She had been ready to tell the entire class that this stuff that looked like cloudy tapioca would grow legs. It didn't *look* as if it would grow legs.

Robert had laughed, and she can't remember now whether the tadpoles had finally vindicated her or not, or even if she had taken them to class. She only remembers that feeling when she'd looked up through the translucent eggs, denouncing herself, how *could* she have been so stupid—before anybody else had the chance.

Now she sits on the porch stairs of the empty house, pulling a long stem of grass to twirl in her fingers. Once she had played at being a princess here, looking out from this porch over acres of pink apple blossoms, the banister about nose level when she was a girl. Maybe she had really had it made marrying Dennis. Maybe that was the best there was. You had a wedding and you lived in a nice house, and you spent money on things and were happy, or close to happy. Everybody had thought she was crazy, wanting out.

He didn't drink, he didn't hit her, he pretty much let her do as she pleased. She ought to have known most men wouldn't have put up with her. Christ, most men wouldn't have *looked* at her twice. But then Dennis didn't look at her twice either. He married her once, and that was the end of it as far as he was concerned.

She was always the one who wanted more from the relationship. He was happy, he always said. She thinks about calling him. It's a wild, veering thought, one chased quickly by another memory—her mother-in-law and the way she had died so quietly, no evidence left, the family waters closing in over her with hardly a ripple.

Gabe listens to the traffic on the road, its noise constant and at the same time varied, a steady stream of cars, motorcycles, rumbling trucks. Now she remembers. Back when the road was quiet, and as soon as the weather got warm enough, all her mother's family took to the oilcloth-covered wicker out on the porch. She calls to mind the pale shades of spring dresses—how her mother used to sit with her aunts, their heads bowed in close together, talking, talking. And how she'd loved the undertone of their voices, taking it for granted, never having the slightest curiosity about any of what they said. That whispery buzz had only been a comfort in those days.

She can almost hear the way the voices sounded as she faced away from them, grabbing the porch rail to see the whole world from that knoll. What can she really know for sure with that eddy of voices behind her, talking, talking, and she uncertain of the words they speak? Visceral thinking, Orbach had said, and all Gabe has is viscera.

April 4, 1984
Five Corners, Michigan

My mother might have been a drunk—it's a theory that could explain some things rather neatly. The summer after she disappeared, the year I was seven, I went downstate for a visit with my mother's family. Apparently Grandma had never approved of my mother's marriage to my father, but she offered to keep me for a while—not Robert, he was too much of a handful. Grandma had ideas about what was proper. She said my mother had always been flighty, spoiled by the big ideas she'd gotten from Grandpa's side of the family. She should have settled down after the scandal that had shamed our whole family then—and ought to shame us yet. A daughter who had given birth to a son earlier than polite society should talk about.

I never heard my mother or my brother named, but I knew who Grandma was talking about. This loss of family face had gone hand in hand with the first tax sale of the farm-land. And bit by little bit after that, they'd had to sell their property off. The shame of her situation seemed all of one piece in Grandma's mind, summed up in the capital irretrievably lost in a daughter who'd married beneath her. She kept asking me, on the tail of any number of stories, stretching the question to fit a lament—how could she have raised a daughter like that?

She didn't need an answer. I was the prop for her soliloquy—my whole family a stageful of soliloquies, it seems to me now. All that summer I listened to secrets about my mother that made me feel traitorous—I'd never seen her drinking and hadn't yet felt ashamed of her. None of what had happened to my family made sense to me. All of it knotted my stomach.

The year before I moved back to Five Corners, the same year Robert got out of prison, my grandmother sold the downstate farm and moved to Florida. We never heard from her again.

Once after a residency at Fond du Lac, I drove the long way back, the whole route around Lake Michigan and up through Benton County, just to avoid my problems. All these places I'd forgotten: Pipestone Creek, along the old Territorial Trail. Land that had once grown family orchards now sprouted rows of stores and close-planted subdivisions of brick ranch and split-levels. It rattled me.

I discovered what I didn't want on that trip. Which only made my conflict with Robert worse once I got home. I remember there being news stories about Wild Kingdom's development prospects and maybe I can find the clippings in Valley's things. Robert and Sid Nichols wanted to bring progress to Copper County with a vengeance, building a ratty tourist trap they'd dreamed up so we could finally cash in on all our excess nature. I hated everything about it. At the time, I told myself Robert and Valley needed the money. I needed the money, since I hoped it would free me of them. But I never could get on their bandwagon, not after that ride through downstate boomtowns.

I think Robert knew better than I did how I felt. I was angry and silent, as my father would have been—and god knows, that didn't help matters any.

APRIL, 1974

It is dark by the time she drives across the Mackinaw Bridge. Its colored lights, amber and aquamarine, bounce in refracted patterns on the water of the straits, reflecting back the arcs that always seem too fantastic and too huge to be real. Once she gets onto M67, she'll be on her way into Copper County, and once past Sid's Friendly, the road will fall away toward Lake Nekoagon and home. She'll wind down through miles of forest tunnel, with banks of ferns crowding the track, and then on a curve just before she reaches Five Corners and her turnoff, the lake will split the valley wide open.

Gabrielle can't help holding her breath for a moment as she rounds that curve. This past summer when she'd arrived in her car, loaded with all she owned, the lake's being there—unchanged and surer than anything—released a forceful sigh in her, something close to a laugh.

It could have been the sun hitting it just right, or maybe she'd just been looking for something. But whatever it was, it seemed to her then that this was the place where things were possible, whatever she was hoping for—right here, where the light spreads like mercury over acres of shining surface and the darkness of trees is so easily left behind.

On a night like this, the lake deepens into ink, and wherever its surface bulges, the moonlight silver gleams. Now she recognizes why Lake Michigan had the same effect on her, back in Chicago. When she was a kid, she used to sit with Shub and Elsie on the front porch of the store to watch color gather in the sky over the water and then darken. Most nights their neighbor Mrs. Snow, with her pug dog on its little red leash, would join them, full of woe about her edema and the tortures of elastic bandages in summer, or the gossip from her daughter who was grown and lived in Clearwater.

Campers would be installed across the street. They'd be cleaning off their picnic tables, getting ready for one more outing in the rowboat before it got too dark. Then they'd build fires in the blackened stone circles on the shore and the kids would run over to Shub's for some popsicles or a bag of marshmallows. Their talk and laughter bounced up from the shore to the porch where she sat.

She thinks of Elsie and remembers she's already been gone three years. She's surprised that she feels an old resentment rekindle, anger at her father for never writing to tell her about the funeral. It had taken Shub several weeks before he'd written her a note, sending her a clip of the obituary. He apologized for his addle-headedness, for taking so long to figure out that she must not know. It was like their father's not having Thanksgiving dinners. No one ever held Henry Bissonette responsible for such things.

The road to Five Corners is still ahead. Its sights are so familiar she already knows them and pictures them, to push away the anger which has already pushed away grief—a little like Shub bringing Elsie up in conversations the way he does, as a substitute for admitting how much he misses her.

Elsie had always crimped her scanty locks with a permanent, always covered her considerable number of freckles with powder. Neither adjustment had ever been entirely successful, but somehow she had managed to be compellingly attractive, always wearing a dress and smelling of soap and talcum, accepting Shub's gruff daily compliments as her due. He had never called Elsie heavyset or plain Jane, though she was both.

If Elsie were still alive, she would listen to Gabe and somehow help her through to understanding, though Gabe would have to get her attention first. Elsie would squint, full mouth pursed, concentrating on whatever she was doing in the store, but once that warm, intense hazel-eyed interest turned on Gabe, her mouth would spread into a smile.

It may have been nothing so much as the habit of years of waiting on people in the store, but for the twig of a girl Gabe had been, that look of expectation had been sunshine and rain. Out back of the store was a screened-in porch where Elsie had made up daybeds for all her nieces and nephews in the summer. Often Gabe was also invited to sleep over, and those were the happiest, giggliest times she remembers. If anything were better, it was waking up in a nest of snoring young bodies to the smell of Elsie fixing pancakes in her tiny kitchen, the sound of her opening and closing the white metal cabinets Shub had decorated for her with water lily decals.

In winter, after summer visitors went home, Gabe and Robert got an even bigger share of Elsie's attention. Whenever they came to the store, they could expect a gift of homemade cookies or clothing or

Gabrielle's favorite—books from the library. The only blessed charge had been spending more time with Elsie, learning responsibility, doing chores around the store, running errands.

Robert was bored by it before long. He had friends who had cars that could take him into Clearwater and Galesburg, but Gabe spent part of every day at Five Corners. When Elsie decided it was time she started saving money for college, Gabe graduated to a paying job. Even when she had to snowshoe to get to the store, she got there.

All these memories are contained in the feeling of being at home as she passes by landmarks that grow more frequent the closer she gets. Up the road, Shub's Economy Mart is heart and soul of Five Corners. As Shub liked to say, it may be out in the middle of nowhere, but by god, make no mistake—it *was* in the middle. Elsie would roll her eyes when he said that, but she went on with her crocheting, decades of it.

Gabe finally comes to the place where the lake opens up the hills, its waters a more radiant jet than night sky, the air softening here, laden with moisture and the smells of spring. On those summer nights when she was a girl, when she hadn't been able to stay with Shub and Elsie, she could still hear the campers. Choppy bits of their talk and laughter would come bouncing over the lake to the Bissonette place on its little peninsula, the sound rhythmic as the waves spanking the pier out front. Gabrielle used to strain to listen, important bits swallowed up in watery murmurs. She remembers feeling happier and lonelier, all at once, for that sound. Now it makes her think of earlier murmurs on her grandmother's porch.

She turns on the dirt road toward the lake, straining to see the water again, but the trees are too thick here. Except for the porch light far ahead, the cabin seems dark. When she reaches the clearing, she notices how little wind there is. She parks the truck, climbs the back stairs, cracks the door open, and calls in, "Robert? Valley? Anybody home?"

For a moment, she feels wildly hopeful that no one is there. But once she's in the kitchen, she can hear a scurrying, the sound of papers knocked to the floor, and also a murmuring—strange, the background sound of her childhood, here of all places. Then, seeing an orange extension cord running into the front room, she deduces what the sound must be—a television.

Valley comes to the doorway, her hair awry, still buttoning the front of her shirt. "Gabe, it's you! We were getting worried, we hadn't heard from you, we were thinking about calling the police!"

"Sorry, I should have called Shub and let you know, I guess."

"Well, how was it? Was it *fun*? What did you do?"

"Oh, it's a long story and I'm so beat. Let's talk about it tomorrow. Where's Robert?"

"He's here, he's coming," she calls back over her shoulder, and he appears in the doorway running his hand through his hair, looking sheepish. He drapes one arm over Valley, letting it hang loose and relaxed in front of her. Gabe guesses she's interrupted sex. But Robert is jolly, welcoming. "Bean-o! We were wonderin' what had happened to you. You said Sunday night, didn't you?"

"Yeah, yeah, but something came up. What's *this*?" Gabe points to the heavy extension cord along the floor.

He walks over to the orange line, pushes it farther against the wall with his foot. "Hey, I hope you don't mind but, really, we couldn't get by without TV. Sid co-signed for us at Monkey Wards, we're gettin' it on payments. We were just watching 'Bonanza.'"

The ads are on; the volume louder, sharper.

"You want some tea, Gabe? I was just gonna make myself some," says Valley, walking toward the stove. "I know you don't like TV, but Robert's right, it's something to do when there's nothing else, and besides, it helps—" Her voice peters out and she opens the stove to toss in a log, then sets the kettle down on top. She looks over her shoulder at Robert, as if she's expecting something.

It is just as bad as Gabe had ever imagined, the tension thick enough to suffocate. She wants to sit down. She will have some tea, she'll sit down and have some tea.

"You got stuff out in the car?" asks Robert, and when Gabe nods, his voice is even cheerier, announcing that he'll go and get it. Gabe protests halfheartedly and lets him go, though he is barefoot.

As soon as the screen door thuds softly behind him, Valley comes to her and gives her a hug, her long hair smelling of coconut, hanging down next to Gabe's face. "I'm so glad you're okay, I can't *wait* to hear about school," she says, fast and breathless. Stepping back, she bends over with her hands on her knees so she can see into Gabe's face. "We've had a wonderful time, but I missed you. How many times can you *do* it after all? Here we go again!" she wisecracks, putting her index finger through a circle she makes with the fingers of her left hand.

Surprised, Gabe laughs. "But, Valley, that *television*—"

"Oh, we do it while we watch TV too, god, doing it to 'Ring Around the Collar'!" and she singsongs the last part and laughs. "You haven't lived until you've—"

Robert kicks the screen door open and comes through, carrying both of Gabe's suitcases. "Whatta you got—bricks in here?" He laughs, setting them down.

"No, books, I'm sorry. They have this great bookstore on campus. I shouldn't be allowed to go in there with a checkbook. Sorry."

He comes over and claps his hand on her shoulder. "Say, it's great seeing you, Gabe. I mean it, *great*! You know, I'm gonna go to school myself someday. I used to read a lot of books when I was at Marquette, had the time to then. Fact is, I could probably get a degree now with all the reading I done. Lots of law books. I thought about being a lawyer. They're the ones who are making all the money."

Gabe nods, not really taking it in.

"You know the old man," Robert says suddenly, sitting down next to her and reaching out an arm to drape it on the back of Gabe's chair, closing her in. "You know what I said about him. Before? When we talked about it before, remember? That's really why we got the TV, he's a lot calmer with the television—even though he's not even looking at it, that's the funny thing—it calms him down."

Gabe stands up, pushing past him, and starts for the front room. "What are you talking about?" she demands, and enters the dark. "You were supposed to talk to me before you did *any*—"

The silhouette of their father's hawkish nose is sharp against the moving color of the television screen. A bunch of kids are spilling chocolate milk on a shiny waxed floor, tracking in mud, trailing a dirty dog behind them.

"We did talk about it, we talked about it, Gabe—you *know* we did. Just look at him, you can't tell me he isn't better off here, with *us*, his own family. You wanna tell me he's not better off? Or maybe you're worried about yourself, I know it's not as easy on us with him here—I know that, if that's what you're talking about. But there's three of us now. Don't you think three of us oughta be able to handle him? Me and Valley managed him for three days now without you. And we can keep on handling him if you're too busy getting yourself another *college* degree, it's all right, I understand—"

"Cut it out, Robert."

"I don't have any scissors," he answers her, the standard response when they were kids. He comes over to her now, and his body blocks the TV screen. He is a wall, no opening in him.

"Look, Gabe, it's important to me. It's really important. It wasn't good between the old man and me, you know that. I wanna make it up to him, I gotta do that. I can't just go and sit in a goddamn nursing home room and have that be enough. I think if he's here awhile, maybe he'll come back. He could, you know. He *could*. But it ain't ever gonna happen in some hospital room. Who would know it, if he did? He might come back and then just decide not to stay around. Here at least he'd know he was at home."

He puts his hands on Gabe's shoulders, and they are warm, warm and, at the same time, hard as November ground. "I know you couldn't have him here when it was just you, it wouldn't have worked. But we're here now. We're together. It can be different now. It's gotta be."

"He's not so bad, Gabe," chimes in Valley behind her. "He really just sits, that's all. Especially with the TV, he doesn't get restless as much."

Gabe, listening to Valley, has turned her face away from Robert. He takes her chin and turns it back toward him.

"Listen, I'll make you a deal. We'll try it for two weeks. Two weeks is all. And if it isn't working, we'll take him back to Pinewood. We will, I promise you. Two weeks and it'll be clear to everybody what we should do. Okay?" He shakes her chin to make her answer. "Okay?"

Gabe stares at him, then closes her eyes with a sigh.

"Good. *Good!* You won't be sorry—we're doing the right thing, I know it. You hear that, Henry? No more nursing home for you! You're back at home where you belong. And me and Gabe are both here with you. See? He's happier already. You see that?"

Gabe acquiesces, too tired not to, and Robert pulls her close to his side, squeezing her tight, shaking her a little. Beyond Henry, something's screwed up on the TV. The same ad is on again, the one that just finished, the same chocolate milk, the mud tracked in on tennies, but here comes the smiling Mom again, the sponge mop, the shining floor restored, and easily.

He kisses the side of her head, and she's so hungry for something to cling to, anything, she finds herself squeezing him back. She wants to do the right thing. She is desperate to do it.

She expects to fall asleep immediately, but the drone of the television, the shock of finding the old man here, the coffee she'd had at the last truck stop just to keep awake, have put her into high gear.

She can't believe Valley just went along with this. She hardly says anything whenever Robert's in the room. She acts her age when he's around, no, *younger* than that.

There was another night with Valley, a good month ago, before Robert came back. They'd been having a heat wave, spring come early. With Gabe, Valley had been the big authority. "Full moon," the girl had said, leaning toward the kitchen window, looking up. "We used to do this ceremony at full moon. Sundew and that group? It's been so warm, I'm tempted to try it, if you'll go with me."

"Go where?"

"To Moon Circle. We can build a fire on the shore. The snow's clear there. Come on, it'll be fun. What else do you have to do?"

Gabe had read every novel in the house, with nothing left except to write her thoughts on the last one she'd read. She'd hated *The Sun Also Rises*. But Orbach felt certain *A Farewell to Arms*, Hemingway's masterpiece of love and war, would change her mind. Instead, it served up a heroine who, when she got pregnant, said to her lover, "But you mustn't mind, Darling. I'll try and not make trouble for you. I know I've made trouble now. But haven't I been a good girl until now?"

Before Valley interrupted her, Gabe had been staring off into space, bored and annoyed at the very idea of having to critique such nonsense—actually wishing for television, she admits to herself now, preferring advertisements and black-and-white reruns of "Hawaiian Eye." She asked Valley, "Is this some more of your granola-bunny stuff?"

"Yeah. Kind of. Come on."

The air outdoors was mild and smelled of mud. Closer to the ground, the wind blew wetter and chillier, picking up cold from drifts of snow. These had looked far gone earlier in the day, pocked and pitted with dirt, leaking water.

The wood frogs were beginning to breed and in another six weeks the peepers would be in chorus, with black terns circling over the lake at dusk, screeching and demanding fish. But this weather was a false alarm, the cold would be back. Now the only sound was a tiny lick of water at the lake's edge, most of the water still capped by rotted ice. The sand under their feet was soft though, a welcome feel after months of frozen earth.

Gabe squatted near a circle of sooty rocks while Valley heaped up dry kindling she'd carried from the porch. She ran back to fetch some slender branches and before long had a fire crackling, sizzling on the damp of the sand.

Pleased with herself, Valley threw twigs from nearby into the flames, laughing at the pops of moisture, the plumes of smoke from wet wood. And Gabrielle, caught up in the excitement, fetched more sticks and fed them into the fire.

"Our first barbecue together," said Valley, when the fire had built to a full, smoky roar. "Too bad we don't have any marshmallows." She coughed when the wind shifted, blowing smoke into her face.

"We've got some hot dogs in the fridge."

"Pleeease. Nitrates."

"Oh. And Nostrates."

"AND Numiluminuminates."

They both laughed. They were getting to be a team, or at least knew what to expect, how to play off each other's cues. They had argued so much about eating meat that Gabe had a standard line, calling Valley a brussels sprout baby-killer. Laughter had given them an out, made a truce between them.

Valley squatted down close to Gabe, hugging her knees. "So. Moon Circle," she said, and cleared her throat. "This is celebrated to honor the great Moon Goddess." She made a sweeping gesture toward the sky.

"Ah. Yes. You learned this from your hippie-dippy weatherman, I take it."

"That's right. Now. You have to think about anything that's troubling you and then you have to talk about it. And you hold this stick up and then you throw it into the fire. And you ask the Moon Goddess to take this thing, not to kill it, you know, but to let it wane naturally, the same way her light does—so that next time you celebrate Moon Circle? Well, the thing that's bothering you will be all faded away. Like this, watch."

Gabe studied Valley as she picked up a stick and placed the end in the flames to ignite it. When it caught fire, the girl closed her eyes, her face suddenly very serious. After a moment, she opened her eyes again and spoke, holding the lighted stick upright. "Oh, Face of the Moon," she said, "you see me and this trouble I hold up to you. This fire is the fear I hide in my heart, the worry that everything I dream is only a dream, that none of what I want can come true. Take this fear and consume it. Watch over my dreams and let them overtake me even when I am awake, till I walk in your moon spirit day by day, with courage to dream even when the sun rules the sky."

Valley glanced at Gabe and whispered a quick and authoritative aside. "See, the moon rules over your unconscious is what I mean. Women, moon, darkness, the inside—all associated. And the sun is more conscious, the male principle. So I'm saying to let my unconscious come to the surface more. That's where the power is. Understand?"

She waited, as if to see if Gabe would get it, then giving up, she closed her eyes, took another deep breath and opened them again, dropping the stick into the fire. They watched the flames tongue the wood, hungry, growing stronger. After a moment, Valley looked at Gabe again. She said, "Now you. It's *your* turn."

A breeze was picking up across the lake's ice and Gabe pulled her hat down a little farther past her ears. "This isn't the kind of thing I really go in for, Valley, you know that. I don't wanna rain on your parade. I'm having a good enough time. But I don't have the foggiest notion what you even said."

"Well, that's okay. That doesn't matter. You can say what you *want* to."

"Look, it all seems a little silly to me, to tell you the truth. I don't want to say anything."

"Well, fine." Valley pursed her lips and scootched to face her more fully, still squatting on her haunches. "Why'd you *come* here, then?"

She waited for an answer and when one wasn't forthcoming, she added, "You are really stuck, do you know that?"

Gabrielle stared at the fire. After a moment she said softly, "You could be right about that." She picked up a stick and was drawing lines in the sand. Finally she asked, "So what is it you were talking about, being afraid?"

Valley heaved an exaggerated sigh. "Well, what do *you* want to know for? You act like you haven't got the foggiest notion about most things. You think I'm silly."

"No, I don't always agree with you, that's all. You're talking about Robert coming home, aren't you?"

"That's pretty good for somebody who acts like she doesn't even know who he is. You could be a little excited or a little mad or a little *something*. I mean, I feel like we're on this big ark, just floating along in this huge ocean, and you'd just as soon stay on board forever. You'd just as soon we never open the door."

"Criminy, what *are* you talking about?"

"Well, that's not what I mean exactly. Oh, I don't *know* what I mean!"

"Look, you don't have to take your frustrations out on me, you know. I'm just an innocent bystander, here."

"There, that's *it*. A *bystander*. You act like nothing that's happening has got anything to do with you at all. It is driving me crazy."

"Well, how am I *supposed* to act? You move in on me like I'm not even here, and then I find out the two of you will be keeping house where I made my own little place for myself, and I had my next year and a half all staked out and then—"

"There! You *see*? You really are furious, aren't you?"

"No, I'm not furious. I'm not furious at all."

"You are too. You are. Look, if I could afford it, in a minute, *believe* me, I would—" Valley's lip quivered so that she had to pause, and then she burst into tears. "What do you think it's going to be like for *us*? Having our honeymoon in the next room from you? Not even having any privacy at all—"

"I scheduled my residency at Fond du Lac for those two weeks! I won't even be around!"

"I mean afterward, I mean—oh, it doesn't *matter*, I know what a burden I've been and I'd do anything not to be in your way and you've already been so nice to me and I'm nothing but a pain in the ass—no, I know it! I know it! Just put this stupid fire out, just put it *out*."

Valley stood up and began kicking wet sand into the fire, sending smoke billowing up into Gabe's face.

"Will you stop that? You're getting sand everywhere. Just *stop* it!" Gabe stood up too. "Stop it," she demanded louder, and the girl took this as a signal to sob even harder and kick some more. Gabe sighed, looking away. Then she asked, "What is it with you? What *is* all this?"

After several moments, Valley choked out: "He got mad at me. He was mad at me the last time. I didn't tell you, I was so upset. Why did he *get* so mad? I don't even know what I did. I don't even know what I saaaaid." This last trailed off into a wail and Valley buried her face in her hands.

"So that's why you're afraid. Because he's coming home and now you're going to have to live your moon dream."

Valley nodded and sniffed.

"I don't blame you for being scared." Gabe felt a little guilty watching the girl cry at arm's length. Had he kicked her under the table? Or was it only words? Words hurt worse sometimes, she knew. Probably she ought to touch Valley, pat her or something. "You probably need to talk to him," Gabe offered, "*ask* him why he's mad. People need to talk when they're married. That's what I heard somewhere— not that Dennis and I ever did."

Valley smiled a little and seemed pleased at this obvious bit of advice. For a hippie, she sure had some *Good Housekeeping* kinds of attitudes. "You *think* so?" she asked.

"Maybe. He's gotta be on edge too, don't you think? But you can't know how you can help until you talk to him."

The girl nodded again, agreeing. She lifted her hands to wipe at her eyes.

"This was really *stupid*," she said finally.

Gabrielle shrugged. "Maybe," she said. But unwilling to lie entirely, she added, "Look, Robert can be mean and kind of touchy. You ought to know that about him. I mean, even when he cares about you, he's that way. Maybe even *more* when he cares about you."

"He is touchy, I know he is. But you know, he won't talk about it. He won't. Maybe we should get him to do Moon Circle or something."

"Yeah. That'd be a big help, I'm sure."

"It would. It *would*. Will you tell me why you are so resistant to new ideas, Gabrielle?"

Valley was angry again and Gabe looked up at the moon's face and felt like howling herself. All of this emotion coursing through the air, encircling her, and none of it hers. On impulse she picked up a stick. "All right," she said and lit the end, squatting back down next to the tiny bit of fire that still remained uncovered by sand.

Valley, placated, immediately squatted down beside her.

"Well, Moon Goddess, here I am." Gabe tried the words on, but her tone warned that none of this was really serious, she'd had her arm twisted. She waited for something inspired to come to her and after several moments, when nothing did, she sent the stick sprawling into the fire. She felt absurd for even entertaining the notion. Baring her feelings in front of this overgrown child, this innocent child—no, she was *naive*, there was a difference. She put Valley off by standing up, looking around at the shrubs, suddenly intent. She said, "I need to find a good hot-dog stick. There's no sense completely wasting this fire."

Valley made a growling sound and stood up too. Gabrielle, searching through the aspen and the sweet gale for a branch the right length, heard the girl's footsteps ringing behind her on the wooden pier.

"You are so *stuck*!" Valley shouted at the top of her lungs, out over the lake so that the sound bounced and echoed, full and deep, filling the dark around them. "Do you know that, Gabrielle?" she demanded. "Do you?" The girl was nothing but a child, Gabe had thought, as she angrily tore a branch, ripping the bark down.

She thinks this now, remembering, listening to the television mutter and picturing Valley out in the front room with Robert and Henry. Nothing but a child.

Probably she has blown this whole thing up to alarming proportions, Gabe tells herself next. Lots of families help each other out like this. Why is she being so selfish? She should give Robert a chance—what's the matter with her?

The pillow she holds close to her chest smells of not quite clean hair and she thinks how old it must be, how familiar the roses of its cover. Pulling it closer she sinks her face into it, drawing up her knees, stroking her calves. She can put her fingers into her ears and almost close out the sound.

V

WILD KINGDOM

The rain had kept on all night, a slow, soaking patter against the roof. Now it's only a drizzle, and Gabe can hear someone up already in the kitchen. She smells coffee and climbs out of bed to find Robert standing by the kitchen window, looking outside.

He has a mug in his hand and the steam from the coffee rises in his face, catching what gray, glowering light there is. When he hears her open the cupboard behind him, he looks in her direction, meeting her eyes. "It's clearing up," he says and lifts his mug to take a sip, turning back to the window.

She feels a reproach in how he holds himself and knows she's been short-tempered, sinking into more silence than usual the last few days. Orbach expects some writing, and she's been procrastinating. It's hard concentrating with so many people in the house. She's run out of time. She has to do her work and quit making excuses.

Intent on this, she only nods and shuffles over to the coffeepot to help herself. Several moments go by as she pours the coffee, finds the sugar, a spoon, then adds some milk.

Robert looks at her over his mug. "You been real cheery," he comments. He'd been home all day yesterday, rained out.

She mumbles this time, nodding again, and several more minutes go by in silence.

"Seems like you've always got your nose in a book or off staring somewhere like you're a thousand miles away."

Robert sends his coffee spoon clattering into the sink. She looks at him then and says, "I got a lot on my mind. I have this paper due and it's coming hard—I can't quite figure what I want to write about."

Robert scrunches his lips together, *poor baby*, nodding, oh yes, he understands, he does, and comes closer to her to pour himself another cup. He almost grazes against her, he is so close, reaching into his shirt pocket to take out a pack of cigarettes, shaking one out. He lights it and looks down at her.

"What are you so hung up on gettin' another college degree for? One's enough for most folks." He exhales and the light in the window behind him illuminates the smoke. "More'n enough for *most* folks," he adds.

"If you want to teach college-level literature, you have to have your master's," she recites, shrugging.

He nods, his head bobbing up and down, up and down, while he takes another drag. He lifts his chin high and blows the smoke out slowly, watching the tendrils curl toward the ceiling. After a moment he levels his head, then turns to the side and down to look at her. "I guess maybe you do," he says. "I guess maybe it beats getting out into the *real* world, doesn't it."

"And what do you mean by *that?*"

He shrugs, pooching his lips up again, shaking his head, palms spread out in front of his chest, saying, nothing, not a thing, he didn't mean a thing at all by that.

"This *is* the real world, isn't it?" she demands, not quite awake yet. The weight of her having fixed this place up, made room for them— having worked a half day at Shub's just yesterday and come home to another shift with Henry and a houseful of people when she's trying to write a paper—brings metal to her tone. "Isn't *this* the real world?" she demands again. "What do you mean by that, Robert?"

"You're right. Sure it is, a course it is. The real world. Knock on wood," he says, rapping on the counter between them with his knuckles, then smiling a tight smile as he pretends to have discovered something new when he knocks against his head. "Real it is. Guess I oughta know about that, with real rain fallin' down on *my* parade. Gonna have to make up for lost time now. Gotta go to *work*," he says and glances at her as he mouths this last word, spoken with precision.

He takes one last drag on the cigarette, then twists it out in the sink. He looks back at her over his shoulder. "Don't be so touchy," he says. "Have another cup of coffee— Haaay, *here* she comes."

He's responding to the sound of Valley coming down the stairs. She's wrapped up to her nose in her quilt. She pulls it up higher around her shoulders as she reaches the bottom of the stairs and greets Robert, wrinkling her nose and kissing him. "Mmmmmm," she says, then smiles bleary-eyed at Gabe, and glances out the window. "Looks like it's clearing up," she says. "You going in?" she asks Robert.

He nods. "Gotta make up for lost time. Probably working extra late."

Gabe calls to him, "Don't forget you promised you'd watch the old man this afternoon. We're going to the library." She scowls, knowing what his reaction will be, but she doesn't care if it does screw him up, he's not getting out of this.

"What? Oh, come on, you coulda gone yesterday when it was raining all day, and I was just sitting around here."

"Well, I didn't have my book read yesterday. Today I do, just like I planned it, some people like to plan their lives a little. Valley, don't you need to go, too? Wasn't there something you had to do?"

"Well, yeah, actually. Belle has got the porcupine stuffed and Sid's all hot to trot, so I thought I'd better catch a ride with—"

"Great, oh *great*. All right, fine. *Fine*. You win," he says and he picks up a pack of matches and shoves them into his front pocket. Grabbing his jacket off the back of a kitchen chair, he snaps, "You come round when you're ready and drop him off at the work site. I understand you got books to read and papers to write and big, important thoughts to think."

"That's right," says Gabe, sticking her chin out at him to say, Yes, more important than what you spend your time doing, more important than any money-grubbing scheme you and that piker Sid Nichols can come up with.

Valley has been following behind Robert, reaching out a hand to touch his arm, trying to stay connected to him. "Wait a minute, Robert, we can work this thing out, we're all adults, there's no need to get huffy about it, honey."

Robert stands and glares at Gabe, throwing off Valley's hand. "We have *got* it worked out, already. We have got it *all . . . worked . . . out*." He pauses between each word, then stands a moment longer, waiting for Gabe to say something.

She doesn't, but she thinks her retort as loud as she can and sends it scorching from her eyes.

He turns to go and Valley, following behind him as he heads for the back door, asks him in her most solicitous tone, "Did you take Henry to the john, Robert? Did you take care of that already?"

He whirls around to face her, teeth clenched together. "No, I did not. I did *not* take care of that." And he shoves her hard, turning to storm out. Because she has socks on her feet, she slips a little and, half-falling, knocks her elbow against the table. Robert pays no attention.

"Ow!" she wails loudly, standing up to watch him exit. They both hear him slam the door of her Volkswagen and pull out with a tire-ripping roar.

"Asshole," Valley says, cupping her elbow, rubbing it as she looks at Gabe and somehow includes her in the name-calling.

It doesn't matter. Gabe isn't sorry. She glares back at the girl and takes a gulp of lukewarm coffee.

April 12, 1984
Five Corners, Michigan

How did I ever go along with the craziness of bringing Pa back home? I didn't really, but deep down I think I'd decided there wasn't any fighting it. Robert would have done it sooner or later. He had to have faith in the idea of family—we had so little proof of it. We both did family the way we did most things—by force of will. Was Robert imagining that Pa would be grateful? He'd have died of embarrassment or stayed drunk before he'd let Robert think he was running things. Admitting that out loud would have broken the spell though. Just like I couldn't say Wild Kingdom was nuts.

I felt smug as Robert's psychologist at the time, but I was doing the same thing—puffing myself up, trying to prove I wasn't as stupid as I felt after my divorce. I thought Robert's scheme was pitifully small potatoes. But what kind of job was I going to get with an English degree? There was something desperate about all of us. Valley believed in my bookish ideas when I couldn't myself. She sold Robert's dreams the way she dressed herself—with sincerity totally at odds with what everyone knew to be true.

Sid never did get rich off Wild Kingdom, although he goes to Florida every winter now soon as deer season is over. What few people come up here to Copper County come because of the billboards he put up, all along I–75, from Gaylord north. They're so sincerely cheesy, I guess by the time people reach the U.P., they must be convinced they can't not see it. But Sid believes, he truly believes he is bringing the people of America something beautiful, however godawful ugly—another example of the power of faith. Or maybe of the fine, evil line between hope and denial. I didn't know about denial in those days. I probably couldn't have told the difference anyway. How can you know which is which, until you see how things turn out?

JUNE, 1974

Valley is poring over the card catalog, then pulling out the books from the shelf in a feverish pitch of self-importance. Watching her from a table across the room, Gabe is trying not to feel annoyed. The trips to the library have become regular for them, Gabe's thesis trying to shape itself, Valley's bits for Wild Kingdom beginning to come together. These jaunts are for fun too, a break from taking care of the old man.

What bothers Gabe most, she decides, is the way Valley deals with Robert, the way she talks so tough when he's not around—she's gonna give him what for, she's not taking his shit—but let him walk in the door, and she's practically on her back, tail between her legs, and it's *Let me bring you your paper, master*. She'd practically lick his *hand*, for Chrissake. Now Valley's in her brusque, professional mode, but it's only an act.

Not that Valley's completely a fake. She's smart enough. Sometimes Valley talks about authors Gabe is only just discovering, Colette and Isak Dinesen and Flannery O'Connor and Katherine Anne Porter—tough-minded women, a little like Elsie. These fill a wide, empty space in Gabe, one she didn't know she had, and she feels ravenous for more. For Valley, it's nothing.

Maybe it's because she grew up with ideas and books, even though she never finished high school. She and her mother had traveled so much in search of part-time college teaching jobs that Valley managed to get out of going. Gabe has deduced that Valley's mom was not altogether in tune with what was good for Valley, more like she was a child herself, although Valley seemed to shrug this off. She'd be bored with school anyway, she said. She and her mother had carted books all over the country, hundreds of boxes of books, going from college to college. Sometimes they sold the books at flea markets to make ends meet.

Strange that Valley could read so many books and not be changed by them, Gabe thinks, watching her now. The girl could discuss theories and sound convincing while she did it, using college words like "dichotomy" and "dialectic." Only none of it translated into how Valley lived her life. She tried on philosophies like the clothes she constantly changed, and she was good at it, skillful. But taking in deeply what she read, being wounded by it or changed by it—that never happened. This is what Gabe finds different and mystifying. And irritating.

Valley is busy doing another of her impersonations, The Writer, this time. She's already read the latest copy of *Writer's Digest* and spent their first hour here whispering about how easy it would be to have a best-seller with the right idea and engaging lead paragraphs and proper query letters. Gabe had been nearly beside herself with Valley's asides, wanting only to be left alone with her unfinished thesis on Hemingway. Finally, Valley went off to work on her project for Sid's Wild Kingdom.

But Gabe picks up Valley's motions and energies across the room, is bothered by her bending over the card catalog like some penitent, zealous to make amends, scratching away on note paper. It's that show of will that bothers Gabe—you let Robert walk in here, and Valley will fold like a fan. How can she *work* after that fight?

Gabe can't. She has found an essay that criticizes Hemingway, something more contemporary that Orbach recommended. The author writes that Hemingway has sold the Romantic self short, that novelists can no longer identify with his idea of suffering as the chief means of transcendence; nevertheless it is a tribute to him that "a number of our recent novelists, Norman Mailer and Saul Bellow, for instance, still think of him as an angel to wrestle with, a father to kill." This last phrase resonates, but she can't decide whether to dare write it down or not.

Valley, on the other hand, has a knack for composition and quickly masters the basic facts, emphasizing whatever is most entertaining, not worrying about accuracy. Each time she tackles a new animal for Wild Kingdom, she adds to her research by asking Gabe and Robert about the animal's tracks and its habits and the local lore. Color, that's what she's after. Gabrielle, in contrast, spends far too much time writing up her notes, wanting to be exact. She decides to write the new quote down, though its meaning blurs, grows darker.

On the way back to Wild Kingdom, Valley reads Gabe what she has written for the latest wildlife scene they're planning. She expects to show it to Sid when they get there. Gabe has never been able to read in the car. It makes her nauseated, and she feels a twinge of jealousy for what seems another unfair advantage. Valley reads:

The north woods porcupine could well be called the "pokey-pine," he is so slow-moving. Sometimes you will see him crossing the road after dark. Armed with thousands of sharp quills, he will demand you stop your car and wait for him. Maybe he thinks automobiles are animals too and trusts sensible creatures to give his prickly self a very wide berth.

If you come upon one of these beasts in the woods, don't be frightened. Contrary to what many believe, the porcupine cannot throw his quills. But don't get too close. The quills are light and hollow and come out at the barest touch—as many of our local dogs could tell you with a painful howl!

The porcupine weighs up to thirty pounds, but with his quills, he looks much larger than that. Fat and sluggish, it seems surprising he is such a good climber. He uses his long, sharp claws to do this and, in fact, spends a lot of his time high up in trees, gnawing the soft inner bark he is fond of for lunch. If you are camping nearby, don't leave out bacon or packaged meats or anything that has been touched by perspiring hands. Porcupines love salt the best of all. He will waddle into your camp and gnaw on anything that tastes of it!

Valley's tone is breathless, hurried, as she adds an approval-seeking, "What do you think?" Gabe can see Valley already finds it very good. She is ready to tackle the next beast. The whole animal kingdom awaits her brilliant write-ups for Wild Kingdom, nothing too great a challenge!

"It's fine," answers Gabe with a tight smile, but her voice lilts up at the end of the phrase, unnaturally high. She concentrates on the road ahead, clearing her throat. Then she decides to add, "You're just leaving the most interesting part out, is all. You should say something about how hard the quills are to get out. Unless you do it right away, they work themselves in because they have little hooks on the end. Each time your muscles contract from the pain," she says, turning to make eye contact, "they go in deeper."

"Oh!" says Valley, and makes a face like somebody poked and punctured. She begins scribbling at once to capture the feeling, then furiously erases a line. Gabe turns back to stare at the road, thinking meanly that at least the porcupine is one animal Valley has actually seen.

Late one night at the end of January, driving home from somewhere, they had come to a section of the woods where pine and spruce thickened. The animal had lumbered across the road directly in front of them. Gabe stopped the truck, leaving the lights on, and glanced to her side. Valley's mouth flew open, her hands on the dashboard.

This was a rare chance. Porcupines generally stay out of people's way. Intending to get out and get a closer look, Gabe had started to open her door, but Valley put out her hand to stop her, shaking her head in a panic. In the dark, the creature's gray mass seemed phosphorescent, overlarge. They watched the rippling, bristling hump go by.

Gabe shut her door. "Well, we might see another," she said. "This time of year, they tend to hang out in bunches."

She put the truck in gear again and as they crept forward, staring into the two tunnels of light the headlamps made, she followed an impulse, partly revenge, telling Valley how her father had eaten porcupine once.

"Oh god, he did *not*! You are just trying to gross me out."

"No, he said it was good. Sweet tasting. He had a Chippewa friend, half Koyukon, who considered it a delicacy. They were glad to have it when they were way out trapping one time, he told me."

"That is so gross. *So* unnatural! You know, it may be mean to say so, but I think it is really no wonder your father had a stroke, clogging himself up with all that animal fat. I am not going to stand by and let that happen to Robert, you can count on *that*."

Gabe thought about challenging her. What was unnatural about eating porcupine? Why should it be people who didn't walk on the ground anymore who determined what "natural" was? Or people who plowed up the earth to grow natural food sold in natural stores shipped by natural trucks? But they had had countless arguments about this already.

"At least I look my own food in the face before I eat it—I know what my life costs, Valley. Life lives on life!"

"Yes? Well, *my* life will live on rice and beans, thank you very much."

"You think that makes you innocent? How much wildlife do you think is destroyed by plowed fields? You think it doesn't matter, your eating the rice plants' little baby seeds? I'll bet the rice plant views it differently."

"Farmers always keep some of the rice to plant next time."

"Exactly. That's what smart hunters do too. They keep things in balance. Why do you think we humans have front-facing eyes? We're predators, Valley! At the top of the food chain. Deer are ungulates, with side-set eyes so they can watch out for those of us who have canine teeth, see?" She tapped her eyetooth to make her point. "That makes it more fair, but life is supposed to be hard. Nature meant for it to be hard."

Valley's mouth had dropped open as she reached her hand up to double-check this definition of eye and tooth and what was just. She was silenced for a moment. But the iron came down in her gaze again, clamping her jaw shut. "Maybe that's our species' history," she conceded. "That doesn't mean it's right." Her chin had come up, her sense of superiority unshakable.

Although since then, the girl had given way on her food rules, just like everything else where Robert was concerned. The night of the porcupine Valley had told her what Robert promised. He had still been at Marquette then. "Oh, he's absolutely committed to vegetarianism. He *is*, Gabrielle. He can't do it now, of course—you wouldn't believe what he has to eat in that hellhole—nothing but white sugar and white flour? But when he gets home, he wants me to teach him all about natural foods. He's open to things, Gabe, he really is," she'd said that time. "Not like some people I know."

Now on their way to pick up Henry, Gabe glances again at Valley, who has finished her scribbling and is staring out the truck's window with a self-satisfied look. It's as if Robert's promises to her had never been made, as if she'd given up every expectation of him, with no need even to talk about it. The way it had been with Gabe, about the old man. Maybe Robert had been right. Valley did fit in with their family.

"What time is it?" Gabe asks, and Valley turns the heavy watch medallion that hangs around her neck to show her. They have promised to come back to the work site no later than 5 P.M. and it's already 5:15. Robert will be madder yet, she thinks. He'll figure they're upping the ante. He makes a good show of being patient with the old man, of sharing the load but, in his heart of hearts, believes that any two women should rightfully be able to handle Pa without him. On a good day, he's a martyr whenever they take him up on his offers to help out. But after this morning's fight, he'd make them sorry for asking.

Valley had tried to explain to her all the pressure Robert was under. He was too busy. He was planning to ask Sid for a raise. She said, "He's doing way too much for what he's getting! He must be bossing a half-dozen men, and he's gone out and recruited them all. Sid wouldn't have any of them without Robert, he pays so piss poor."

"Believe me," Gabe had said, "it must be killing Sid to pay them anything at all. He usually doesn't have any waiting time between paying out and getting back. Something this big—going to a bank and all? It's not his usual style."

Now she decides to bring up the porcupine again. There is something she wants to say, something surrounding the animal she isn't ready to give up yet. She had remembered telling Valley about the patterned strap her father's friend had made out of the porcupine quills, an old Chippewa tradition to honor the animal giver and make it more visibly a gift. With this in mind, she adds, "You didn't talk about the quillwork in your porcupine piece."

The girl looks stymied, until Gabe adds, "The quillwork my father's friend made, remember? The one who ate porcupine?"

"Oh." Valley rolls her eyes, looking annoyed. "What about it?"

Gabe shrugs. "I just thought there might be some way you could include it, the way indigenous people live that's different from us, the way they use everything and make it beautiful, even something as plain as a gray porcupine quill. I was thinking it might give your piece a little more substance."

Valley stares at her a moment. "And what makes you think people who come to Wild Kingdom are going to want *that*?" It does sound absurd, put so starkly.

They pull off M67 within sight of the Friendly, into a wooded area a work crew is tearing up. Gabe drives by this site regularly, but the project is getting bigger. Every time she passes, there's something new. There isn't a tree standing for the length of a football field and a dozer is making a racket near the back, pushing over more trees.

"Good god, what *is* that thing?" Gabe asks. She is looking at a weird wooden structure in the foreground, newly raised this afternoon. Two men are on scaffolds pounding nails into a two-by-four frame.

"That must be the cave part," says Valley. "The man-made mountain Robert's been talking about. They're going to stucco it over. Big, isn't it?"

Valley gets out, the slam of her door barely heard above the roar of motors, the pounding of hammers, the metallic whine of saws. "I bet that's the entrance, Gabe. See the doorway?"

Gabe nods even though she doesn't see it. Earlier, when they'd dropped the old man off, it'd been lunchtime and quiet. Now it's like an ant colony, everyone scurrying.

She follows Valley across the open field toward a tiny trailer. On the right, a crew of men are laying pipe in trenches. Another crew, using a crane and a massive chain, are lowering a big cement tank into a hole deep enough to bury six Cadillacs. The septic system of course, Gabe thinks. Rest rooms would figure mightily in a place like this.

Dirt blows into her face, stinging a little. Ahead, she can see Robert come around the corner of the trailer to meet Valley. She braces herself, but he seems in a good enough mood, smiling as he turns to watch them come nearer. "Come to get the grand tour, did you?" he calls. "Whattya think? Pretty big operation, isn't it? Getting bigger all the time."

"I had no idea," Gabe says. "You're building yourself a small city."

Robert grins, glances at Valley, lights a cigarette. "In a way, we are. That's right. Parking here for half as many cars as fit in Clearwater. No meters either, all of it free." Robert swings his arm, showing the expanse of this generosity, including Valley and Gabe in the grace. All is forgiven. Visibly relieved, Valley clings to his right arm, entwining her fingers in his.

"Over there will be the gift shop part. It'll look all Indian-like. People nowadays like that. And over there, that big roundish thing? That's the heart of the whole idea. The Wild Kingdom cave. Sid's got this guy will make it look just like rock. We're gonna put copper and iron ore chunks in the plaster, and Valley here will write all that up. About the mines, and how whole towns went boom and bust. Remember that from history class? You must, you always liked history, Gabe. I hated the stuff, never thought I'd use it! Well, we're gonna have lots of that here. A lot of people like that."

Gabe knows this reference to school is a sop thrown her way, but she doesn't let this register on her face. Valley is being eager enough for the both of them.

"Over there—see? That's gonna be the railroad depot. Valley tell you about that yet?"

The structure looks about the size of a short outhouse, and Valley shakes her head. Robert smiles wider and puts one arm around Gabe's shoulder, pleased, gesturing with the hand that holds his lit cigarette. "We're putting in this miniature railroad track. I just talked Sid into buying the engine today. We'll take the track back down to the river, over by where the Chippewa had their pit mines? No, I know what you're thinking, but we're not going to hurt anything. We'll treat it just like it's holy, which it *is*, I know that—in fact, we'll play it up that way. Put a make-believe graveyard over there, with those little bark houses they used."

Gabe nods, turning her head away from the stream of smoke that is blowing back from Robert's hand, and Valley says, "I can't believe you talked Sid into it! I thought he was going to keel over with a heart attack last time I was here and you were handing in some bills."

"It's been making him kinda crazy," Robert says, and flicks his butt down to the ground with a snap of his forefinger. "But I told him that's how you gotta do things now. Take a chance and go for the big time. Like the men working overtime. Yeah, it's gonna cost him, but the sooner we get this thing done, the sooner the money starts rolling in." He puts his head forward, raising his shoulders in an exaggerated shrug, hands open and imploring in front of him. "Can you imagine the money we'll make if we get some of this thing open by July Fourth? But he's like some old lady. It's startin' to piss me off a little!" He steps on the butt then, twisting his foot into soft earth.

When he looks up, he's calmed himself. "But hey," he says, shrugging again, "I got my way on the railroad track. All I want is my piece of the action, is all."

Without thinking, as if quoting some familiar Bible verse, Gabe speaks an ingenuous truth. "Nobody I know of ever got a piece of Sid."

Robert pulls back from her, dropping his arm, face swept clear of expression, mouth set in a firm line. She knows she's made a mistake.

She mumbles something incoherent, which seems to mollify him. At least he looks away from her then, hearing a worker coming up behind him. The two talk a moment, aside from the women, the short, dark-complexioned man gesturing in the direction from which he just came, over near the trees in back.

"Shit! God*damn!*" Robert explodes, and then to Gabe and Valley, he says, "Look, I gotta go check this out. Some of these guys wouldn't know their asses from a hole in the ground without me there to tell 'em the difference." At once he sets off with the workman, his walk a determined, quick jabbing. The smaller man has trouble keeping up, and looks back at them, the whites of his eyes standing out against his sunburned skin. He scoots to catch up with his boss.

"I wouldn't just stroll around," Robert calls back to them, "especially with the old man here. Keep an eye on him, will you?"

He stops dead in his tracks then, as he stares at the figure sitting in a lawn chair near the trailer. "Jesus, will you just *look* at him?" he calls, and his face clouds over for the second time, his mouth grim, eyes lit with rancor. "Look, just get him out of here, will you? I've had about all I can take for one day. I'll see you back at the house, about seven-thirty." He turns then, his back and shoulders stiff, striding off with the little man just a pace behind, keeping his face in the shadow of his hard hat.

Gabe follows his gaze to Pa to see what has upset Robert this time. She and Valley look at each other, unsure what is different about the old man, what has triggered Robert's reaction. Henry is sitting hunched over in a green metal chair, staring without interest in the movement and the noise all around him. His expression is about something internal, the usual shocked incredulity. He needs a shave and his hair looks shabby and frayed in the lowering sunlight.

"He can sure be touchy sometimes," says Valley, bending over to pick up Robert's cigarette butt. "Comes in handy, I suppose, whenever you want somebody *else* to do all the work. Maybe I'll just start having a burr up my butt."

The women's eyes meet then, and they both know better.

Valley sighs resignedly and tries to push tight lips into a smile but it flags quickly and becomes a grimace. "Oh, the old man's all right. It's not so bad. Come on," she says, "let's go give a hand to poor old *En-er-ee.*"

She doesn't say she knows full well that Robert will not be home at seven-thirty. He never comes home when he troubles himself to name a time like that. It becomes a gauntlet thrown down, a rule that then has to be broken to prove he is boss. She knows this as well as Gabe does, but neither of them say it.

April 30, 1984
Five Corners, Michigan

Kate's questions circle around, but I see where she's leading. It's a place I've been to already. Wondering what made us so angry. What did Robert and I fight about? Taking care of Pa. Or the way we managed our schedules and transportation— all of it supporting or complicated by Fond du Lac or Wild Kingdom at opposite ends. We didn't have to speak, we could sleepwalk our diverging paths—taking the detours around my big education and his paramount project. If one of us slipped and said what we actually felt, we'd back off and be careful not to repeat it. Otherwise Valley would scold us for being stubborn. Or worse, try to smooth it over with some sweet gesture or ceremony, which was so different from the way she plied me with questions when we were alone, guessing and shrugging until I was shrugging back. Robert and I were both dead certain we were right about the world and how it was put together.

A taxidermy museum is all Wild Kingdom is. Finished off by a guy whose specialty was figurines for miniature golf courses. When you go inside, brown-painted footsteps on the floor lead from one glass-faced grotto to the next, where beaver, wolf, and deer are molded into scenes, like moth-eaten Disney nature films minus the music. Valley framed her little descriptions on the wall and painted animal tracks next to each yellow button, which, when pressed, lights the scene and activates a recording that describes animal sounds: the blackboard screech of a broad-winged hawk, the slap of a beaver's tail, a chattering porcupine. In the last scene a white-tailed deer crosses the yellow line of a highway, looking stupefied by the lights. Press the button and you hear the funny cough deer give when they're startled, and you learn how many are killed by cars each year.

The painted footsteps finally lead to coffee and popcorn and candy bars and souvenirs back in the room Robert worked so hard on. He faced the walls with white birch bark and glued-on twigs to look like a Quonset hut, or a tourist's idea of a Quonset. Crammed to the ceiling, it's got tiny birch-bark canoes, rubber tomahawks trimmed with fuschia-dyed chicken feathers, turquoise and copper jewelry, ceramic ash-trays shaped like toilets that say "Rest your ash here," and little redwood outhouses stamped with "Wild Kingdom" on the front, "Made in Philippines" on the back. Velvet portraits of white-tailed deer or dressed-up dogs playing poker. Shell grotto TV lights with crucifixes. Butterflies glued on wood with thick varnish. And conch shells.

Conch would freeze to death in Lake Nekoagon in the full of summer, much less survive a single winter. But people stand in line at Sid's cash register to buy them—pink, gaping shells, souvenirs of the north woods. Better than rainwater turning orange wherever it pools on ore-rich ground, or columbines growing wild. Those sights are too fleeting—full of scratches and bug bites for your trouble. You can't sell that in shops.

So Sid sells them their nature bottled and stuffed, electri-fied with sound effects. And the tourists are grateful. How do you fight that? Sometimes I couldn't keep my mouth shut and would say something sarcastic, but Sid would only answer that he didn't make this world. He just lived in it. Wild Kingdom wasn't the first of its kind in the upper penin-sula. A thirty-foot-tall Paul Bunyan with Babe the Blue Ox had been standing at Tower Rock for years. Like Robert used to say, If Sid didn't do it, somebody else would, sure as shit. I'd shrug and agree, but Robert knew it was for the shit part.

Wild Kingdom was the blind Robert and I hid behind, blasting away. What did I know then, except what I didn't like? What is it I know now? It's like my being so sure of what I hate about hunting or what I hate about progress—I go half the distance, disapproving of what I don't like, never naming what I love. And after all this time of being silent, how do I open my big mouth to say what I thought Robert and Valley ought to have done? Some logging? Some trapping? Maybe selling some real estate? Valley said I was stuck. Maybe I was.

You don't live through something like this and not change, Kate says. She thinks it impressive, my having sorted out so much already, but I worry about claiming anybody else's hope. I can't go by other people's beliefs again, not even Kate's. She's waiting for my big insight, wanting for it to match up with the one she's already had. So am I in denial? Her talking about survivor's guilt made me angry. But I don't think I was being defensive at the time—I was angry.

I've been happier this past year than I remember having felt before—maybe ever. Not all the time, but a lot. Doing what I set out to do—with no one disapproving or interrupting or barging in when I'm not looking. That year, I learned how dangerous it is to be numb. But how important can that possibly be, to make it worth what it took to wake me up? That would put me back at the center.

JUNE, 1974

It is Friday night and Valley and Gabe have brought Henry down to Shub's store. Valley has dressed up in shorts and a tank top, with a plastic poodle pin on her shoulder and a cowboy handkerchief around her neck. She's wearing lace-trimmed cotton anklets with her Mary Janes for the occasion.

They have told themselves that Pa likes to sit on the porch like old times, listening to neighborhood gossip. In reality, it is something for the two of them to do to escape the loneliness of the cabin. They are weary of the quiet.

"Supposed to get even warmer tonight," Shub is exclaiming. "Can you beat that? Warmer as soon as the sun goes down? It's just more of the kinda thing I mean. Folks should pay more attention to these things."

"It's the Gulf Stream," Valley says.

"You mean the jet stream," Gabe corrects her.

"It's just one more sign, I'm telling you," Shub persists.

Gabe is pushing the porch swing back and forth with the nudge of one foot on the floor. Turning her head to the left, away from their talk, she can watch the sky over the lake turning pale yellow, with wispy clouds like brush strokes colored lavender. These will deepen to purple as she watches.

She has been here so many times before, everything the same: the smell of barbecued meat and behind it the watery smell of the lake. The sky will yawn gold and rose-pink and violet in the space over water, while the pines blacken at the edges, cast into saw-toothed rim as the sun lowers. In the background, like raucous birdsong, come Shub's dire warnings that everything is threatened. His portents and omens make her feel cozier, the threats a part of what feels familiar.

"This is the best thing for him," says Valley in a preachy tone, patting Henry's knee. "He likes it when we talk like this. But you have to just act like he's part of it."

"It's not like he was ever much of a talker, little girl—I hate to burst your bubble," Shub answers. "They never get better, not when they're this far gone. I've seen it too many times, too many times." Now that he knows her, he never quits trying to look for an argument with Valley, who is full of positive thinking. But tonight she's quiet. Shub is stuck with his restlessness, left aching for a fight.

"Here comes Robert," Gabe says after a moment, having spotted a dot of orange in a plume of dust.

Valley stands up immediately, smiling. Watching the VW pull into the lot, she walks over to the wide stairs on the side, bouncing a little on the balls of her feet. It is Friday and he's come home. He hasn't gone drinking.

"You have a good day?" she calls, and her voice lilts up to soprano.

Robert makes a face, says, "Shit, *no*," but then he beams broadly, coming up the stairs. "I'm gonna forget all my troubles and take you out to the Clearwater Drive-In, honey-lamb. We're gonna take in a show. Gotta get going if we're gonna make it before dark."

"Did you eat already?"

"Shit, yes, had a nice thick red *steak* at Sid's. Oh, I love it when you squirm like that. You're afraid I'll bite you—might turn you into a carnivore yourself!" He growls and dives into her neck, making her squeal. Then he grabs her ribs. "You need some meat on these bones, girl! You are wasting away, eatin' nothing but sprouts!

"What was I *thinking* of?" He straightens up with this last exclamation, still teasing her by calling to the rest of them. "Bringing a goddamn granola head up here? Tries to feed me *tow*-fu, for god's sake!"

They have heard this sort of thing over and over. There's no need to respond.

Red-faced but smiling, Valley straightens up. "I didn't know you had a drive-in around here—god, I *love* a drive-in," she says, bouncing more, and landing a quick kiss on his cheek.

"We gotta get us some treats though. Hold on a minute. Don't trouble yourself, Shub. I'll put my money on the register."

Valley is grinning, pleased to have Robert's attention. She glances at Gabe then, looking guilty for leaving her alone with Henry, belatedly remembering to say, "Is this okay, Gabe? Can you handle him by yourself?"

"Go on and have some fun. But *don't* let him take you to the drive-in, Valley. Do something else. And make Robert take Pa to the john before he leaves, will you? He can do that much at least."

Robert swears when Valley asks him to take Henry to the bathroom, but he acquiesces, handing Valley the Hershey bars, the bag of marshmallows he has bought, a six-pack.

"Robert," she says, "you are going to do terrible things to your metabolism. Meat is one thing, but I thought you told me no more white sugar—"

"Peach-face, don't worry," he answers as he helps Henry up and walks him into the store past her. "Just you get in the car and wait for me. *You* don't have to eat none of this stuff."

"Where is it you're going?" Shub asks, turning in his chair toward Valley.

"It's a surprise," Robert yells to him before Valley can answer, and Shub shrugs and calls to Valley with a raised hand, "Well, have fun."

When Robert comes back to sit Henry down in his chair, Gabe looks at him, catches his eye, grabs his arm. "Why don't you take her somewhere nice? It's a shitty thing to do to her, she'll hate it," she pleads.

Robert gives a scoffing laugh, waves an arm at her in a swatting motion. "Aw, you used to like it, didn't you? Besides, you worry too much."

"Where is it they're going?" Shub asks again.

"To the Clearwater Drive-In," Gabe enunciates, staring at Robert.

Shub makes a face like he smells something bad. "Judas-*priest*, boy! She's not gonna like that! You think you'da outgrown that kind a stuff by now, wouldn't you? Right here in front of your old man. Ain't you ashamed? Valley! Come on back here, girl!"

Robert throws his head back, smiling from ear to ear. When he sees Valley stirring in the Volkswagen, curious about what they are saying, he motions to her to stay put.

Shub goes on, "And I told you I don't want you buying no more beer from me. I am not about to help you break your parole. That's all you need, isn't it? Sid too, for that matter."

Gabe demands, "Will you think about her for once? Will you?"

Robert only laughs without making a sound, laughs and laughs, turning to bound down the stairs. "See you two later!" he calls back over his shoulder.

She and Shub sit in silence, listening to the tinny sound of the VW, heading back up the road toward Clearwater.

Gabe sighs, sliding down into her chair a little, and decides not to think about Robert or what he is doing to Valley. She's got to concentrate on the last essay chapter she's working on, the critique of Hemingway that won't quite come. Probably she should go home and get it done.

Shub announces, "Here comes Mrs. Snow," and the two of them watch the old woman in her slippers, ankles wrapped in flesh-colored bandages, waving at them while her pug dog stops to squat on the grass. The dust from the car's passing sifts down in a cloud behind her. Only Henry stares out to the lake.

May 17, 1984
Five Corners, Michigan

Why doesn't Kate just come here so I can talk to her about this? As if that would be easier for me. It's this last bunch of questions. The nerve of her, using my suggestion, a trick I use with my students. Sometimes they'll get up on their soapboxes and start expounding on beauty or evil. So I like to ask them, "When?" Asking when always prompts a scene, a specific event. I say, "Tell me a time you felt this, you saw this, you believed this. Don't give me an abstract word to describe it—give me an example, show me." I told her that sometimes when they do this, they open their minds and see more. Rhetoric is a fine thing, but outlines and labels don't hold up when real people are pressing against time and space, in a world with limits.

So I say I wasn't helpless—how could I have acted so helplessly? And now Kate asks me, When? Tell me, when.

JUNE, 1974

Gabe sits at the typewriter, staring at the blank page. Hemingway is a great writer, she rehashes. So how come she resents him? She still can't think of how to put it for her paper, but this time Orbach is insistent. She's got to produce this last part. But about what?

His women. That's part of it. They're such mewling little twits. First Brett Ashley in *The Sun Also Rises* and then that childbirth scene in *A Farewell to Arms*. She hasn't given birth any more than Hemingway has, but she knows she could write it better than that. For one thing, Catherine Barkley *would* have to die, wouldn't she—when most women don't and never rate a book for their trouble. Dennis's sister said giving birth felt like shitting a pumpkin. Gabe's heard stories about women cursing their men at childbirth, but not Catherine Barkley. She apologizes. "I'm sorry I'm taking so long, darling." She doesn't even protest when they scold her for saying she won't make it. "You will not do any such foolishness. . . . You would not die and leave your husband. . . . You must not be silly." At the end you're only glad when she finally shuts up—*dead*, simpering Catherine. But Gabe can't say that in her paper, it's not scholarly. What can she write?

It's late and still they're not home. Maybe the show was late getting started. Maybe Robert had second thoughts and had taken

Valley somewhere nice, the way Gabe said he should. But she really doesn't think so.

The Clearwater Drive-In—count on Robert to think of a name like that. Gabrielle was taken in by it when she was about thirteen, the same year he was supposed to graduate from high school. Just like him to quit school with two months to go, trying to prove something—though what exactly, she still can't say. Stupidity was what the old man had called it. He'd refused to talk to the boy, for months that time. She'd felt so sorry for Robert she tried to make it up to him, kept him company when he needed it. Like that night he took her for ice cream—he had a job pumping gas—and he'd said, "Come on, I'll take you to the Clearwater Drive-In."

They'd gone way out, almost to Galesburg, then turned onto a dirt road going back into the woods, back and back until it was two tire tracks. They bumped over grassy hummocks, crouching down in their seats, lowering their faces because the branches whacked the windshield and scratched the sides of their truck with a sound like fingernails on a blackboard. She could feel the tall grass folding over, pressing back against the floor of the cab.

"Robert, where are we going? What kind of a drive-in is it, all the way out here? It isn't X-rated, is it?" She remembers how the thought had scared her. Sometimes Robert said things he shouldn't to a sister and looked at her breasts, just budding that year, though she had told herself she was overly self-conscious and probably imagining it. She couldn't shake her uneasiness though, had begun to dislike his having to walk through her room to get to his own. She asked for the room downstairs, but hadn't been able to say the real reason to her father for fear he would have thought she had a dirty mind. As it was, having thought of dirty movies made her feel ashamed.

"Better roll up your windows," Robert said, ignoring her. She had thought he meant because of the night air and mosquitoes and her being dressed in shorts, though really it was warm and too early in the year for the mosquitoes to be bad. She did as she was told.

Then she saw light up ahead, throwing the trees into silhouette. Robert turned left. An odor, sour and rotten, seeped into the truck despite closed windows. The trail widened into a clearing. A ring of cars with their lights on faced them. Robert pulled into a space next to the nearest car, nearly completing a circle, and Gabe could see the headlamps were illuminating a dump in the middle of the space. Small hillocks of green plastic bags, some of them ripped open like full bellies, spilled eggshells and coffee grounds and tin cans full of grease. There were piles of yellow corn kernels—Copper County's favorite vegetable—and spatters of mashed potatoes and home fries mixed in with plastic blister packs and cardboard tubes and toilet paper and cans and bottles, all of it stinking to high heaven, worse than the sum of its parts.

"They oughta be coming in over there," Robert had said, dipping his head toward a red station wagon, three cars over.

"What will come in over there?"

"The bears. This is the bear dump I been telling you about. They come in like clockwork, you'll see."

Gabe held her breath. She knew there were bears in these woods. She'd come across their scat but had never spotted one. Hardly anyone saw them anymore. The old man had a bearskin with the head still intact rolled up under his bed. But the fur was dry, the teeth yellowed with age, and he'd given up hope of ever finding another to match its size and replace it. He'd had chances to bag smaller ones, he'd said, but didn't have the heart. No sport in that.

Robert opened the door and got out. "Gonna make this more exciting," he said.

"What are you doing? Get back in here!"

He took some Hershey bars out of his pocket and smiled, holding them up for her to see. Then he went down to the edge of the pile of plastic bags and debris and unwrapped one of the bars. He stuck it upended into the trash. Next he walked back to the truck and, smiling again, like a magician pulling a rabbit out of his hat, reached into the bed and pulled up a bag of marshmallows. He returned to the chocolate bar and surrounded it with marshmallows, walking backward to trail the confections to the truck and up onto the hood where he partly unwrapped a second chocolate bar and slipped it under the wiper on Gabrielle's side.

She was panicked by then. "Robert," she said, rolling the window down a crack. "You'd better get in here, come on, you'd better get in."

He smiled, waving away her concern, pointing across the dump to the darkness, bobbing his head in excitement. "Lookit there," he said. "Here they come."

"Hey, Roberto," someone hollered from a car across the way and waved out their window. "Show time!"

Gabe looked where Robert had pointed and saw something blacker moving against the dark—the bears, she thought, and, with heart pounding, she rapped on the windshield. "Come on, Robert, come on!"

Robert waved back, grinning, and then took his sweet time, unwrapping a third candy bar, placing it on the roof overhead. "Hey, Dancing Bear, come over here, why don't you? Smokey the Bear, come and get it!" he yelled. By now a parade of black bears, heads down, mouths open in a pant, was shuffling into the light. Robert lobbed marshmallows at them, hitting them more than once, though they didn't seem to notice, or to have the slightest interest in the source of things. Instead, they focused on the ground, gobbling up the white goodies, almost stepping on them.

There were three of them, one a little larger than the other two— possibly a mother and her cubs. Robert finally got into the truck and Gabe said, "Lock it!" He laughed, shoving against her a little. "Don't get yourself in an uproar. Watch what happens. Look at 'em, will you?"

The bears swung their heads from side to side as they walked, laying their feet out ahead of them heavily, plodding. They seemed to have already learned that these cars had nothing to do with their business. Maybe they thought of the lights as part of the landscape. The bears poked their noses into piles, using their paws to overturn bags or rip them open, and once something interested them, they sat down on their fat rear ends.

"Look at that big one lift that can, will you?" Robert said, laughing. "You'd think she was sitting at a bar, swigging a big one, wouldn't you? God, they kill me," he said.

Gabe would have laughed, but she was tied tight in the middle, so that she couldn't take any but the shallowest breaths. "Robert, won't they come up to the truck with those marshmallows all over? Will they come up that close?"

"They might. That's what I'm hoping. Maybe not, though. They seem pretty happy with stinkin' garbage. Maybe they can't even smell chocolate with all this stink. I can't smell it, can you?" He sniffed his fingers, then held them out for her.

"Robert, I'm not kidding. Please, I don't want them over here, not close."

"Don't you worry about a thing." Sympathy overblown, his mouth stuck out in a pout that gave itself away, corners turned up a little, a smile playing there.

Suddenly he swung his door open again, and stood up next to it, lobbing more marshmallows. "Hey, Bruno. Over here!" he shouted.

Gabe could hear the guy in the next car over. "Sit down, asshole. You won't think it's so funny, she comes over and shakes your hand." Embarrassed for Robert, Gabe turned to look at the man, who had children and a wife in the car with him, probably tourists. The man cursed again for her benefit, so she could see how disgusted he was.

"Robert?" she tried to call out, but her voice came out short of a whisper, as if her body were conspiring to keep her presence a secret from the bears.

The mother bear was sitting on her haunches, her paws waving slowly in the air, balancing her weight as she studied the arcs of marshmallows falling near her. Then she flopped down on all fours and began vacuuming up the morsels, stepping with a gait that, while clumsy looking, nevertheless brought her neatly, effortlessly, little by little, closer to the truck.

Robert got back in, though he didn't shut his door all the way, keeping his hand on the knob. "Now she's got the picture. Here she comes, watch this, watch this, she's coming over."

By now Gabe was quivering in her seat. Feeling nearly cut in half by steel bands, which were cold, cold as the draft she could feel coming in Robert's door, she turned her body away from the sight of the black bear coming toward her. The bear's coat was remarkably shiny and clean looking for a dump bear, she thought, glancing for a moment that seemed to go on and on, the shiny coat coming at her, fur shimmying, sliding loose on the bear's muscles, slipping on shoulder blades as the animal walked nearer. The bear nuzzled the ground next to the truck, following Robert's trail.

"Come on, what are you nervous about?" said Robert, putting his arm around Gabe, trying to turn her face toward the bear at the same time. "Mamma Bear's not gonna hurt you, look at this—where else you gonna see such a show?"

She had wanted to say, I'm not *afraid*, except it wasn't true. She

was afraid, but more, she was ashamed—*he* should be ashamed—
and he wasn't, he wasn't at all. She worried she might throw up.

"Com-ahn, Momma Smokey. Come on to papa," Robert called
out, watching the bear that had all but disappeared in front of the
truck, a black shadow the lights couldn't pierce. They felt her body
push against the bumper, moving the truck a little. Then they saw the
bear sit up again, facing toward them, a little to the side of the truck,
her nose wet and alive. Moving deliberately, she turned her head
toward Gabe, still sniffing. Her small eyes moved, searching, backing
up and checking on the nose's intelligence.

The bear's mouth came open and Gabe could see its pink tongue,
the wobbly black lips, and behind them, pointed pegs of teeth. The
bear looked like an old woman, intent on some all-consuming memory,
gape-mouthed, as if her adenoids were troubling her breathing, and
drooling a little. Leaning forward, she lay her head on its side, right on
the hood, and stuck her tongue out, coiling it around one marshmal-
low, then a second, drawing them into the black of her gullet.

That close, she may have spotted the half-wrapped chocolate bar,
or maybe she smelled it with that moving, twitching nose. But suddenly she reached out a paw to unlodge the candy that Robert had
placed under the wiper blade. Instinctively, Gabe turned her face
away, tucking her head to protect her neck as she heard the click of
the bear's claws on the glass, the hard, clacky scrambling.

Robert laughed, short-breathed and quick, watching the bear
slobber on the glass, following up the unsuccessful claw work with
her mouth. By now the bear was standing, leaning her paws on the
fender. "Lookit that!" Robert said with such intensity that Gabe
turned to see. The bear's head appeared huge in the windshield,
seeming to fill it up. Having smeared the chocolate on the glass, she
was licking it with a languor that was sensuous, maddeningly drawn
out. Her strategy worked at last. The bear sat down, upright, with
what was left of the candy bar between her big paws, looking around
absentmindedly, chewing paper and all with open-mouthed enjoy-
ment, like a fat, happy kid at a barbecue.

Once the chocolate was gone, she came snuffling up to the side of
the truck, finding a few stray marshmallows and then, either because
she had caught the scent of the last chocolate bar on the roof or
because the arrival of one of the smaller bears brought competition,

she made the grand effort. Standing straight, she walked upright on her hind legs, belly in full view until she came smack up against Gabe's window, pressing against it, rocking the truck with her weight. The hair on her chest was longish and coarse, but it swept in from either side to meet an invisible line in the middle, as neat as the duck-tail that Robert combed a hundred times a day. Underneath this belly coif, Gabe could see a row of nipples mashed against the glass.

"Holy shit," Robert said then, and Gabe could see that the bear had mounted the running board. One of the full fleshy pads of the bear's back paws was up against the window now, the claws dark and long, clicking against the glass as she tried to get a grip and climb on board. The truck swayed from her weight. She got one hind foot in finally, still struggling to flop forward and reach the chocolate. The metal of the truck bed made a hollow booming noise.

Having an extra passenger wasn't what Robert had planned. He threw open his door with a loud whack. "Get out of here," he yelled, standing up on the running board on his side, pounding a fist on the roof with a thud. "Get out of here, you fucking garbage hound!"

"Robert, watch out!" Gabe shouted. The second bear was making its way round the front of the truck, getting close to Robert's door. "Behind you!"

"Jesus," Robert said, turning to see the smaller bear stand up too. Robert threw the door open wider, flat and hard against the small bear's front. It made a whumping noise, echoed by the bear's whining grunt, repeated each time Robert smacked him with the door.

Moving quickly, Robert squeezed into his seat to slam the door shut, but the second bear had one paw on the top of the door frame. Gabe could hear the clatter of metal against claws. The door bounced back open. The bear dropped down to all fours. Overhead, the thunder from the first bear persisted. Mama had managed to stand up in the truck bed by this time and was leaning against the back window, her front splayed across the roof. She was still after the last candy bar.

"Jesus, shit!" Robert said, slamming his door shut. Reaching his arms up overhead, he straightened them like a weight lifter. "Christ!" he said, feeling the tonnage.

He started up the engine, eyeing the second bear, hoping the roar of the motor would scare them both off. The second bear sat up on his haunches, watching his mother in the back of the truck. He kept complaining, a whine that ended in a deep grunt, repeated over and over.

Laughter rang from around the ring of cars. "Hey, Roberto!" the guy across the circle was yelling. "Good show, man!"

The attention drove Robert crazier. He hadn't planned on this, he hadn't planned on this at all. He reached to pound his fist against the glass behind him, where the belly was still in sight. Then he gunned the motor and slammed the truck into gear, releasing the brake with a pop. "Come on, Momma Bear, let's go for a ride," he said, gritting his teeth in a smile.

The truck lurched forward. Then Robert slammed on the brakes. One paw from the up-top bear slid onto Gabe's window, the bear's balance toppled. It scuffled back into place.

"Jesus!" Robert swore, pounding the steering wheel. His fists slipped and the horn honked. Inspired, he leaned on it, letting it blare. The noise felt earsplitting, but he kept it up. The cars around the circle joined in. Some honked in long blasts, some in tentative toots, all in good fun, laughter, and shouts, the noise melting into cacophony.

"Stop it," Gabe said. "Stop it, I can't stand it!"

The bear to one side stood up to listen to this strange night bird-song. He dropped down to all fours and swung his head from side to side. Then he strode off in that swaying, foot-slapping stride, back to the middle ground of the dump. Overhead they heard the rumple of steel as the mama bear's paws slid down the glass behind them. She sat in the truck bed to survey the situation. Robert jerked the truck forward and back.

"Let her go now," said Gabe. They sat still, turning to watch the bear tumble over the side. She started off toward the dump, falling in behind her offspring, her big round loose-skinned rear-end straight ahead.

Robert gave the truck some gas. "C'mon, asshole," he said to the bear, to himself. "Com-*aahn.*"

He rolled up behind the bear, giving chase, Gabrielle crying, "Robert, *please* let's just go home, come on, let's go *home!*"

He took the truck to the edge of the garbage, trying to bump the bear's behind, making her speed up into a loose-jointed trot. He didn't let up until he'd smeared garbage on the front tires, sending junk whipping back into spatters when he got stuck and had to put the thing into reverse, spinning the tires, roaring backward, turning sharply to exit. Within moments, they were tearing back down the trail in the dark, branches screeching against metal. The truck hit bottom on potholes Robert couldn't see.

"Are you crazy? Robert, slow down, can't you? What are you doing?"

"Shut up! Shut up, you fucking little bitch!" He pounded his fist on the dashboard.

This had worked. She didn't dare say another word, not then, not later. Not even after the story came out in town and made him out a comedian, and he made the story another joke between them.

Gabrielle hears the teakettle whistle and gets up to make herself a cup. She has left off the paragraph she is writing with these words:

He is masterful at drawing a detailed scene with the clean prose he became famous for evangelizing. His unembroidered rendition of the retreat from Caporetto in A Farewell to Arms *makes every word resonate with the weight of what is not being said. This technique is doubly effective for his having chosen a topic that had traditionally been omitted from fiction. The spaces in his prose speak of lies about warfare that his generation had been seduced into believing.*

Similarly, he uses plain-speaking in the story "A Natural History of the Dead," showing us despair only between uncluttered lines: "Can any branch of Natural History be studied without increasing that faith, love and hope which we also, every one of us, need in our journey through the wilderness of life? Let us therefore see what inspiration we may derive from the dead. . . . In war the dead are usually the male of the human species although this does not hold true with animals."

Gabe is pretty sure she's got the part about clean prose right. Yet acknowledging Hemingway's literary innovation, how could she take him to task for his depictions of women? His straightforward prose, his unshrinking gaze, all the more reason to find him trustworthy— maybe he was right in what he saw in women. Maybe Catherine Barkley really was that way. Think of the way she'd been that time at the bear dump with Robert—but she hadn't mewled and fawned. She'd been right to be afraid. She'd been sensible.

Headlights flash in the living room through the porch windows, a sight familiar by now. She braces for Valley's and Robert's homecoming. He will bluster with loud, profane stories, and Valley will go through the motions of protesting. "Oh, Robert! How can you?" she'll say, and then he'll pooh-pooh all of her shock and her fear, or her sense of propriety or morality, or whatever it was this time. The whole scene is predictable, and not even original. *You make me feel strong and brave, and I'll make you safe, little kumquat, so you won't ever have to take care of yourself or worry.* Robert's job is to make up for whatever she lacked, and hers is to help him define how capable he is, in the light of her inadequacies.

Gabe sighs and squeezes out her tea bag, laying it on the counter. The lights flash in the window again—and curious, she walks to the porch door. She sees a motion in the darkness of the trees and makes out Valley, stumbling in the shadows.

Gabe opens the door a crack and calls to her, guiding her with her voice. "Valley?"

There are rustling noises, then Valley's hoarse whisper, "The goddamn bastard. He better think twice, he better think twice before he lays another hand on me."

"Valley? Are you okay?" Gabe meets her at the bottom of the stairs.

"I'm okay, I'm just mad, that's all." Valley has both of her fists held up in front of her chest and it is ludicrous, this pose. "Oh, I am so *mad!*" she repeats.

"What happened? Did he have too much to drink again?"

"Of course he did, what's new? I am telling you, I am really having second thoughts. Who the hell does he think he is, who the hell—?"

"You've been drinking too."

"Self-defense, isn't it? Only be worse if I didn't. Do you know where he took me? Do you know what his idea of fun is? To see these poor, dreadful bears, these morally bankrupt bears, digging around in the dump like bums, like poor, awful bums, it was—"

"I should have warned you. I'm sorry."

"You should have *warned* me?"

"He took me there, years ago. Did he put out the chocolate bars and try to scare you?"

"Yes! My god, *Gabe!* Why didn't you *tell* me? I would never have gone there, *never.* The way he—he *forced* me to look, put my face right up against the bear's face, on the other side of the glass, and he thinks it's so goddamn funny, like I know there's *glass* between us, but I don't care, it's goddamn scary, he had no *business!*"

"Come on," Gabe says. "It's hot inside. Let's go to the shore and sit on our logs. I'll make us a fire."

The lake wind breathes into their faces, cooled by its journey over acres of water, and soothes them both. It licks at the fire, feeding it until the warmth is another kind of comfort, crackling at twigs, mirthful.

"I should have warned you," Gabe repeats, not knowing what else to say.

"I'd have probably gone anyway," says Valley after a moment, and both of them know this is true.

"Do you see anything here?" she says and turns away to bare her neck to Gabe. Gabe comes closer to look.

"You've got a bruise started, I think. Is that from Robert?"

"Yes. From later. I mean, I was really scared, I was so scared. But he was *too,* that's the part that drives me crazy. He had that bear sitting right on the top of my car and we thought for sure the roof would cave in. My little Volkswagen, and here we are, riding around the dump with this bear on top, and everybody laughing. And we had nothing but this lousy coat hanger on Robert's door! That bear could have just—oh Jesus."

She puts her face into her hands for a moment, then looks up. "But that's not what this is about," she says, pointing at her neck, "not the bear."

Gabe sits and watches Valley's profile, waiting for her to speak. Valley stares into the fire for a while before she goes on. "Afterward we went tearing down this little dirt road—not a road really, just a track, and I thought it might rip the doors off my car, or he might bang out the bottom, you know? So I'm blubbering like a baby and I'm saying, 'Robert, Robert, come on, slow down, what's the matter with you? Look at me, will you, I'm scared to death and you're making me worse!'

"And about then, we come out onto pavement and he turns the corner and stops and all of a sudden he puts his arm out, like he's gonna punch me or something? He grabs me by the throat and his teeth are gritted and his eyes look ready to pop. Like this, see? And he snaps my neck with a jerk and he says, 'That's enough. Shutup, *shutup* with your goddamn whining!' And I'm coughing—I'm *choking* before he finally lets me go."

She looks at Gabe then, incredulous. "So then he fucking lets go. And I stare at him, like I can't believe it, I'm just, like, *crying*, and he says, 'I don't need that kind of shit from you.' He's biting off the words, like this," she says and bares her teeth, snapping once, twice. "'I don't need you fallin' apart on me, like some little kid,' he says."

"So we go down the road a little, and he starts to laugh, this quiet, breathy little laugh." She imitates the sound and Gabe recognizes it, feels herself in the car with Valley because she's heard this, like the bobble of a glass knob on the lid of a boiling coffeepot.

"He starts laughing, louder and louder, pretty soon his shoulders are shaking he's laughing so loud. 'That's right,' he says, 'you *are* a kid, aren't you? What's the matter with me? Acourse you're a kid.' He reaches out his arm again, and I flinch, you know? 'Cause I think he's gonna hit me, but he doesn't. He cups my jaw the way he does when he's being sweet. He pulls me close and starts in stroking me, saying, 'Little girl, my poor, scared, little girl,' only his hand on my chin is like some vise!"

"So where is he now?"

She rolls her eyes, shakes her head a little. "Says he's gotta see a man about a dog." She pulls a clip out of her pocket then, fiddling with a roach she has left in a plastic bag. "Got a light?" she asks, holding it out to Gabe.

Soon the lake air is sweetened with the smell that makes Gabe think of secrets. After months with Valley, Gabrielle has learned to associate the stuff with the telling of what is hard, what is usually not said. If positive thinking doesn't work, pot will. Remembering her father, who is still inside alone, Gabe declines the lighted joint when it's offered. Valley gets stoned easily. By the time her eyes are heavy-lidded, she has accepted her situation, expects Gabe to accept it too. Valley begins to feel benevolent toward Robert, is ready now to forgive him, though still she is mystified, she says. She can't figure him out.

"He was scared as I was," she insists, half asleep. "That's the whole thing. I *know* he was scared as me."

June 11, 1984
Five Corners, Michigan

Mouth-shutting guilt. I wanted Valley to get what was coming to her for fooling with my brother. I thought, Let Miss Pert-and-Certain learn a few things—giving everybody advice, taking none of it herself. This isn't Kate's survivor guilt—it's vengeance.

How do I tell her that? And why am I surprised? It's the reason I didn't want to think about Valley. Admitting that I wished she'd get hers is all the more galling, since one of the local explanations was that I was jealous. Couldn't find a man of my own, skewed by my too great love for my brother.

Is that all there is, then? Denial? And all my journal work to come up with the obvious? What everybody's been saying all along? How can I tell Kate that? She doesn't look at stuff the way folks up here do, changing their stories to suit the situation. Oh, but the other version was even more colorful than jealous sister—the two of us were dykes, people said. Too bad we weren't. Instead we were fools—and god, when I say that I still get so mad. I could flatten her myself, I swear I could.

It wasn't that way then. I didn't have to do a thing at the time—just keep quiet, obsess over Hemingway, and let Robert's chips fall where they may. I was trying to write objectively about Hemingway's women, but it always got too personal. I had no business getting angry—what did a great man's relationships have to do with his work? What did my brother's love life have to do with anything that really mattered?

I wasn't consciously connecting my family and Hemingway and vengeance and storymaking then. But now I recognize Robert's using Valley this way—his making her over in his own mind, the way Hemingway recast women in his fiction. I think I was mad about recognizing Valley in those nurses Hemingway created, knowing she wasn't like that—

not really. Why would a man want some stick figure to love him? What good is that?

It was the real nurse, Agnes, that Hemingway fell in love with. Wounded and full of feeling for her, he felt entitled to marry her. When she rejected him, he raged—his brother said he got violent. Later when he started writing, he straightened her out as nurse Barkley in *A Farewell to Arms*, killing her off, while Brett Ashley, his other nurse in *The Sun Also Rises*, suffers endlessly. Both unlike Agnes, the real nurse who got along quite nicely without him. But what sort of hero would put up with that story?

I'm no better. I'm writing, writing away, remembering myself as loving sibling, brave friend, finding instead, incestuous sister, dyke. Everything I've feared is untrue and of course true—because words are a snare, either/or, this or that, when both are, both always are.

Valley—asking me if I thought she could learn to shoot a gun. I laughed, loving the crazy way she could turn on a dime. She wouldn't hurt a fly, not to save herself, I reminded her— and she made a face, wincing as she agreed, smiling finally because it was so rare for me to put an arm around her.

JUNE, 1974

Robert comes down the stairs stiff-legged, stumbling to the refrigerator. He pours a glass of tomato juice, then spikes it with the vodka he keeps under the sink. "A little hair of the dog," he says, lifting his glass in Gabe's direction, saluting her. "And a vicious bastard it was. Bit like a . . . bit like a Russian bear." He laughs. He sets the glass back down and studies Gabe, who is sitting with a book, having coffee. "You okay?" he asks.

"I'm fine. I don't know about Valley. I told you to take her someplace nice. It wouldn't have killed you."

He blows out his breath, scoffing. "Oh, she was fine, she had a *good* time. And anyway, it was research. She's always talking about her animal research. Now she can write her little story about the black bear and know what she's talking about."

"Wild Kingdom's going to have a scene at the dump, is it?"

"No, we're gonna have a scene like everybody wants to see it. Out in the woods, with the bears eatin' nuts and berries, all happy and bloodless so even Valley can stand it. Shit, I'd have Belle Nichols put a fuckin' smile on the bear's face, maybe put a hat on his head like Yogi if I thought people wanted it." He sipped from the glass again, watching her over the rim, then set it down, the tomato juice coating the glass. "You got a problem with that?"

Gabe has been stirring her coffee. Now she taps the edge of the mug with her spoon. "No, I love the whole thing. You know that."

He watches her and a smile spreads across his face. "I know that," he echoes, nodding. "You and the old man with your nature shit—you don't know how weird you are. You'd just as soon stay stuck like it was a hundred years ago." He gestures toward the wall, a rude hitch-hiker's thumb, a jab. "I'm having a phone installed. Right here. Gonna put us in touch with modern technology. Quite the concept, isn't it? You pick up this thing and you can talk to people, same as they were in the room with you. Amazing."

"Well, I'm glad we all talked about it first."

"No need to talk, Bean-o. I knew what you'd say. You're wrong is all. You're wrong about a lot of stuff. Wild Kingdom is the best thing that ever happened to Copper County. I put daddies to work who are feeding their families now. That probably doesn't mean much to you, what with the wad you must have walked away with, from Dennis. Maybe you'd like it better if I started myself a drugstore, but Clearwater's already got one, and I don't happen to have the college degree you need to push pills into them little brown bottles."

Valley's footsteps are coming down the stairwell behind Robert. He stops and turns, walking over to the stairs to wait at the bottom, just out of sight.

When Valley's steps pause, he says up to her, "Good morning, sweet thing. You sleep tight?"

Gabe can hear Valley mumbling, and pictures her sliding her hand over her face to scoop hair up out of her way. "I'm awright, I guess."

"I was just tellin' Gabe about the telephone man coming today. Ain't that gonna be good, being able to use a telephone? Damned dangerous not to have one out here, isn't it? Come on down, now, sweetheart. I got something for you."

"You got something? What?"

"Well, come down here and I'll show you. Come on."

The sound of soft footfalls resumes, then Robert's voice is murmuring affections, she can hear the smack of kissing, and they come around the corner, Robert's arm around Valley's shoulder.

"Now where'd I put that?" he thinks out loud, going through all the pockets in his pants in back, in the front, finally in his shirt pocket. His face lights up. He looks at Valley again, relishing the tension he's created. "Here it is," he says finally, and pulls out a silver ring. "You like it? It's turquoise, the genuine thing. Gonna sell these in the Quonset. You can have all the ones you want, kumquat. Same color as your eyes almost."

He cups her chin in his hand. "'Cept your eyes are nicer. You are such a pretty thing," he says and kisses her with a murmur like someone savoring his favorite pie. "Isn't she pretty, though?" he asks Gabe, and she has to admit that it's true, nodding that Valley is.

Valley smiles at her, sheepish, pleased.

Last night is beside the point now, it's clear. Everything beside the point. Gabe looks away from the scarf around the girl's neck, away from the blood blooming dark under Valley's skin.

VI

GRAND OPENINGS

Gabe waits for Valley to come back down, looking out the flank of windows in the living room, sitting next to Pa. The two women have decided Henry's smell of urine and stale sweat is more than they can bear, but she can hear Robert and Valley arguing about it upstairs. She pats the dry, fragile skin of Pa's hand, tells herself the open window helps, the sight of lake water and sky helps.

"Jesus Christ," Robert is yelling. "My one morning off and you have to hound me, you won't let me just stay in bed?"

"He's too heavy for us. And besides, it's embarrassing. You've got to be the one to take him into the shower. Or do you want me and Gabe to strip and get in with him?"

"What about a bath? Can't you just sit him in the tub?"

"We half-killed ourselves getting him out the last time. Half-killed *him*. No, it's got to be a shower. We've already talked about this, Robert. You promised me."

"Oh Jesus Christ! He never used to shower this often."

"I'll bet he never used to wet his pants!"

"Jesus *Christ!*" The sound of Robert's stomping down the stairs is so loud, Gabrielle turns her head to see him, a juggernaut, headed straight for her and their father. She starts to ask him if he wants some coffee, but he is busy proving a point, ignoring her. He strides to Henry and grabs his arm.

"Come on, you old bastard," he says. Putting one arm around Pa's back, grabbing his belt, Robert hauls him to his feet.

"Robert, not so *rough*," Gabe says, standing up, trying to help. "You don't have to be in such a *rush*, he'll walk with you—give him a *chance*."

Robert ignores her and puts the old man's arm over his shoulder, pulling one of the old man's legs along with his own. Valley, who has followed Robert downstairs, has to step back out of his way as he drags Pa toward the bathroom.

"You had better have him sit on the toilet first," Valley says through the open door, and Gabe hears the shower go on, full-blast, watches Valley saying, "All right, suit yourself. Do you want any help? *Do you?*"

The door slams in her face so that she has to swerve back to avoid getting hit.

"Fine!" she screams against the door. "That's just *fine,* you asshole!"

She looks at Gabe, then up at the far corner of the ceiling, shaking her head. "It isn't even worth it," she says. "Next time I'll just do it myself, I don't care if he is my father-in-law. Just get in with him, tits and all, and see how he likes *that!*"

"Great," says Gabe. "That'd be great. How about if we just put him back at Pinewood where he ought to be?"

"Sounds good to me."

"Oh shit!" comes Robert's voice through the closed door. "I can't believe this! Jesus Christ! *VALLEEEE!*"

She yanks the door open and billows of steam come pouring out. "What *is* it?" Valley yells, her tone exasperated. "What's the matter?" she demands, thrusting her head and shoulders into the fog.

"Jesus Christ, he has gone and shit right in the bathtub, down his leg, right here on my foot. Will you come in here and help me?"

"Didn't I tell you? Didn't I *say* he had to go to the bathroom first? Why don't you listen to a person once in a while, Robert Allen Bissonette. *Pissonette* is what it should be! Move him over a little. Here, no, let *me*—get him over!"

Gabe has gone to get paper towels and now she steps into the room, holding them out to Valley. A horrendous smell has joined with the steam and weighs on the skin, clinging. Valley gets on her knees, paper towels in hand, and reaches in behind the shower curtain. Gabe asks, "Do you want me to—"

Robert is cursing a blue streak, a steady background to Valley's instructions. "I've got it now. There. No, it's all right. Hold his foot out a little. Now rinse it off. Turn him around. Go on, use plenty of soap, all over. That's right. There." Valley straightens and stands up, water streaming down her hair into her face. "So much for modesty," she comments. "It's not like he knows a thing."

"Oh, he *knows*," yells Robert through the shower curtain, though the remark was meant for Gabe. "Don't give me that. He knows more'n you *think* he knows."

"Use plenty of soap, Robert!" Valley answers him. She has dropped a wad of paper towels into the toilet bowl at arm's length, put her forearm to her face, and pushed wet hair back. "Too much fruit, I guess," she comments, reaching over to flush the toilet, not thinking. But watching the water rise higher, she comes to, suddenly panicked: "Oh no, get ready with the *plunger*, Gabe, I put an awful lot of paper in—here it comes!"

Gabrielle had seen it coming and has grabbed the plunger. She pumps away and gradually the water recedes, but she half-whispers, "You shouldn't flush when the shower's on."

Valley, realizing what Gabe means, clasps her hand over her mouth and scrunches her shoulders up around her neck, listening to the water spraying in the tub, waiting as the toilet tank starts to refill.

Meanwhile, Robert has begun to enjoy himself a little. He's humming rock and roll bits while he makes reassuring comments to Henry. "That's it, old man, just lift your arm a little—Jesus *Christ!*" Robert yells. They hear him fumbling to turn the faucets off, watch the shower curtain billow. "What are you trying to do? Put us *both* in the hospital? In the burn ward? Jesus *Christ!*"

By now, he has sworn so many times that Valley laughs softly behind her hands. She stops immediately when he reaches out for the towel, groping, then laughs silently again as the shower curtain swells and bulges, attesting that Robert will be damned before he will ask for their help again, not for anything.

Valley makes eye contact with Gabe, who by this time is smiling from watching her. "Jesus *Christ!*" Valley mimics in a whisper and ducks into her hands to laugh some more, trying not to break up and failing.

"Just what the fuck is so funny out there," Robert yells from behind the curtain, but some bluster in his tone gives him away. He's like a father laughing at his naughty children, trying not to let them know he's amused. "Or maybe you think it's what's in *here* that's so funny. You think shit between my toes is funny? Yeah, and tub-fried balls are funny too, I suppose. That's right, I can *hear* you laughing out there. Here we come, ready or *not!*"

He yanks the shower curtain back and leans forward at Valley, grinning at her, and she takes this as permission to laugh uproariously. There is still a trail of soap bubbles down one of his shoulders. "TURD TOES and FRIED BALLS!" he screams in his best long-hair rock and roll voice, standing with the curtain hiding him, strumming the air with his free hand, shaking his head, which is sopping wet, hair standing on end. He leans to hold Henry up next to him, though the old man is only partially visible. Valley doubles over, she is laughing so hard at them.

"Funny, huh? What are *you* looking at?" Robert asks Gabe, laughing a little himself by now. His face is flushed, and his teeth gleam white, hair in wet coils next to steamy red flesh. "You better get out of here or you're gonna see a lot more, you two. The family jewels. Both generations. Yeah, and *crown* jewels they are too, ain't that so, kumquat?" he says to Valley. "Yes*sir*, little sister," he says to Gabe as she closes the door behind her. "You wait out there a minute and we will all be out, pink and squeaky clean," he calls and then she hears him talking to Valley, "Hey, doll, give me a hand—yes, *you*, you laughing hyena. Gaaabe! Get me some coffee ready! That's it, baby, hand me his robe. You got it."

Another ten minutes and they are dressed and smelling of soap, just as he promised, sitting at the table, drinking coffee. Gabe has made toaster waffles in celebration, since it could have gone either way. More often than not, it has gone the other way lately, with slammed doors and muttering, slights and cold silence. For the moment there is camaraderie, only Henry unmoved by the sunshine coming in the window and the smell of strawberry jam and butter.

"Sit him up some more," Robert instructs, and Gabe leans against Pa to push him straighter into the crook of the armchair, smoothing his napkin in his lap. Robert pushes the forked waffle piece into Pa's mouth and they watch him chew reflexively, Robert with fork still extended, ready to retrieve whatever falls.

"Never thought I'd see the day he'd come to this," Robert says as he says nearly every day, as he's said a hundred times in the past month at least. He is serious, staring at Henry's expression, which hasn't registered any reaction to their anger or their laughter. Like an aged newborn, Henry is in some other universe of contemplation he can't tell them about. But, unlike a baby, he never progresses, never makes eye contact or smiles, no matter how patient and attentive they are.

Gabe sighs, watching Robert with their father. "Well, it happens," she says, tired of hearing it, "to a lot of people."

"Happened to my great-grandma," chimes in Valley. "You know the one," she says to Gabe. "The saint?"

"Hmmm," Gabe says. "After your mom died?"

"Yes, they had to put *her* in a home. Wasn't anybody to take care of her, with all their family just too busy."

Robert assesses the two of them, judging they're in cahoots. "Well, some people have got their family close by," he says, daring one or the other to take him up on it, staring each of them down in turn. Neither responds and he gives Henry another bit of waffle.

"We are the only family some people have," he adds, and again they are silent. At least Robert is in a good mood today. He will finish feeding the old man this meal. Afterward Pa will be their worry again, until they can prevail upon Robert for some smidgen of help. Although they don't say they resent this or want it to be different, for a moment their silence suggests they may be thinking this. Robert answers, "No nursing home would take care of him this way. Sitting here with family—it's gotta mean something."

They all look at Henry. He appears ready to let out a moan, his eyes staring off at that vacant place. There's waffle in the middle of the moan, so he chews it, still staring, intent on not losing sight of whatever it is that no one but he can see.

"Wouldn't it be great," says Valley out of the blue, "if long-lost Margaret finally showed up—your mom, I mean. Maybe that'd get through to him—don't you think? What if she walked in and sat down at the table and said, 'Henry, here I am.' He'd pay attention then, I'll bet."

Robert closes his eyes briefly, shaking his head.

Gabe shifts her weight. She looks at the girl, saying, "Where do you come *up* with this stuff, Valley? What're you thinking? That he's Snow White—you think she could wake him up with a kiss?"

"You have got to be the world's *ditziest* broad," Robert adds.

"What do you mean?" Valley is hurt. She was only trying to build on the good feelings.

"Don't even start in," Robert says. "You don't have the fucking slightest idea how it was for him. He had to get a *factory* job after he married her and he had to *buy* her things, and they had to have neighborhood *parties*, and went to see her *parents* and all *their* social crowd. He hated all that stuff. That's what she'd want *now*, if she came back. That's what she wanted when she left here. She's probably someplace getting ready for a dinner party right now, probably found somebody could give her a crystal chandelier."

"You make her sound awful."

"No, she wasn't awful, that's not what I'm saying. She thought she could do better than my old man, that's all."

"You don't know that's true," Gabe puts in, thinking of the photo Shub has shown her, the worlds of possibility that no one has considered. "Neither one of us knows what she was really like. Probably she's not even alive. She must be dead or something. Even Grandma Farleigh never heard from her, never knew *what* happened."

"Never *told* us what happened. It's not like she was the old man's best friend exactly, or ours either. Grannie didn't want anything to do with *me*, remember. Now *she*—she was awful." Robert tossed the fork down onto his plate with a clatter.

They waited for him to pick it up.

"Looking back, I'm not even sorry for what happened. I used to fantasize how wonderful it would be if she'd stayed here with us, or if we'd all stayed downstate. But that's a crock. For kids. Just like talking about her walking in through the door, how wonderful that would be. Jesus, Valley, I gave that stuff up when I was about twelve. How old *are* you?"

"You were just talking about her last night, Robert."

He closes his eyes, taping some inner fracture back in place so he can sit up straighter. When he opens them again, he looks at Gabrielle, not Valley. "I never *told* you about Silver Beach, did I? That was one story I never told you, all them stories I told you over and over—remember, upstairs, Gabe? Never told you *that* one."

"What's Silver Beach?"

"You remember the place—remember going there? You were little, only three or four, I think, and I was maybe nine. They had a big merry-go-round? And these little boats you really loved. They went round in real water and you could ring a bell. Remember?"

"Yeah. I do remember that. Cotton candy. Getting stuck at the top on the Ferris wheel." Begging Robert to stop rocking the thing, please, *please* stop rocking—but she doesn't mention this.

Robert laughs. It's coming back to him now. "A really great old place," he says, "and we went down there a lot, a lot of people did on the weekend, and you could walk out on the pier to the lighthouse. There'd be people fishing and people walking, and you'd see folks you knew, the whole town was out, and we'd talk to 'em. Well, our old lady would talk to 'em anyway. On a nice day the wind would blow in and Lake Michigan made these big, choppy waves. Sometimes they'd splash hard on the pilings and you'd get sprayed and everybody'd run away, laughing—you know, having a *good* time."

As he talks, Robert makes a gesture with his hands to show the waves smashing against the pier, water arching up, and Gabe can see and smell the silvery spray, hear the sucking pound of it.

"This one day, all four of us, the whole family, were walking on the pier. Walking out to the lighthouse, other people walking back on the other side, and I see this guy coming. He came over to the apartment when the old man was at work, this guy who smelled like aftershave. I'm thinking Ma is gonna *say* something to him. Only I get all nervous, you know—like maybe I know something I shouldn't, or maybe I think something is gonna happen. Or maybe I pick this up from the old lady because I'm holding her hand and she's got it real tight, like *this*," he says, grabbing Gabe's hand and squeezing it hard.

"I look up at her, scared. I don't know *why* I'm scared, just trying to guess what to do. And she's looking straight ahead, she's just smiling with her mouth in her best *Sunday* face. Walking along like nothing's happening, until I start thinking maybe *I'm* wrong. Maybe it's a different guy just *looks* like him. So I look real *hard* at him, and I look back at the old lady. And then I see the old man. He stares at me and then at Ma. He looks like I've answered some question and I didn't even know what it was! Back then, I didn't know what the fucking question *was*! But he keeps on walking too. Neither of them says a thing and the other guy doesn't speak. He just walks by in his fancy coat and tie. Doesn't so much as look at us—*you*, Gabe, you were busy watching the gulls!"

"You think the guy you saw was the one your mother was having an affair with?"

Robert raises an eyebrow at Valley in answer.

"You think *Pa* knew then?" asks Gabe.

He closes his eyes and shrugs. "It was after that when he came home from work and caught them that time," Robert says, opening his eyes to meet Gabe's stare. "I think maybe I gave them away." He gives one breathy laugh, a silent scoffing sound. "Pa sure wouldn't have known it from the old *lady's* face, she was *that* good."

Valley reaches out to touch him. "Oh, Robert, you can't blame yourself. That was between your parents!"

"I'm not *blaming* myself," he says, jerking his arm away. "*She's* the one, had us right there, Gabe and me right there in the house with her, fucking her boyfriend, right in the house! And what about when she left? Left Gabe and me too, didn't want *any* of us. If I was the old man, I'd a done the same thing, beat the shit out of the guy. Beat *her* too—the old man let her off too light, that's *his* whole problem."

He closes his eyes again, like something's come loose, some worthless lacing that keeps coming untied. He shakes his head, picking up the fork to stab another piece of waffle, stabbing two, three, four bites.

"He's better off without her—we all are. Here, open up, open *up!*" he demands and shoves a too large bite into the old man's mouth.

Watching Pa chew, a blob of jam hanging in suspension from his bottom lip, Gabe holds her breath. She feels her mouth moving to help him masticate.

Robert's teeth meet in a line. His eyes are stones. When his shoulder jerks back, Gabe flinches, expecting him to cuff Pa or throw something, but it's an unintended movement, just tension.

"Jesus *Christ,*" Robert mutters suddenly, glancing at his watch, and tosses the fork down to his plate, metal clinking against glass. "It's almost noon—I gotta get to work, *you* finish this," he says, slamming down the hall, and is gone.

June 18, 1984
Five Corners, Michigan

Bad dreams. Heavy legs. Had this dream a lot after Robert came home. I woke up last night sure that he and Valley slept upstairs, afraid they might hear me the way I sometimes heard them. Staring into the dark, panting through my mouth, it slowly came back to me—they're gone.

I should get myself a dog—a big one to sleep on my bed. A dog would help me figure out the difference between imagined fears and real threats. Dogs only growl at real things usually. I'd like to wake up and hear his tail thumping louder than the thumping in my chest, or to hear him rumbling if something real ever endangers me.

I know Kate would notice how willingly I'd trust the dog to know what is real and what isn't. How I automatically assume that whatever's inside me can't be real. Maybe Kate's right about this being a false distinction. Feelings don't come out of a vacuum.

When I think about what I was feeling then, I can't remember rage—I mean, something close to rage shakes me now sometimes, but not back then. There was too much fear. I felt fear all the time. And I felt fear last night, waking up. What was chasing me? My own emotions? I know I must have felt some anger back then. But I couldn't let it show, not the way Robert could. Maybe to Valley a little—but not really rage. I couldn't have spared the energy for something so large. I was using all mine up, trying to discern what was real. Not knowing what was dangerous, thinking everything was dangerous.

Kate says females sometimes delegate violent feelings to the men in their lives, empowering them to act out the whole family's anger—I suppose she thinks I might have done this. But how can I know for sure? I have to stop being afraid of what I see, what I feel.

June, 1974

"You have the old man's will. It's *your* place," Valley says, as she lifts her chin to look down her nose at Gabe, the smoke making her squint. Artfully, she cups her chin in the curve of her hand, one finger stretching up to her eye in a graceful assertion that on anyone else would look contrived. It looks contrived on Valley too, but somehow natural because she never pretends to do anything but pose. Her little finger lifts up to touch her lip as she speaks. "I wouldn't put up with his shit for a minute if I were you."

She's talking about the argument Gabe has just had with Robert about tax money coming due. He doesn't have time for that now. He has left the cabin in a huff, claiming pressure at work though it is eight o'clock at night. Valley's response had been to light up a joint.

Gabe says, "What are you talking about? You put up with his shit all the time."

"But you don't *have* to. You're not married to him."

"Oh, and that groupie wedding, that five-minute swearing in, that's something sacred, is it? That means you've got to let him knock you around because you're man and wife."

"He doesn't knock me around!"

"The hell he doesn't."

"He never! I wouldn't stay with a man who did that. I left Jack, remember, when he started in thinking he could. I'm outa here, he starts in with *that*!" Valley rolls her head around on her neck, stretching, then lolls it back on her shoulder and sighs, shutting her eyes. She opens them again, head still back, looking at Gabe with eyes hooded. "I'm outa here," she repeats, taking a deep drag.

She offers the toke, but Gabe says no, shaking her head, putting her lips together in a hard knot. On the wrist that Valley holds out is a blotchy blue and yellow ring, as if someone had tied something too tightly around it. There have been other bruises, usually explained away or, more often, ignored.

Valley lies back, sinking into the pillow she's brought downstairs, lifting her arms over her head. "I am going, going, *gone!*" she says in a singsong, playing with words, making them trill and fly, then plunging into the deepest tone she can reach. "Gone!" she says again, trying to make it sound like brass struck with a padded hammer. "Gone!" she laughs.

June 23, 1984
Five Corners, Michigan

Going through boxes, looking for clues. Easier than tearing out words these days. A door feels shut. Locked. I should send Kate my thesis—she might find it interesting. I felt like I was being so radical, but by today's standards, it's tame. Compassionate even.

I think Kate's right about Hemingway being my saving grace in those days. Keeping my nose to the grindstone—whirring rock close to my face—a needed distraction. I was naming things I saw in my brother—paragraph by orderly paragraph—and what a relief that must have been from the chaos of living with the real thing. Valley said I could see myself in Hemingway—that's why I hated him. I think it was really Robert I saw, though we all three did share a particular article of faith—that there is no meaning and things will go wrong and people will suffer for their stupidity.

Valley used to say she couldn't be so certain. Don't good things keep sneaking up on a person from out of nowhere? she'd ask me, shrugging her shoulders. I knew she meant like we had surprised each other, becoming friends. By then, I did feel like her friend.

I found a parchment in the box. A legend on the Chippewa left unfinished. She'd smudged the border, these little moccasin prints she drew with brown ink. The finished one is hanging on the wall at Wild Kingdom next to a tiny model of when Lake Nekoagon was a summer gathering place for the people she learned had called themselves Anishinaabeg. I can still hear her say this.

On days when I didn't have to go into the store, Valley and I would both work in the cabin, she upstairs, writing out her parchments, me downstairs, close to Pa. If he slept in the afternoon, we might go for a walk up the hill, or if he were restless she might bake something to fill the cabin with good smells—these carrot muffins I got really fond of. Or zucchini bread. Something Robert wouldn't eat. Just for us.

People don't believe a woman would lie like that about the guy who's knocking her around, but she was protecting herself as much as she was him. What are you admitting when the man you love hits you? That you're not as valuable in his eyes as he is in yours? That you've screwed up, some-how? There's this element of trust in the wifely role. Valley wanted that. Part of me wanted it for her, wanted her to have a feeling of safety, the same feeling that makes me want to get a dog. We want trust in the house. When you're a wife, or a big, good dog, and your master gives you a kick, it's because you were lying in the wrong spot on the rug—no need to talk about it. Just move and hope for the best.

I get so mad at Valley for not trusting me, and that's stupid—of course she didn't tell me everything. I'd already been right about Robert's romantic sweetness and his vegetarianism. She was damned if she was going to let me act told-you-so about something else. She saw it coming, Sid's edging Robert out. Of course she hedged her bets—it was all she could do, the best she could manage. It's no good believing in evil—not in your own home.

I found a photograph I'll send Kate—the only one I have of all three of us, taken on Shub's porch. Valley would tell you I'm the one who looks like a lumberjack. Robert is the photogenic one—with his arm around Valley. Looking at us from this distance, I can see why people suspected me. I look tense and miserable, the way you might look if you were guilty.

JUNE, 1974

"I don't know why he called you, Gabe. I could have gotten a ride."

It's after six and Gabe has shown up at Wild Kingdom to pick up Valley, and has come inside the cave building to find her standing in front of the beaver grotto. It is one of the last to be finished. Valley wants to rearrange the scene to include three new specimens, young ones that Belle Nichols has finished stuffing.

Valley can't bear to touch the bodies, which are more like dry little furry logs, she tells Gabe, shuddering, reaching out her hand to show her the beavers in a cardboard box. Then she goes back to squinting through the glass window, trying to imagine where she wants them.

It isn't working, she complains, she's got to see it. She needs August Santee, she's going to go look for him. When Gabe protests, she calls back over her shoulder, "You didn't even need to come, you should have *checked* with me first."

Gabe is pacing in the hallway, considering heading back without Valley, when August walks in with her, his posture straight and formal as he listens to her instructions. He nods in greeting to Gabe, then crouches to enter the scene through a low door, pulling the box of three beaver young with him, and places them as Valley motions with her hands: Two go close to the mother at the water's edge, next to the fallen birch, and one joins the father in the water, which is actually blue-painted plaster. This last beaver's position is giving Valley the most trouble.

"I'm trying to picture the way he'll look," she calls to August through the glass.

"The plaster can come up in little waves on the side. I can paint them so they really look real," August answers in a muffled voice. He cups his hands around the third small body as he shows her, "Like this."

She nods and Gabe watches their eyes meet. Their gaze is held longer than what is strictly called for to mark agreement and, when Valley looks down, she seems flustered. She pushes her hair back behind her ear, raising her arm, which is soft white underneath. When she looks at August again, she's smiling.

"That'll work fine," she says. "Don't you think so?" she adds as she looks at Gabe, wanting her to approve.

"I guess so," Gabe answers. She sounds as insincere as she feels, like a traitor somehow, though why, she doesn't have the chance to put in to words for herself, interrupted by loud voices coming down the hall.

Sid and Robert barrel past, on their way to Sid's office on the other side of the Quonset hut. "Look, it's shortsighted as hell to skimp on this," Robert is saying to Sid's back. "That train is going to make us a lot of money, a *lot* of money. You ever know a kid could pass one up?" he demands.

They can't make out what Sid answers, though the gist is clear from his tone. He sounds angry and out of patience.

August doesn't seem curious to know more about it. "I gotta go," he says after crawling out of the grotto, and disappears back down the hall.

Gabe asks, "You ready to head home now?" as if Valley hadn't already made herself clear.

Valley is looking down the hall after August, then turns her head to listen to the argument in the other direction.

A door slams and Robert comes striding back to them. "He finally listened to reason, the old skinflint. I gotta truck on down to Escanaba for a special part. You go on home with Gabe now, Valley."

She answers, "I was planning to stay *late*, Robert. I wish you'd *check* first before you go around ordering my life for me. I wanna stay and finish this *grotto*, I'm not gonna have another chance before the opening."

"Well, how you gonna get home? You ever think two jumps ahead? Or is it always just whatever comes to mind? I had Gabe come all the way out for you. The old man's probably baking out in the car right now."

"That's what I *mean*," Valley says, sticking out her chin at him. "First you just take my car like I couldn't possibly have any use for it, and then you plan my day for me. Did I just say my *day*? My whole life—without even talking to me first."

Robert puts his lips together. He gets red in the face, looking around as if searching for something he's misplaced. "Jesus Christ," he says, "like I don't have enough on my mind."

He spots the cardboard box inside the grotto. "Now what the hell is *that*?" he demands, striding over to the glass front. One of the baby beavers appears to be walking on water.

"That's what I was just *telling* you," says Valley, coming closer. "August has to add some more plaster. He's gonna put the baby beaver *in* the water."

"Like hell he is, not this way. Looks like amateur-city. And not anytime soon. I gotta few other things for him, before he can get around to *this*, and then—Jesus Christ, he has got this all wrong, all wrong. I have to watch everything Santee *does*!" He crawls inside and begins tossing the bodies back in the box, more roughly than he needs to. Then he shoves the box back out.

"He's always bitin' off more than he can chew when he's already up to his neck in plenty of stuff," Robert says, standing up and holding the box in one arm. "And don't you be battin' your eyelashes at him either," he says, thumping her on the chest with his middle finger. "You think I don't know how you operate?"

"Who put *you* in charge, anyway? Belle gave these to *me* to do, not you, and Sid says if I want August to—"

Gabrielle swings her arms out, letting them drop again. "Look, you two, why don't I just head on back—"

"You stay put!" says Robert, but he doesn't take his eyes off Valley and his voice is loud. He grabs one of the beavers. "You want to *do* this, then you do it," he says, shoving the body at her. Her hand curls back, trying to avoid contact with the fur, but he grabs Valley's hand, pulling it to him. "Here," he says, cramming the furry body into the crook of her elbow, sliding it up to her neck. "You love the little animals so much, here, *do* it!"

His eyes are riveted on her face, his teeth meeting perfectly as he presses the dead pelt against her bare arms. "Make him swim," he says in baby talk, "the sweet little baby beaver. Come on, *swim!*" he yells, bobbing it up and down, bumping it against her. "Isn't that what you want? Isn't it? *Answer* me."

Gabrielle grabs his arm, says, "Robert, that's enough!" and immediately he flings the body back into the box, smashes it down, as if the touch of it and of Gabe's hand repulses him. He shoves Valley away with his other hand.

"Do what you want," he says to her. "Do whatever the fuck you *want*," and he stomps off past Gabe without so much as looking at her.

Valley brushes her arms off, her cheeks, underneath her neck, squirming and groaning with a quiet, forceful breath. Gabe brushes her too, picking off dark, long hairs. "He probably ruined that one," Valley says, looking down at the creature in the box fearfully, as if it might jump out at her.

"That was a mean thing to do to you," says Gabe, trying to make eye contact, wanting to convince her, but Valley is too overwhelmed to hear. She keeps brushing herself off, backs away from the box, stumbling toward the door.

"Come on," Gabe says then, as if leaving were her idea, catching up with Valley and cupping her elbow in one hand. She steers the girl out to the waiting truck.

They ride in silence for the twenty minutes it takes to reach Lake Nekoagon. Gabe's attempts at talk have fallen flat, awkward with Pa squeezed in between them. She resorts to imagining conversations she will have with Robert later, talk that will set the record straight; she will tell him just what she thinks of him. The girl had compromised her deepest feelings, working on this project for him. It wouldn't kill him to be nice to her.

Valley wipes her face with the back of her hand, trying to get herself together again. They are almost home when she pipes, out of the blue, "So how is Ernie?"

"Ernie?"

"You know. Ernest. Hemingway. Who'd you think!"

"Oh. Oh. He's okay, I guess."

"Okay? Don't you have to give a presentation pretty soon? Aren't you getting nervous about it, talking in front of all those college people?"

"Thanks for reminding me. I wouldn't want to be lax, not worrying myself sick about it every minute. I was thinking about you, Valley."

"Oh. Sorry. Hey, I'm all right. But you gotta know, I'm really interested in what you're doing. I *am*. I've been so busy with the opening, I'm sorry. I'll bet your paper's really good. Is it ready for me to read yet?"

"Not quite. But I want you to. I've got a little time yet."

"Well, not much."

"So do you think Robert went to Escanaba?"

"I dunno. I don't care."

"Yeah—"

"I don't. I have really had it with his temper tantrums. It's just as well he goes off somewhere else to have them. I think he's on something. He says he's not, but he is. You watch him."

"He's gonna get busted again, he starts in with that stuff."

"Yeah. Probably. He'll miss going to see Dirty Harry or something and that'll be the end." Dirty Harry is Robert's name for Harold Rosenthal, his parole officer. "He won't listen to anybody. Some people have to learn everything the hard way, I guess. No skin off my nose."

"No?"

"Like I said, I am outa here. Did you think I was just stoned, saying that? I'm just waitin' for my ticket is all. August Santee has his next job all lined up in Indiana, an auto dealer who wants a big gorilla out front in the parking lot. They'll put this car in the palm of the gorilla's hand, isn't that a hoot? You know, you'd be surprised the demand there is for chicken wire and plaster sculptures, a lot of money to be made."

"So how'd you get to know so much?"

"Well, I have to work with the guy, no matter what Robert says. He's not so bad, really. He has a nice smile."

"I noticed."

"Sid really likes him. He has this great manner about him, you know, so serious, and then he bowls you over with that grin. You have noticed—he's cute, isn't he? I mean, really, Robert has cut his own throat, if you want to know the truth. He makes Sid out to be a lot worse than he really is. After all, Sid's gotta get his money out of the place, he can't just give it away. But Robert gets a burr up his butt and that's it! Always right and righteous about everything. And *mean* too. He doesn't have to be so *mean*."

They turn onto the cabin road and Gabe parks the truck, but Valley isn't ready to get out yet. "I have to be on the q.t.," she says to Gabe, but looking at her fingers, studying them. "I have a lot to figure out."

Gabe doesn't know what to answer. She doesn't want to think about what Valley is saying.

The girl sees this but, surer of herself, feels generous. "You worry about your Ernie," she says, reaching out to touch Gabe's wrist. "It's not that far off, your leaving for school, you know. I'd be scared sick, if I were you."

"Thanks a lot. I'll try to remember. Look. Valley, you want to come with? To Fond du Lac?"

"Nah, I'm not leaving my little orange Bug behind. She's all I've got." She looks out the window, studying the trees for several moments, and then she confides to Gabe, as if she's telling herself. "He'll be all sweet when he comes back, but it's not gonna be the same this time. I'll stay until you get back, Gabe, so you won't have to worry about the old man. But it's not gonna be the same."

Gabe looks up to the rearview mirror, then glances at her father in the seat next to her. He is staring out past Valley's shoulder. She wishes, she wishes he'd say something.

July 7, 1984
Five Corners, Michigan

I found Valley's clippings of Wild Kingdom's grand opening. Can't believe how I burst into tears, seeing the picture of her standing with Sid and Belle outside the man-made cave. Valley pointing to the legend she's written explaining the rocks.

Robert's nemesis is there in the picture too. I remember now. At the time I tried to tune that rivalry out. August Santee.

All week I've been trying to remember his name. I've dreamed about him and his smile—completely disarming—maybe I had a crush on him. The day of the picture, Valley complained Robert couldn't be in the photo because he was off seeing to some business. But later Robert twisted this around into some kind of plot against him. Robert and Valley revised August, good or evil, depending on what was needed on any given day. He must have been confused by all our free-falling emotion. I never saw him after that Fourth of July. I wonder if he ever built that gorilla.

Sid had his grand opening, though the project was unfinished. Everyone was there. Natty Raison and his boss, the guy in charge of the state park, the county commissioner, the state representative, the sheriff, even the president of Michigan National who financed construction with land as collateral. Shub and I were the only ones who found it all too much— the grandstand set up outside, the red, white, and blue bunting, Nixon's portrait between George Washington and Abraham Lincoln. I'd brought Pa in a wheelchair and pointed him toward the President, thinking Pa's expression right for once. There were speeches, band music, carnival rides (to make up for the train's not being ready yet). Shub won a nail clipper in a powder-blue zippered case, pitching baseballs. I traded him for the orange plastic dinosaur I'd won throwing hoops on bottles.

In a spare moment Valley confided that Robert was mad and not going to show. His playing hooky for the big occasion seemed typical. Robert would make the most of any conflict, would make himself out the wronged one somehow. None of this is in the clippings or was even in my head at the time. The air was too full of all-American spirit. You'd have thought the Fourth of July commemorated moneymaking, with everybody doing their patriotic best. Between booms and cracks of bursting fireworks, you could hear the ring of Sid's cash registers.

WILD KINGDOM'S GRAND OPENING IS GRAND, one clipping reports. Sid was the KING OF THE KINGDOM, says another. But my favorite story is the one from *The Clearwater Gazette*, the one I'll send to Kate. The picture of Sid's ribbon-cutting is so clearly small potatoes, compared to the pageful of reader responses to an earlier story on doe season.

Every year the old debate with the Fish & Wildlife Department heats up the letters section. I remember the winter kill that year had been especially bad, and whenever that many deer starve, it's always fuel for the state biologists to argue for thinning the herd with a doe season. Handled scientifically, this will prevent the deer population from outstripping winter forage. Judging from the letters in response, though, doe season is no matter for science—this is war and holy and—God knows—only barbarians go around killing females.

Last November you could have read the same arguments in the same paper, probably from the same families. Nothing has changed, except back in 1973 doe season opponents had the example of a war on their side. If Americans went along with such a plan, next the government would be wanting our wives and daughters to get drafted and go off to Vietnam and come home in body bags. Doe season always seemed part of a Communist conspiracy to some folks. And just like people here understood that their sons and husbands had to go off to be right-gendered cannon fodder in southeast Asia, so everybody in Copper County knows that the female of the species has to be protected.

Likewise, they know who to blame if the deer kill gets worse or a war goes sour or a president gets run out of office—all of it linked to the same loss of plain old common sense, pushed right out of people's heads by biologists and peaceniks and book learning. Only a bookish person like me would be deluded into thinking it was wrong to send Robert off to get shot at, while I was let off the hook.

So I was supposed to be grateful. Only when was I let off the hook? How have we females been spared? The does starve. Women carry home the body bags. I've been piecing my life back together for years now. How have we been spared?

JULY, 1974

Valley is tired, having finished the last of the Small Mammal legends today. Now there are only a few birds to do, the kingfisher and some of the raptors.

Gabe wonders about Valley's beavers, but doesn't bring it up, because Robert has gone out again and Valley says she's just glad to sit on the porch and stare at the lowering sun. This is all that is needed to keep Henry company, and it means both of them will be out of Gabe's hair.

Gabrielle wants to concentrate on finishing the presentation, which, on Valley's advice, she's calling "On Love and Hate and Hemingway." She's marked it up to a fare-thee-well, and now she rolls the third sheet of paper in and immediately, so as not to lose momentum, begins pounding away:

Many critics give an explanation of war novels of this period that would apply equally well to Hemingway's writing over several decades. One author says there is small place for love in such novels because it creates an oblivion, improper for a man in war whose existence depends on preserving a tight hold over himself. This "tight hold" seems evident everywhere in Hemingway's thinking and writing. It fits well with the writer's own writing motto: Not too damn much.

Gabe pauses a moment, considering whether there isn't another way to express what she wants without using a personal pronoun, but then decides it is precisely the personal she wants to use, she will dare to use—the reader expressing her ideas, nothing more than that, nothing wrong with that, and she continues:

I describe his sense of superiority as "desperate" because of what others have commented on, a self-confidence born of anxiety. To admit that one is less than superior or merely on a par with the rest of humanity can be terrifying. Tremendous energy can be spent denying it—whole novels can be written.

Hemingway's strongest denial of his vulnerability can be seen in his characters. Even when his male protagonists face life's meaninglessness—and to Hemingway life is above all meaningless—they suffer but never concede. Better to hitch up their pants, jut out their jaw at the Being who seems to delight in their misery, and respond with a jaded "What the hell" before fading into gray or dying at the end.

Valley has tiptoed in, headed for the refrigerator and another glass of wine. "Can I get you anything?" she whispers when Gabe pauses.

Gabe shakes her head furiously, not wanting to break the thread of her thought and starts typing again, hitting the keys, making the paper snap. This is where Valley says Gabe has hit a nail on the head. About an earlier draft, Valley reported feeling the same way, and her voice had sounded girlish, enlivened by the gossipy shock of Gabe's frankness:

And if there really are women who are such great ninnies as Lady Brett Ashley or Catherine Barkley, it is certainly a mystery why any writer of Hemingway's caliber would think them worthy of a central place in a novel. They might be acceptable in a parody, such as his famous one of Anderson. But it comes close to an embarrassment at times to discover that Hemingway's depictions of male relationships with women, which seem arrested at the preadolescent stage of life, are a part of Hemingway's writing about which he is most nearly serious—perhaps even approaching the seriousness of bullfighting or trout fishing.

Gabe pauses, smiling a little at this jab, not wanting to take so much pleasure in the very combativeness she is criticizing in him. Writing this hard feels good, she discovers, like throwing a left hook. She is at the spot where she wants that quote about his art, the place where he takes himself the most seriously. It's in *Death in the*

Afternoon. Damn, she thinks, fumbling through her stacks of books, looking for the index card. She has it marked.

"What was that?" Valley asks, coming in from the porch again, glass in hand. She looks a little frightened, staring off outside where she's heard something.

"What was what?" Gabe echoes her question, preoccupied.

"That sound. There it is again. Do you hear it?"

"Yeah, rifle fire. Somebody must be practicing."

"No. No. Not practice. It's Robert I think."

"Robert? Well, maybe he's practicing then," she answers glibly, ignoring the way her stomach takes a dip. She is wanting to finish this section, damn it all.

Valley comes close, sets her glass down, puts her hand on Gabe's arm and grips it. "You've got to come with me," Valley says. "I know, I know you're in the middle of this paper and I really want you to finish, but I mean it, I've got to go find him—J. Gordon, I'm afraid he'll hurt J. Gordon."

"What do you mean? It's not even season."

"I know. It doesn't matter though! Robert's been teasing me about him. He took a rifle tonight. Yes, in the car earlier, I just didn't know where he was going, I didn't want to think about it." She gets more breathless as she speaks.

Gabe wills the girl's eyes to hold contact, touches her arm, lowers her voice to calm her. "There's no reason for him to do something stupid like that. Why would he hunt out of season, or for that matter risk breaking parole over something so stupid? He knows how you feel about that deer."

"That's why," Valley says, and her voice takes another bound, panting. "You said it just then. He wants to hurt me."

Finally their eyes meet, and Gabe knows this is true, knows an insane thing for its logic. Valley goes on, "He thinks Sid is going to fire him and I dunno, it might be true, and he's feeling sorry for himself and he's really acting crazy, Gabe—I didn't want to tell you, he's acting really crazy."

"Come on," Gabe says. "You've convinced me. Let's go find him, put your jacket on."

"Well—wait, what about Henry?"

They stop and look at Pa for a moment, who is staring off at the lake, still about to break into a howl.

"We'll put him inside. What can happen to him? He hardly even twitches. If he gets hungry, maybe he'll get up and help himself for a change. Here, help me get him up so we can set him in the living room. We can close the door at least, he'll be safe enough."

Valley struggles to put her jacket on, bouncing in Gabe's truck as she tells how Robert had looked over in the direction of the deeryard when they were coming down from Sid's place. They'd seen J. Gordon in that area before, plenty of times.

"J. never was overly smart. He's probably right where Robert will look first," Gabe says, and turns north, toward the same stretch of road. Up from the lake, where the cedar begins the long climb that curves round in a drop-off to the north of the cabin, they spot the orange VW pulled over to the side of the road.

"I told you," Valley says, slamming her door.

"It doesn't mean anything," Gabe says, setting out. "He could be practicing. What the hell are you so guilty about?"

Valley has trouble keeping up with her. "I'm not *guilty*, what do you mean by that, Gabe? I haven't done anything wrong. You can be just like him, do you know that? You can be just as *mean!*"

"Shut up, will you. How are we going to find anything in this woods, with you scaring everything off? Just shut up."

They walk for several minutes, their strides long and driven, nothing but the sound of pant legs rubbing together in a swishing rhythm and the huff of their breathing, here and there the loud snap of a twig underfoot or the smack of a branch flung back.

"He's been through here," Gabe says at one point, picking up an empty shell and putting it to her nose. "Somebody's been through here," and they pick up the pace, breathing louder, heading for the deeryard.

"Will the deer be up here this time of year?" Valley asks after several more minutes of walking, her voice chuffing.

"I don't know," Gabe answers. "I honestly don't know," and she thinks how Pa would certainly have known and maybe had taught Robert. He'd spent a lot more time with Robert in the woods. Robert had the advantage.

They've been following the trickle of the stream and now they can hear a louder rushing of water, Brushy Creek, thirty feet down, cutting through the sandstone ravine on its way to the cabin's peninsula.

"The footbridge," Gabe says. The moment she says it, it seems impossible the thing could have left her consciousness for a moment.

It spreads out in front of them, formidable, unavoidable, a good twenty feet across the ravine. The cable is slung low, like the belly of some beast, the air visible between its wooden ribs, the slats. The handrail on one side looks rickety and ends with that makeshift rope.

Valley's already started. "Oh no, *god*, I forgot about this thing, I can't go across that, Gabe. What am I gonna *do*, what'll I *do* if I—"

"Just shut up, you don't have to do anything." Gabe reaches out and shakes the handrail, checking it. She half-turns, grabbing Valley's arm. "Keep quiet is all." She raises her voice, calling: "*Roberrrt!* Are you there? Robert! It's me, Gabe! Where are you?"

They stand and listen, but there is only the sound of water rushing far below them. After a moment, Gabe says she is going across and Valley should just stay put.

Gabe places her foot out on the first step of the bridge and tests it, telling herself this is easy. She's not loaded down with a gun on her shoulder this time. There's no ice. She's done this lots of times. Skipping over nightmares, she thinks only about last deer season and the moment she sprang off the thing, elated, victorious.

She takes another step and remembers the rhythm, reminding herself to ignore how the bridge moves. And don't, definitely don't, think about the place where the railing ends and the rope begins. Keep stepping. Step, then pause—step again.

She reaches the place where the bridge sinks lowest, swing deepening, where it answers her footfall like a living thing would. She hears Valley beginning to cry behind her, a nervous, exhausted kind of crying.

"I can't stand to *watch*—"

Gabe pauses to look behind her, holding onto the end of the wood railing with her right hand, her left out for balance. She knows instantly that stopping is a mistake, all wrong. "Never mind," she calls back to Valley. "It's okay." Her voice gives lie to this, words plummeting, heavy as rock. Every one of her cells feels aware of its individual weight and together they testify to the implausibility of being suspended midair. A breeze, wet from the creek below, pushes against her, threatening her balance.

"I'm all right," she calls back. From some biological place she finds the will to step out again and feels the sway underfoot. She watches her feet. She pauses, steps again, transitioning to the rope, then feels a sudden jolt behind her. Bending her knees to ride the responding undulation, she grabs the clothesline with both hands, then grapples to reach back for the wood railing.

She turns to look and there is Robert. Silent, coming out of nowhere, he has jumped onto the footbridge, six arm's lengths behind her. He revels in his weight. In one hand, he holds the Mauser out over the chasm, balancing with the other hand, showing off. His expression taunts her, and so does the way he stands with shoulders back. He can fly if he wants to.

He points his rifle at Valley, who is cowering near the white pine, and he makes an exploding noise with his mouth. He pretends to feel a kickback from the force of it and jars the bridge again, laughing when Valley screams, "*Gabe!*"

Gabe can see he's both contemptuous and pleased by Valley's fear. He turns around toward Gabe then, looking for more.

Gabe's body fronts the railing and she still grips it with two hands. Her face is turned toward him, enough for him to appreciate that her breath's been knocked away. He leans forward, arms still out, not touching the handrail, searching for the right inflection in his voice. It comes out a blasé drawl, stretching for the limits of her terror. "And just what the hell are *you* supposed to be doing?" he asks, eyebrows up.

"Looking for you," Gabe answers over her shoulder, careful not to vibrate the air too much, and to keep her head balanced on top of her spine. An about-face will mean letting go with her right hand before she can fully turn around. She takes tiny steps, feeling her way until she has to straighten, hoping one hand is enough.

Robert is saying, "Just what the hell is the matter with you two? Can't a guy just come up here for a little recreation?"

"No, Robert. He can't." Gabe is surprised by how loudly, how quickly she says this, standing, not crouching. No, he can't, he can't, he can't keep on doing this, she thinks, but the railing moves then, and she stiffens.

Beneath her, the water gushes on and on, ranting. She has to get to Valley. She calls out, announcing, "I'm coming back now."

Her teeth clench; she keeps her head steady. Even her thoughts are a careful monotone. Look where you want to go, Gabrielle. There, that ground beyond Robert, not at him, not at your feet, don't look at your feet, not the air, don't look at the falling-away space between those slats—shut it out.

Robert has turned away to talk to Valley, but Gabe tries not to listen or to notice he's still blocking her way. "There's no need for you to come up here and baby-sit me," he is saying. "What did you *think* you'd do anyway? Take my gun away? Make me come home? *Slap* me? Ohhh! I'm gonna *cry*, I'm gonna *cry*," he mocks Valley. Lifting his arms while the rifle dangles, he screws his fists into his eyes, the corners of his mouth turned down, bottom lip pushed out, wailing and making the bridge sway, "Boohoohoohoo. . . ."

Gabrielle steps, pauses, steps again, almost reaching him.

"*Boo!*" he ends, swerving toward Gabe. He jars the bridge deliberately.

"Robert!" Gabe hears Valley scream. Underneath Gabe's feet, the slats on the cables twist. She's on an airplane wing, banking into the ravine. It dips farther, too far. Her right foot slides off into air, her left foot sliding.

She sinks onto her haunches, extending her foot, holding the railing that seems ready to snap. But it holds. The bridge straightens.

She pulls her leg back in, squatting on the swaying motion. Beneath her, the sound of water has become a throbbing roar. "You *ass*hole," she breathes.

"Just stand up," Robert says, but his voice gives away that he is scared, like when they were kids. He's gone too far and he knows it. "You're okay," he says offhandedly, but he steps back off the bridge to make way for her.

She straightens up, knees shaking. The railing moves but she places her left foot forward, steps once. She waits a moment for runaway heart, lungs that won't deflate. Again. She blows with her mouth. She steps. Once more. Again.

Finally across, she jumps two-footed to the bank, throwing herself at Robert's chest, both arms hammering. "Don't you *ever* do something like that! I could be dead now! You asshole! I could be dead." She thumps him with both forearms, throwing her whole weight into it, *ever, dead, asshole.*

He is glad for the blows. Payback. Hit me, he says with his eyes, hit me, harder.

"Don't you ever, *ever*—" she says, slapping him some more, furious she can never make it better this way, she can't hurt him, it can never be equal between them—and who is she kidding, playing this ridiculous, childish game—and she can't stop herself.

He is saying, "I didn't *mean* to," and his arms are open, embracing the blows. "Look, I didn't *mean* anything—"

"What is that? Your life *story*? Just what *did* you mean, if you didn't mean to scare the hell out of me? What makes you think it's all right you didn't happen to *kill* me? Because you didn't mean anything by it? What *does* mean anything? What *else* do I have to go by?"

From the safety of the white pine, Valley calls, "Gabe, are you all right?"

"And what about your pointing the rifle at Valley—are you *crazy*? What the fuck are you doing with it up here anyway? You can't touch a firearm or they'll lock you away again." Gabe blows out a breath, having trouble breathing, talking.

"I'm okay," she calls to Valley, who has fled to a more distant pine. Then wobbly, weak in the knees, Gabe sinks down and sits flat.

Robert watches her a moment before he reaches up to his shirt pocket to grab a cigarette. He lights up and exhales. There's agitation in his movements, a glittery flutter of his eyes. He's unsure of where to put his arms, crosses them in front of his chest, swings them free as he paces a few steps, then back. He glances over at Valley and takes another drag, flings the butt away from him, walks over to squash it with his foot. Leaning his weight against a beech tree, he twists and, with the Mauser he holds in his other hand, strikes the smooth silvery bark, once, twice, cracking metal against wood, thud, thud.

He stares off into the woods a moment, then comes back to squat down next to Gabe. Laying the rifle down on the ground, barrel pointed into the woods, he reaches out one hand as if to touch her, but lets it fall short, fingers touching the sandy ground between them. "Here, you take it," he says, pushing the rifle closer. "Just *take* it."

"Save it, will you?" Gabe cuts him off. "Don't make me puke." She means this. It's a possibility.

He's quiet and when he does touch her, the heaviness of his hand shakes a little. She is not so sickened she can't see the curve of his face and that beautiful mouth, the line down to his chin backlit by the sun of late afternoon.

Asshole, she thinks, and puts her face down into the dark of her elbow, waiting for the ground to stop moving.

It's crazy but she knows there's something she's been wanting, something she's been struggling for, something she already knows. Robert always wanted full control, somebody small enough—and if he owed anything, his creditor became an enemy, he'd make things up if he had to.

"I was just up here *practicing*," he says in a tone that doesn't even try hard to disguise his lie. "You didn't have to come up after me. Why did you do that? You guys shouldn't push me like that." He moves in closer. "Hey, come on." He presses the space next to her. She can feel the bulk of his body, the heat from it.

"I was just coming up here to remember being with the old man is all," he goes on. "Sometimes I get so sick—you know, looking at him, the way he is now, so different from what I want it to be. Everything's *wrong*." His whisper is harsh, insistent. He looks at Valley and the corner of his mouth twitches, holding back something, nearly giving way.

"Christ, what was I thinking, marrying a *kid* like that?" He tries smiling next and wants to laugh about Valley, wants to share a joke between the two of them, but Gabe doesn't smile.

"Don't you put it on *her*."

"Hey, I *love* that little girl," he says. "Why do you suppose she makes me so mad? You think I don't understand that? I know what my problem is. But you gotta believe me, I would never hurt either one of you, I swear to God."

Gabe, breathing more normally, meets his eyes. His arm weighs on her shoulder. She feels muscle against her cheek, the pressure of his weight held in check by the fulcrum of his elbow.

"Gabrielle?" calls Valley again, though she still keeps her distance.

"She's okay, honey, she's okay," Robert answers for Gabe, and then quietly, just between the two of them, asks, "You're feeling better now, aren't you?" In the crook of his arm, where he had always held her whenever he got too rough, he breathes, "Jesus Christ, I almost really fucked *up*."

His regret is warm in her face, the smell of his skin, familiar, entering her mouth, going down, spreading out through her lungs to fingers that still tingle. He is there in the breath she releases.

Slow-motion running, legs leaden, something nameless chasing her, and a crackling, sweeping noise, the sound of underbrush and running footfall behind her—

She sits up, eyes open. None of it real, she understands at once. The dark welcomes her into a hush that becomes more blue as she watches. She finds herself smiling, a fish returned underwater, her relief as instant.

She listens and the cabin is silent. Beyond her bedroom door, the kitchen is deep in darkness that blurs the edges of everything familiar. Outside, a fingernail of moon, a sliver of white, grows brighter.

She looks down at the luster of her palm, half-expecting to see her four fingers laid out in it, another part of the dream. Four fingers, the image of wholeness, the number four, but fingers bloody at the end, nipped off, and no pain to it, no feeling. Her fingers? Someone else's? And after that, the chase, no time to look more closely.

She won't be able to sleep now. She pushes back the sheets, sits up and puts her robe on, goes to the kitchen, pads over to the stove and lights a burner, filling the teapot. In the living room where Henry sleeps on the daybed, the bit of moonlight is reflected on the span of lake seen clearly out the front windows. Pa's breathing comes soft and steady and strong, as if nothing were wrong. Nothing is wrong with *him*, she thinks, looking at him, at once admiring and despairing of how impregnable he is and always has been.

If he were himself, nothing would be different. He and Robert would be fighting is all. He might be annoyed by Valley and find little ways to slight her, and then if she confronted him, he'd deny there was anything wrong. He was always good at that. He handled Gabe the same way, and it seems to her suddenly, she has done this herself. Played this part with Valley. She feels a little ashamed. Pa put up with Gabe because she was so useful, so anxious to please, but Robert was the one he wanted. She always knew that. Now Robert wants her. For what?

There is an incident, an insignificant, small incident decades ago, too small for a story, never told to Robert or anyone—back when they were still downstate. It was her turn to give the gas station man the dollar bills for the gas, and she hung on to the back of Henry's seat, asking to be the one to hand the money out the window. She wanted to be the one to get the service man's smile, the tip of his hat. She is sure it is her turn—has been learning about turns and what is fair, and now she uses what she knows, puts her faith in it, and asks.

But Henry gives the money to Robert to hand out, smiling while he tells her that gas station attendants really like to get their money from little boys. Her mother is dressed in a navy blue hat with veiling. She glances at Gabe and smiles, acknowledging this higher truth. Robert is so beautiful, Gabe saw in that moment, his milky skin, those blue eyes. He will always be more beautiful than she.

Odd, this coming to mind. It may have been the last time she let herself feel crushed for not being the preferred one, after that, allowing herself only the stone of pride, the bloodless reward of knowing better than to ask. That was the beginning of her taking care of herself, she realizes now. She had better continue. She had better think about herself.

Behind her, there is a rustling sound. Someone cups her elbow and, standing behind her, places a chin on her shoulder. "Couldn't sleep?" Valley whispers. Gabe nods. This is not the first time Gabe's awakened and found Valley up. Valley loves to interpret dreams and visions.

"Come on, sit *down*." She pulls on Gabrielle's arm and Gabe lets herself be led to the table. Valley takes over, making them both tea. "Chamomile," she says, holding up the box. "Very soothing," she instructs, then puts her finger up to her mouth, shushing herself, reminding them both they had better keep quiet.

In a moment, she brings the steaming cups over and places them in front of Gabe, leaning over and pressing her cheek against Gabe's, wrapping both arms around her in a loose embrace. After a moment, she sighs. "It's not like I can save every deer in the world," she whispers against Gabe's face. Her tone says she is trying to get used to the idea, practicing. "J. Gordon will just have to take care of himself from now on."

Gabe nods. They have both been thinking the same thing. There is only so much a person can do.

"You don't have to stay. Leave when you need to," Gabe says suddenly, turning in her chair to look at Valley.

"I told you. I'll wait until you get back. But after that, you and Henry are on your own. And then what, Gabe? For you, I mean."

Gabe turns around again and looks for the milk-crescent of the moon. It's gone. But there—just beyond the white pine—its light throws leggy shadows.

"I don't know," she says after a long moment, allowing herself to dive the depth of her not-knowing, the fathoms of emptiness. Yet at the bottom, she's discovered a bedrock of fear—oddly, a kind of gift to move her past uncertainty. "Right now, I've got to get my presentation at school over with. I'll deal with your being gone and whatever that does to Robert. And after that—I'll do *something*."

"You'll *miss* me." Valley's face comes close again, her breath a soft pressure on Gabe's cheek, familiar.

"Yes. I'll miss you. Maybe I'll move somewhere closer to the college on my own. Robert can deal with the old man himself. Without us here, he'll probably put him back in the home, and I think that's the best thing. Meanwhile nothing really *bad* could happen to Pa."

Valley says, "He could get a *rash*." She smiles, trying to make Gabe happy, less guilty. She pulls her chair up close, sits down, puts her feet on the rung of Gabe's chair. Then she picks up her cup and lets the steam dampen her face. She seems calm, relaxed.

Too much so, Gabe thinks. Like J. Gordon. She wishes Valley were more frightened. "Will you be all right till I get *back*?" She hopes the girl will hear the warning in her voice.

Valley only nods, seeming surer of herself. "He's always nicer after something like this. Butter won't melt in his mouth. Really, you did me a favor, your timing was great. Even though it was *awful*, I'm *sorry*—" she says, putting her hand on Gabe's knee, wanting to show that she knows what Gabe went through for her sake, going on with, "Robert will be okay unless things get worse at Wild Kingdom. You know? Which they might. But one step at a time. That's all we can do."

They sit, listening to Henry beginning to hit stride with a gentle snore, in, out, in, out.

"The bitch is, Gabe, I really *love* him. If he just weren't so mean—
he can be so sweet or—I dunno, so *lovable* when he wants to be,"
Valley says, shrugging. "I feel sorry for him."

There is no need for Gabe to agree. Valley knows. She puts her
hand into Gabe's, holding it, patting it with her other hand. "In the
morning," she whispers, looking up toward the staircase, "I am going
to make kasha for your send-off. No bacon and no eggs. He can
damn well eat it or go hungry."

The girl pats Gabe's hand, smiling and patting, patting.

VII

DOING THEM HONOR

From a water glass on the counter, Shub's Alka-Seltzer sends off tiny bubble rockets, his first defense in the war against stomach acid. Though it is only seven o'clock, he's been up all night with indigestion he says, and today will be checking in new people at Cabin Three. "The Pasquales or some such Eye-talian name. Three kids, all boys, probably ornery. They better teach 'em how to swim in Evanston, where they come from. I'm not about to be lifeguard to no wop city kids."

He covers his mouth for a little burp and asks, "Where is that Valley these days? Haven't seen her for a while."

"Oh, she'll be in likely, sometime soon. She's trying to finish writing up her animals. Got the kingfisher left. Some hawks. She might have trouble finishing though, managing the old man alone the next couple weeks, I mean."

"Robert'll help her," Shub says, straightening the rows of Frito-Lays, stacked on the wire shelves. His tone is so matter-of-fact that she looks at him. Does he really think Robert and Valley are just like he and Elsie were? "Have him bring your dad in here," he suggests. "I can watch him. The old guy likes coming in here."

Gabe closes the receipt pad where she's written down her gas charge. "They'll think of it, Shub. I won't be seeing them for a while. I'm leaving straight from here. Be gone the next twelve days."

He's forgotten why this is and knows he shouldn't have. His eyebrows raise up in an arch, asking his question for him.

"Fond du Lac," she reminds him. "Another residency. I have to give a presentation this time. Gonna read a paper I wrote."

"Aaah," he says, lifting his chin, meaning of course, now he remembers the importance of her event. His not taking the subject further also shows what he thinks of Fond du Lac, what he feels about grown women going off to school and studying literature—hoity-toity stuff nobody reads—and also something about his good manners because he steers away from unpleasantness; he changes the subject.

"Well, they have some terrible tornadoes over that way. That place have a basement? You better make sure it does, in that part of the country. Elsie, she'd never even go traveling, much as she complained about being stuck here, 'cause motels, they usually don't have any basements. Built on slab." He shakes his head sadly, thinking about the irresponsibility of most motel owners.

She hands him the Jay's Ripple Chips from the lower shelf, helping him to rearrange the space. It's not good business to show any holes.

"You ever read Hemingway, Shub?" It strikes her how audacious this simple act is, her coming back to the subject he has so cordially ignored, drawing attention to herself and things she knows about.

He thinks a moment, put on the spot, then shakes his head. "No," he says, "don't think so. I know *about* him, of course. Never thought he was any great shakes. Think I saw a movie he wrote once, with Spencer Tracy?"

Gabe nods, crossing her arms in front of her. "Hemingway's dead now," she says. "But he used to come up to Michigan from Oak Park. His folks had a summer place in Petoskey. He wrote about it."

"Is that right?"

She thought that would get him. There are possibilities here for storytelling with the Pasquales—a famous writer from Illinois, summering in Michigan—he'd tell them all about it. Maybe one of the Pasquale boys would follow in the writer's footsteps, maybe someday Five Corners would be as famous as Petoskey.

Gabe says, "He's the one I wrote my paper about."

"Is that right? Well now. So how long ago was this, he came up? You know, Elsie's cousin Babe lives in Petoskey. Might be she mentioned him to me one time. Where exactly was their place? I'll ask Babe about it. You know, that spot they're surveying across the lake, we've been hearing stories some writer bought it up, some woman writer, makes a lot of money writin' romance novels. Now, what was her name? Belle knows it, Sid was telling me at the fireworks— Rosemary Bethune? Benoir? *Beauvoir*, was it?"

"Shub, I doubt she's in the same league as Hemingway—"

"Well, I don't know, Gabe, they're making a movie out of one of her books."

"I know, but you can't just go by—" She thinks of Hemingway's lion-hunting story, "The Short Happy Life of Francis Macomber," another that made the woman a villain falsely—abusively even, at the end. She had thought only this morning about adding this example to her talk. Yet now she wants to defend the rhythms of Hemingway's language, admiring most where he had spoken as if he were the lion himself:

"He trotted, heavy, big-footed, swinging wounded full-bellied, through the trees toward the tall grass and cover"—this bloody-headed lion who charged against all odds, whose courage shamed Macomber even in his dreams.

"Bennington, was it? Belleville, maybe." Shub gives up, shrugging it away. "Probably a rumor anyway," he says. "Not the first time somebody rich and famous was supposed to come in and have a place across the lake from us. Would make a pretty spot," he says, and that's the end of that talk, about people too good for *this* place.

She capitulates, nodding. Shub isn't the one she should be trying this out on, anyway, this new determination of hers not to follow the unspoken law, to remain invisible. It was never Shub's law; look at Elsie. She should leave the old guy alone.

"Well, I have to be going," she says. "You might keep an eye on things, you know, I mean if Valley and Robert come in. See how they're doing. Valley says Robert's been worried, thinks he's gonna lose his job or something."

"Well! No wonder if he did! Sid doesn't have to put up with his malarkey. He's cost Sid plenty, him and his big ideas, one thing after another, always losing his temper! You know how much that engine cost? They can't even get the thing running. The track's all screwed up. They just up and put it on soft ground. First turn it took, the whole thing just tipped right off the rail."

He makes a shushing noise at such nonsense, shaking his head. "You gotta know what you're *doing* with those things."

"Robert never did lack for confidence. You can say that about him."

"Say, *yes!*" Shub agrees, pulling his head back so that his jowls fold and his head shimmies from the impact of this fact. "But you can overdo a good thing," he says. "You gotta have *some* common sense! But you know Sid, he's to blame just as much as Robert. Always trying to save a nickel. Probably figured it was cheaper payin' the boy half rate than doin' the job right. Guess maybe he learned a thing or two."

Gabe nods her head, pretending this is all stuff she's heard about already in great detail—though actually she's heard a strikingly different version. This one makes more sense.

"No doubt," is all she comments. "Sounds like them both, doesn't it? Well, Shub. Gotta go."

She raises her hand to say good-bye, glancing back as she reaches for the screen door. He is leaning both hands on the counter, pursing his lips, nodding after her. Something about the way his head inclines tells her he feels smaller, despite all his blustering, for not having been able to follow her down the path to Hemingway and other glories he has only heard rumors of, from far away. The way he holds his head—like bad weather coming—in need of some elaborate theory he'll have to work up.

"Bye, Shub," she says and smiles, trying to reassure him, thinking, Really, he's a good egg.

JULY 22, 1974

It is seven days into the twelve-day residency. Tomorrow is her first presentation. Eight students, including Gabe, sit on folding chairs in Orbach's office. Other groups are meeting in other faculty offices, and there will be more lectures and student presentations later. These eight have arranged themselves to face the stone fireplace, filled with philodendron in summertime, expecting to learn about indigenous ceremonies.

Orbach crosses his leg, yawns into a hand, then smiles, catching Gabe's eye, nodding. All of them are tired. It's been a long day, including an art show and now this film. There's a bottle of wine on a table in the corner, a platter of cheese cubes and clusters of grapes. The light from the green glass shade on the desk lamp and a floor lamp in the corner behind Orbach warm the dark wood paneling.

"Now the Haitians," says Greta Pritchert, another one of the graduate students, as she pulls the movie screen and hooks it in place to stand it in front of the fireplace, "practice a form of shamanism, using a ritualistic, very hypnotic drumbeat. You'll see in this film, the shaman's dominance, the obeisance paid him by all participants in this initiation ritual, and actually in every aspect of their lives."

Greta walks back to the movie projector, signals Orbach to turn off the floor lamp. She starts the film, then reaches over to turn off the desk lamp. There is no color, no sound to the film, a rare documentary that Greta has discovered in her research. This is her master's presentation. She has already been accepted for her doctorate at the University of Chicago.

"Now you see that everyone except the shaman is in a pair, and that the movements are strictly dictated by the accompanying drumbeats. Though you can't hear them, I'm sorry to say." She laughs a nervous apology, pushing up her sleeves. "They're planting the pole in the earth in the place where the spirits can enter, where the vertical line crosses the horizontal line of the earth. You see the circle they've drawn. There are symbols inside the circle, which I'll talk more about later, that have implications for Jung's archetypes."

The projector clicks and whirs. Gabrielle finds herself involuntarily yawning, wineglass still half full, but she sits up straighter, wanting to pay closer attention. The vertical, the horizontal—spirits entering a cross, though this has a feeling of being older than the cross she's known, which has death and self-sacrifice at its center. What about the circle? The other symbols? She sets her glass down on Orbach's desk.

Across from her the door opens and lets in a crack of light and someone's head appears. "Is Gabrielle Bissonette in here?" the head asks and Gabe shifts in her seat, raises a tentative hand, then admitting the truth, raises it higher.

"I'm sorry to interrupt," says the head, "but you have a phone call downstairs."

Gabe gets up, apologizing as she makes a black silhouette on the screen, getting to the door. She enters the lighted hall, closing the door behind her, and follows Jeannie, one of the coordinators of the program. She is tall, lithe, with a mass of dark curls. She smiles and half-turns toward Gabe as she walks ahead, saying, "I thought it might be important. A young woman. She sounded anxious to talk to you, I didn't think you'd mind."

Gabe murmurs her agreement, picking up her pace. What could it be? Valley's never done this before.

She enters the office, goes where Jeannie is pointing to a phone receiver lying on the desk. Gabe picks it up. "Hello?" she says, waiting for Valley's voice, but instead the line is dead. "Hello? Valley? Are you there?" No one answers.

"You have to push the 'hold' button," Jeannie says, walking over and releasing it. She stands watching Gabe, eyebrows up in inquiry, as Gabe repeats, "Hello? Hello?"

"That's odd," Jeannie says. "I'm sure she understood me. She insisted on staying on the line. I should have gotten her name for you." She shrugs, frowning.

"I think I know who it is. I'll call her, if that's all right. I'll reverse the charges."

"Don't worry about it," Jeannie answers.

The operator lets the phone ring a good ten times, then says that no one appears to be answering. "A few more rings, operator, please," Gabe says, and waits, listening to the ring repeat and repeat.

"I'm sorry," the operator says. "Please try your number again later."

They go back into the hallway, Jeannie stopping to click off the light in the office. "Maybe your friend was calling from another number," she says. "I'm really sorry I didn't get more information for you." They walk to the end of the hallway and Jeannie clicks off the light behind them. They start up the stairs to Orbach's office and the movie. The phone begins ringing in the darkness below them.

Jeannie makes an irked noise, a "tsk" against her teeth. "Come on," she says, descending again. "Maybe this is she." Gabrielle follows the trail of light Jeannie blazes, flicking the switches.

Jeannie picks up the phone. "Hello? *Hello!* Who is this, please?" She cups her hand over the bottom end and says to Gabe, "I think there's someone there, but they're not answering."

Gabrielle takes the phone from her hand. "Hello? This is Gabrielle. Who is it you're looking for, please?" Like Jeannie, she knows that someone is on the line, but no one answers. "Valley, is that *you?*"

A click, then the line buzzes again.

"Very strange," she says, hanging up the phone. "Don't ask me why, but I think it *was* for me."

"Well, the call earlier certainly was. I didn't want to alarm you, but frankly, she sounded beside herself. I had a hard time understanding what she wanted exactly. She just wanted you very badly, I think."

"Oh," Gabe says, feeling her stomach turn over. "You know, I'm a little worried. I think I have to go home . . . my sister-in-law. Will you explain to Professor Orbach for me? I'm scheduled to give my presentation tomorrow, but I'll have to reschedule. You can make him understand, can't you?"

"Sure," says Jeannie. "I'd do the same myself." They enter the hall again, turning off lights, making for the back door this time. "She's not *ill*, is she? Your sister-in-law?"

"No. I don't think so. Maybe. Why do you ask?"

"Oh, her voice just sounded odd, all breathy. I'm probably making it out to be more than it was, with all this mystery." She smiles, laughing a little. They step outside into cool night air, where the path leads to Nicolet Hall, its windows rows of rectangular lights just beyond the trees. "Things happen," says Jeannie, touching her arm in farewell. "Try to come back as soon as you can, but if you can't make this residency, we'll just reschedule with another of our graduate cycles. The worst that can happen is you'll be in some other group, that's all."

"Thanks," says Gabrielle, already heading down the path into the dark, her eyes on the lighted windows of the hall.

It is a good three and a half hour drive back to Lake Nekoagon. Gabrielle diverts herself with memories of Valley that would explain the phone call—if it was Valley who called—she can't know that for sure.

Valley could get panicky over practically anything. She imagined her arteries clogging up just from breathing the steamy smoke from fried bacon. Swimming scared her to death. She was always frightened of finding a successful mousetrap, insisting that Gabe put them in out-of-the-way places where she couldn't possibly discover them.

The first month Valley had been at the cabin, they'd had a terrible scene over the buck Gabe had shot. She had needed the venison to get by for the winter, what with her not working except at Shub's. But what a commotion.

They'd had a second snowstorm, not long after Thanksgiving, and were stuck again in the cabin together, both of them tense, feeling each other out. On impulse, when Valley was upstairs moving furniture around again, Gabrielle had decided to take care of the buck, a week earlier than would have been ideal for aging the venison, just so she could have something physical to do, to divert herself.

"I'm going outside," she'd called to Valley, not waiting to see if the girl had heard her or not. Gabe cleared the snow out in front from under the porch, so she could swing the door open to get to the cooler where she'd hung the buck. Her father had the room well set up for butchering—a table saw, a chopping block, another table for wrapping the meat in paper.

She would take the buck down, but first she had to skin him. Inwardly, she addressed the deer, remembering the way her father had. A dozen times she had watched him stripping skin from muscle, murmuring instructions in a tone that was close as he ever got to worshipful. His deft hands had moved quickly, and she tried her best to do the same, as if sparing the buck.

"A lesson to us in purpose," she addressed him, guiding the knife with her finger close to the point, pulling, cutting. Shub used to say that like all good things, the deer's gifts were difficult to claim, only right to expect it to be hard.

Gabe stopped to sharpen her knife on the whetstone he had used, and looked around for the saw she needed to take off the buck's rack. She had decided to nail the antlers to the porch eaves overhead, where her father has put each of his. They were up there in a long row, a set of antlers for each of the years he'd hunted here, except the really big ones he'd had mounted for Boone and Crockett.

She went outside and nailed her six points into place, then stood back, studying them in context, comparing them with others for symmetry, not so much for size. Satisfied, she walked back down to the cooler, keeping the doors wide open so the light was better, and began to scrape the hide clean of meat and fat, and afterward, to salt the skin down, rolling it tight, fur side out. Her plan was to take the cape to Belle Nichols, who bought them if they were in good shape.

She was nearly done with the hide when she heard a small gasp and looked up to see Valley near the doorway. The girl was staring at the head of the deer, scalped of its antlers, which Gabe had propped upright against the open door, and at the four handsome hoofed feet which she had cut off and propped next to it, planning to have Belle convert these to a gun rack for Shub for Christmas.

The knife lay on the table next to her, the weight of the carcass swinging behind her. Still crouched over the hide, following Valley's gaze, Gabrielle looked at her handiwork with new eyes. In the winter's dimness, with a single bare lightbulb hanging next to the carcass, it was grisly, this stickum of blood, the blue-white of fresh-cut bone. The body was too red, its ribbons of muscles and ligaments shining and sheathed in a pearl-surfaced membrane—dreadful, what lies at the bottom of motion and power.

"What are you doing?" This was almost whispered, as if Valley were afraid to affront the demon corpse. But no, Gabe saw it then. She must have grown horns and a trident-tipped tail herself, *she* was the demon Valley saw.

"How *can* you?" she said next, and turned on her heel, going back up the hill to the kitchen porch where she came from, leaving Gabe blinking, trying to come up with an answer she could live with. She decided not to bother and picked up the salt to resume her sprinkling.

Valley came storming down to the door again, her face blotchy and red from crying, her mouth a puffy torn edge. She wore her ridiculous wool cloak and was carrying a garbage bag filled with her things. She attempted to say something but couldn't speak, then shot Gabe one resentful glance and stomped back up in the direction of her car.

Gabrielle heard the tinny roar of the VW's engine starting. She heaved a forced sigh and picked up her knife. Little idiot. How far did she think she would *get* on these roads? Let her go then, if she thought she could get anywhere. She heard the Beetle getting stuck, its tires whining and screaming, forward, backward, forward, backward. The car door slammed shut and Valley came stomping back into view again. "Where's the shovel?" she demanded.

"Over here, I used it earlier." Gabe motioned to the corner and went back to rolling the deer hide.

Valley grabbed the shovel and marched off again, calling, "I'll bring it back, don't you worry." Gabe didn't look up, but she had noticed Valley had her Mary Janes back on, along with the wool socks Gabe had loaned her.

A fury of chopping and slicing, the stinging sound of metal shovel on snow floated back to Gabe. She was trying to stop listening to the racket of Valley digging out the VW. The girl would never get out to the road, and even if she did, the lake road probably wouldn't be plowed for a good while yet. Gabe began wrapping cuts of meat in freezer paper, putting the packages in plastic bags.

More shrieking of tires and the painful sound of motor pushed too hard. More slamming and shoveling and, from time to time, words—Valley exclaiming, swearing possibly—though it was the tone Gabe made out, not the language. After a while, she was certain the girl was crying again.

Eventually Gabe didn't hear anything, too engrossed in the work she was doing. When she was finished, there was only bone left of the deer, and even this would go into the freezer for soup stock, nothing wasted. She carted armloads of freezer-wrapped meat up the slope to take inside. Coming around to the kitchen porch, she could see Valley's car was still running. She realized then that the sound of struggle had been quiet for some time.

Gabe put her tools away and in several trips carried the meat to the room off the porch where the freezer chest sat next to a squat water heater. Then she took a single slender leg bone and walked to the nearest young beech tree, placing it as high as she could reach, in the crotch. This was something she had seen her father do, a good luck charm he'd learned from his Koyukon friend.

Curious because Valley's car remained still, Gabe walked over to the driveway and approached the vehicle. Her shovel was buried in a mound of snow next to the car, the whole area ripped and spattered with ice and dirt. The car's windows were steamed up and clouds of white exhaust swirled at Gabe's feet and rose in spirals. Through a haze, she could see Valley sitting in the driver's seat.

She tried the door and when it caught on something, she remembered it was wired shut, from the inside this time. She went to the opposite side of the car, yanked open the door and stooped over to look inside.

Valley didn't acknowledge her. She was hugging herself and rocking, staring at the dashboard and rocking, rocking. She had finished with her weeping, face streaked and blotchy from it. Her upper lip was swollen, its edges blurred and only a little darker red than her nose.

"Valley?"

The girl didn't answer. She kept on rocking.

Gabrielle used a harsher tone. "Valley, stop this and come inside. You'll be frozen again."

It was then that Valley looked at Gabe without turning her head. She looked with her eyes only, her eyes impotent and filled with sadness that spoke of broken things, a life filled with broken things that could not be fixed.

"Come inside now," said Gabrielle. "Come on."

Valley turned off the engine and lifted herself up over the gearshift. Gabe steered her by the arm, carrying her garbage bag. They walked back up the driveway and the porch stairs, past the crime of bloody bones. They went to sit in the living room where the couch faced the row of windows that looked out on a sky that was almost clear by now and blue, the color of indifference, its brilliance too vast.

Valley began rocking again, a tiny motion at first. There was something about it that cried out and, without thinking, Gabe put her arms around Valley and joined in the movement. Back and forth, back and forth, all the comfort they could find, this movement on and on, give and take, life and death, back and forth.

Gabrielle catches herself rocking slightly behind the wheel and she stops, mid-motion. She sighs, knowing she is almost home. She sees the turnoff up ahead and blinks her eyes open, wide as she can, wanting to be alert.

Hand over hand she turns the wheel, veering onto the private peninsula road that winds back to the cabin, straining to see its shape. Then through the trees appears the roof's outline, the small light on the back porch seeming to blink on and off, on and off, blocked by the trees she's winding through as she comes closer. She pulls up next to the house and sees that the Volkswagen is not there. They are out then, Valley and Robert. She has driven half the night for nothing.

She thinks about turning around and driving back, straight through, going back again to try to make her presentation, but she's too exhausted. Calling Orbach, it's going to sound like an excuse generated by a student with cold feet. Without a doubt she will sound just like one, since she is. She wonders suddenly if she has manufactured all this fear, creating an elaborate diversion to escape her presentation.

Climbing the back stairs, Gabe's feet are leaden. She'll leave the two of them a note on the table, go into her bedroom and crash.

She opens the back door and a strong smell hits her. Garbage, stale cigarettes, damp rot, and what is that—kerosene? The smell alarms her. If Valley and Robert have gone out, then where's the old man? She turns to face the kitchen, feeling for the light switch. She flips it up, but nothing happens. Burned out, probably. Damn.

To the left, the porch light is shining in the bathroom window and she notices how that room is a mess too, damp towels strewn on the toilet tank, over the shower curtain bar, on the floor. Valley's makeup bag has been knocked to the floor, pencils and sponge applicators scattered. The plastic hose to her hair dryer sprawls on the floor like a snake.

The lightbulbs are in the cupboard next to the kitchen sink. She walks over in the dark, feeling her way with her hands, knocking over an empty beer bottle and what sounds like a potato chip bag, the whole table, every flat space, cluttered with food and dishes and abandoned projects—pencils, paper, a bottle of window spray.

She reaches the sink and bends to open the lower cupboard, and the rotten smell comes closer to her nose. There is something dark in the dish drainer. She hears flies droning, their buzz deep and resonant. She makes a face, sucking in her breath, holding it, not wanting to inhale again as she reaches for a new bulb.

Back at the table, she pulls out a chair and reaches overhead for the fixture, unscrewing the knob that holds it in place, carefully letting down the glass, making room on the table to set it down. She unscrews the lightbulb next, then sets it down, finally twisting in the new bulb. The room fills with light. Her eyes sweep over the litter of bottles, dirty dishes, empty containers, a stack of wire hangers on top of the stove. She starts to climb down off the chair as her gaze reaches the sink, half afraid of what might stink there, and startled, she stumbles a little, misjudging the distance to the floor.

The head of a buck, antlers just budding in velvet, lies in the dish drainer on the counter. Flies hum at the corners of its closed eyes, at the moisture of its nose and mouth, their dark bodies gliding down in swoops to the puddle of juice that is pooled in the rubber pad beneath the drainer, not blood but rose-colored, scummy water.

Walking closer, she sends up a flurry of buzzing. She holds her breath against the too sweet stench, tipping the deer's head away from her a little, studying it. It looks as though it's been partially buried for a while, at least there is dirt mixed in with the bloody juice, she sees, and that surging movement on the cut edge, maggots. In the same moment, she admits it is J. Gordon, understands why Valley had called.

Despite holding her breath, the odor has entered her stomach, intruding past clenched teeth. Through her shoes she feels dirt underfoot, hears its gritty scratch as she walks quickly to the bathroom, barely making it to the toilet in time. She heaves until she hurts. She can't get rid of the fetor of spoiled meat, the motion of white worms. She waits a moment before standing up, then flushes, and after a pause and clearing her throat with a cough, goes in search of that other smell—kerosene.

She lights the lantern, an arc light, and stumbles into the front room, holding the lamp high. Chaos spills into this room too, an empty pizza box on the table, surrounded by more beer bottles and saucers filled with cigarette butts, a week's worth of junk mail, rumpled jackets, shoes and socks, a gun bore, and rags.

Gabe attempts to walk nearer the gun case to check out the smell and nearly falls. She reaches out her hand to catch herself and gasps, recoiling from the touch of warm flesh. Henry's chest, his shirt half unbuttoned.

"Oh, *Pa*," says Gabrielle, relieved, pulling her hand back to the base of her throat, speaking before she has time to remember that talk is a wasted exercise. He won't hear her, won't be able to answer any of the questions that are begging for answers. He is standing behind the wing-backed chair, the seat of which is filled with greasy cloth, almost as if he'd been cleaning his guns. What has happened to move him from his seat? Why is he there, crouching almost? Holding up the lantern, she cups his face in her hand, studies him, trying to judge whether he's all right. His chin is whiskery. No one has shaved him and his hair hangs in oily strings.

She lifts up one of the rags on the chair and smells the corner of it. There the kerosene is, just as she thought. Simultaneously she sees lights playing on the wall in front of her, the bounce of a car pulling into the drive. Valley and Robert, she guesses, and her heart begins to drum against her sternum, anticipating their discovering her here. What will she tell them about why she is home early? But never mind—she is *angry*, angry at *both* of them, for being so irresponsible—so damned *predictable*, their childishness, just like last time! What a goddamn mess.

She steps back then, listening to the sound of Valley's car door closing, off-kilter, gathering herself, getting ready for a fight, and her foot bumps something solid. She twists around to see what her foot has met, something oddly soft but wooden, an object that does not yield and makes everything clear—a thigh she has bumped, a smooth thigh—the back of bare knees and calves, ankles ending in small, arched feet—those feet she'd know anywhere, those pale bone-filled feet.

She sinks down to her knees next to Valley, putting out her hand instinctively—Valley, who is splayed out on her stomach, face turned to the side, dressed in shorts and a tank top and that ridiculous bandanna. Valley—who feels cold.

Gabe raises both elbows up high, hands curled next to her face, throwing her head back to moan, ohgod ohgod, god *no*, horror swelling to a howl, but caught there in her throat.

The sound of footsteps on the back porch brings her breath up short, tight in her chest cavity—too late—her car is clearly visible, the kitchen light on—

She puts out the lantern and scrambles on hands and knees, her breath coming in quick gasps now, making her way to the gun case in the corner.

"*Gabe?*" comes Robert's voice, and his tone is loud, demanding.

She hears footsteps.

"You there, Gabe? *Gaabe! You there?*" he calls. Each time the tone is different. She hears him thinking out loud, practicing tentativeness, bluster, then trying a phony innocence.

She clenches her teeth, listening. She's made it to the gun case. She slides the glass door from the bottom and, still kneeling, eases out her .30-30. Her hands shake so badly she has to use both of them to steady the gun.

Sitting back and laying it across her lap, she pulls open the bottom drawer and reaches in for a shell, pressing it into the rifle, cocking it into the chamber. She does this noiselessly.

"I know you're in here, Gabe," Robert calls. "Whyn't you come on out now, huh? I don't wanna fight. Look, I *know* what it looks like, but she had a *handgun*, Gabe, and I—we *fought* and I—oh, Jesus, *Gaaabe?* That stupid buck? I shot it for *meat*, I had to, seeing I don't have a job anymore. She's acting like I'm some monster. Can't show me a little *sympathy* at a time like this, for Chris*sake*—"

Self-pity cringes in his voice, a whine that touches fire to Gabe's tinder. She clenches her teeth harder. Rifle loaded, she pauses on her knees before putting one foot flat on the floor, ready to raise herself upright in a single movement.

She yells, "Don't come *in* here, Robert! I'm warning you! You're not doing to *me* what you did to hhh—" She attempts to breathe the word "her," meaning Valley, meaning green place, meaning love and home and safety, but the word won't come, sliding out instead in a groaning growl, which surges up, surprising her with its force. She grits her teeth to stop herself, afraid she'll lose control.

Robert is too quiet. She strains to hear him, trying to figure what he is up to. More steps, but they are wandering ones, not forceful or full of direction, and occasionally there is also a metallic clunk, a sound she can't quite recognize. A stronger smell of kerosene wafts into the room and Robert's intentions come to her on streamers of smoke that hover close to the ceiling above her. He is getting rid of the evidence.

She looks down at Valley, glances at Pa again. "*Roberrrt!*" she screams.

No answer. Listening for the sound of his getaway, she plans to run and put the fire out, or escape as soon as he's gone. But he's waiting. There is only a gathering whisper in the next room, a gentle crackling.

She risks standing up then and, glancing to her right, sees the flank of porch windows, an easy enough escape route. She can lower the gun out first, drop down, then run for her truck, though probably it is blocked by the VW now. She glances back over her shoulder to make sure Robert hasn't appeared behind her. Moving quickly, she smashes the butt of her rifle through the glass, shattering it, and immediately realizes her mistake, giving her position away.

"Don't *do* it!" he calls and his voice is abrupt, closer. "Gabe, *don't*, I said!"

She sinks down, hiding, and makes a squatting turn to see him in the doorway. His outline is hard with angles, legs parted, arms held away from his body. He is trying to place her, a small revolver hanging in his right hand.

She is ready for this moment. She has pictured it over and over since she first heard him call for her.

"I never asked for this to happen," Robert is saying, and his head jerks from tension. He shrugs this away in an undulating shoulder motion, like a fighter waiting for an opening. His eyes sweep back and forth across the room, looking for her, and his face is strangely defenseless, open as a child's. As he speaks, the handgun comes up.

"I'd never hurt Valley, I would never *hurt* her," he says, and glances over to where the body gives lie to his words. Gabrielle recognizes his shrug, misery wringing him, twisting his head to the side. Firelight behind him sparks his eye with brightness, a glitter.

She stands, puts her rifle up, and stares down the barrel.

He's already sighted her and finished raising his gun. He laughs a mocking, breathy laugh. "A Mexican stand-off. Go *ahead*," he dares her, meeting her eye, and in the next move—such a slight one—points the gun into his mouth, takes the noise into his brain, reels backward to hit the floor with a sprawling thump.

Already she's squeezed the trigger. Her gun stock kicks her shoulder and thrusts her head back so that ever after, she will see Robert go down in a slow-motion arc from under the fringe of her bangs.

July 18, 1984
Five Corners, Michigan

Shub likes to say the hardest rock in all creation, the continental shelf, reaches all the way from up here to Niagara Falls. All the crashing water there ever was has never yet worn this rock away, and people here take the stuff up through their boot soles. It's part of their jawbone and their tooth and you see it in their eye, he'll tell you. North of here are pit mines thousands of years old. The first people here—the Chippewa—the Ojibway—Anishinaabeg—believed that copper ore was full of healing spirits, the best of what the earth has to give. When the Jesuits came, the Indians didn't like to speak of how they used it. Later, finally worn down, they granted "mineral rights"—whatever those were—I can almost see them shrugging—leading white men to big pieces of the stuff as a distraction. Sparing their more sacred sites. They thought these would stay protected if they didn't speak of them.

The power of secrets—the protection of what is never said. But of course the copper was discovered. And removed. And so was the iron and the bauxite and every other kind of mineral up here, and still men are looking for more. Once Valley told me that whatever is female has traditionally been pictured as dark and hidden—as secret as the sacred copper, I suppose. But most people no longer think of the earth as sacred. Or as female. Female secrets these days are anything but holy. We've forgotten something, twisting our remembering—Kate's questions have made me stop and think more about this. Why should I have kept myself a secret? What holiness is left to protect in this story?

Courage? Not that I can recognize—I mean, how did I manage to put out the fire in the state I was in? What was I feeling? The log walls had such mass, they're only blackened in places—it must not have been that difficult to put out. The kitchen table and cupboards and the windows had to be replaced, but I can't remember them burning. The newspaper stories haven't helped me, hardly mentioning me except for the way I was known to handle a gun. That made me a novelty, I guess, something sinister. They cast Pa as silent witness—a romantic figure, the brave father standing before the flames. I remember him in a corner, facing away, terrified. Robert always said he knew more than we thought he did.

I remember I couldn't figure out how to call the police. I managed to call Shub's store to ask him to. I told him Valley and Robert were dead. There was such a long silence on the other end, I knew he thought I'd done it. I felt as if I had.

It's all a blur. Cops talking into their car radios, a rude, blatting noise coming back at them, which they ignored, mumbling code numbers. Cruisers everywhere, zapping blue strobes. An ambulance, its red lights whirling.

The cops took me into the kitchen to question me, but it stunk too badly. We went into my bedroom and I sat on the edge of my bed, which is high enough that my feet don't touch the floor. I felt like a child—being taken care of by the deep-voiced policemen.

They were kind enough—it's not surprising given what they told me—something I've tried hard to forget. Valley had called them the day before she called me. "There wasn't much we could do," one of them said. "We warned Robert to behave himself. Must have made him madder, though." The other cop slowly shook his head, shook his head at what a shame it was.

Two empty gurneys rolled past the doorway, sheathed in white, and I panicked, desperate to find out what had happened, afraid until then to look closer at Valley's body. How did he do it?

"Not with the gun," the head-shaking policeman answered, holding me back.

"She was a tiny thing," the other commented, leaving it to me to imagine how easy it must have been.

They asked more questions. I heard myself answer. A loaded gurney rolled past with a small form under the sheet, everything clean and tucked in. I stood up, wanting to follow, but the second gurney, spotted with crimson, came by and blocked my way. I had just enough time to grab the wastebasket by my desk. My stomach was empty, but knotted again, refusing the smell of paper, of ink, of air.

The nearest policeman put an arm around my shoulder, insisting, "It's okay." He kept saying, "It's okay," while they took Pa off.

I know the coroner and the forensics people from the state police came, and the reporters must have been there by that time. Everyone was composed and businesslike—their voices mumbling to one another, their footsteps sounding on the wood floors. I remember volunteering that I had armed myself, intending to kill my brother. "I fired my gun, maybe I killed him," I said, knowing I had wanted to, expecting they would lock me up.

I think I remember this, but it might be from some crime movie—the investigating officer looking at the spot where Robert had been, marking it with white tape, walking back to the log wall, making some notes on his pad. I was shown the handgun I'd never seen before, the one Robert used. I told the police what Robert had said, that it belonged to Valley. He probably was lying, but she'd been talking about leaving, I admitted.

The district attorney's office found the case a murder-suicide. None of the newspaper accounts mentioned my shooting at Robert. They only implied my ability. But word got out. And if I felt guilty, other people must have blamed themselves too. Any of a dozen people could have predicted what would happen, could have intervened somehow. So folks needed a scapegoat. And the more silent I was, wandering around half asleep from tranquilizers—the more they remembered. They remembered bad blood between Robert and me. They remembered arguments they'd overheard between me and his wife.

Shub said Sid and Belle were the worst. Maybe they felt responsible because they'd fired Robert. That was one of the theories to explain what had happened, but others were circulating. Theirs were among the meanest. They said I was heartless, I was jealous, I wanted the cabin for myself, and never volunteered a helping hand with Pa or Wild Kingdom. And the most brazen rumor, in Shub's opinion, surely gave away its source. Nobody but Belle would've dared use the word dyke, he said.

My best hope was to become a secret. Odd not to have ever thought about how different this was from Robert. If we'd all gone up in smoke, Valley and Pa and me, Copper County would have come to our funeral and Robert would have cried and gotten sympathy. Even if people discovered his premeditation, he would have become a tortured individual in their minds, pushed into a corner, acting out of desperation. Without his even having to ask—and they'd respect him more for not asking—he'd be forgiven, he has been forgiven.

July 26, 1974

"The damn hypocrites!" Shub is saying, and Gabrielle makes her way across the church basement, past him, looking for a place to throw her paper plate. He is talking about the Catholic priests in town. They wouldn't bury Robert's body in the Catholic cemetery because of the suicide. Shub has told this story to everyone, outraged enough, he said, to become a Unitarian. Leastwise, they will take you whether you've been baptized or not, whether you're a member or not, he has said, over and over.

It had been a strange ceremony. Both of them, Robert and Valley together, buried side by side. It was what the funeral home recommended, what the minister said would heal Gabe and comfort the community. Love had gone bad, but everyone knew that Robert and Valley had been happy together once. They had been such a romantic couple. Everyone would want to mourn this with Gabe. Two funerals would be harder on everyone.

Gabe pushes her lips up into a smile, nodding, as an older woman with a pillbox hat, draped with black netting, reaches out a hand to touch her arm. She won't like it that Gabe shrinks from the touch, barely tolerating it. Already they have noticed that she hasn't cried. They have probably taken account of the fact that her dress isn't black; it is gray and not a deep gray, probably not gray enough, she worries, sure of their disapproval.

The woman is saying something about her husband having died, about knowing something of loss herself. Gabe can't bear to listen to her. Does she really think this is the same? Gabe manages the slightest smile, nodding some more, beginning to take sideways steps away with her dirty plate.

The kitchen is empty, and Gabe leans back against the counter and sighs, letting her arms hang limp. It is exhausting, holding one's face in line. If only she could weep. She could scream and that might start it, but it wouldn't do to make a scene, only a *few* tears expected. Even Shub had looked askance at her once during the eulogy, tears standing in his eyes. She knows he was embarrassed to find her so unmoved. But she can't take any of this seriously. The eulogy read from a book. All the reception small talk. A joke. It's not as if any of them *knew* Valley or Robert or would *want* to know what really happened. None of them had been at the scene. Yet all of them act careful to keep what really happened *from* her—that's how they behave, as if they need to protect her from it.

They talk in whispers behind their hands, but to her they say, "I'm so sorry for your loss," as if all her losses are equal, Valley and Robert on a par, just mysteriously dead somehow. They follow the script for a generic funeral play. "I'm so sorry for your loss," when really they ought to have said, "I'm so shocked you are still alive," or "I'm so appalled you could let this happen," when really she would like to say back to them, "They gave me drugs to keep me together for this" or "Don't believe my smile—you all can go to hell."

Oh, Valley, she breathes, and senses at once how able to weep she is. The chunk of wood in her chest is protection. Don't start now, she warns, not yet—believing that once she begins, she will never be able to stop. This is only the surreal beginning of an unimaginable journey, and none of these people will be coming with her, she thinks. She would just as soon get on with it. Shove off. But in a way she belongs here. She's as dead as Valley and Robert. She feels just as dead.

The lady with the black-netted pillbox and some other women are standing next to Shub when she comes back out. Gabe catches the tail end of what he is saying, "She's still in *shock* is what the doctors say, it'll take a while." His eyes meet hers and his voice takes on an almost cheerful tone. "But time heals all wounds, they say."

Listening to optimism from Shub the doomsayer, she pushes her lips up into a smile, reminding herself to nod.

AUGUST, 1974

The evenings have been growing colder. Gabrielle has put out mouse-traps to protect her pantry from the onslaught of field mice searching for winter haunts. There are millions of mice, she argues with Valley, they'd take over the cupboards if she didn't do this. She mutters, complaining about the slick black seedlike turds she finds even in the corner of a drawer. They carry germs—she can't have this; she *can't*.

She sits wide awake far too late again, looking out on moon water, having given up on reading. She's had to take time off from Fond du Lac, unable to concentrate, not doing much of anything these days except waiting on customers at Shub's. She's ashamed to let others know how hard she is taking this, and she also knows how far from being over it is. It will never be over.

When she isn't fantasizing about moving away, somewhere far away, anywhere, she fears this infinity—scared to death she will not be able to grow around this grief. Most days she takes long, rambling walks and has come to identify a misshapen spruce, weirdly grown up around a schist of angled rock, as her marker. She had never noticed it at the bottom of the ridge before. Now, whichever direction she comes from, the tree leans in a familiar way. It says, This way home, hanging onto thin topsoil with tenacious, wiry roots, holding stone to its heart.

She hears a mousetrap snap in the hall linen closet and gets up to check it. The wire has done its work, clean and quick.

The mouse body is warm yet limp, its eyes shut as if asleep. She holds it up and sees the yellowish curved teeth, the silvery whiskers, the tiny bare feet, almost like hands. In the corner behind the towels is a neat pile of shredded paper, the beginnings of a nest. Gabe wants to say she is sorry. She welcomes the blame for everything. Whatever it is, she's sorry. She decides she could live with a few mice, it wouldn't be so bad, and promises Valley that from now on, she will trap them only in the kitchen. Only there, to keep them out of the food. But that's impossible, she thinks, they'll overrun the place.

Mice won't keep to any such deal. There's no bargaining with mice. You have to keep them out. I *have* to kill them, Valley, she argues, and bursts into tears at how horrible the world is. Hours go by before she can promise the moon this: She will get a cat and she will never again throw dead mice into the garbage. She will return them to the earth, bury them decently.

She remembers this too: Robert was no mouse.

SEPTEMBER, 1974

Whenever she's bothered to eat at all the past month, she has lived on rice and beans, but this morning, Gabe awakens feeling ravenous. She rummages in the freezer for what is left of the deer she downed last year, the sausage she made with apples and onions, Shub's best recipe. Even Valley had thought it smelled good enough she'd been tempted to taste it, though she never had, and now she never will. Frozen packages knock against each other like so much wood.

Gabe finally finds the small foil packet. She puts a little water, and then the frozen links, into the iron fry pan, remembering how grossed out Valley had been by the casings. Gabe had held them under the faucet, rinsing them before stuffing them, arguing, "They're *clean,* don't be so anal," irritated at the time.

"*Pig* intestines! How *could* you?" Valley said. "How would you like it if someone did that to *your* intestines?"

"At least I wouldn't be going to waste. It'll be the same when I donate my organs to science someday."

"That's *different!*"

"*How* different? Eating, surgery, birth—" Gabe jammed the words, shoving the ground meat into the casings as she talked, "all bloody, all to keep people alive. It's no crime, staying alive. It's not respecting the *sources* of life—that's the crime—thinking it all comes from *stores.*"

Valley watched her, but as she listened she lifted her chin in a way that Gabe knew meant she wasn't convinced. Ashamed, Gabe also remembers being provoked enough to dangle the casing when she was done, grinning as if it were a filled Christmas stocking.

Valley hadn't been amused. She turned on her Mary Janes, going out to the porch with chin still lifted high. "There's dying and blood *enough* in this world already," she pronounced.

Water evaporated, the sausage begins to sizzle in its own fat. Gabe looks up, almost startled to have the sense that Valley just exited the room—a shoulder, the hem of her skirt swishing past the doorway's corner, almost visible. Other times she's believed she just heard the pad of crocheted slippers on the floor or the cupboard doors opening.

Gabe follows the wraith out toward the porch, steps into the front room she had kept closed off, preferring the darker kitchen or her bedroom, darker still. She finds the space full of morning light. The room is empty as her stomach, which rolls over now at the sight of clean, uncluttered surfaces, windows a searing blue.

She goes back to stand in front of the stove, appetite vanished. She has to eat, she tells herself. It wouldn't be right to waste this. That's what's *wrong* with the world, she thinks, suddenly angry. "I'm so sick of your squeamishness," she argues, flipping the sausages over. "Everything dies. But some deaths serve life, others destroy it. Blood has to be terrible. Whatever's holy is frightening. Don't you see the difference? To wield it like some club or to measure how big you are—it's not *useful* like this deer."

She knows Valley would be unimpressed. She can almost see her raise her nose as she stares Gabe down. "Different to whom, I wonder? Useful to whom?" she demands. "Your mouse might have different ideas about holiness. Your deer might."

"You have to understand—" By now Gabe is begging. But the cabin answers that Valley is wasted, and Robert too—the very word he might have used for what he did. Gabe places the sausage on a saucer. She puts it away in the fridge. She can't eat this yet. Not yet.

JANUARY, 1975

Professor Orbach looks bewildered, is probably uncomfortable because of all they are not talking about. "You know you could wait, Gabrielle, there's really no pressure on our end to have you do this before you're ready."

"No. I'm ready. Really. I want to do this. I've lost months already. Getting this presentation over with is what's important."

He looks nice, dressed in a tie for the occasion, but she doesn't care about making it easier for him. She doesn't want to talk about Robert and her tragedy so that he can feel more in charge. She knows what she wants to do, and this is not about Robert. This is her life and something else, something new. She is thinking about herself. She demands what is important and repeats, "I *want* to do this."

The other students trickle in. She shuffles her papers, waiting for Orbach to introduce her on the subject of Hemingway. It feels tense at first. Orbach has invited the resident undergraduate students to join them; she doesn't know most of these people. When Orbach signals with an open gesture in her direction, she begins. She struggles to read slowly, stopping to look up from the podium, the way she had practiced with Valley, making eye contact, connecting. She's already through several pages by the time she notices Orbach is squirming in his seat. He had advised her to get rid of that "tight hold" part. And the "Poor Scotty, this, Poor Scotty that." Too personal, he said.

The woman next to him looks as if she were let in on a secret she's always suspected, pleased to have things out in the open. Gabe comes back to her often for eye contact. By the time she's reached her closing pages, she can feel the other students listening too, and her voice is growing more at ease. She is getting used to speaking in front of them. She pauses, then continues:

We can listen in on Hemingway talking about his own high standards for craft, in a scene from Death in the Afternoon. *He was arguing against "skillfully constructed characters," and he said, "People in a novel . . . must be projected from the writer's assimilated experience, from his knowledge, from his head, from his heart, and from all there is of him." I remember reading this with a jolt, because it is almost precisely a statement of my criticism of him: I accuse him of careful construction.*

Hemingway urged the novelist to bring himself to the page, whereas I would argue the novelist cannot do otherwise. Any storyteller will project heart and mind and experience—including all its tricks and holes and all that remains unconscious. This is what any of us are stuck with, and that self will inevitably be colored and shaped by our times, our beliefs; it comes complete with defenses and compensations. So Hemingway, believing that he must write with "a tight hold over himself," in that very choice, reveals his vulnerability.

Gabrielle looks up at this, to mark her place with Orbach. He is grimacing, clasping his knees where they cross, upper foot bouncing a little. She takes a drink of water and notices the woman next to Orbach appears tense, possibly anticipating what could come next. Yet the woman gamely smiles, nodding, wanting Gabe to go on. The audience is whispering now. Gabe wonders whether they are realizing who she is, recognizing her notoriety. She can see them changing positions in their chairs to see and hear her better. She clears her throat, then continues reading:

I find myself agreeing with Van Wyck Brooks, one of Hemingway's contemporaries: I too would like to hear the story of despised Robert Cohn, "the young man in The Sun Also Rises *who behaved so badly from the point of view of his little set because he had the courage to admit his feelings." Hemingway's Robert Cohn openly adored Brett Ashley, his female protagonist, and she, of course, rejected Cohn, in love with somebody else, because in Hemingway's world, women are cruel or they are silly, and men who let themselves love women deserve rejection.*

In the world I know, men and women are more complicated. Robert Cohn would have no trouble finding a woman who would love him in return and I think he must surely have had another tale. He might have learned to choose more wisely, to choose a wiser woman. But Hemingway will not be the one to give us that story. He couldn't see its possibility, perhaps even when it happened under his nose. I wonder, could all his marriages have been so empty of love? Why would he rely on and write to his wives even after he divorced them? Van Wyck Brooks once asked with William James: What proof is there that dupery through hope is so much worse than dupery through fear?

No proof, it seems to me, no proof at all—Hemingway's violent death at his own hands, a marker for us in the dark forest of our hearts.

She looks up to signal she is done then, and just in time. Her voice has begun to quaver, her knees so wobbly she can barely stand a moment longer. "That's all," she says, and the students clap, but she can see the questions on their faces, can hear uncertainty in their clapping.

Orbach stands up then, smiling, spreading his arms to draw the answering applause to Gabe. Then he asks, "Questions, anyone? Comments?"

One soul dares ask, "Isn't your brother the one who shot his wife in Five Corners?"

Gabrielle nods, turning red, though shooting isn't precisely accurate. "Yes, and then himself."

No other questions emerge. The group is crowding toward the back for wine and cheese, gathering in clusters, talking privately. Orbach comes closer, leaning in toward her. "Is dupery *all* that is possible?" he asks softly with that unpleasant smile and chuckles. "Sorry, Gabe, but I remain convinced a man's marriages can hardly figure in a critique of his literature. You see the simplistic leap the audience made—did your brother ever *read* Hemingway, I wonder? Many have and never killed their spouses *or* themselves. How do you explain that?"

"I don't think I was suggesting anything *simple*," Gabe put in, upset that he seems affronted. She knew he wouldn't like it, but she hadn't expected him to take it so personally.

By now the older woman who had been sitting next to Orbach comes forward, reaching out to shake her hand. She confides, "You know I always hated Hemingway too, and could never admit it. Thanks for that talk. Imagine, 'knocking Turgenev out of the ring!' Afraid of his own softness, if you ask me—afraid of his feminine side, you think?" She smiles and puts four fingers up, scrunching them in quotation marks when she uses the word "feminine."

Gabe doesn't answer, only gives the briefest smile because she's uncomfortable with the woman stepping past Orbach. She looks in his direction, wanting to include him somehow, but he's gone already, heading for wine and cheese. The woman adds, "Listen, I'm *so sorry* about your brother and his wife. That must have been *awful*."

July 29, 1984
Five Corners, Michigan

Kate brought me up short. She thought I'd appreciate her sharing Anita's confidence that my colleagues at school find me difficult to know. Ridiculous! I thought, reading Kate's question. She asks, Do you realize how intimidating you are at first impression? Meaning my poker-face habit of looking straight at someone when I talk, I suppose. Too much for Anita and her bunch to handle—like Valley, I decided. I always hated the way Valley tipped her head when she smiled, a sign of submission in the animal world. I never would do it.

No wonder I'm lonely. I make a good impression. But is this the courage Kate says that people admire in me? Maybe it's another kind of craziness. I'd like for people to know me.

That's new, I think. I've remembered where I met that woman who recommended me for my job—the retired professor I didn't realize was a professor at the time—embarrassed to associate myself with someone who made silly quote marks in the air. She liked what I said. How many others have I shut out?

Was Valley really baring her neck in submission? I don't think so. It was more a willingness, an affirmation—a risk even. Letting me know I needn't fear her and that she wasn't afraid of me either.

Kate's coming here for a visit. All year I've felt her listening. To see her smile will be even better.

Late July, 1975

The whole summer has been a blur of soft green, the wettest, muddiest summer ever in Shub's memory. He says even the weather feels it. He can't make sense of anything anymore, he shrugs, meaning the clouds and wind, meaning a year gone by and there is still only loss and bewilderment. It doesn't even bother him that the cabins have been quieter, that the tourist business is down from all this rain.

Gabe still comes over to help on days when stock is delivered. They've had some clear, cold nights the past week. Things are bound to look up. Before long, people will be flocking. The maples will turn orange and fringe the lake, looking brighter against a backdrop of hemlock and spruce. Autumn, when everything comes closest to dying, is the time everyone thinks the place most beautiful.

Gabe has made Shub and herself some of Valley's peppermint tea, her prescription for Shub's perennial bellyaches. They stare out at the water, commenting at length on how cold it's looking. Gabe weighs whether to bring up something, something that has been on her mind as she rattles around the cabin, walks in the woods. Halfway convinced it's better to keep it to herself, she lets words stumble out, testing them: "It occurred to me the other day, Shub—I wanted to ask you something."

"What's that?"

"It's kind of crazy. Horrible, really, but it crossed my mind the other day."

Shub looks out of patience, waiting for what she still struggles to encase in syllables. "You spend too much time thinking," he comments. "That's your whole problem, right there."

"Could my pa ever do to my mother what Robert did, you think?"

Shub has not seen this one coming. He lets out a breath like she's socked him in the stomach and answers in a vexed tone, annoyed at their peace being spoiled. "Godsake, child. Where do you come up with such stuff?"

"I want to know. Did you ever see any evidence of that?"

Shub pulls in his chin and shakes his head vehemently before giving himself time to think. "No," he states. "Uh-uh, absolutely not."

"What about Elsie? Did she ever say anything about my mother?"

He puts out his bottom lip, looking up at the ceiling as he shakes his head again, this time slowly because he's considering it, going back through his memories. "Nope," he decides. "Nothing like *that*."

Neither one of them can bear to say what "that" is, exactly, but both of them know what they're talking about. "I wish *I* could ask her," Gabe says after a moment. She sips her tea, looks away at the lake again.

"What do you mean?" Shub is miffed, hurt that she thinks he might have missed important clues. But he doesn't openly protest since they have both clearly missed a great deal already.

"I mean, there might be something. Maybe that's why nobody ever heard from her. Not even my grandmother. Did it ever cross anybody's mind?"

"Course not. Never. We knew they'd had their troubles. That's why they came up here, I guess. But then she decided to run off." This rings a warning bell. He stops himself, his expression searching as he continues, less sure. "Can't say as we blamed her for it, but she run off. That's what we always thought," he adds, looking upward again, wobbling down mental corridors that are dark, half forgotten, trying to find his way.

He discovers something and looks back to Gabe, satisfied: "There was a suitcase. The police asked about it. Hank told them she took a suitcase, and the rest of her stuff he got rid of."

The police, she thinks, and breathes a short scoff. Yet in the next breath, she decides Shub is right about this. He must be right. She cannot think of the other possibility. Besides, there's no way they can know anything for sure, not now.

She watches Shub looking up at the ceiling again, still exploring. "It half-killed him, her leaving," he comments after a moment. "I know that much." After another moment he adds, "I mean, he took it real *hard*," arguing with Gabe, when she is only too ready to believe. They finish their peppermint tea without saying what they know has changed for both of them forever.

NOVEMBER, 1975

"He's resting quietly, miss. You're welcome to look in on him, but I doubt he'll know you're here."

Gabrielle nods yes, she understands. She's been told his condition many times, but since this is nothing new, she thinks the nurse must have just started here. She doesn't yet know her father, his family, his friends.

He is tucked in under a blue cotton bedspread, his skin pale and papery, unhealthy looking next to green-patterned pajamas. His hair is lighter, thinner, beginning to streak with silver. He is snoring with satisfaction and suddenly she is happier to have found him asleep. In sleep, he seems almost himself. It is easier to imagine his waking and being different.

She has a Polaroid shot Shub has taken of her with the doe she dropped this year. Last year she hadn't even tried. She props the picture up against his water glass. It's crazy maybe. He still never seems to know a thing. But she will leave it because it is as close as she can come to telling him all the fears she has had to conquer, just to pick the rifle up and load it again. Maybe he will know it, all the trust she had to place in herself to do this. But on the other hand, he wouldn't like it. He never approved of doe season.

That moment when the deer had walked out, she'd been sickened by the sight. Everything she'd ever decided about what was right and what was natural went out the window then. There was only this slim-boned creature, the same sex as Valley, same as her mother, only viewed down her rifle. Afterward she'd realized it was silly, the spiritual experience she'd been hoping for—what had she been expecting? That the deer would see her and turn to give her permission for what she was about to do? Here, take, eat of my flesh, my blood.

It wasn't like that, no communion of the sort she had wanted. Only a clean kill, taking her down with one shot while the doe looked off in the wrong direction. Nothing spiritual feeling about it. Afterward, Gabe had tried to conjure the gift, searching for gratitude as she wrestled with the body's limp warmth. Homage is full of grief. The doe's side-set eyes stared away as Gabe thought how its body would nourish her, how she would do the doe honor by going on living—that would have to be spiritual enough.

Now she looks out past the glass louvers of Pa's window. She sees her predator eyes reflected in the glass. The doe stands stock-still in her mind and she knows she couldn't have spared it, couldn't pretend it had no stake in what happened in the forest, or that its life would be safe otherwise. It wouldn't be.

She listens to Pa's breathing behind her. His window overlooks a parking lot, not the trees of the sitting-room view. A man gets into his car, slams the door, turns the ignition, and the thing gives a sound like someone bearing down, a hysterical grunting, a dry, dissatisfying birth.

August 10, 1984
Five Corners, Michigan

I told Kate again in a letter I started this morning, I had never felt rage. But then something came floating up—something else remembered.

When I stood up to face Robert, holding the gun the way my father had taught me, I wasn't just defending myself. There was music in me—a symphony stood me on my feet. Jubilation raised my gun. It's not supposed to feel so good. Anger and violence shouldn't feel this way. But it did. I admit now it did.

What hope can I have then, with no difference between me and my miserable brother? I've been sitting here and staring from the bottom of a hole that used to be my moral high ground.

That same pleasure destroyed Valley and Robert. I mean that Robert had as much capacity for loving, for taking care of, for staying connected as I did or as Valley did. But long before he pulled any trigger, Robert had killed that in himself. I could do what I did for the same reasons he was able to— numb as he was to everything but fury by then. Rage fools you into thinking nothing else matters, when so much else does.

I see every day how complex and allied all of life is—in the woods, in the lake, hanging in precarious balance with everything invested in surviving and thriving—nothing central about what I happen to want, nothing disconnected from what I do. Only the ballast of desires of all kinds around me, entangling. I don't ask for forgiveness. I can't afford to be appalled. I was answering weight when I stood up to measure Robert in the balance. That song that raised me to my feet— here—my pulse.

NOVEMBER, 1976

She dreams she is out hunting with a bow when she meets him. The eyes of August Santee smile at her but his mouth is solemn, held fast in a hard, straight line as he holds out his palm for her to see. There her fingers are—four of them, the ones she's been looking for. He gets out a deerskin pouch and puts them into it, pulls the pouch strings tight and hands it to her.

Until that moment she has thought of him as friend. But as she takes the pouch and feels the softness of the deerskin, somehow he is transformed into someone dangerous and terrible-intentioned. The leather bag with her fingers bears down, heavy. He smiles more fully. She admires it, thinking how ingenuous his grin, but at once also sees that expression reveals eyeteeth—and how pointed they are, how cleanly they might tear.

She no longer is hunter. Santee follows her into the woods, and his step behind her jolts, transforming her to prey. He gives chase when she runs, and is joined by a woman partner who appears out of nowhere, racing next to him, with long hair streaming out behind her.

Sprinting ahead, Gabe can see them both from over her shoulder, and then, like a mirror image, she feels her own match running beside her, his stride powerful, muscular. The pair of them pound the earth with bare feet, sprint in a rhythm to match their beating hearts, pant the pulse of the ground and, melting green and black, become the trail itself.

She wakes, sits up and blinks, trying to think who the woman with August could be. Mirror images of her own dark side? Valley? she wonders. The woman had long blond hair. Valley—the *hunter* this time?

Gabe laughs a little, recognizing at once that if this were so, she would gladly feed her life to Valley, to go on living *in* her. Please, she breathes, wanting only for Valley to be again. She asks for forgiveness, and this comes so easily, answering inhale to her exhale, that she lies back down, overcome by generosity. The world is full of favors.

It occurs to her then. The fleeing runner beside her—it could have been Robert. She remembers this Robert from when they were children, both running down the road to the lake, laughing and gasping together for breath. He lives too. She wants it to be possible, but not without punishment.

Though that's how life is, she remembers, simply going on. Valley was *like* that—too easy, a soft touch. The best, the most vulnerable thing about her.

It shouldn't come so easily, she protests, sinking back into sleep to wrestle some more, though grateful, holding her pillow close.

August 20, 1984
Five Corners, Michigan

How to share this with Kate? As often as I've told myself, it sounds mushy-headed as soon as I write words around it. It happened just before I went to her conference. I had been walking for over an hour and had crossed the place where you are separate—I mean that I wasn't different anymore from where I was or from the air I was breathing or the leaf mold underfoot, I was all of it—sunlight on my skin and everything alive and not split off, divided and named as something other. I saw the blue buck, the one my Pa had everybody in town talking about.

I always thought he'd been imagining it, though I see now, he was never like that. He was always half-ashamed of the story. But here I was, making all kinds of noise, churning through the woods. And this buck, who ought to have run the other way or stood out of sight until I was past, came up over the ridge as if to meet me. He held my gaze a split second before he lunged away, big and topped with a rack and blue—blue as they always said he was.

I followed his trail. Put my fingers in the tracks he had left in the earth. Never caught another glimpse of him—not a haunch, not an ear. The sun was sinking down behind a hill, turning the sky a peach color, and I lectured myself that here was the explanation. The light must have been hitting him right, turning gray to indigo. There's always room for doubt. Even now my mind stretches to fill the open spaces he came crashing through.

What do you do when a place you know as well as your hand reveals a mystery you would swear couldn't be there? What else might remain unnamed? What you see is a matter of perspective. Like the ruffed grouse who roosts in snow tunnels, where birds clearly ought not to be, bursting out when you get too near. One frightened Valley when we were walking to the deeryard once, and when she screamed, I turned around. She said an explosion had gone off by her feet, pelting her with snow that still sparkled in the air. I remember being annoyed at the way she was more awestruck after I explained what it really was—a plain brown-feathered bird.

So here I am, swinging my arms, taking steady strides and this crashing sound comes over the rill—a sound like I'm making with my own feet so that when the buck appears at the top of the ridge, I'm taken off guard. And so is he—holding his head like a woman's loaded with baskets of fruit, his rack full and curvaceous. When he turns his head, his side-set eyes meet my straight-on eyes, and all our shapes are contained in a moment of whirling molecules—male-female predator-prey—and species before us and all those that come after.

I get this secret out of its pouch a dozen times a day. What on earth will Kate make of it? Will she say it's projection? My shadow, transformed? I don't care really. Any brown-bird explanation will do.

People know these things. We recognize the weave of dark and light when we see it—in our dreams at night if we shut it out. She'll understand what I am trying to tell her.

ACKNOWLEDGMENTS

Grateful acknowledgment is made for permission to reprint excerpts from the following material:

Van Wyck Brooks. *The Writer in America*. (Copyright 1952, 1953, renewed 1980, 1981 by Van Wyck Brooks. Used by permission of Dutton Signet, a division of Penguin Books USA, Inc.)

Daniel Fuchs. "Ernest Hemingway, Literary Critic." *American Literature*, 34: 4 (January 1965), Duke University Press.

Harold M. Hurwitz. "Hemingway's Tutor, Ezra Pound." *Quarterly Review of Literature* 5 (1949–50), 140. The Johns Hopkins University Press.

George Plimpton. Interview with Ernest Hemingway. *The Paris Review* 18 (Spring 1958), 60–89.

Robert Penn Warren. *Selected Essays*. (Random House, Inc., 1951.)

Permission is also granted by Scribner, a Division of Simon & Schuster, for use of excerpts from the following works of Ernest Hemingway:

Selections from *The Complete Short Stories of Ernest Hemingway*:

"A Natural History of the Dead." (Copyright 1932, 1933 Charles Scribner's Sons. Copyrights renewed © 1960 by Ernest Hemingway; 1961 by Mary Hemingway.)

"A Clean, Well-Lighted Place." (Copyright 1933 Charles Scribner's Sons. Copyright renewed © 1961 by Mary Hemingway.)

"The Snows of Kilimanjaro" and "The Short Happy Life of Francis Macomber." (Copyright 1936 by Ernest Hemingway. Copyright renewed © 1964 by Mary Hemingway.)

The Sun Also Rises. (Copyright 1926 Charles Scribner's Sons. Copyright renewed 1954 by Ernest Hemingway.)

A Farewell to Arms. (Copyright 1929 Charles Scribner's Sons. Copyright renewed © 1957 by Ernest Hemingway.)

Death in the Afternoon. (Copyright 1932 Charles Scribner's Sons. Copyright renewed © 1960 by Ernest Hemingway.)

Although only alluded to in this text, a debt is also owed to Bernice Kerts's biography, *Hemingway's Women* (W. W. Norton, 1983), and to Morley Callaghan's memoirs, *That Summer in Paris* (Coward-McCann, 1963). Thanks also to John W. Aldridge for his insights in *The Lost Generation* (McGraw-Hill, 1951).

Many books have been invaluable to this novel, but teachers and friends were even more so. Thanks to professor Richard Hathaway, who first encouraged me to think my own thoughts about Hemingway and his work. I'm grateful to Norwich University's Charlotte Gafford and my first mentor in the MFA in Writing at Vermont College, Gladys Swan, neither of whom discouraged early versions of this story but wisely sent me deeper into my interior forest. Beth Delano and the Delano family instructed and strengthened my respect for what it means to live closer to what one eats. Michelle Ahearn and the Families of Inmates Support program, along with the St. Albans Department of Corrections and their inmates, inmates' wives and girlfriends, helped me better understand the complexities of families in trouble. To all those who responded to early readings or written chapters, I'm grateful, but especially to Linda McCarriston, Dru Daugherty and to The Writers' Potluck: Michele Clark, Sue Burton, Jane Bryant, Fran Cerulli, Leslie Williams and Norma Skjold. Thanks too for the demanding vision of the Calyx Books' editorial collective. And, finally, a thank-offering and alleluiah for Stephen McArthur, my heart's companion for the duration of this long, long turtle race.